Praise for *The Rags of Time* by Maureen Howard

"Many novelists today are bold and noisy in language, voice, or plot, but without a thought as to how to defend the necessity of the novel itself—the means of connecting form and feeling to grand effect, once literature's bread and butter, now a maddening puzzle. Maureen Howard is the opposite: stringent, subtle, unsure, ironic, acutely reflective about means as well as end, and yet stunningly determined to take on the mantle of tradition and press forward toward the large questions in both old and new ways. . . . *The Rags of Time* casts a shadow back on its three predecessors, and reveals that the real subject of the whole series has been the artistic endeavor itself. This extraordinary book is a last reckoning, a reflection on the success—or, just as possibly for Howard, the failure—of a gamble already made."

—Sophia Lear, *The New Republic*

"In a literary landscape that is fast, crowded, and desperate to astonish, Howard's books offer something else. They are heartbreaking, huge, unsolved, and uncannily close to life. . . . Howard has structured her vast web so that we are constantly un-learning or re-learning what we think we know about a character or relationship. In each and every season, knowing becomes suspect and subject to revision. . . . The intimacy of the final volume is the intimacy of a story and characters that have been lived with for a very long time. . . . At the end of the fourth book I wanted to start all over again. What could the first volume say about the last? What could the early lives tell me about the later ones?"

—Emily Austin, The Faster Times.com

"I see you, Maureen, in your *Rags*, not just in your fictional writer but in the very structure and style of the book. You've made something that can contain different points of view, contrasting impressions, and your characteristic blend of past and present. And I sense that behind the multiplicity is an author who remains acutely concerned about the future."

—Joanna Scott, *The Believer*

"Narratives, Aristotle suggests in his *Politics*, work best if they are arranged around some preexisting unit of time: sunrise to sunset, January to December. Maureen Howard has taken this advice both literally and extravagantly in her tetralogy of fictions based on the seasons; her novel *A Lover's Alamanac* (winter); a collection of three novellas, *Big as Life* (spring); another novel, *The Silver Screen* (summer); and now, finally, *The Rags of Time*, which comes described as a novel, but is more a kind of late, meandering overture, part meditation, part postscript, part appendix. Like autumn, it flares and fades, rages and dissembles, not wanting to give itself over to its inevitable end."

—Jess Row, *The New York Times Book Review*

"Howard, a writer of gorgeously elliptical, droll fiction, brings her richly figured cycle of the four seasons to a beautiful and resonant conclusion. Each book in this finely modulated quartet juxtaposes psychological acuity with gleanings from history, science, and biography. . . . Slyly riffing on meanings of 'fall' and slipping pieces of autobiography into a rag rug–like design, Howard creates a novel of exquisite synthesis, rare nuance, and deep conscience."   —Donna Seaman, *Booklist*

PENGUIN BOOKS

THE RAGS OF TIME

Maureen Howard is the author of nine novels, three of which (*Grace Abounding*, *Expensive Habits*, and *Natural History*) were finalists for the PEN/Faulkner Award. *The Rags of Time* is the last of a boldly structured quartet of novels (including *A Lover's Almanac*, 1998; *Big as Life*, 2001; and *The Silver Screen*, 2004) whose characters and themes are woven across the cycle as a tapestry of the four seasons. Her memoir, *The Facts of Life*, was the winner of the National Book Critics Circle Award. The recipient of an Academy Award in Literature from the American Academy of Arts and Letters, she lives in New York City.

MAUREEN HOWARD

The Rags of Time

PENGUIN BOOKS

PENGUIN BOOKS

Published by the Penguin Group
Penguin Group (USA) Inc., 375 Hudson Street, New York, New York 10014, U.S.A. • Penguin
Group (Canada), 90 Eglinton Avenue East, Suite 700, Toronto, Ontario, Canada M4P 2Y3
(a division of Pearson Penguin Canada Inc.) • Penguin Books Ltd, 80 Strand, London WC2R 0RL,
England • Penguin Ireland, 25 St Stephen's Green, Dublin 2, Ireland (a division of Penguin Books
Ltd) • Penguin Group (Australia), 250 Camberwell Road, Camberwell, Victoria 3124, Australia
(a division of Pearson Australia Group Pty Ltd) • Penguin Books India Pvt Ltd, 11 Community
Centre, Panchsheel Park, New Delhi – 110 017, India • Penguin Group (NZ), 67 Apollo Drive,
Rosedale, North Shore 0632, New Zealand (a division of Pearson New Zealand Ltd) • Penguin Books
(South Africa) (Pty) Ltd, 24 Sturdee Avenue, Rosebank, Johannesburg 2196, South Africa

Penguin Books Ltd, Registered Offices: 80 Strand, London WC2R 0RL, England

First published in the United States of America by Viking Penguin,
a member of Penguin Group (USA) Inc. 2009
Published in Penguin Books 2010

10 9 8 7 6 5 4 3 2 1

Portions of this book first appeared in different form in *Conjunctions*.

ILLUSTRATION CREDITS: Page 1: © Lee Friedlander. Courtesy Fraenkel Gallery, San Francisco
• Pages 87 and 185: Drawings by Todd Mauritz. • Page 142: Photograph by Andre Emmerich. By
permission of Susanne Emmerich. • Pages 112, 140–1, 145, 160, 163 (top), and 221: Photographs by
Ali Elai • Page 152: National Portrait Gallery, London • Page 163 (bottom): Photograph by Ken Fang.
• Pages 177 and 184: Courtesy of the National Park Service, Frederick Law Olmsted National
Historical Site • Page 191: Sara Cedar Miller, Central Park Conservancy • Page 236: Paul Strand:
Bombed Church, Moselle, France, 1950. © Aperture Foundation, Inc., Paul Strand Archive.

THE LIBRARY OF CONGRESS HAS CATALOGED THE HARDCOVER EDITION AS FOLLOWS:
Howard, Maureen, date.
The rags of time : a novel / Maureen Howard.
p.   cm.
ISBN 978-0-670-02132-1 (hc.)
ISBN 978-0-14-311789-6 (pbk.)
1. Fiction—Authorship—Fiction.   2. Central Park (New York, N.Y.)—Fiction.   I. Title.
PS3558.O8823R34 2009
813'.54—dc22   2009015167

Printed in the United States of America • Designed by Nancy Resnick

To Mark, and to Nicholas Howard Fudge——time bends

Acknowledgments

My family—husband, Mark Probst; brother, George Kearns; daughter, Loretta Howard, incalculable thanks for their support and correction. Richard Powers for his generous editorial reading; James Longenbach and Joanna Scott for their care and honesty with a work in long progress, this last of my Seasons. Binnie Kirschenbaum for her spirited commentary. My agent and friend, Gloria Loomis, patient with me over the years; and Paul Slovak, my gifted editor, at once exacting and imaginative. I am indebted to Jeri Laber, Patrick Keefe, Mohammet Yildiz, Harish Bhat, George and Sonya Tcherny, Cleo Kearns, Brenda Maddox, Ann Weissmann, Ed Park, Paul La Farge, Bradford Morrow, and to Drs. Iris Sherman and Mary Anne McLaughlin for their consultation; to the Mercy Learning Center for letting me camp on their porch, and the Bogliasco Foundation for a residency at the Villa dei Pini.

Love, all alike, no season knowes, nor clyme,
Nor houres, dayes, moneths, which are the rags of time.

——John Donne, *"The Sunne Rising"*

The Rags of Time

Central Park

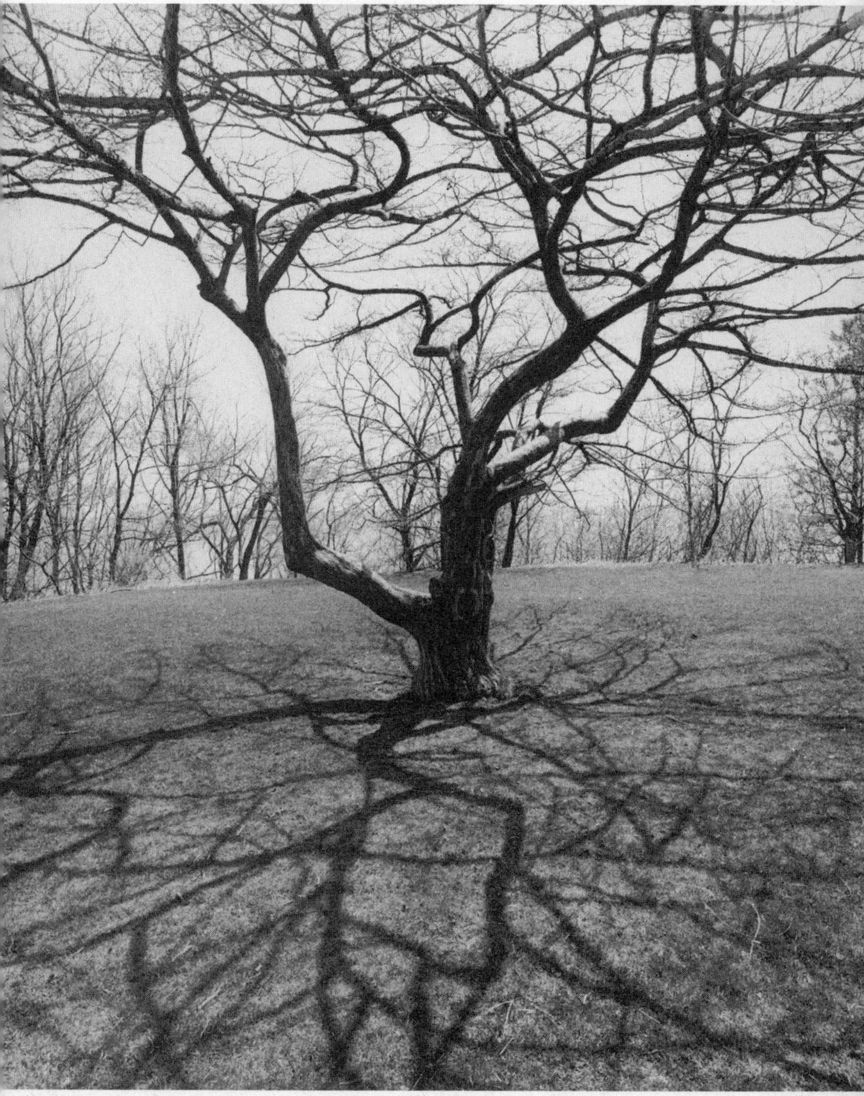

THE BOOK OF DAYS

> *In soul-baring confessional writings (maximum honesty with regard to oneself), the third-person form is better.*
>
> —Max Frisch, *Sketchbook* (1970)

In God We Trust. She notes these words inscribed on a five dollar bill she sticks in her pocket, heads for the park. Odd, how she no longer sees the motto on twenties and tens, on every coin in her purse. Did she ever believe in that trust? When the patrician voice of the president declared *a date that will live in infamy*; when her brother was drafted during the conflict in Korea; perhaps held that tarnished belief when she marched with thousands against the wars in Vietnam, Cambodia, Laos. Even then believed, though her trust was in the marching, not *God* on a dull penny, in the slogans and songs, trusting something worthy would come of her effort, more than camaraderie or the glow of self-satisfaction. Her picture had been snapped with the hippie academics. She's in the tie-dye T pushing through the police barrier, storming onto campus when Governor Reagan punished children who stepped out of line, said oh no you don't teach your dispiriting lessons against the war, not on my watch. These days she would not be sure of her footing if herded into the courthouse in Santa Barbara to be charged with unlawful assembly.

The Sixties were so performative! This contribution from her daughter who lives nearby.

What does that mean?

Well, she can no longer march. In Central Park she walks the short distance set by her failing heart, delights in a warm day, an amber wash of Indian Summer.

She would like to know who proposed the motto *In God We Trust,* and when unseasonable days were first called Indian Summer, as though knowing might steady her flip-flop pulse. These are almanac questions with almanac answers available on an Internet service. Suppose, just suppose, this time round the easy answers will not heal by way of distraction. *I am outraged.* She repeats this phrase in the lilting, stage center voice that entertained students in the classroom and readings of her work in years past. *I am outraged. What crimes are they committing at their Black Sites?* Delivered to her husband, her brother, to Cleo and Glo—whoever will listen, and they are outraged, too, repeating the day's dreadful news. *We have not been given the full count of the injured.* She is caught up in gestures of dollars and cents where *In God We Trust* came into her story—on greenbacks, coinage in the pocket of her old black coat, though it's her credit card that registers the small donations of her protest. So it goes.

She is still in her bathrobe at noon, her flighty gray hair unwashed, strange crust on her cheek, a new hillock of puffed flesh on the wrinkled map of age. She turns from the mirror. Not much for mirrors anymore. Let the body play out the days with a handful of pills adjusting the heartbeat, thinning the blood. Till well after noon she stays in her back room writing the last of her seasons, Fall with its showy splendor. She predicts year's end may be her end, but that's one of her stories. Her body will float on a bier of books and first drafts down the Lethe, or bob in Olmsted's Lake, which appears at a distance, an elegiac vision she may have to revise, a cold wind ruffling the glass surface. Seldom given to self-pity. Consolation is across the street in Central Park with its Bridle Path, Pinetum, Reservoir Track, all that prospect of a healthy, if halting, afternoon walk, thus the five dollar bill in her pocket for the needy or a threatening encounter. She loses her glasses, forgets her cell phone and what's for dinner, repeats her riff on outrage, remembers in some detail disturbing events of the past filed away under *Wars I have known,* one scene oddly persistent in recent days.

* * *

As a freshman in college, she stayed up late with her new friends. It must have been the first weeks of October. Three little girls at school with no bedtime, few rules. What stories did they have to swap? Empty vessels. She is harsh as she thinks of them in their flannel nightgowns, their French grammars and Lattimore's monumental *Greek Tragedies* thrown aside for idle chatter. The woman came to their door, which stood open a crack. Looming, mysterious, she waited in the dim night light of the hall for a long moment, then invited herself in. The girls made tea on an electric hot plate, the red coil dangerously close to a curtain her mother had sewn to make life homey away from home. She figures how old their guest was, a graduate student from Austria studying Government, as they called Political Science then. Perhaps in her mid-twenties—big breasts, heavy thighs, the pulsing of her neck as she told her story. The plait of honey hair she drew round the fullness of that neck was a noose snapped free to reveal a silver cross. The three girls were children who listened obediently to the woman's steady guttural voice with now and again a German word translated for them to English. The salty odor of sweat from the Austrian woman's ragged ski sweater. They were all sitting on the floor of this room in a dormitory for mostly privileged young women. The rug was lumpy, braided of rags by the mother of the old woman who was then a girl listening to a story she could not comprehend, how their visitor's father was taken away, the brother, too. Tap, tapping her cross, the woman said the Cardinal came to lunch. Her father had thought His Eminence's visit a good sign. She knelt to kiss the Cardinal's ring which smelled of laundry soap. They might find that the strangest part of her story. Come the next year, a knock on the door in Innsbruck and they were gone, the father, the brother taken by brutal men these girls had seen in newsreels and movies. More tea, and though they had not asked, the Austrian student with a woman's body said as the war was coming to its end a soldier spoiled her. *Schande.* Never saw him, her face covered with a pillow. Soon after, the Russians came.

For years the woman who lives across from the Park recalled the shame of her relief when the foreign student left her college room, shame at her inability to feel nothing more than embarrassment, to wonder at— the harsh soap of suet and lye embedded under the princely ring as though the honored guest in the magenta beanie joined in a humble washday task. Had the woman found other children in the dead of night to listen to the calm recitation of her story? Today the warm dormitory room appears again with the two friends who went their separate ways by the end of that year, the poster on the wall—*Carnation, Lily, Lily, Rose*—Sargent's little girls in white summer dresses, their Japanese lanterns illuminating a garden beyond lovely. And there on the floor, the discarded textbook in which the Greek chorus mourned what had come to pass as in the chant—*We are outraged*—or warns what will come to pass, but tragedy had gone out of business. Her own initials were incised on her tea mug, MK—a gift from her father—a gruff, sentimental man, who never wanted her to grow up, leave home with new clothes—a lumpy rag rug, gauzy curtains fluttering near the hot coil of the burner.

Not much for mirrors, and not happy with my attempt at third person. In my book, confession begs for absolution, but my sins are not wiped away like sweat when you've run too fast or too far; and now I can't run at all. Today I am outraged by the use of camouflage in the desert. Disguises nothing, you've noticed? With sophisticated surveillance devices, there's no need for blotches simulating mud and sand. Camouflage of a sort is worn by the Cheerleader, his business suit, navy or gray. You've seen him bounce down the steps of Air Force One, sprightly, airy. Crossing the tarmac, he waves us off, the palm of his hand denying access as we watch the evening news. Thumbs-up, he gives us the finger; his tight-lipped smile, mum's the word. The boy who painted our fence has gone to his war—a kid who worked in a toy store at the mall, had no future in that line and asked what I worked at since I am seldom at the little house in the country. I showed him a book. He took it in his hands. Bewildered, he laughed as though at a useless brick, slick and lighter than the ones that edge the front path but do not keep weeds out of the garden. It's a book with false moves written at the turn of this century, not this sketchbook, album, field notes of the past and passing days.

I'm comfortable with first person, don't mind drawing back the velvet curtain, coming onstage. I was born in the city of P. T. Barnum, the impresario who never feared facing his audience even when the music was too highbrow or the freak show failed to amaze. On *Good Morning America*, a marine amputee is learning to walk on metal stilts to carry on in our three-ring circus.

I have my troupe, my regulars, bring them center stage as they are needed, one by two by three, duets and line dancing, solo turns throughout the seasons, not lives of the saints, yet not lives of the sinners. The improbable mathematician, his lapsed artist wife, the foreign student with the heavy rope of hair who appeared one night vowing never to return to Innsbruck where she grew up in extraordinary comfort. Call them my cast: in shameless imitation of Papa Haydn and Vivaldi's *Four Seasons*, I give you Sissy, a waif with golden hair and a bad habit; the Jesuit cousin—godless man of god; Audubon, who killed, stuffed and gave life through his art to our American birds; my parents in their molto adagio, who have long been defenseless. And you, brilliant in your supporting role, flipping the calendar back to take as good as you get, as though we are still in our prime. I look forward to your corrections, to my reply as I turn to the next blank page.

You advise me against bringing the Cheerleader into play, writing of here and now, allowing editorials to seep into my stories, spoiled fish wrapped in yesterday's *Times*.

Let's not get into shelf life.

You say: *Outrage is a bumper sticker, one of many sentiments parked side-by-side in Kmart Plaza. Proud parent of an honor student at Monument Valley High. Honk if you love Borges.*

There's a picture of Charles Dickens sitting at his desk. He's not writing, not addressing his next cause—illiteracy, pollution, tax laws, copyright, child labor: the list is long. His biographer tells us he's imagining. Time out to conjure a story. His characters paper the walls, enacting their memorable scenes. A miniature girl sits on his knee; asking what next, she looks to her maker. Will she marry after many trials, or be awarded the famous deathbed scene? This picture of Dickens is on a card which reads ALL GOOD WISHES OF THE SEASON, a bland greeting he'd never put his name to, yet I have recently posted it above my desk to remind me how inadequate my dreams. Boz, partner me in a pantomime. Hold me aloft in a cold season. You'd be outraged at our accidental killing of Arab girls in a cement block school. Dip into the ink pot, Lover, imagine more than my bitter words. Write a gay or plaintive story about your desk to be auctioned this year, proceeds for the children's hospital in Great Ormond Street to which you contributed ten pounds, a theatrical skit, and your precious time.

Today I forgot the name Panofsky but remembered a review I wrote a long time ago in which I took issue with *Slaughterhouse-Five,* a war novel that became famous, much praised. Vonnegut was imprisoned in Dresden during the firebombing, *carnage unfathomable,* just months before the Allies won that war. I could not begin to understand how the writer worked his story in a somewhat comic vein. Wall of flame, overkill, body count, his banal refrain—*So it goes.* In honesty, I was still something of that girl, flannel nightgown buttoned to the neck, listening one night to the seductive report of a survivor, to a foreign student who could not guess my . . . emotional incapacity.

In God We Trust: the national motto was first used during the Civil War, when religious sentiment was running high. The Secretary of the Treasury responded to pleas of the devout that it be printed on our currency.

Indian Summer: a few days of blessed warmth after the cold weather has set in; or the time when the Indians harvested their crops; or a time before frost when they attacked European settlements storing their food for winter. The settlers retaliated with cumbersome muskets. So it goes.

I live in the city. I share the garden across the street. If you would like to know with maximum honesty about my loves or further shame, my faltering heart, it's none of your business. My brother is switching channels, expecting the bombed mosque in Mosul will be shown in more detail. Was it them? Or us? No matter, he is outraged. We all are. My husband, who works with numbers—market up, market down—figures to the nth dollar the military contracts dealt out to the Cheerleader's friends doctoring the books, the outrageous rip-offs. There will be a candlelight vigil. We will stand with our homemade placards: WAR IS NOT THE ANSWER. Song, piety, mulled cider in the Park. It will only be effective if we wait till the sun has set, well after dark.

Daybook, October 8, 2007

1929, the year of my conception. What were they thinking of, bringing another hungry mouth into the world? Perhaps not thinking—her red hair aflame on the pillow? I must not make a drama of that cool October night, perhaps Columbus Day, in the little house with its peaked gingerbread roof and curlicue hasps on the door. The cottage had just been built for our middle class comfort, for a night of their fumbling and fondling under the blanket in the front bedroom that faced North Avenue. In the throes of discovery they were blessedly not thinking. Who am I to say fumbling at this very late date, casting my mother in the role of shy schoolteacher rescued from spinsterhood by the brash boy detective? I have portrayed them too often, Loretta and Bill, made them my subjects.

I throw down the book I was reading, nothing to do with an October night in Bridgeport at the start of the Great Depression. The false memory of my begetting was a digression, an off-bounds stop on the way to a disturbing story. This very day I had searched the pages of a novel I'd written as though checking an old bankbook to reckon where I spent foolishly, what interest accrued that I might go on with and ended up broke, wishing dramatically to have never been born. I was attempting to make some connection, this daybook with my rants against the war to the book thrown aside. To my discredit, that love story was of the Second World War, yet all I called up, attempting to balance the account, was to switch the scene to my parents' bedroom, muslin curtains flapping in a welcome breeze while I read *War and Peace* in a creaking wicker chair. Why was I allowed to invade their space through the long Summer days while I read Tolstoy's great work? I was fourteen years old.

Today I can no longer look at my war story, the novel with the gold medallion on the cover declaring my prize. I put on an old black coat with the buttons dangling, as though covering tattered jeans might conceal the shame of conjuring my parents' embrace on the four-poster. Is the coat needed on this warm day?

Your topcoat, Mimi. Better safe than sorry.

I put words in my mother's mouth while Bill strikes a match, cups his hand around yet another Lucky. In this way we keep track of each other, though they're long gone.

If egg whites are stiffly beaten, the meringue never falls.

Just brought the fellow across the state line into the jurisdiction, don't get a hold on your lefty complaint. This rendition? I set myself up for their corrections, begging their care, their tolerance, my indulgence of the past, I suppose. The picture of him in the *Bridgeport Post*, Bill, plump, choirboy handsome, the jaunty brim of his felt hat casting a shadow on his smile. Handcuffed to a mobster of note: *Simple police work, extradition.*

May Day 1978

> *I write to you on his birthday, the wrong day for my father to be born. He voted Conservative down the line. You pulled the Socialist lever long after McLevy was thrown out of the Party. The one blip in your near perfect pairing? There's no evidence to the contrary. In any case, thank you for having me.*
>
> —A note never sent to my mother,
> her mind fleeting, soon gone

So in the old black coat I headed to the Park across from our apartment house designed in '29, a year of public and personal disaster. I aimed to cancel my debit column with fresh air, bracing city views. Just a walk, yet, waiting for the light to change on Central Park West, I felt I was off on a redemptive journey. Turning to see our apartment house as though for the last time, I noted the familiar storybook façade—the lofty terraces, crenellated towers, fake balconies and dungeon gridwork of each window. Do you recall the grande dame at a meeting in the lobby after we'd all bought our co-op shares and could now think of the golden concrete bulk with silvery doors as our property? In a voice steady with the assurance of old money, she brandished her cane, protesting any alteration to the building that would not be a landmark till 1985. Most particularly she defended the casement windows that screeched open on their hinges quite easily enough for men who'd lost everything in the market to jump to their deaths on Black Tuesday. Not accurate, for it would have been, at the earliest, the winter of '31 when the first tenants moved in, but she was grand with a blue rinse permanent wave and bright lipstick of a past era. And who knows if it was only a story made up in defense of our iron windows, which, though not sturdy, are handsome to this day?

You said: *There's no one among us to challenge her. The small triumph of the survivor.*

I walked into the Park slowly, as advised, and headed straight for the slope running up to the Reservoir newly enclosed with a black iron fence, replica of the Calvert Vaux original. There was not a ripple on the water. The ever present gulls squatting on the pipe that spans the Reservoir appeared two dimensional, so many ducks in a shooting gallery. For a long moment no one in sight, all the better to cherish my melancholy brought on by eavesdropping on my parents' bedroom with its crisp dresser scarf and the wicker chair in which I spent most of a summer reading *War and Peace* for the love story, skimming the pages of Napoleon's retreat from Moscow, understanding less of that carnage than I did of the *Bridgeport Post* mapping the D-Day Invasion, or the White Russian Division advancing on the Germans. That war progressed on the nightly news my father listened to, head tilted toward the speaker of our bulbous mahogany console, while I set the table in the kitchen. When I finished my chore, I'd come into the living room to hear the roundup; then my father took his place at the head of the table and softened the bloody events of this day for my mother, who absorbed the news in silence, then took off her apron to serve our supper. One night, with adolescent bravado, I declared that the defeat of the Soviets at Minsk was much like the fall of Napoleon's Grand Army in the very same city, history repeating itself as our table talk mixed tidbits of neighborhood gossip, my brother's mastery of Latin declensions and my father's unpatriotic grumble at his paltry serving of meat.

Now, Bill. How often she'd sneak her chop or chicken thigh onto his plate.

Taking up my route round the Reservoir, I determined to leave behind these girlish memories of war, more honest than my invention of Nazi espionage in the novel I'd thrown aside. Looking to the first lap of my forbidden journey, I saw the runners coming upon me, a full cadre of men and women in red jerseys training for some competition. Their leader swiveled his gleaming shaved head to check on the pack falling farther and farther behind. It is only in recalling the moment of the runners straining to catch up with this lean man wound tight, clearing me out of his way, that I clung to the fence, saw in the tranquil Reservoir a mirror image of the bright sky that banished all thought of my troubling intrusion on the lives of Loretta and Bill, subject to my telling their tales. In a Chaplinesque strut, sure to leave my fraudulent war novel behind, a love affair trumped by betrayal, I began my route around the Reservoir Track. The body took hold with its thoughtless demands. The level course is rimmed with limp mullein in this season and untidy wild asters. I'm not part of the jogging scene. The heart that's failed me improvises its bebop arrhythmia. I take caution as ordered, slow to a stroll, but never give in to a bench, not even as I approach the bridge joining track to parkland, where a gathering of athletes, maybe just neighborhood friends, pay court to the old runner, Alberto Arroyo. He's at his post every fine day, some not so fine, the gold medal dangling from the patriotic ribbon round his neck. In running gear, silk shorts this crisp day. I catch sight of the swollen blue veins in his legs, fanning out on the weathered cheeks the handlebar mustache white as his gleaming halo of hair. His gestures exuberant as always, though by his side the steel cane, rubber grips on its claws. It's said he ran the first New York Marathon, indeed was a founder. Who knows if that story is true or with time became legend? The time before the old legs gave out, before he sported the Mylar toga each cold day, conserving body heat at the end of no particular race, before he became a figure of reverence at the South Pumping Station, fashioning himself as local patron saint, grandee of the Running Track.

A mere walker in down-at-heel tennis shoes, I thought how neat to be of that company, to know I might scramble up to the Reservoir, pay homage to the old runner, listen to his words of wisdom or enjoy the gossip of the day to set me free of the reading chair which this day brought me back to the place of origin, my voyeuristic tale with its many variations—how on an Autumn night when the barberry hedge was not yet planted in the patch of front yard to absorb the noise of traffic, with the green linen shade drawn against the streetlight, my parents felt their way to each other in the dark. Felt their way with what purpose? I heard the footfall behind me, the huffing breath of the next trotter. All passed me by. As though I was stuck on a treadmill, the Fifth Avenue side of Central Park with its swirl of Guggenheim Museum seemed no closer. Soldiering on in my invalid pace, this day's outing was a strategic maneuver against the assault of memory.

This stretch of track is more carefully tended, though the ornamental cherry trees have dropped their end of season pips and, sloping down to the police barracks, ferns flopped, yellow and limp. Tourists had found their way into the Park with museum shopping bags and guidebooks in hand—Germans with camera gear; Japanese lovers delicately holding hands; a party of Brits, the Union Jack on their sweatshirts. Clouds swept in, a sudden surface rippling, and a mallard, floating free of the rushes, ruffling her wings, was joined by a male with brighter plumage by far.

Name of the laike? Sharp Cockney diphthong.

Walking on I called out: *Reservoir.*

Can't they see it's man-made? The wonky circumference distorted by a hydraulic bulge on the south side. The slight undulations of this carefully plotted shoreline bear no resemblance to nature's random design. Turning, not to be rude to visitors, I called out again, *Reservoir.* The Japanese man put an arm round his girl as though to protect her from my shrill cry. The Germans had set up a tripod for a picture of our Fall blazing an Oktoberfest across the shimmering expanse of water. That shot can be bought from a vendor outside the Guggenheim, but it would be their own view, recall a hike in New York. Yes, they carried burled walking sticks as though to conquer an alpine height, but our Track is level, the water piped in, no racing streams, no cascade. My breath came short, unsteady as I turned round again to call out another correction.

Jacqueline Kennedy!

Reservoir, I meant to repeat, but the Brits had gone their way. She would have recalled the old Croton Reservoir piping water down to the city after the raging fires that consumed Lower Broadway long before the Civil War. Keen on preservation, she might have winced then, aware of history's erasures, accepted the memorial renaming with grace. On a slick little map, I'd seen the blot of blue water *Lake Jackie,* too familiar by far, yet she'd know her name would *convey* to the Germans, the Brits, even to the private school kids who replaced my Japanese lovers, kids awkwardly entwined on a bench, a lacrosse stick balanced between them.

Drawing back from the heavy breath of his ardor, the girl shrugged him off. I was their embarrassment, old lady in tennis shoes, buttons dangling.

Needle and thread, Mimi. Don't let yourself go.

Old party pretending to look away, not to admire the girl's mane of long honey hair, the neat muscular knots in her legs. She's baiting this guy. The awkward gesture of his hand hovering in limbo above her bare knee; his face, broad and earnest, Slavic perhaps. The affront of his rejection sends me back to the creak of the wicker chair in my parents' bedroom as I settled each Summer day into the romance. How inevitable of Natasha, that enchanting child, to love the careless Prince, not the worthy suitor, Pierre. But worse, morally worse in my view: when Tolstoy finally marries her to the good man, she plays their last scenes as a frump, a plump housewife and mother.

Still reading your book?

Yes; they fed horse flesh to the Turks, did you know? Proclaimed at the dinner table to alarm. *They,* the French or the Russians? I was uncertain, but the shocking tidbit was mine. *Which we may be eating now.*

Rumor that Kunkel, the butcher on Capital Avenue, minced horsemeat in with the beef. Now that recall does stop me; the supper table lesson on the bloody retreat of Napoleon's Grand Army. The lacrosse player, lolling on the bench not two feet from the Track, was the girl. The bright blue jacket of her team thrown open, breasts on display. Let me make that clear: nipples, erect in chill Autumn air, poked a T-shirt which read, EVERYONE LOVES A CATHOLIC GIRL.

So untrue. I could tell her stories along that line. We were not embarrassed by each other.

Me—reading her chest.

She—slouching in a phony embrace, humiliating that boy. Then, ditching the flirtation, she ran off, lacrosse stick cradling air, boy trailing after. Dismissed from their after school tryst, I felt a sharp pang of shame, the lot of a voyeur. Had I invented my parents' embrace in the four-poster, then hovered over these hapless kids to dismiss my guilt? I had manipulated history to write a love story. Printed and praised, there could be no erasure. Playing a shell game—that war, this war, did I hope for a reprieve with the feeble cry of my outrage at the Cheerleader, at the coaches directing his boyish strut as he comes to the podium on the White House lawn? We are audience to his grotesque performance at halftime, his bounce, joy in atrocities. Whatever happened to Civil Disobedience? The essay not assigned in college. Fellow grew beans, lived by a pond, nothing as fine as Central Park, what we've got here.

When I turned back to see the distance I'd come, the Germans were still in the photography business. Finding the pin oaks dull at end of day, they'd set up a white screen to reflect what was left of sunlight on tarnished bronze leaves. *Give it a week. Our grand finale will knock your Birkenstocks off.* My heart beat a fierce catch-up thump. I was breathless as I came to the open view at last, the point of full exposure. Clear across the Reservoir loomed the house I fled a half hour ago. From this vantage point, the trees, still leafed out, erased all other buildings on Central Park West. Our turrets caught the last glitter of this day in false gold.

Yes, the El Dorado. The presumptuous name of the house where we live with ancient plumbing and electric circuits updated with vigilance, with those casement windows sanded and painted against rust and the mural in the lobby of a phantasmagoric pilgrimage to a futuristic city of heavily varnished gold. And in a back room where the sun never shines, my failed book thrown aside.

Get out in the sun, Mimi. Take your bike for a ride.

My secondhand Raleigh, tires gone flat while I turned the pages of Tolstoy's very long story renewed and renewed. I feel the hard surface of its indestructible library cover (dark green), title stamped in the spine. And see, as of this day, the slick dust jacket of the war story that garnered my prize.

REVISION

> *I could but dream the whole thing over as I went——as I read; and bath-ing it, so to speak, in that medium, hope that, some still newer and shrewder critic's intelligence subtly operating, I should have breathed upon the old catastrophes and accidents, the old wounds and mutila-tions and disfigurements, wholly in vain.*
>
> ——Henry James, *The Art of the Novel*

On the flap of the book which bears a gilt medallion on its cover, *The Normandy invasion of the Second World War is rendered in cinematic detail.* Flap copy performs its duty. *With detailed care the writer illuminates* (!) the baby face of a soldier who figures in the opening pages as disfigured beyond recognition. The dog tag hanging round the kid's neck with a Star of David recalls his bar mitzvah, Torah in hand, that side story set in a clap-board temple on an unlikely back street in the Berkshires, but then it's all unlikely——the body count of those left behind on the sands of Normandy fails to elevate a misbegotten romance. The boy soldier——he's well out of it, out of the plot. His commanding officer had studied physics with Heisenberg at the Kaiser Wilhelm Institute whereby hangs an oper-atic tale. *Liebestraum,* my story of an American Captain's puppy love for a soprano he occasionally slept with in Bayreuth, the Führer's favorite Art Site, is *searchingly honest.* Blurb on, elicit kudos from readers before they turn the first page. Too late to be sorry. Terrible thing to do, conjure that kid out of a squat brick high school, flagpole at the ready in a dusty playground. Note of pathos, fakes his age to fight the Nazis. Stunning body count of the D-Day landing, the Captain's doomed foreign affair, his postwar prize of suburban survival. Was that last bittersweet chapter all I learned from Tolstoy's true and dark story? That war, this war. I think now of the boy who painted our fence in Monterey, Mass. He waited some months till he was the age to enlist, but writerly ambition stirred my plot line years before he quit the toy store, that job with no future. He is now serving his third deployment in Iraq.

Today, reading in my airless back room, the landing gear grunting onto the shore of Omaha Beach, my soldier boy—jaw shattered, chill waves pulling him under—ticked off the memory of my father turning up the volume of the Philco on the evening when all America, so the story goes, listened to Roosevelt call a benediction upon our troops, *the pride of our nation.* My mother coming from the kitchen to hear *we shall return again and again,* while I stood by the console. The clatter of knives and forks when I dropped them during the President's prayer.

Mimi! My father scolding.

History demoted to domestic anecdote, the uncontrollable urge to bear witness, write myself into the scene.

Where was I when the first mushroom cloud rose in its ghostly threat on the black-and-white screen?

The sun parlor, where my father had set up a twelve-inch set to watch the Yankees.

When Kennedy slumped into his wife's lap?

London, a rented flat in Chelsea. The neighbors we'd never met came to the door with flowers.

Bobby bloodied on the kitchen floor of the Ambassador Hotel?

Walking my daughter to first grade, streets strangely empty. The assassination posted on the school door.

Let me unscramble time. In the personal almanac: my solemn attention to the landing of Allied Forces in Normandy, June 6, 1944, was broken by the kettle shrieking on the stove. I let go forks, knives and dessert spoons to savor rice pudding still warm from the oven. The following week, the school year ended, I turned to the opening pages of *War and Peace*. Mastering the difficult Russian names, I pursued the romance, admiring the wealthy landowners, suspecting the impoverished royals might be up to no good. In my parents' bedroom I settled into the creaking wicker chair by a side window. On the few dark days, I read under the soft light of a silk-shaded lamp. Scraps of my mother's old skirts and my father's worn trousers had been braided into a lumpy rug at the Women's Art League, wool gathering history. On their Victorian dresser, her soft chamois nail buffer in its ivory case lay beside the empty leather holster for the County Detective's gun. I am no longer sure why I plotted, or why they tolerated, this incursion into their room.

The next year, watching the first A-bomb do its unspeakable thing, I was reading nothing at all. That summer was one long orgy of desire at Fairfield Beach. I blistered my fair skin parading in front of a wheezing asthmatic boy mustered out of the army. He never took notice of me— *Everyone loves a Catholic girl*—his name irretrievable, while I bear the near-invisible scars where the basal cells were removed from my chin. Looking across the Reservoir to the El Dorado, I stopped on the track remembering the good doctor who zapped the offending growths with such skill, Bernie Simon, who lived in the north tower of our building. He had worked with the team of plastic surgeons when the Hiroshima Maidens were brought back to New York, twenty-five Keloid Girls mostly kept out of sight by their families. Nine years after the bomb, they arrived at La Guardia, June 1955. Their disfigured faces and limbs were to be reconstructed. Many of the maidens were billeted with Quakers, peace-loving people. By October some had discarded kimonos. Others posed for the camera in saddle oxfords, twinsets, cultured pearls, the costume of American college girls; others wore prim secretarial suits cut close to the body. In the photographs, taken at a distance, you can't really see the thick, dead flesh on their hands and faces.

Today, the mighty block of Mount Sinai hovers over the eastern skyline of the Park, but it was in the old hospital at 100th Street and Fifth Avenue where the A-girls were slowly, painfully transformed into something like normal—that can't be the word—poster girls for an act of reparation, cruel footnote to history. Dr. Simon lost a spirited maiden on the operating table, though he massaged her bare heart with his hands. Tomoka had wanted to wear summer blouses with short sleeves, not much to ask. The year before his death, Bernie worked out in a loping run, an easy stretch on the Bridle Path, the flesh of his legs and arms burnished with a healthy tan. As though to figure in my story by a masterful computation or throw of the dice, an honored mathematician, Peter Lax, lives other side of our building. When called to Los Alamos, the Project he worked on seemed to the young lieutenant "like science fiction. There were all these legends everywhere."

Here's a true story you might recall if you're getting on in years: *This Is Your Life,* a popular show, bottom of the TV barrel, in which the unsuspecting party is brought onstage and confronted with someone long lost who "made all the difference." A programmed occasion for faked embarrassment, tears of joy, shrieks of disbelief: *Oh, my God!* Which is exactly what the pilot and bombardier of *Enola Gay,* the plane of infamy that dropped the bomb on Hiroshima, cried out, *Oh, my God!* upon viewing the shadowy forms of two Keloid Girls hidden behind translucent screens, lest the audience of 40 million be disturbed by their Barnumesque disfigurement. The pilot died this past year, ever sure of his mission. Well, that's the story folks, entertainment trumping science fiction.

I managed to make my way huffing, puffing to midpoint in the eastern stretch of the Track. Windows high above Fifth Avenue flashed the bronze setting of the sun. I will never understand how that brilliant display, mostly blocked by the apartment houses on Central Park West, leaps the Reservoir's expanse. And do not care to understand, demanding magic from this forbidden journey, though the simple refraction of light at end of day may be grammar-school science. Breath coming short, halfway home, no use turning back. Feeling my considerable age, I settled into a simple touch of the blues. Not a jogger in sight, as though an official blew the whistle—ending play. Loping on, heart racing ahead, I was alone on the loop that leads to the North Gate House, thinking the tennis courts would soon come into view, might still be open at dusk with the *plunk-plunk* of balls and the mercy of a public drinking fountain. But there, under the flickering cover of trees, were two figures, still as statues until they heard the slow shuffle of my feet, then the woman put out her hand. With a swift gesture demanded I stop.

Perched above—an owl. In the lens of his unblinking golden eyes, the bird possessed us.

The quiet, spooky at first, was then pleasantly prolonged, the owl joining our conspiracy of silence. The woman's attention consumed her. The man lowered his binoculars to feast on his wife's pure pleasure as she wrote in a little book. I presume wife. Now I place gold rings on the birdwatchers' fingers. Matched beyond their Nike jackets and billed caps, they became one in their attention to the bird. It's only now I frame them as young lovers in a chill season, intent on their pursuit of nature; not shepherd and milkmaid tumbling in the hay, stockings in telltale disarray. I presume they are blessed with each other beyond this bucolic scene. Or not blessed, for he withdrew a few steps, looked somewhat paternal, admiring the quick strokes of her drawing, the ardor of her attention. For a moment he took me in—disheveled old lady with no claim to bird lore—then flashed me a smile as if to say, *We're not among the converted.*

His wife would know, without benefit of my Audubon Guide, the long-eared owl to be ubiquitous in the Northeast. She drew us to our observation again. A sudden movement in the undergrowth broke the spell. We waited, we three, for something tremendous, the owl's dive for its victim, a chipmunk or Reservoir rat. The bird would not perform. Then, in that still, suspended time, thump-de-thump declared itself, the heavy off beat of my heart. Random, the turbulence does not follow fast moves or exertion, drops in like a petulant neighbor with its complaint. I waited for the fibrillation to tap its way back to something like normal. When I skipped off from our hushed encounter as best I could, then turned back, the birdwatchers had also left the scene. The flat Track seemed uphill all the way, the North Gate House much farther than recalled. As it finally came into view, I heard a creature's high screech of death, and the owl's cruel laughter—hoo-hoo-hooting, having deprived us the thrill of the kill.

Clouds moved in with surprising swiftness, dusk turning twilight.

I approached the dreary granite of the North Gate House, or houses—
two on the Reservoir shore—straight and tall like giant rooks abandoned
in a game of chess. Their black iron doors bolted, double padlocked. I
take the notice personally: KEEP OUT. As though I would trash, pollute the
works, while in the backwater sloshing between the towers my fellow
citizens have deposited plastic bottles, deflated soccer balls, dead sneakers. Skeletal ribs of an umbrella float in thick green scum. This debris
seemed placed here to call the city to mind—its waste, fumes, and general congestion of the grid in which Frederick Law Olmsted and Calvert
Vaux staged their pastoral drama, drew up plans for a park with hills and
vales, rusticated nooks, and the folly of a castle to be viewed from the
grandeur of Bethesda Terrace. The people of New York, high and low,
would take pleasure in this otherworld that would never admit crumbled cigarette packs, milky condoms, a dismembered iPod jauntily floating in a tangle of weeds. Just beyond this detritus, the water was clear
across to the South Pumping Station. The gulls, drained of color in the
approaching night, held their post all along the pipe that dissects the Reservoir. I'd always thought a pipe's a pipe. Not at all, when the water's low
you see their perch to be handsomely paved with stone. Above, the moon
was translucent, a nibbled host in a starless sky. The programmed lights
shone brightly on the tennis courts for players who would not give up on
the day.

Home before dark, Mimi.

Take care.

Repossessed by their warning, I found myself, dark end of day, round
the block on French Street—its empty lot with shanties, idle men out of
work. Our mother never called them tramps.

*Watch out for the Gypsies your father runs out of town, rabble that follow the
circus. Duck the Commies at Workmen's Circle. Steer clear of Benny the Drooler.*

I can take care of myself.

As I crossed the Bridle Path, the last child in the playground struggled
against his mother's embrace. The fiberglass hippos and jungle gym clung
to their stations while the kid was dragged off protesting. He did not
want to go home, nor did I. How I hate that antique locution—prissy,

at arm's length from my fear the escape route ended where I began, the backward glance at my storybook with its claims to a sorrow never felt for the reality of a war and its aftermath I did not—may never—fully understand. With the doctor's warning and the day's meds, I had accomplished the loop, 1.58 miles, still subject to parental correction. Why the twinge of disgrace, sharp as a stitch in my side? Why my childish name? What's more, they were right, I do not know how to take care of myself, simply enjoy the day's adventure, cut free of the past. I'd been seduced by the contrived beauty and small adventures of Central Park, hoodwinked by an owl, affronted by black iron doors. My playground was closed for the night. I was home, Chez El Dorado, elevator at the ready.

You were there, waiting. I passed you by in the hall—rudely, I guess—ran to my workroom, made a note—*Everyone loves*—lest I forget the self-serving legend of the *Catholic Girl,* forgetting I'd had a Bic and small pad in the pocket of the old black coat, two of its three buttons now missing.

I called to you, *Put on the pasta pot.*

By my reading chair, the book I threw aside. On a knockout cover, a single Rhinemaiden swims for the gold. By the sparkling stream, the author's name is printed in Third Reich Gothic. I had aimed at important: that took the prize. *Liebestraum,* now reissued with a student guide, should have a query on the writer's plagiarized emotions: Does the note of doomed love underwrite the inexhaustible horror of *that* war? My journey down the well-trodden path into the dark woods of National Socialism was pure Grimm. I cast myself as the clever troll to lead the way.

But if, you suggested in a reality check way back when, when I was in the heady spin of my misdirection, *if, before the war, that lieutenant you're writing about studied physics with Heisenberg, he should have been stirring the hot pot at Alamogordo with our neighbor Peter Lax, not slogging through enemy fire on D-Day.*

Captain. I promoted him toward the end of the war. Yes, or he might have been translating at Nuremberg and not so easily betrayed by a Rhinemaiden bitch; but D-Day it was for the sake of my PLOT, the *nefarious name, in any flash upon the fancy,* so advises Henry James. As though calling upon the Master would make amends for my *patter of quick steps,* the forward march of my story. Did I then presume the glib balance of an aphorism, sum up the argument: *Memory prods History. History corrects Memory. As in—*

Where were we when Al Gore won the election?

In Seville, the Grand Hotel. We went to bed happy.

This evening you appeared at the door of my workroom, no longer costumed for the office. For the first time this year, you wore your old wool vest, offered me a glass of wine. You had news of the children and the world, urged me to take off my coat.

Stay awhile.

The children, you told me, by which we mean grandchildren, have moved on to pumpkins and plastic masks of action figures unfamiliar to oldies, but the options are still open about what they will actually *be* for Halloween. Transformed, as we were, to tramps or ghosts in homemade costumes?

It's only Columbus Day, a day off school, a parade, no treats. Buy them too early, their pumpkins will rot.

I noticed the scar on your nose which I lose track of over the years, a perfectly round patch of slick keloid, large as a dime. One day you had a chat with Bernie Simon in the lobby. *I'll take care of that,* he said, saving your life. In those days we were cavalier about the ravages of time. Heartburn, toothache, a touch of vertigo—our vision of the future blurred by cheap drugstore glasses.

Where've you been?

The Park.

As though just another jaunt, breath of fresh air, not a reprieve from the heavy sentence of the book I'd thrown aside. What might I have said that was truthful? That I too often looked back, not to presume upon the day's blessing, isn't that how my mother might put it? Channeling that cultured voice—*Best get on with your business, Mimi. Remember Lot's wife.*

Well, I do, I remember that wife is given no name, no space in the story, and no say. She disobeys, turns to look at the sinful city in sulfurous flames. Swift chapters in the good book don't miss a beat turning her into a pillar of salt. Whatever the indulgences of body and soul in Sodom, she was leaving home with nothing like the comfort of Central Park to run to.

You took *Liebestraum,* the offending book, from my hand. *Leave it.*

Burn it?

You knew perfectly well what I'd been up to, picking at the gold medallion on its cover like a kid with a scab on my knee.

I said, *Let's give some thought to supper.*

The new flat-screen TV in the kitchen brought cut-rate news. Corporate Greed, Celebrity Breakup, DNA Frees Convicted Rapist, Dollar Drops Against Euro. As president flops off mountain bike, I shed onion tears. High school bands march down Fifth Avenue: NYPD, Mayor Bloomberg, Senators, Sons of Italy, Knights of Columbus. Car Bomb in Haifa, Helicopter Malfunction in Mosul. Five marines, their deaths verified. Sipping my wine—tears, the real thing.

So tell me, what's wrong?

The Knights of Columbus. My grandfather.

Who made the money and lost it?

Nothing to cry about. Those kids.

Their photos: two in camouflage, three in dress uniform. Tonight the oldest is twenty-three. I could see you didn't buy my tears for the cruel fate of those boys shipped home, RIP. Onion knife in hand, I left you to go back down the hall to my workroom. Behind the confusion of old postcards and printouts, there's the photo of my grandfather sitting on the steps of the Knights of Columbus, an ample brick-and-shingle house spiffed up to rival the Masonic Lodge. Bridgeport, 1918. He is broad-shouldered; craggy forehead shelters his eyes from the sun, mouth rather too generous with a twist of a smile. George Burns is remarkably handsome, big hands clasped on his knees to ground him while this picture is taken with the fraternal brothers, important men who run Main Street, the harbor, City Hall. He is the only Knight in a soft shirt and tweed cap that a worker might wear on a Sunday. The rest of the

Templars sport confident fedoras, stiff collars, four-in-hand ties. All of them Irish, and it's a wonder to me still how these Paddys-come-lately tied up with Columbus when they had little to do with Italians other than renting them tinderboxes in the Hollow or granting the occasional loan. Burns built houses for the men who worked on his crew, all Italians, paving roads in the city outgrowing its limits. At sixteen, when the landscape firm that bore Olmsted's name extended the breakwater in Seaside Park, he'd carted stones, scythed the bulrushes of Long Island Sound and lost half a finger.

Back in the kitchen, I hand over the photo dulled to amber photogravure. You've seen it often, yet I launch the whole roundabout story while the water in the pasta pot boils away, tell how I circumnavigated the Reservoir, hooting at tourists when I came to that bend in the road, and end with the devalued holiday, the grandfather I hardly knew, an old man bankrupt, shrunken, silenced by age, dealing his grandchildren pennies from a jam jar.

Thank Grandpa.

I'm small, with few words. He reaches out, strokes my cheek with the stump, the slick flesh of that terrible finger. I'm ashamed of my tears. Pennies clink as my mother drops them one by one back into the jar.

Last night I told you of my slow progress round the track, the reflection of clouds skimming the water, Fall not yet in its glory as balm to my passing fit of despair, the fabled Reservoir drained to the events of my day. Outwitted by an owl. I did not mention shortness of breath, my heart's marathon beat pumping for the booby prize. It took the evening news in the kitchen to connect me to Columbus Day, the great Christoforo aiding and abetting my notion that history prods memory, serving up fragments of postcolonial lore.

Not arbitrary like strands in my mother's rag rug, carefully chosen.

Plotted?

We've lived too long together. I feed you your lines.

Yes, plotted, and on I went turning back to serving my life sentence for the story I committed, that Nazi soprano who betrays a smitten officer, his love doomed from the first page, American innocence exposed as plain foolish but *always forgivable. Liebestraum* (*Love Story* in plain English); a touch of irony to leaven my story.

Come off it. Your tone not amused, not indulgent.

I wound back to the comfort zone, the course of my flight through the lobby of the El Dorado with its homey grandeur—sofa, club chairs, flowers stiffly arranged—past the kindest of men at the imperial front desk and the doorman who would never comment on my coat with its last buttons dangling, bleach spots of a misbegotten wash day splattering my jeans, then my crossing to the park with the comfort of its stories. Waiting for linguine to test al dente, I confessed I had not cried for today's boys blown up by the side of a dusty road.

I'd be awash in tears, every night's news. I cried for an old Irishman I hardly knew who stroked my cheek with the thick flesh of half a finger, a Knight, mind you, of Columbus. So, I cried for myself. Isn't that a shame?

Take it down a peg, Mims.

I could barely distinguish between my mother's correction and your tolerant smile at pennies in a jar. I moved on to the owl, claiming the bird as my discovery of the day, how he tricked me into submission. You said, *Watching the pot?*

Daybook, October 9, 2007

In the morning I phone my brother; he of total recall.

As we talk, I pick at the medallion still stuck on my book. When I have it off, Alberich comes into view, the gnarled dwarf who grabbed the gold ring. The Rhinemaidens, all three laughing at his plug-ugly body; at his rejection of love which set Wagner's whole Ring Cycle rolling on and on, fable begetting fable. By family telepathy my brother gets the message. I'm in the dumps. I protect myself with a pawn, tremor of uncertainty in my voice: *My Summer of* War and Peace? *That creaking wicker chair? How come I hung out in their bedroom?*

Don't make a fuss. Grandma Burns came to stay. She displaced you. They set up a cot in my room. I can still hear you snore.

I don't snore.

But yes, that Summer I set one more place at the kitchen table. *And the war news? Before supper we gathered by the Philco.*

The Magnavox.

Trust he's right about the Magnavox, but I know for certain that on D-Day FDR's message of sorrow and hope was cut off by the clatter of forks, knives and spoons.

Mystery solved: *I dropped the good silver 'cause Grandma came to stay!*

My brother's voice is strong today, sharp, lighthearted: *What are you on about?* He gets it. *D-Day? Your prize story—rubbing salt in the wound of success? All that old stuff.*

Calendar stuff. Like Grandpa in a dinner jacket at the Grand Knights of Columbus. They served oysters Rockefeller, don't you know. Santa María, *remember?*

That was my brother's ship in a bottle. I recall his concentration with glue, pincers, scraps of a linen napkin dipped in tea for the sails, button-thread rigging. He remembered pebbles brought home from the school-yard, painted gold. The treasure chest stuck to the balsa wood deck of the Admiral's flagship, *Santa María.*

All that glitters . . . Columbus, he's discredited.

Untarnished in grammar school.

You're a day in arrears, Mimi, but give him a try, one of your bios. They always set you up. Lives of the Rich or Famous. Your calendarial Book of Days.

Calendaric.

Calendarial. Promote and demote, that's what history amounts to these days. Admiral of the Ocean Seas, prop the old sailor up, easier than ship in a bottle.

I heard the *Times* flop down on the table that lives by his side with amber bottles of pills for the daily doses aiding and abetting stealth moves on his body. We compare systolic over diastolic achievements, scoring low for the gold star.

He knew, this brother who was there from the beginning, that I was out of sorts, weighted with more than my displacement to a wicker chair, what big eyes you have Gramma, sleeping in my bed—all that old stuff. He groaned slightly as he rose. I heard the slow squeak of his walker as he made his way across to the bookshelf in his tidy study. Now he would pick *The Anatomy of Melancholy* off the shelf, the book so heavy as he flipped through its pages to find clever bits to amuse me. We had been into Burton's big book of a lifeline before:

Of Seasons of the year Autumn is most melancholy. . . . Fools have moist brains and light hearts. They are free from ambition, envy, shame and fear; they are neither troubled in conscience nor macerated with cares, to which our whole life is subject.

Stop!

It be, melancholia, a kind of dotage without a fever.

Stop!

If there have been any suppressions or stopping of blood at nose, at hemeroids or women's months, then to open a vein in the head or about the ankles.

Till he induces laughter. *So, you think while they listened to war news after the dishes were dried, I read Tolstoy by lamplight? Flies batting the screen.*

Stay on message, he says. *Honor the holiday, one of your brief lives, Columbus.*

There's nothing left to explore.

We're still hoping for water on Mars. What about your time in Genoa? Just writing your stories at that villa. No grand tour.

I'd launched a piece on Columbus but it sniffed of embalming fluid, seemed a replica of his statue commanding the Piazza Acquaverde, the bus station in Genoa. We did tour the house where Christoforo was probably not born, and in a nautical museum viewed waxy simulacra of the Admiral with a first mate, and selection of sailors costumed for the journey. His instruments of navigation, the quadrant and the astrolabe, while  never useful, were beautiful, and in yet another funky museum, a plaster cast of his hand. Why his hand? *It's so undiscovered, Genoa. The well-worn joke . . . À tre scopertede . . .*

Prego, *not to tell it again.* **Do Columbus.**

Like the old days, I obey his command.

DEAD RECKONING

October 12, 1492—Cristoforo Colombo, Italian Navigator, born near Genoa, discovers the Indes East of the Ganges.

For some days Columbus noted in his log: *weeds in abundance with crabs among them;* a whale, *they always keep near the coast;* pelicans and a turtle-dove. On October 11 he sighted a flickering light in the distance as though from a candle. That proved a mirage. The true sighting is attributed to Martín Alonzo, who sounded the alarm at 2:00 AM, according to orders. Columbus knelt on the shore of Guanahani to claim San Salvador for the King and Queen of Spain in the name of Our Lord Jesus Christ. He had reached the Indies. In the heat of his discovery, his account flips from third to first person. The natives are recorded as *an inoffensive people.* He gave them glass beads, red caps and various trifles in exchange for par-rots and skeins of cotton thread. No need to say who got the better of the bargain. These Indians had no fireboxes, no candles, no weapons. The naked bodies of the men were decorated with red and white powders in mysterious designs, but it seemed to the Admiral they would make good servants and *would readily become Christians as they have no religion.*

Adam with an agenda: he named each island in this earthly paradise—Trinidad, Fernando, Isabella, Santa María de la Concepción and so forth—bringing it all back home. Best that he did not invoke the Lord in naming Puerto Grande, a sculpted harbor of Cuba we know as our naval base, Guantánamo Bay with its history of detention and "outrages upon personal dignity" (Geneva Convention). On first sight, the vege-tation of the islands recalled the beauty of Andalusia, but deeper into the rain forest's dense thickets of vines and lush trees the humidity was overwhelming. The natives, friendly and instructive, alas had no vein of gold. They offered stone glittering with something like mica, and the story of a great king who lived by an inland lake. Or perhaps the golden man was lord of a distant island? Could he be farther up the dangerous waters of the Orinoco, this godlike figure in some versions named El Dorado, with coffers of the precious stuff in his city of Manoa, enough to fill the royal treasury impoverished by holy wars to convert infidels to the one true faith. Now Colón's calling was to be as much missionary as miner, persisting in his duties until on the island of Hispaniola he might find the river of gold in the waters of the Ciabo, might find enough glitter to show in Madrid along with curiosities and his captives. He settled the crew he left behind to set up shop. The book of Colombo's discoveries was a best seller; his tales wonderful and so wonderfully told they might be the adventures of Marco Polo, which he read and reread in Italian, his mother tongue, preparing for his discoveries and for the writing of his own extravagant tale. After the success of the first voyage, Columbus drew up a contract, *The Book of Privileges,* in which Don Colombo demanded and received a title, a coat of arms, and a share *in perpetuity* of the profits of all the lands of his discovery. On the second voyage, he brought chickens to this handsome race quick to learn words of a strange language and the value of a farmyard egg. Prospects did not turn out for the best.

The High Admiral of the Ocean Seas proved to be a slack administrator of the greatest real-estate deal of all time. He was unfortunate in choosing his lieutenants. Christoforo's gift was for mapping the sea, not transatlantic politics, not sorting out quarrels between gold diggers and the indigenous people. Among the curiosities brought back from his first travels—lemon seeds, a necklace of fish bones, tobacco, cinnamon bark, corn—were strange birds and slaves. He had assumed his captives would submit to this arrangement, though the Queen found their possession a bad show when they were put on public display—perhaps the beginning of his fall from grace. And where in advertised abundance was the gold? At the outset of his third voyage, he was becalmed in the Doldrums under the sign of Leo, which, given his belief in astrology, foretold the severity of his fate. When at last the Admiral landed at Santo Domingo, the ungrateful settlers he had left behind revolted. His powers dissolved, Columbus was shipped home in chains.

In a homey museum just above Genoa, we discovered him in two roles. A white marble statue portrays a pretty boy with abundant curls, dreaming the glorious future, longing for adventures at sea. This charming Christoforo sits on a shelf with the crusty oil painting of a broken man, scant white hair, swollen feet, tattered robes. *Shackled below deck,* you said, *head bowed to darkness.* Upon his return to Hispaniola, the settlers had not thanked him for their hunger, war with the natives, death and disease. And yet again he returned. Now here's the pity: the Don came back that fourth voyage, sailing with his young son and brother, to find the route to China described by Marco Polo, confusing fiction with geography, presuming that the estuaries of Panama might be the rivers of Cathay.

Cristóbal Colón, Colom. Or Colombo—an Italian-Jewish name. A wool carder, weaver, boy sailor. Instructed by his brother Bartholomew in cartography, he mapped the known world. In Portugal and Spain, cartography was a Jewish profession. According to Christoforo's calculations, the world might be shaped like a pear, and so he sailed round this fruity globe to bring back spices and trinkets of the Caribbean. His true quest had been for the wonders of China or Japan. He figured the world too small, America lay in the way. It is said the Admiral, bitter and nearly blind, passed his last years consumed with the defense of his *Privileges* and his title. It is said the Genoese bankers drew on his *pesos d'oro* in Hispaniola, which supported him grandly. If true, he died rich. A devout Christian, he was deeply religious yet a confessed mystic who communed with the stars, though he never mastered celestial navigation. Five hundred years after weeds and a pelican foretold the most promising landfall known to man, a colossal statue of Christopher Columbus was refused by five cities in the States and Puerto Rico. A Taino woman, descendant of the people who first greeted Columbus, debunked the memorial enterprise: *To allow the ultimate symbol of mass murder, genocide, oppression, colonialism . . .* Enough! There is never enough outrage to fully tarnish a symbol. We are left with the navigator, son of the wool merchant, possibly illegitimate, the bright ambitious boy who went to sea.

The public television documentary turns folio pages from his log book, voice-over reading the translated text on-screen; model of the

Santa María; an animated map of each voyage, with his fleets bobbing over the sea: the professors disagree about the date and place of his birth, perhaps a hill town above Nervi. A facsimile of the chart used on the triumphant voyage of discovery is pegged as it was every four hours, pinpricking the distance achieved each day. The flow of sand in an egg timer tracked navigational hours. A quadrant and an astrolabe are displayed: the nifty new tools he carried on board. But the Admiral could not fix his latitude; in bad weather could not site the North Star. In a letter to the King of Spain, Columbus claimed he had determined his latitude off Cuba by use of a quadrant. In truth, his readings were off. He did not have the math, laid the instrument aside, sailed the parallel by dead reckoning, pinprick by pinprick, a ship's boy, perhaps his son, turning the egg timer until the last willful voyage was done. The astrolabe behind glass case is not of his period, so the tag says in all honesty. When we left that museum set in a park just down from the villa in Bogliasco, we took a wrong turn into a boccie-ball game, old men, old as we are, passing the time. They were welcoming to *i stranieri* with museum pamphlets in hand. One with a grizzled beard could not resist the old Genovese query, *À tre scopertede Genoa sono?* I answered: pesto, banking, and America. We laughed in bilingual accord.

Columbus Circle, newly refurbished with trees that brave the exhaust fumes, stands at the southwest corner of Central Park. The Admiral wears the familiar cloak of his best days, fur trim and rich wool stiffly flowing. The puffy beret we remember from a school play. Perched on a mighty pillar, he stands sentinel to the traffic that circles round him, his back to the Park and to the outsize pylon that bears the competing statue of Columbia Triumphant as she heads toward Broadway in a golden shell. Layer upon layer of gold leaf covers her body and windblown gown. She commemorates our Victory in the Spanish-American War, 1898. Columbia and Columbus join in our urban allegory of Empire as empire sails on.

October 13, 1492. *The fish so unlike ours that it is wonderful. Some are the shape of dories and of the finest colors, so bright that there is not a man who would not be astounded, and would not take great delight in seeing them. There are also whales. I saw no beasts on land save parrots and lizards.*

On shore I sent the people for water, some with arms, others with casks; and as it was some little distance, I waited two hours for them.

During that time I walked among the trees, the most beautiful things I had ever seen. . . . —Don Cristoforo Columbus

Among trees. On the Mall in Central Park, he stands under American elms with the poets. Blinded by disgrace, the Admiral could not see Literary Walk flashing green to gold on the day marking the discovery, nor hear the distant blare of a high-school band, so I backdate him to full possession of his *Privileges,* walk him along Columbus Avenue a block west of Central Park. In the neighborhood of the El Dorado, two restaurants are Italian with inferior *trenette al pesto, pandolce* of sorts. The Mass at St. Gregory's on 90th Street is said in Spanish and French, *Salve,* a poor parish of immigrants—Hispaniola, San Salvador, Port-au-Prince—its school basement once the last refuge of unruly priests who protested the Vietnam War. That war, this war. Many of the indigenous on the avenue are dusky as those once noted in his log. On this unnaturally warm day, a few men and women display markings of mysterious designs on their naked arms and legs. We might stop at the narrow shop with birds in the window—zebra finches, parrots, canaries, the exotic creatures he captured for the delight and edification of Her Majesty. Past the flower shop with Peruvian lilies, maranta, Queen's tears, a bouquet gathered from his *Discoveries.* We will stop at 86th Street. Two banks on the corner. That should amaze the Genoese sailor. His swollen fingers fumble with the knot on his purse. The high ceiling and terrazzo, all so familiar, but the deposit slot rejects his *pesos d'oro. . . . And that henceforth I should be called Don, and should be Chief Admiral of the Ocean Seas, and that my eldest son should succeed and so from generation to generation forever. . . .*

The woolen cloak heavy on his stooped shoulders, strands of white hair poke out of the jaunty tam. Through infirmity of eyes, he sees at last this Manoa, the strange land of his discovery. We head east on 86th, back to the Park. *Thanks be to God the air is very soft like April at Seville; and it is a pleasure to be here, so balmy are the breezes.*

On the Promenade, a Hispanic peddler of gelato. *Limón, por favor.* Pinprick by pinprick, back in time when the world was fresh. Near blind.

A small whale near shore? A stalk laden with rose berries, in plain light of day birds flying from winter. Heaven on earth awaiting his discovery of a flickering mirage.

Daybook, October 20, 2007

We are plotting a surge. Our Republic—mine, yours. It's dumb to sign off on this country, like some old lefty still humming "The Internationale." Ten, twenty thousand troops will tidy up, bring *them* round to our way of thinking. Not thinking, just watching the reality show. It comes on after the weather, which has been lovely, day after day of sun withholding the sharp promise of Fall. I still speak of my outrage launched some years ago. The edge has dulled, needs to be honed. Time was, we took out the whetstone, sharpened the blade. In the past, wars beyond our recall were taught in school. How the Civilized Tribes were sent off on the Trail of Tears, *that from these honored dead, that we here highly resolve* (each child in turn reciting by the schoolroom flag); how during the Mexican-American War our town in the Berkshires chose the Mex name, Monterey. This war, that war, how the Austrian girl was instructed to kneel when she kissed the Cardinal's ring; how the Spaniards got rid of the Moors, a costly operation, so Columbus shipped out for the gold. How the pilot of the *Santa María* sang a chant marking time, first note to last, forward to aft. Depending on wind and tide, on flotsam and jetsam near shore, on words lost in the wind, *Salve*, the ship would make harbor. How men have always been intimidated by animals they fear, nothing new siccing dogs on prisoners. And did I go on about Walter Reed, while deplorable, it's nowhere near as unsanitary as hospitals were in the Civil War. *This war, that war, my father deliced soldiers who survived the Battle of the Argonne. Ran a hot rod up the seams of their clothes, much like the iron instrument once used to curl hair.*

You said: *Take it down a peg. You're edgy.*

I thought we hated that expression. You're the one warned me off here and now, how stale today's incursion seems tomorrow.

These treks across the street may not be the best prescription, for your spirit, I mean.

You flapped the *Wall Street Journal* against your thigh; a respectful review of a movie we might want to see.

Elizabeth, The Golden Age. Biopic, right up your alley.

Your instructive tone is troubling. It's the Park I have going for me, new material—tourism, birding, our looming towers preserved in bourgeois splendor. I spoke then of my Scheherazade mode, of watching the clock run down, of my balancing act that's solo, though often I depend on a fellow traveler. *Like Chaucer, don't you know?*

Whan that Aprille?

It's Fall in *Central Park*.

Time Bends: The Student's Tale

> With all the senses of my body I have become aware of numbers as they
> are used in counting things. But the principle of numbers, by which we
> count, is not the same. It is not an image of the things we count, but
> something which is there in its own right. If anyone is blind to it, he
> may laugh at my words: I shall pity him for his ridicule.
>
> —St. Augustine, *Confessions*, X, 12

We had been best of friends, boyhood friends. A possible way to begin? My profession, such as it is, does not lend itself easily to words. Numbers are my game. At times I must explain as I chalk the blackboard. Given $x + y$ and xy find x and y, simple stuff, but this is a confounding story. Bertie, Chairman and CEO of Skylark, a telecommunications empire— so his enterprise is called in the business section of the *Times*—Bertie is charged with conspiracy to commit fraud. I am waiting to take the stand as a character witness, have been waiting for two days, as you well know, since I deliver Cyril to school while you stay home with Maisy, our congested girl once again prisoner of the nebulizer. But this is not a family story. Cyril delivered, I head down to the Federal Courthouse we've often seen on cop shows. The echoing hallways are unfamiliar off-screen, dismal. I have been called to testify that Bertie is an upright player in the financial games of this republic, in sum, a good old boy, has been since I first knew him, eighth grade. He is charged with backdating his options, tinkering with the books of his corporation so that gain became loss, or vice versa, good tricks that would please my students, many of them preparing for their future in the business world.

I am writing in the small green notebook in which you record our sightings of northeastern birds. It has been years since I scribbled more than a quick note with pen on paper. Attorney Thaddeus Sylvan informed me that Security might not look kindly on my laptop, though my life and times are easily accessed, from the incompleteness of my Yale degree to my credit rating to the theorem I am attempting to work to its probable conclusion. Your notebook slipped easily into the pocket of a gray flannel suit worn to Wall Street by my grandfather. I rescued it along with his pocketwatch, so that I might wear it when called to testify on behalf of Bertram Boyce, who's between a rock and a hard place. Silenced, I resort to the shorthand of clichés; sequestered in a small room with unforgiving metal chairs and a behemoth of a scarred wood table. It seems, as I look over the page, that I write in a retro voice much like my grandfather's. Cyril O'Connor was a gent who was formal at breakfast, who muted his affection at bedtime and contained his exuberance when our Yankees won the game. A shame you never knew him.

Bear with me, Lou. I will ease up. I'm attempting to describe the occasion when I reattached to Bertie, who I must claim as my good friend. You were along for the ride. It is best to turn back to that day on which Bert and Artie found each other again, embraced in a Judas moment, though who betrays, who saves the day is yet to be determined. Should anyone audit this memory bank or question its inventions, they must know you cannot testify against me, insofar as you are my loving wife.

Field Notes: October 12, 2007, 3:30 P.M. U.S. Weather Station, Central Park, 65°–70° (trusting to memory, therefore guessing), possible afternoon shower.

A volley of shots in the distance. A thrasher fluttered into the bulrushes. I faked a pistol with my hand. *Backfire.*

A great egret flew to the island in Turtle Pond. Displaying his annoyance, he chose not to perform his strut. In something of a huff, you lowered your binoculars. We'd come for songbirds stopping off on their migration to pleasant winter climes. The day was unseasonably warm, as though the years flipped fast forward and phoebes had long abandoned the sheltering grasses round the pond.

Lou, there was nothing to fear on a Monday afternoon in Central Park. Above—swift sailing puff clouds; below—still water glazed in sunlight.

A second volley.

I know it's backfire, you said, convincing yourself no sharpshooter crawled the swampy undergrowth. Took me a week to get you to come birding, never my great thrill, yours. I wanted to see your pleasure at the green gold of the warblers, observe your full attention sketching their pinstripe tails. I wanted you to breathe easy, Lou, for a few hours of the day. Our Sylvie, more than friend, who often looks after the children, had gone off, a visit to her stepdaughter in sunny CA. You checked your watch, opened this small spiral notebook to record our sighting of the egret and the single thrasher in the reeds repeating his mockingbird cry. This outing was going as well as could be expected, given we had abandoned our children to a student of mine with no experience in kid care other than a brood of brothers back home.

Turtle Pond lies directly below Belvedere Castle, once a stone shell, a hollow stage set built to enchant the eye. All such notes, Lou, come by way of my grandfather, a would-be historian if life had not ordained his career on Wall Street, allowing only an occasional Sunday walk in the Park to instruct a boy. So, if I include the Delacorte Theater with its seats facing an empty pit, we might have been a couple of lost groundlings from a pageant of heroic legends. Tourists and a busload of schoolchildren were on the viewing terrace above, looking down from the battlements on the little body of water and the island both, as their guide blasted through a megaphone, ENTIRELY MAN MADE. A disappointment to his audience surely, but there we were by way of entertainment, Louise Moffett and Arthur Freeman, playing our observation of the birds for all to see. With the next volley of earsplitting pops, you mimed fright. If these outlanders had simply turned from us, looked down other side of the Castle, they might have seen men in their Conservatory jackets attempting to deal with a disabled tractor backfiring at the utility shed. I enclosed you in the rough body hold of a protective embrace. How long had such childish fun been in short supply? Shrugging free of me, your cap tumbled down the embankment. Artie to the rescue. In a princely gesture, I set it atilt on your head. Worry lines not permanently etched in your brow were hidden in the shadow of the bill, but your cheeks were ghostly pale in the bright light of day. You tucked in the ponytail. That day plays a PowerPoint show in my head: Here's the moody egret, here a lone phoebe seeking shelter in the reeds from the guide blasting Vista Rock with misinformation, here's my wife, gorgeous and plain. Mind if I put that down? You insist you are a throwback to Household Mom in black-and-white reruns. I might say *a fading American rose*. I still call you *Miss Wisconsin. Cheese, say cheese.*

Pen poised above this very notebook, the stern set of your mouth would not give way to a smile as you estimated the great egret's height. I brushed the wet grit of the embankment off my khakis. Then, as though to amuse in a game of I Spy, I trained my binoculars on the foot soldiers above. The schoolchildren, you may recall, waved little flags—red, white and green—but the tourists seemed puzzled or plain embarrassed by their bird's-eye view of us horsing around. What had they seen? A private moment, always lovers in the Park, though not often caught in an act of observation. Adjusting my lens, I dictated notes to you on the enemy's shaggy plumage, their slack mandibles and splintered beaks.

They could not hear me describe them as goosey gander, common tern, but no doubt heard you cry, "Oh, Artie." The high chirp of your laughter reached up to include them as they watched our tussle, your love punch to my ribs and my gentlemanly gesture, taking your arm as we climbed toward the Great Lawn, where soccer practice was in progress, boys in the blue jerseys of Trinity School. Next the Pinetum, where you hoped for a red crested kinglet, then the Reservoir, expecting the arrival of grebes basking in the sun. Again you checked the time. Our Maisy had the first cold of that peculiar season, which did not deliver crisp Fall days. I'm uncertain how much to recall of our encounter with Bertram Boyce, not yet charged with backdating options of Skylark shares, but I am certain I lured you away from the apartment with Maisy's congestion, with Cyril's trembling tower of Lincoln Logs. I offered you the consuming delight of birds in their citified migration.

You hurried ahead, past dog walkers, babies in slings, past the elderly taking the air, skateboarders—illegal on the walkway. The pretzel salesman had resumed his Summer post. A fat boy in a red shako, much gold braid on his breast and belly, began a melancholy taps on his bugle—*Day is done, gone the sun*—broke to drain spittle from his mouthpiece.

You were not amused by this touch of Fellini. Checking your watch: *Four-fifteen.*

Columbus Day, I said. *Parade long over.*

I wish they'd stop fooling with the calendar.

The holiday stuck on to the weekend. Cyril had wanted to go to school that morning, always wants to go to school, where he outwits his classmates less endowed. His cleverness is a cross he will have to bear. Only now that I recall Bert Boyce and Artie Freeman breaking through the Fifth Avenue crowd when Columbus Day was kept in its place, the disruptive twelfth. Snotty nerds lusting for the drum majorettes and their flock of twirlers from the outer boroughs, those high-stepping girls far beyond our reach.

In the Pinetum we did a swift look-see searching for the red crest of the kinglet. There was only the resident clown in a battered derby prompting his flea-bitten parrot—*H'lo there! 'Lo there!* Impatient, you took the Reservoir Track the long way round. Not a merganser in sight as we headed to the crosstown bus to get home to the children. Our pretense of pleasure seemed a failed duty until you caught the noiseless swivel of an owl's head, flick of tufted ears.

The long-eared, napping till end of day, did not deign to acknowledge our ogle eyes trained on him. Drowsy creature, yet I believe he heard every step of our approach, listened to each shallow breath of our silence, a comfort compared to the panting of joggers. We had discovered him fully disclosed on his perch. If he'd been in a story, he'd be wiser or at least crafty, the role he's often assigned. You wrote in this very notebook, the turn of the page noiseless. Flipping back, I see with what care you drew the eye stripe cutting a perfect V to the owl's beak. In any case, I had my prize for the day in your extended moment of delight, which swept aside Maisy's catarrh, the terrifying pops of an old combustion engine, and the anxiety, never mentioned, that my work was not going well. I might not find my way through the knots of higher mathematics to the solution of one small problem. In clear sight of the owl, the troubling world dropped away. Louise, confess your thing about owls, starting with barn owls on the farm in Wisconsin. The first prize you ever won, sketch of an owl perched on a downspout, every night watching that bird from your bedroom window until the dive for its prey, the death shriek of its victim.

Our binoculars captured the Halloween mask of the owl's flat face. I must not deprive the bird of his owlness, see him pompous and befuddled, like Owl in the book our son loves. An uncertain shuffle brought the prolonged silence to a halt. Do you remember the old woman huffing and puffing her way round the track? You signaled her to stop? With a flip of your hand ordered: *Look, look up.* A party of three sharing the vigil. In a contest of wills, this urban owl might outlast us. Finally, the shabby old girl broke the spell, shuffled toward the tennis courts, her breathing audible—uneven. The sky had darkened, leaves rustled underfoot. The long-eared was surely gloating as we headed toward Fifth Avenue, his unblinking eyes on us. I preened at coaxing a laugh at Turtle Pond, and for some time, long minutes of owl time, you'd been lost to the world.

This is Bud's story, Bertie's. I was the only kid allowed to call him Bertie and will use that boyhood moniker when I speak of our friendship, rekindled that very day, the day of our birding. My "guard" in the waiting room is a court attendant, Tim McBride, gabby Irish, "been in the job since." What follows is the real dope on Jimmy Hoffa disappearing into a cement grave, not the void, same year as bilingual signs here in the courthouse rest rooms. "My case" will most likely not be called today. The parties still in judge's chambers. McBride releases me till after lunch. *My case,* an odd way to refer to the troubles of Bertram Boyce, far from mine. His are unfortunately dated. Bert took liberties with time. My problem was clocked— will the scholar-in-training triumph over the odds or fail to make the grade in given time? That question troubles you, Lou, though the solution is solely mine.

Released into the city at high noon, I could head up, or downtown. History lies in both directions. Downtown is Wall Street, where my grandfather went to the office every working day. He invested, bought and sold, made money. We are living off him now, Louise, though he's gone these six years if I reckon correctly, which I should be able to do, since he has willed me the luxury of going back to school to pick up my love affair with mathematics. So I had the choice of walking down the blocks to look at the Stock Exchange that rang the market to my grandfather's attention each day, though not going as far as the Trade Center wound or taking the route up to SoHo, where we lived our first years together in your loft, the materials of your trade all around us—paints, charcoal smudges in progress, canvases stacked against the wall. I was in that empty waiting room at my request, the privilege granted by the machinations of Bertie's lawyer, who believed I must fiddle on with statistics and correlations for my class in applied mathematics. Furthermore, I did not want to spend time under the surveillance of Attorney Sylvan, famous for finding loopholes in the law. I had been coached by him, his every slick word put in my mouth, thinking when the time comes I'll say what I have to say truly—my schoolboy adventures with Bertie, my larky jobs at Skylark, more play than employment.

My choice was not to travel downtown for recess, Lou, not to recall the dutiful life of Cyril O'Connor, not indulge in Lower Broadway, where we were so gone on each other our nights of love consumed us. I've loosened up, though *consumed* is too heady a word, or too visceral. My tongue freed by a hot dog with the works as I perused the discount junk on Canal Street, odd lots of T-shirts with Goth symbols of the Reich, dog beds, doll heads, faucets, copper wire, cruets labeled Oil and

Vinygar, framed posters of Che and the Eiffel Tower. Products in their mass graves guarded by their keepers, who seemed to be doing swift business of sorts, perhaps as subject to investigation as Bertram Boyce's deals at Skylark. Troubling.

You were well acquainted with troubles that day in the park, your fears crossing the line from daily concern to manic organic. Alar in the apple juice, bacteria flourishing in plastic bottles, *E. coli,* tuna with its dose of mercury—all loomed large as the national debt. A whiff of the super's stogie in the hallway, Asian flu, Teflon and faulty seat belts—right up there with toxic waste. *Nothing to fear but fear itself,* attempting the noble line, I fail to amuse. Along with your catalog of horrors, there is Maisy's persistent congestion, and the uncertain course of my career. Love, in one of its many distortions, allows you never to speak of my possible failure, though I work hard, harder than I ever have in my life. Lou, there is the one unspeakable word—*talent,* if in fact the gift of numbers was ever mine to squander. No longer nimble, one step behind the beat? Better to record the owl's composure on a warm October day.

That night when Cyril and Maisy were safely stashed in their bunk bed, I discovered you were keeping an account of the current war's fatalities, though only *our boys* were admitted to your file. You had copied each soldier's name, age, rank and hometown into a baby book, a present from your mother intended for Maisy's vital statistics—first tooth, first fever, first word. On the cover a stork carts a swaddled newborn in its beak. I suggested the death toll of Operation Iraqi Freedom is online, www.Iraqbodycount.org. *Oh, that's only information,* you said, transferring Private First Class, 20, *Linden, NJ,* and Staff Sergeant, 34, *Shreveport, LA,* from the *Times* to your register, inscribing each name, your pen dipped in India ink. Kind of crazy, the record made personal, and then Louise Moffett, once an artist on the cutting edge, now invested in the role you embrace as housewife and mother, costumed in apron and sensible shoes, closes the baby book, takes up a mystery, British. *Potboilers,* you call these murders set in the manse or vicarage. The gardener did it or the village doctor you thought so kind. The night of our birding, you challenged the sly smile of my bewilderment.

You know the satisfaction, Artie. Puzzles, solutions.

Our pleasant ongoing argument in which I point out that a problem chalked on the blackboard is without motive—no adultery, sibling rivalry, not even greed to provoke a crime.

Ambition?

You win.

And fell asleep with the murder unsolved. I scanned my preparation for class—harmless proofs completed, then lay your book aside, turning down the page not to lose the place in that story. Even in sleep you looked troubled, gone from me, but earlier that day I had you back. As we headed along the sidewalk to 86th Street, I was hopeful till worry surfaced in tightness around your mouth, an audible sigh as you looked across Fifth Avenue at the apartment house where I lived with my grandparents when I was a boy, an orphan. You won't *go there,* a slippery expression, though you take care to avoid the wounds of my childhood, which I believe long healed. I have hoped that Bertie, with his troubles, all too real, might release you from conjuring the demons of my past, and from free-floating angst that pursues you. OK pursues us all, but we get Cheerios in the bowl before reading the morning paper.

Some of us. Some do not.

I imagine how gently your might cut me off. Backdating to that day of owl and egret, your ponytail slapping air, for no reason at all, gave me hope. That night, the night of our birding in the Park, while you slept I turned on the tube, muted it to indulge in our nightcap addiction to the comic turns on the dysfunctional state of our nation. The pantomime without clever words and background laughter seemed as inadequate, to wing a metaphor, as a Band-Aid on a suppurating sore. Or merely electronic—a fleeting message held in our hand: *pick up juice, organic snacks at the market.* We'd lost track of the sand castle blown away in Desert Storm. So it's ever been while Rome burned, though have you noticed there's no tune for this war? *Where have all the flowers gone?* My mother strumming, *Long time passing. Long time ago.*

I am writing in a new notebook with unlined pages, bought at Pearl Paint, where you ordered supplies when you were still invested in your art. Your little green notebook is, after all, for the birds. When I returned to the courthouse, Tim McBride presented me with a sealed envelope. Lawyer for the defense—that is, Thad Sylvan—asked me to consider in my testimony the charities of Bertram Boyce Jr. and the corporate goodwill of Skylark. And what did I recall of the Boyce family holidays, and the religion of their choice? I remember that the mother (divorced) went to Aspen for Christmas, Bermuda at Easter. She took Bert along until he was old enough to be abandoned to the Park Avenue apartment or sent to visit his father, a mysterious tinkerer in Bethesda, Maryland, who held patents on medical apparatus that paid the bills, saved lives. I did not share these memories. Sylvan should do his homework. Why not ask poor Heather Boyce who, in *Newsweek*, walked up the courthouse steps arm in arm with Bertie, a couple properly suited for good works. Their names are printed in programs of the symphony, the opera—Bertram and Heather Boyce, right up there with the heavy donors. Black tie at the Modern and the Met, drives you crazy, Lou, their attention to couture. And Project Hope, the llamas with big, soulful eyes, Heather supplying indigenous folk with herds of the beasts for costly sweaters. Shearing, carding, spinning for a week's handout of rice and beans.

There's this. I had a few beers during recess. Observe, dearly beloved, that I was ever so slightly greased. Up for the self-portrait, not the idealized Artie Freeman you once sketched, boyish with a thatch of hair gone early gray. You demoted my smile to an air of bemusement. Forever looking on, not part of the show, the squint of my eyes at every sleight of hand, moral or monetary. Jimmy Stewart, you suggested, one of those innocent heartthrobs.

Clark Kent without glasses.

A wimp?

In disguise.

Back to Bertie, back to business. I have written more of me and more of you than the subject of my deposition. *Testimony:* corrected by Tim McBride when I attempt the legal lingo. I put the two of us on the stand while the accused awaited his day in court. Birding in the Park, the day we met Bertie, I now understand as a confession. The only one I ever knew who confessed was my grandmother, Mae O'Connor, the least sinful of women. She was shriven, strange word, at Ignatius Loyola a

few blocks from the apartment. I waited on
the church steps facing Park Avenue expecting a hum of holy about her when she emerged
from the blessed darkness, but it was only Mae
fumbling in her purse for the list of groceries
we must pick up at Gristede's. A shame you
never knew her. I see this memory business,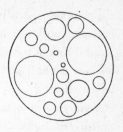
this getting it down, might be a simple image that I use for my class. You
can't, Louise, fill up a circle with circles that do not overlap, but if you
allow the overlap, then there can be many if not infinite circles which
will allow Mae O'Connor to take her place in my story.

Circles within circles as on that day heading out of the park. *Past five.
Five,* you repeated, in case I missed the urgency in your voice. Across
Fifth Avenue, the apartment house where I lived as a boy was encased in
scaffolding to update its limestone façade. The window where my mother
stood with her *love child* (my grandmother's version of the tale) was
draped in netting, misty as the occasion of my birth. As a boy I wanted
to be born on Krypton where, by improbable chance, my father lived,
but where was the dynamic logo, my soaring flight over Metropolis? Two
lapdogs nipping and nosing each other blocked our path. I stopped you
crossing as a siren cleared the way for an ambulance racing down from
Mount Sinai. A cab jumped the curb, an ordinary mishap in the city.
The electronic pedestrian, trapped in the stoplight, raised his arm in a
friendly salute. Safe, safely across. Chill coming on, cloudy sky if memory serves. You checked your watch again, *five-fifteen.*

Day is done, gone the sun. Now, why? Why did I sing that funereal tune?
From the hills, from the lake . . .

To get the laugh, *Oh, Artie.*

Speaking of the old woman in the floppy black coat, jeans shredded at
the cuffs, I said, *Wasn't she a funny duck?*

We recalled her look of offense when you ordered her to silence the
heavy pit-pat of her tread. You suggested the heavy gasp of her breathing
put the owl off its kill.

Though she got into the bird . . . and the two of us.

I question the two of us. In the past, our eyes and ears were in accord when birding, specially in the city, my admiration for you on display, the milkmaid walking with a proprietary air through the whole spread of Central Park as though tracking the back acres in Wisconsin. That day we were not in sync. Our argument, could it be called that, had little to do with sighting.

Kind of a washout, you said, *birdwise.*

You're missing Our Sylvie.

That must have been it, Sylvie, a legacy of my grandfather's, her love for the old man embracing us beyond blood relation. Our kids' Frau von Trapp. No need to recall the untidy woman squinting up at the owl, coat stretched across her bum. Same age as Sylvie, give or take a few years, yet in no way like our friend, who is slim and stylish, the cap of white hair carefully sculpted to her head, *Like an angel,* you said, *ageless, one of Fra Angelico's darlings.* And if Our Sylvie had been home to take care of the children, you would have been free to enjoy a few hours of the Fall migration in the Park. I hustled you by the apartment where I lived with my grandparents, a motherless, fatherless boy. Why fear him?

McBride believed the case—mine and Bertie's—might be deferred. Have I made it clear that Tim came round now and again for a chat with the professor doing his math? I hadn't the heart to correct him. He admitted me to the empty room, then went off on his assignments, slapping at his hip, searching for lost authority in the black holster of Security. I'm not dangerous, so left on my own. Or dangerous only to myself, writing not one word in defense of my old friend, but these many words of self-incrimination, backdating my limited options to the incident of birding, recording only personal discoveries of that Columbus Day, avoiding our chance meeting with the accused.

At the bus stop: teenagers comparing test scores in shrill, competitive voices. I can't forget one sad striver with a mini-tattoo on her wrist, silver stud in her nose, concave chest weighted with schoolbooks. You stepped off the curb to see if the bus was coming while I took measure of the distance I ran from my grandparents' apartment to the museum. "Take measure" is a Cyril O'Connor phrase, prudent, unlike these pages written for you. I stood at the corner judging the distance I crossed to the Temple of Dendur, ran up the steps of the museum, through the massive door, cut right to the Egyptians. So familiar to the guards they never stopped me for my pass, sharp kid eager to show them my ill-drawn barges to the underworld circa 2 B.C. Not so strange after all, my obsession with the Pharaohs and their vast company of underlings to serve them in their tombs. Even Bertie, conspiring with me in all plots against the popular faction at school, was not privy to my devotion to Isis. My fix on the goddess was a reasonable accommodation to my mother's death, a way to believe in the afterlife, not as my grandmother believed in the apparatus of heaven with angels surfing the clouds, saints in cumbersome robes. Reviewing my route to the tombs fitted out for the long run of afterlife with the comforts of home, I maintain it was not the worst idea, writing to my mother in hen-scratch hieroglyphics. So why does it trouble you when my clever tactics for survival are long packed away? True, I wasted time searching for the phantom father, now only the loose end of a story. Never fear, Lou-Lou Belle, the grief of my childhood is not a genetic disease.

The crosstown came toward us. I stepped free of the students, drawn into a circle of noisy flirtation. You called to me, frantic. Waving your cap, hair flying, you stood by the open door of a limousine, its extravagant length blocking the bus stop. Passengers decamped in the middle of the street. Slowly, yet grandly, an emaciated version of Bertram Boyce stepped out of the long black car that established his importance. In the courthouse, I should have been figuring the next problem built on the last, but this business of writing without chalk or computer is rewind—back, I go back in time while Tim McBride stops by, hand automatically patting his missing piece. I replay the scene, Bertie helping a woman with babe in arms to collapse a stroller. He steers her up into the bus. The private school kids observe Mr. Wonderful with teen irony; then the boss, once my boss, takes me in hand, settles me in the beige leather of his limo. The old authority in his order to the driver: *Downtown.*

You said, *A ride across the Park will do us.* Something like that, cryptic.

Bert did not introduce us to the girl with a cell plugged in her ear, a spill of mahogany hair veiling her face. We spoke softly, not to interfere with her compelling business.

Bertram Boyce, dry as a pod with a terminal tan. He seemed an endangered species in a fringed . . . serape? Poncho? We watched Bert stroke the girl's leg up to the black leather skirt that ended far above her knee.

He said, *Long time no see. Better part of a year?*

Christmas. Ah, the holiday visit. Bert's family in suburban splendor. You will not forget the extravagant gifts. Bert, dispensing goodwill of the season, offered a priceless claret, Lafite-Rothschild: *Some prefer '85.* He found '86 more than OK. A fete out of the nostalgia manual—Dickensian goose, Bud with the girth of St. Nick. Better part of a year for that rotundity to scale down to skin and bones.

You surely remember Heather Boyce flashing Santa's watch ringed with diamonds. Boyce children, bored with our kids, dismissed to their Game Boys.

Heather, *So what can you do? The holidays.* Something like that, putting words into her mouth as I've put them into yours. Isn't that the idea of writing it down? Call back the day, things said in passing or by intent, translation from the foreign film of memory into the subtitles of here and now.

Hear her? See her? Heather, who has never shed the yearbook smile of savvy innocence, the pleasant efficiency with which she packed away your offerings to Fern and Bertram III? Sketch pads, Chinese brushes, from ye olde curiosity shoppe with a bell over the door. The Christmas invite, an awkward duty for both parties.

Court dismissed for the day. My keeper, McBride: *See you tomorrow.*

Same time? Same cubby?

Cubby brought a scolding. I did not value the privilege, Attorney Sylvan having procured this cell to prepare my schoolroom assignments. Had Thad slipped McBride a gratuity?

Tim ran his hands over the digs and stains of the table. *This room, interrogation room, used to be.*

Did money change hands so that I might sit among the ghosts of the guilty? Released for the day, I drew circles within a circle on the

Broadway Line. Students will guess a scribbled infinity at one glance, though this simple visual has nothing to do with their progress in Math for Business Dummies, everything to do with my notebooks, with this spill of words written in ballpoint on paper, circles within circles. I could not run word count on the inked page, *that's only information,* closed up shop on the Broadway Line listening to the muffled beat of my neighbor's music, having written not one word in defense of my friend.

I am reminded of Einstein's letter to someone famous in which he confessed that images ran in his head long before the difficult search for language. The notebooks stored in my backpack with their weight of words seemed . . . well, wordplay skirting some image central to the story that is mine as much as Bertie's, as though we are still competing as we did first day in the schoolyard. Let the image be the soccer ball with its patchwork of pentagons he shot my way, and my penalty kick these many years later, roughing him up in my version of our story. We were tough on each other, always outside the varsity game in progress.

Gina! As though I could forget the fourth party in the limo. Her commanding presence, uncomfortable at best. She swept back the red hair. On second glance, not a girl.

You're Freeman, the boyhood chum.

Backdating, Bert filled her in on the apartment where I lived with my grandparents. *Where we picked them up, a block from the old homestead. Grandpa was Wall Street, last of the ticker-tape honchos.*

Gina stayed in the present. *You're the guy working on knots.*

Your Ghostly Honor, I may have actually joined the prosecution in my estimate of that leathery woman, she of the great legs who tossed off what might, or might not, be the subject of my dissertation when she apparently hadn't a clue that we, the Freemans, had for some years moved uptown? Why get into it, Lou? She seemed well aware that I was a Boy Scout tangled in a stubborn knot of string theory. This Gina sneaking up on the site in which my theorem depended upon the work of others. She would know that the problem was not mine alone, and further know we broadcast our progress with a sense of camaraderie, as though still low on the ladder, we might settle into a Viennese café, spell our answers out on paper tablecloths, though the acrobatic dream of my climbing a rung up while scribbling through cigarette haze may not work out, not at all. You see how precarious it was, yet how available my various routes to solvation.

Perhaps that Gina was even aware that Ernst Gottschalk, our leader in the quaint Hall of Mathematics, is the man I dodge even when he's gone a-conferencing, not settled in his endowed Chair, elegantly tailored beyond the three dimensions of the world we inhabit in out-at-elbow Gap, worn student jeans. The door to his office flung open, no appointment needed, as though we play in time gone by—kindly teacher welcoming a confab with befuddled adjunct in need, though mostly unavailable as he publishes the next and the next paper, the only one that counted back in '78, the dark age of a quantum past. Gott, who still holds with No. 2 pencils, red erasers, an ancient's belief in *the contemplated mark on the page, the rubber crumbs of correction.* I slouch by his door each day. Idle fear, Louise, as though he might catch me out in a miscalculation. Tut-tut shake of the ponderous head with its unruly ruff of white hair. For now I will call it a touch of paranoia connecting that Gina, Bert's Munster mom, to Gott, a legendary figure of fun and fear you have never, may never, meet. Our leader does not frolic at math parties, partake of our pizza sweating in the cardboard delivery box, sip our tepid beer.

Gina, this is the professor. Her bangled arm raised in greeting. *Gina multitasks, nanos, surveillance.*

In the past, Bert claimed the title Entrepreneur—telecommunications in Africa, oil in Belarus, gold in Peru—seemed multi enough. At his emporium a job arranged for Artie when in need, so I'd run the books on the screen, always this side of the law, or play pixart, imaging whatever the boss imagined in his climb to the heights. I trust you recall Skylark's shot at a weather channel, Bertram Boyce controlling the elements. *Make it rain, Freeman. Give us a blustery day.* More often than not, reality echoed my cloud cover or the mist of a Spring morning. Snow fell softly on the tristate area, credit of Arthur Freeman. We marketed the sun, the rain. The atmosphere in the limo that day was heavy with a climate of restraint, a forecast of possible grief.

The 86th Street transverse allotted little time for my sorry tale. I was not and, as you feared, may never gain the dimension of professor. The Park glowered above its stone walls, trees and sky dimmed, blur of a dirty white cloud. Bert scrolled a window down to admit a wave of fossil fumes, then, skeletal hand on your thigh, made his move, the old one-on-one maneuver.

How's the art business?

You sweetened your answer with a smile. *I'm not in business.* Let it play out, the uncomfortable silence enclosing us at the stoplight.

Then Gina on the wireless canceling out the old friends of Bud Boyce. *I'm on the board,* to whom it may concern, *so I'll go in that direction.*

Feathering her nest?

Fast forward: Bertie is ushered up the courthouse steps, spiffy with a silk handkerchief in his blazer pocket, Heather tottering behind on perilous heels. Cameras that day. I was ordered to keep my distance by the defense, T. Sylvan, Esquire, who does not deserve his arboreal name. I am well aware of the unkind view I'd taken as the case presented itself at the distance of judge's chambers. My day in court, I'd have said nice things, believe me. Bert, devoted father and husband, simply lost his way in the prevalent culture of greed. Why not skim off the cream? My grandmother, Mae O'Connor, taught me about top o' the milk when milk came in a bottle, when children were instructed not to skim or backdate, though everyone's doing it. *Mea culpa,* another of her lessons, came to mind as I opened the new notebook each day. McBride brought me a mug of coffee, a friendly gesture. He sat with me, took the weight off his legs. Phlebitis goes with the job. Forty years he's been at his post, forty! Knows how they swing, the Scales of Justice. Tim feared a motion to dismiss. He looked with a trained eye at the words covering this page as though to ask, *Where, Professor, are the numbers?*

Topology, that's a crowded field, Gina said.

You remarked upon the jangle of her bracelets, her assessment of your canvas jacket with Maisy's spit-up on the shoulder. In the gathering gloom of the limo, you rapped your binoculars for attention: *We don't have much time away from the children.* Protecting me, not yet a postdoc, from this woman's superior smile and, as you noted, excessive eyeliner and smart mouth, this Gina with tasks insufficient to keep her from surveillance of Artie, the boyhood chum. So you rattled on, *abundance of species. A long-eared today. Owl, that is.* You attempted the great egret's mournful cry, though he had been out of sorts, silently strutting on pipe-stem legs.

Bud offered door-to-door service. You said, *Just drop us, we like the walk.* That's how I remember it, a conjecture which need not be proven, strange when you'd been counting the minutes to get home to the kids. Something desperate about Bert's air kiss aimed at you, corner of CPW, Gina's ringtone ordering him back to business in the limo. Tapping me with a skeletal hand, Chairman of Skylark said: *Don't be a stranger.* Not an offhand remark, a plea. We faked one of those embarrassing male embraces. Bert, transformed to dry skin and bones. What was left of my friend's solid state? There's your problem for topology. And why that woman?

Many questions, though on our way home in a taxi, I simply asked, *Can you believe it?*

I believe it. Poor Heather.

Why the peasant costume?

Turista. Hides his wasted body.

You wondered about that—poncho? About the design woven into the gray wool, a pattern circling in on itself, the fringe of dangling strings with the weaver's knots you thought might be read, knots forming words, and the alarming sight of Bert's manicured toes peeking out of rough sandals. You never liked Boyce. Till that day I did not know he once suggested the two of you *get it on,* the boss and my wife riding downtown in the old Boycemobile, fitted out with a screen tracking the commodities market. And yes, I was pissed or at least affronted, but you awarded the incident a girlish disbelief you can still call upon in honesty. The current floating palace less office, more lounge of a first-class hotel. Smoked glass of the windows mutes the city. Did Gina *get it on* with Bert? He seemed too frail, flesh fallen away under the floppy gray garment.

Such a find, you said, *in the chili-bean market, unwearable when you get it home.*

Bud had looked a sad clown. You carried on about that Gina, then disapproved of yourself as a prude. That woman intimate with the small problem I worked on, suggesting I'd never find my place in a crowded field. You haven't much of a clue about topology, only that my superiors are attempting to map the world, beginning to end, without landmass or bodies of water. You remain a tourist in this geography of abstraction.

Remember the logo? I called to mind the wingspread on the web site. Skylark, on the annual report and the simplified wings of my design woven into the corporate carpet. *Bird that never was.*

Bird thou never wert, correcting your husband, Humanities dropout, comic relief man chirping *wert, wert.*

Oh, Artie, checking your watch again. How long had we waited for the crosstown, then malingered in the stretch while Cyril and Maisy were abandoned to my student, a strange girl they'd never met?

Gone the sun from the river, from Riverside Park. Darkness falling as I sorted through bills to pay the cabby.

All is well, safely rest, God is nigh.

Now, why? Why that melancholy tune? To beg a smile.

If I relied on the memory of my laptop with its stellar capacity, I'd not have the full story—day of our birding, even less of the present. Could I have imagined Tim McBride's educated guess as he let me into the abandoned interrogation room? The Boyce case might never go to trial. So why was I absent from my classroom duties, simmering on a back burner? Why reconstructing, as though with imaginary numbers, the events of a day on which we sighted the long-eared who, noted in our communal notebook, would not ruffle his *speckled cascade of feathers?* I had come in good faith to speak my piece to judge and jury and find I am defending myself, still telling the story of the Castle in Central Park that now harbors the Official Weather Station, Your Honor, and the timeline of that day, as in: It was well after six when my student really could not, Professor Freeman, consider the money pressed on her, and besides it was fun helping Cyril with his homework. Cyril, who is five, does not have homework. And Maisy, she was sorry to report, had been coughing, running a fever. A well-brought-up girl, sweetly rejecting my offer to walk her home in the dark.

It's only six twenty-seven. Cyril, flashing his digital watch, grown-up gift from Our Sylvie. The student was gone with high fives for the children. A last gift of the day.

That night I couldn't get near the extra dimensions that may, in a very long run, anoint me a professor. *Don't be a stranger.* Bert's look searching me out was desperate, but we were exactly that: strangers. He knew it, yet sent that woman, whatever part she played in his life, to ferret out my small problem. That Gina who seemed to know I was sulking in a corner of string theory appropriately called *flop-transition,* as though the tilted rubber ball of space named the failure of Artie Freeman.

It was no go when I attempted to work on while my family slept. That is how I think of it now, my family safely tucked away. I logged off, took up the birdwatching diary, which lay by your chair along with the discarded mystery. I have now violated the green notebook with an account of my courthouse days, flipping past the pages on which you recorded Columbus Day 2007. *Great Egret* (*Casmerodius albus*) *4:30 Turtle Pond, should be on its way south;* your lovely sketch of our owl (*Asio otus*) *4:50 Reservoir Track,* lacking the observation as to sex or probable age, though you had noted: *Boyce, a molting Goshawk, predator, 86th & 5th Avenue. Wears a gray tunic to hide his wasted body. The fringe is patterned with knots that must mean something if you can read them. Is he sick, even dying?* I left the book open, believing I was meant to answer, then carried it to my grandfather's desk, took a pen from the secret drawer and wrote: *Dying or trashing his life. Lou, it's numbers in those knots that dangle from Bert's gone-native garment, not letters that tell a story. Numbers, an accounting or tracking of days tied in by a woman in the Andes, a bit of pre-Columbian string theory I might at best master, at least understand.*

It occurred to me that night of our birding, not for the first time, our family life in these rooms was inauthentic, no need for our children to be stacked in a bunk bed, Maisy below nestled in her plush menagerie, Cyril above clutching his tyrannosaurus rex. No need for us to fear toppling his tower of Lincoln Logs. Just behind me the hamster tumbled incessantly in its cage. A cluster of shrinking balloons hovered on the ceiling. No need for this pretense of student life. We should look to our own migration, a refuge sustainable for more than a season of uncertainty. I'd sold Cyril O'Connor's apartment on Fifth Avenue, glad of the take. You said we must move from the loft downtown, the contaminated air of our injured city the first of all your fears. So here we still are in cramped quarters, a little late for growing pains self-inflicted. Is that what Bud, costumed as a starving peon, was up to? He had stroked the leg of the all-knowing Gina as though under a spell.

I opened the baby book with the stork on the cover, flipped back to the day of our birding, first day you had not noted each verified death in the war. The blank page was marked with a postcard from Sylvie Neisswonger who is more than our friend. The Oceanographic Institute in La Jolla sat firmly on its hill. *Waters rising! Love to all, natürlich.* Sylvie's hand schoolgirl perfect, *natürlich.* What's more, you did not read a mystery that night, no body in the library, no clueless inspector from Scotland Yard. Then, as I finally attempted to set the course for the next encounter with my students, more pedagogical tricks than math, you stood beside me, Maisy in your arms. You had affixed a disfiguring nebulizer over our daughter's face. Mucus sucked in little blips from her nose and mouth.

I said: *Now, this is the scariest thing.*

You shifted Maisy, left shoulder to right: *Not really.*

Her temperature would be brought down by pink sugary drops, nothing magic. I understood the pleasure of your control, your soft lullaby voice. Do you remember the only thing that mattered was to wait in silence for the even draw of her breath, for the moment when Maisy pushed the plastic tube away? Then we waited for the sleepy smile on her flushed, rosebud face. Together we put her down with the bear and the lion, the tortoise and speckled snake. I said, *All that's missing is an owl,* an attempt to keep our vigil light.

When Maisy breathed easy, I noted that you wore the nightgown, the one I like, though it buttons to your neck with difficult pearl buttons, the blue nightgown now dimmed in the wash. And I saw, not the first time, streaks in your pale hair, dark as dull bronze.

A full week of delays. Like that Gina, I opted for the present, waiting for a judgment to be handed down; that's the feel of those courthouse days. Skylark in ruins, unlike the midscale Buick that shares its name, more the frail body of my equations towed to the scrap heap of rusted ambition. When it finally came, the reprieve, McBride was proven right, proud of himself predicting Bertie would not be charged with cooking the books. The case was too flimsy, but the plaintiff is not off the hook. Boyce must be a good lad, suffer a slap on the wrist, a year's public service. Skylark may never soar again, spread its wings over the dusty pits of Peruvian gold or peck at the infinitesimal grains of nanotechnology. In the first flush of their victory, Bertie and Heather, losing their cool, embraced me, but I had not testified that my friend discovered Freeman, the new boy at school, inscribing hieroglyphics in his algebra text, that he had a slim chance of besting me at chess, that the neighborhood was ours, every alley, shop, embassy and elegant doorway between Fifth and the Boyce apartment on Park, where we played games of my invention on a primitive DOS system free of interference from Bert's socialite mom. Play—we had played hard and long—which kept me from diving for salvage in my mother's watery grave. Back, back then Bert finally psyched out my trips to the Egyptian collection, but the Opening of the Mouth was never revealed. Only now comes to mind, Louise, the ritual I enacted in the back bedroom of the apartment you dread, King Tut mumbo jumbo that might bring the goddess to life so she might breathe, speak to her boy, play a song on the lute. That was private, middle-of-the-night stuff. Still, never-call-me-Bert was my buddy, and the alliance began in which I was to play office boy as he rose to corporate power.

On the courthouse steps, we lingered in a light drizzle, Bert, the payback kid, almost fully restored, as though that desiccated version of himself reflected the misdemeanors of the dated past. My walk-on lines were written out of the script, though where, may I ask, was that Gina?

Refurbishing her nest? Bertie and loyal wife were escorted to a modest black livery by their lawyer, licking his chops, swallowing the canary, brittle bones and all. They turned back, suggesting a triumphal lunch.

Can't bring to mind how I begged off. *Rain check?* Or work, I suppose, heavy duties of my professorial life.

Justice was deferred, which brings to mind my grandmother, who said something like that about our sins, most particularly sins of omission, that we would face them come Judgment Day. McBride in his various roles—prosecutor, defendant, jury, judge—went on to his next case. I was free of the interrogation room.

Tonight as I stood at the window looking through the leafless trees to the Hudson, I saw a familiar boat not yet stowed away for the season. It will sail downstream to safe harbor, the 79th Street boat basin, I guess. A ship with a single mast, and it was only then that I remembered *skylarking.* When we were in high school, we came across the term in a computer game we played too often, signing off on an early version of Myst. No knights defending a phony castle, only the crew of a pirate ship. Apparently Bert did not forget the perilous game played by these black-hearted sailors. Climb the mainmast, latch onto the rigging, swing out far over the sea. City boys making our mark in the classroom, we never had the occasion to skylark beyond the virtual, but we climbed too high, Bertram Boyce and Arthur Freeman.

That first day, post-courthouse, I returned to campus, homecoming of sorts. Our leader, Gottschalk, caught me out, called me into his office, a stage set, this proper old-fashioned realm with wooden bookshelves to the ceiling, an oak desk of modest proportions on which the sole computer looks a prop, screen saver of dizzy double helix spinning. We know in Mathematics Hall that this room with its arched windows looks on the livelier courtyard of the business school sheathed in glass, endowed with incorruptible steel. But it is here in Gott's office, we confer under the water-stained ceiling, the dim overhead light, and take our course assignments from our Chair. Gott, attempting a youthful look that day, had gelled his white hair (cockatoo in breeding plumage), a double-breasted blazer overdosed with brass buttons, the stud of some prestigious award in the lapel. Tap-tapping a printout in hand. Tilted dumbbells of extra dimensions floated to a decorative purpose. He turned to a back page. Under *Also Noted* noted:

Fellow at MIT, Gott said, *an elegant paper.*

Squared it away, so to speak, the very problem I had been working on. Fellow at MIT beat me to it. We had stalked each other. Had I not been at the courthouse, I would have known of his triumph without our leader's old news. So it's a slice of humble pie, happens all the time, Lou, fellow edged me out in the crowded field. It was then suggested— Gottschalk's no-nonsense words—that I am "a live wire" in the classroom, perhaps not a perfect fit with the theoretical, as though I wear a pinched shoe. Then again, sequencing has taken an energetic turn in the human-genome race, not to mention the tech market, nano coming into play. At the end of the day, end of the story, I have been advised to limp on to new fields.

You have computational skills, Freeman.

Like Cyril, that's our bright boy. Now, why did I say that?

Not to get the laugh, though it was all quite pleasant after the tight shoe dropped, Gottschalk suggesting how I might recoup. Move on? Einstein tells us that to move on, to take the next step beyond the signs and images of numbers, *conventional words must be sought for.* It is no consolation to know that he never solved everything, though he sure tried. Every last thing—how the universe got it together in this, our long allotted space-time. Well, I'm no Albie, apparently not much of a mathematician at all. But there is an endgame to the mystery that may give you some pleasure. Why had I not known that the problem was solved? Up there in Cambridge, fellow at MIT looking beyond his successful calculations to a bright Autumn day on the Charles. Because I had not accessed the information that a boy's quest for an answer had been, in fact, answered. In those courthouse days, I became devoted to words written down, addicted to news of the past, which suddenly seemed more pressing than the tabloid headline: FREEMAN FLOPS TRANSITION. Early on, I had failed with hieroglyphics, with demotic script invoking my mother. And in our time, Louise, lost the scavenger hunt for my phantom father. Perhaps,

after all, Bertie's troubles were a dodge and this is just a family story. I
see that these pages did not come easy at first, then too easy—spilling
off the backlog of our birding, the meager discoveries of a day in Central
Park. How I mocked your catalog of fears, my possible failure right up
there with e-waste, habitat loss.

Conventional words, Lou: I am sorry.

One night not long ago, pre-courthouse, when your mystery was neatly
solved, we laughed as usual at the festering state of the nation, unhealed
by comic turns on TV. We looked forward to the midterm election that
might salvage what was left of our honor. For a moment all was right
with our little world. I attempted to join in the fun, deliver my layman's
praise of your recent work. The homey vision of your art—mind if I
use the word?—which you have all but abandoned. You'd been working
ahead on what Cyril calls Mom's project—*it's cool.*

I said: *A turn on the kids' refrigerator art, Lou.* Cyril's precise launch pads
and rockets, Maisy's scribbles freehand. I believe, post-courthouse, care
must be taken honoring your vision, so let me correct and revise.

*Moffett's paper memorial to our soldiers dead in this war decorates the glass
shelf over the stove in our kitchen. The names of the dead are not memorialized
in black marble, just written in ink on fragile paper scraps stapled one to two,
two to three, three to four and so on. They were first recorded in a book meant to
track the weight, height, amusing words, and fevers of our sickly child, but that
record is long gone. Moffett's memorial is now inscribed on strips of brown butcher
paper that winds between the measuring cups and the copper stock pot that was my
grandmother's prize, then circles back on itself and sweeps round the broken coffee
grinder. Where have all the young men gone?*

*Bonifacio, Jerry L. Jr., 28, Staff Sgt., Army National Guard; Vacaville, Calif.;
First Battalion, 184th Infantry*

*Escobar, Sergio H., 18, Lance Cpl., Marines; Pasadena, Calif.; First Marine
Division*

*Hodge, Susan M., 20, Specialist, Army National Guard; Ridgeway, Ohio;
612th Engineer Battalion*

Johnson, Leon M., 28, Sgt., Army; Jacksonville, Fla.; Third Infantry Division

Kimmell, Matthew A., 30, Staff Sgt., Army; Paxton, Ind.; Third Battalion, Fifth Special Forces Group

Sneed, Brandon K., 33, Sgt. First Class, Army; Norman, Okla.; Third Infantry Division

Though each link holds steady, as the months pass, Moffett's work is in need of repair. Gone to graveyards every one, sadly forgettable names weep in the steam, which I believe is what the artist has in mind. Looping down dangerously close to the flame, it is eerily festive, her Möbius strip with no inside, no outside, no end.

In our cottage industries of art and science, we do move on, discovering the last stale breath in the shrunken bladders of this year's birthday balloons, the hamster replacement spinning in his cage, Bert's sentence called off pending our further interrogation. Again, I place my updated notebook by your chair. You will remember the owl, the cold eye of that Gina, our Maisy's congestion, your impatience one day in the Park, the ten dollar bill pressed on my pretty student who couldn't possibly, Professor, a girl with no fear of the city dark, though big readable numbers on Cyril's watch told us 6:27, *gone the sun, from the hills, from the lake, safely rest.* . . . That is the trouble with memory: it sorts through the chaos, brings images to mind—watchtower of a phony castle, Bert sniffing his claret, the rough stuff of his poncho, rigging and mainmast, a gold doubloon for the scoundrel who takes a death-defying chance.

Louise, notebooks in hand, stands before her husband, the plaintiff's side of his desk.

"Our Sylvie," she says, no need to say more. The children are safe at home with Sylvie Neisswonger. Louise has seldom been to Freeman's office, a bleak room atop the curious little temple, Mathematics Hall, a cast-off aerie he shares with his aspiring pals—an acknowledged genius, boasting baby fat, who brings cookies to the children when invited to supper, devours them before the kids get a chance; an Indian woman who affects biker gear to counter her astonishing beauty, her great reserve. Artie is alone as Louise knew he would be, his schedule posted on their home page, *Works and Days.*

"Your version of our birding? What you wrote, down there in the courthouse?"

She begins her case against him, then turns to the blackboard, of course. Of course there must be a blackboard screwed to the wall. An elaborate problem covers most of its surface. Underneath in the old wooden frame, some joker, or serious student, has carved PYTHAGORAS SUCKS.

"You left these for me to read as though we can no longer talk."

"Lou-Lou."

"Don't Lou-Lou me."

"Easy way out, writing it down."

Artie comes round the desk, turns his wife to the window. A spectacular Autumn day, the sky wiped new blue. Students denying the chill in flip-flops and shorts litter the steps leading down to the broad campus from Low. The view from this height trumps that from Gottschalk's office. Homer, Plato, Virgil, the usual suspects inscribed in the limestone cornice of Butler Library catch the late sun.

"Computation?" she says. "He's got to be kidding."

"Gott doesn't kid. Demographics, genomes. Think small."

"Not what you wanted, not ever."

"Just different. I will not *contribute*. Love that terminal squeak? The Big Bang, first or last, will blast off without me. Fellow's paper beating me out by a mile may be published too early, pie in the sky, amount to nothing at all."

"Then why is it elegant?"

"You hear me talk solutions—beautiful, stunning. Some friend of Einstein's said elegance ought to be left to the tailor, the cobbler. Take Gott, for instance. The proof of his pudding may amount to nothing more than his elegant labels—Gucci, Armani, or so we students suppose."

But she wasn't listening—as she had so often—to the tolerable lectures attempting to make his work real to her. When they lived downtown in the loft, she had followed his every word, or tried to. At the turn of the millennium, Louise understood perfectly why the world would not end in a slippage of time, Y2K snuff the soul out of our computers. With reparation we would move on. Artie had called his return to mathematics the makeup class in whatever the world might be made of, that his scribbled lineup of symbols and numbers were the merest foot soldiers to a general theory of everything, don't you know? At times he would attempt to draw strings coupling, or make visible the loop-de-loop of quantum frenzy. She never quite got it but took the pencil from his hand, shaded in, crosshatched to get the depth of possible dimensions. Her own work had given way to house and children as though, much like old Gottschalk, she wiped away the rubber crumbs of her art, leaving the smudge of line and perspective unsolved.

On the South Lawn below, a card table flaps its antiwar poster. No patrons to read the leaflets, sign the petition. Too brisk, too bright a day, the message worn, ineffectual. *Long time ago,* 1968, that war, the students had stormed the president's office, but that siege doesn't come to mind; she just wishes he had not used that gentle folk song in his account of her work. She must tear down her kitchen art. The private notice of her mourning seems foolish today, Art Speak to no listener other than Artie. Once she had drawn the arrow of time for Freeman, a birthday card, and once exhibited a cloudy solution in a bottle of water, half empty, half full, a show playing with uncertainty, the assault of time on the body, that's all. Time passing as we know it, day by day. *Not mere numbers,* he had said of the evaporating water in a hand-blown bottle—his judgment kindly, self-effacing. Now as she listened to his babble of knots and loops, she did not try to understand, not this time. Perhaps she was never meant to. From the rising pitch of his voice, she guessed he was going on about proof. What matter whether the conjecture was true or false? Something absurd, how he fell into the swamp of the excluded middle, laughing, still foolin' around.

He said: "Oh, Artie," imitating the caress of her incalculable scolds.

"Don't," she said, "don't go there." She held the notebooks to her breast, his new one from Pearl Paint and the old greenie with her bird notations, heard the shuffling of papers into his backpack and the familiar snap of his laptop as he prepared to walk Cyril to school each morning. Closing up shop, but she did not think so, not now, perhaps never. He couldn't give up playing the numbers. On the way home, they would speak, a few words with a bitter edge to be glossed over. Then they would talk for how many years? They would move, though never far from a classroom, and she would again have a studio. Change of direction might not suit them, not again. They would honor the yearly trip to the farm in Wisconsin. What mattered was here and now, the probable life just outside the city, a garden perhaps, doghouse, sandbox, but never a plastic feeder to fake out the hummingbirds with sugar in a bowl. She would plant red flowers to lure them, though she could not yet name them—cardinal flowers. Our Sylvie would discover her young friends still within range of their starting line, Lower Broadway. He would make light of Lou's fears. She would endure his mixed metaphors, his puns, the dated phrases of his grandfather, Cyril O'Connor. The difficult pearl buttons at the top of every nightgown would be snipped off for the hope of easy access on nights reclaiming their eager bodies in the loft, skin to skin. Nightclothes came with the children. She wished he had not used that song. It belonged to his mother, to her mother, too. Or perhaps he did not remember the appropriate line: *Where have all the young girls gone? Taken husbands every one.* Though that was not true, not true of his mother, who left him by accident to an orphan boy life. He switched off the buzzing fluorescent light, the room behind her in semidarkness now. She thought, how unfair: Artie lost, Bertie won. Would they still go to Connecticut for the Christmas goose, the tasteful Boyce glitter, snubs from their spoiled children? She would not speak; the anger was still there, a clutch in her throat that he'd never told her, that he'd written his failure out as though it's no more than a story. Put words in her mouth. On the way home, she would relent, hand over the notebooks, say *good job* to his account of their day in the Park, entirely man-made, their birding, her fears. But that would never do, for that's what she said to the kids—*good job*—when they showed her their brave efforts with Play-Doh, Legos, with Magic Markers of their refrigerator art.

The sun at the window was still bright, almost blinding. Squinting, Louise could see a Frisbee fly over the patch of lawn on the campus designated for play, and a tour guide leading prospective students and their parents up the steps into Low, where they would be awed by the dome of the rotunda, for sure a temple of learning. She could hear Artie scrape back the chair from his old desk, funky like Gottschalk's. As though there for a show at the end of this day, birds flitted from tree to tree on Campus Walk. She would not call them city pigeons. Pale mourning doves, she named them in a coo. *Colum-um-bidae.* When she turned, her husband was erasing the intricate problem on the blackboard. Chalk dust fell in a haze. Not to steal his words, she waited for him to say it.

"Clean slate."

Daybook, October 25, 2007

The children, by which we mean grandchildren, have carved a pumpkin for us, lest we forget. He—it's a he—sits on our front hall table. His snarling smile, jagged teeth, triangulated eyes don't scare us at all. Part of their pleasure was making the mess. They are scheming, wacky tricks, I presume. We're stuck in the waiting game. The costume I've been wearing these many years, middle-class woman in the last days of the Holocene, surely belongs to someone else, though the plot as it plays out, remains the same. Conception to the grave. The rest is filler.

In Tolstoy's *Death of Ivan Ilyich,* read just weeks ago, a posturing public servant reviews his life to discover that his ambition has been a burden to his family. As it was to Tolstoy's, so we are told by Nabokov, spreading the guilt around. Prompted by this confession, I swing toward you on my ergonomic chair. You are at the door of my workroom. I speak of the years you've put up with my scribbling.

Apology dismissed, you suggest we close the little house in the Berks this year, *As a precaution.*

Caution on your mind these days. While I have a formal gratitude for your care, what might happen if I throw it to the wind? I mourn the loss of our wrangling, the way you screen my fancy through reality check. We will miss the view of the garden safe in its blanket of snow. Still, we are in perfect accord.

Not yet, not in October!

Settle into your books.

You closed the flue, discarded the ashes good for the garden.

Here in the El Dorado the fireplace in our apartment was sealed up

before we settled in. A pretentious display of marble. The mantel's cren-
ellations and brass rosettes refer to some striver's hope in the wake of the
Great Depression. *Elegance*—now you see it: now you don't.

In any case, the little house is closed as a precaution. I'm confined to
the safety of our twin towers and the Park, all stories within reach, legends of the season. I mean to say: more than a magician's trick, though
plain as the nose on my face, the decorative dead wood in the fireplace
is not *seen* anymore. The screen to protect us from hot embers, useless.
Antique Roadshow stuff—an astrolabe, highboy, cradle, *Death of the Virgin*, Goya's *Disasters of War* (second state).

Our Sylvie: A Fireside Story

> And God said to Noah, I have determined to make an end of all
> flesh; For the earth is filled with violence through them; behold I will
> destroy them with the earth; Make yourself an ark of gopher wood;
> make rooms in the ark, and cover it inside and out with pitch.
>
> —*Genesis 11:13–15*

Sylvia Neisswonger is strapped into her seat heading east. To her right
she sees the image of a plane on a small screen. To her left, bright blue
sky stretches above suds of cloud as far as the eye can see. Perhaps that
distance can be figured. Martha, her stepdaughter, measures depths of
the sea, so why not the distance to beyond? The plane on the screen is
trailing a red line as it flies across America, eating up the distance from
San Diego to JFK. Sylvie can't figure how to call this image up. She looks
to her seatmate's screen. He's a young man, young to her, with a beak of
nose on a fleshy face. To Sylvie he looks assembled—floppy ears, receding chin, his body a soft bulk. He has fallen asleep, thumb in the page of
an airport thriller, not thrilling enough, though a car bomb in the act
of exploding a U.S. Army vehicle is blazoned on *Run for Cover*. Soldiers
in splotched camouflage stand, thank heaven, safely aside. Carts with
salty snacks and beverage of choice have been wheeled down the aisle.

In the hum of the pressurized cabin, she hears the occasional cough, a shrill cry, perhaps the baby who gave her a grin when infants, the old and infirm were boarded first. She pops the flesh-colored hearing aids out of her ears. The dumb show in the cabin surrounds her.

Quite deaf, though not infirm, as the guards at the Oceanographic Institute in La Jolla might tell you, tell that every day of her visit, Mrs. Waite, as she is properly known, climbed uphill to have lunch with Martha. They were more than welcoming. "Gallant": that's the word she searches out, Perez and Bonfilio not checking the visitor ID that hung round her neck, quick to escort her up the steps, open the door as though the Institute were a first-class hotel, not a temple of science. Perez has three children. His wife's name is Lola. Bonfilio is studying bookkeeping at night. Calling out loud and strong—*Beautiful day, Mrs. Waite.* How they did love to chat when she made it to the top of the hill, breathed easy. Waite, her legal name on two documents submitted at the airport in New York, is the name of her stepdaughter, Dr. Waite, Martha. Checking through Security brought back the memory of her first U.S. passport and the name she was born with: von Neisswonger. Yes, her mother, Inga von Neisswonger, had charmed the American consul in Toulouse. The papers he procured were not fraudulent; her passport with the photo of a wistful girl, stunned by the camera, hair braided tight, perfect little snowflakes knit into her Tyrolean sweater.

My brother Otto had a sweater with the very same snowflakes. Absurd, our father said,—snowflakes never match. Each one has its own crystal network. Pleased with herself for telling Martha that story with its bit of crystallography, for it's hard to find common ground, always has been, to come upon a moment when she was not the woman with the trace of an accent, with words sought for in plain English. When she was not that intruder— *Call me Sylvie*—who came all of a sudden years and years ago to an old house in Connecticut to take the place of Martha's dead mother.

My brother Otto . . .

Your brother Otto?

Yes, older by three years, already at the gymnasium. Always showing off, explaining the workings of the Jacquard loom as though our father would not know a thousand snowflakes, if you like, might be programmed, woven exactly the same.

Martha said: *Most likely not woven*, then held forth on the invention of knitting machines, correcting Sylvie not as sharply as Papa Neisswonger had corrected his son. Sylvie understood about the Jacquard loom, that it didn't knit sweaters. She was ten years old at the time, some years older when her mother told the story, the way Inga told family stories to her new friends in New York, always leaving out the name of her son as though *Otto* might scratch, a painful burr in her throat. It is quite ridiculous, this loose strand of a childhood sweater that will lead Sylvie where she goes too often this past year, to the stucco villa in Innsbruck with its red-tiled roof, handblown glass in the windows transforming the garden to a shimmering mirage. Shuffling memories, laying out the cards.

Both von Neisswonger and his son were escorted out the double front door to the purring Mercedes by Nazi officers with thick Berlinerisch accents, Otto clutching his scuffed football like a ruined globe in his hands. Sylvie had once planned to go back to see the house, now a small hotel—how odd it would be to see her room rented for the night, her little bed with its white coverlet transformed to the vast comfort of king-size, the frieze of twined edelweiss painted out. She had once thought to return with Cyril, show her old lover the house on the river Inn, the imperial squares of the city, the Alpine mines her father worked, summer and winter. She will not go now, now that he's gone, lies with May, his wife of many years, leaving Sylvie the comfort of his family. A wonder how they have sorted themselves out. As she packed for the yearly visit to Martha, *My trip to California must do me*, said to the neighbors who knew nothing of her abandoned journey to Innsbruck but would look after the house in Connecticut, take in the mail, overwater the plants. The house of Bob Waite, her late husband, she had explained to one of Martha's pals at the Institute. *Late. I have never understood that expression.*

Better late than never, the fellow said, a rude remark now she thinks of it. They were a funny crowd, these men and women who keep track of the wind, who search for holes in the sea, who count time in the millions of years, a time when the waters rose, a time before the Great Flood became a Bible story. Now the deluge was all too real, happening fast in their calculations of melt. A stargazer, declared a crank by these scientists, believed he had found Noah's Ark, what was left of it, poking up in a satellite picture of Mount Ararat. The waters were now rising, not receding, so what did he hope to salvage, they asked—a blockbuster script? The animals, two by two, cast from the San Diego Zoo? The *Titanic* in biblical dress? Sylvie had thought to stop their laughter—*The ark was sturdy, sealed with pitch*—then thought not, for she was their guest, the powdery old lady listening in at the end of the table. Martha took her side. Prehistoric sea creatures found at Yellowstone, so why not? Plucking a hair from Noah's beard, DNA coaxing—could be *Jurassic Park*.

Sylvie believes that as soon as she left each day after lunch, the scholars went back to talking their winds and waves while she braved the freeway in her rented Toyota, found her way back to Martha's cottage. Still, they seemed to her quite silly, these brilliant seashore observers laughing at last night's TV, making jokes of the State of the Union. Well, the State of the Union was perilous, they well knew. She did not cut into their play, though it was all too easy to translate White House blather they laughed at to the German propaganda of the Reich. *Heimat. Vaterland. Ehre.* As for Noah, the one just man, she searched the shelves in the cottage wanting to read what God ordered by way of an ark. Martha did not own a Bible. Sylvie is certain about the pitch, the viscous caulk Bob Waite applied each Spring to his trawler. The smell was god-awful, impossible to wash the black stuff out of his clothes. Each year when he finished, that thrifty man threw his ruined jeans and work shirt away.

Far as Sylvie can see, these lunch breaks at the Institute and an occasional barbecue are Martha's only life beyond the lab. There's her bicycling team on Sundays and a correspondence with a professor at Woods Hole that seems to have gone beyond ice cores and ocean sediment. Martha, well into middle age, is flustered as she speaks of coming east to present a paper at a conference organized by her—pausing for the appropriate word—her *mentor*.

So mentor it is, though Sylvie hopes he is more. She will call Martha when she gets home to Connecticut. Still early in California, her big athletic girl with clipped gray hair will answer on the cell even if she is in the midst of climate calculations or e-mailing her prospective lover of an event some million years ago. What she remembers of Martha's industry, what she told the scientists at lunch one day, was the story of when this

Sylvie was brought to the house on a hill, Bob Waite's unwelcome surprise. She took his children to the shore, the rim of sand on Long Island Sound, that small puddle, and the girl she did not yet know dug, dug until the water seeped up from China, saving the pebbles and a necklace of slimy seaweed to examine at home. Martha's future, Sylvie told these men and women plotting the fate of the Pacific coast, was written in the sand.

And she sleeps as the red line makes its way across New Mexico up to Denver, till chicken or beef, hard to tell, though she recalls cupping her ear to hear the selection. She eats only the bland cookie, sleeps again, and when she wakes, the big screen at the front of the cabin displays a young man with a smirk on his face driving a mountain trail, a treacherous journey, though Sylvie's seatmate is laughing—the hearty ho-ho of that *Mitteleuropa* actor in the old movies, jowls shaking in joy or despair. She imagines the thrill of the chase, the tough words of a cop who looks fierce . . . well, not really. Laughter across the aisle as the clown drives off the cliff, a well-known clown, and next thing he is jumping the cables on the set, flubbing his lines for the retake. Oh, they are only making a movie. Sylvie enjoys the pantomime, easily guesses the stuntman's flirtation with the script girl, then nods off again, a dreamless sleep without fear, without longing—and when she wakes, the little plane on the small screen's heading toward western Pennsylvania, and the long descent toward New York and home.

Her seatmate comes on friendly—*I'm in sales*—though she's not asked, can't hear the name of his product.

Resets the digital devices in her ears. *Sales?*

Heavy equipment. Farming, construction. Nurse the infrastructure of developing nations . . . Jed does not offer a last name. He's Jed; she's Sylvie. Developing nations—*you've got your Asians, your South of the Border*—will continue to need his backhoes, cranes. Jed flies business class. *Coach this trip, personal time.*

But suppose, Sylvie suggests, *suppose the fields in Asia are underwater.*

Wall-to-wall rice paddies? That's a good one. On his laptop he brings up pictures of his daughter, a piglet with her father's floppy ears, blessedly not his beak.

Lovely bright eyes. Sylvie says, *Not rice paddies. Where there is now land-mass, we may experience seeping salt water, estuaries. I have been visiting my step-daughter.* Sylvie attempts a quick course on the Gulf Stream, *temperature twelve degrees above normal, while in the Pacific we may experience*—finds her-self tangled in alien language—*short cycles of stability.* From Jed's indulgent nod, she suspects he's heard it all, figured it into sales of his products—mapping the deluge, the snowless peaks of Kilimanjaro as seen on TV. She retreats to the airline magazine. Jed finds his place in *Run for Cover.* Sylvie flips the pages with many items the efficient traveler might need—inflatable hangers, golf bags, foldaway tents, bug zappers, ponchos for rainy adventures. Home is addressed in doormats, tea cozies, safety grips for the bathtub, electric heaters. Martha has said to come live with her for the warm weather, said it so cheerfully Sylvie barely detected the duty in her stepdaughter's voice; and then she thinks of the chill Waite house in Connecticut, carpenter ants chewing hand-hewn beams to sawdust, mil-dew in the basement, but the pearwood mantel is sturdy and there's the fanlight over the front door. Sunshine or shadow, each morning as she comes downstairs, the delicate tracery puts on its show, a subtle retort to squared-away Yankee design.

Still, the Federal house is not her home; and the broad stucco villa on Lundstrasse is not home, though she can tour every room with por-traits of ancestors, all men with trim whiskers, several with military honors of the Austro-Hungarian Empire. The Dürer woodcuts were hung between mirrors in the dining room. So predictable, Inga said to her new friends in New York, and so dreary—*Death of the Virgin. Pas-sion of Christ!* Well, Inga would rather not partake of *Melancholia* with her schnitzel, *Danke schön,* and one day said as much to her husband, whose home the villa was in every detail. The famous etching of that brooding angel with her mystical apparatus and a sleeping dog at her feet remained in its place. Each room replays with its legend, how her father turned the incident of the Dürers to his benefit when an emissary of Cardinal Innitzer came to lunch. Otto was allowed to sit at the table while Sylvie had been instructed to kiss the Bishop's hand, then sent belowstairs. Yes, Albrecht Dürer was son of a goldsmith, his iconography decidedly Protes-tant. Now his art graced the walls of a Catholic silver-mine family, a step

down in the metallurgical table. An amusing story told by Neisswonger and retold by Inga with a mocking smile. Later, much later, Sylvie would understand the anecdote was not about the Master of Nuremberg or his works, gloomy though great, but about the slights a country girl of no account often suffered having married the honorific von with a sloping Hapsburg jaw, about how Inga dare not speak in the presence of the prelate come on behalf of Innitzer, who folded when the Germans appended Austria, about a move already in process had she looked up from her Apfelstrudel to advise the Jews to pack up, or simply noted the collapse of the Empire in a fistful of marks dealt out for a loaf of bread.

When they were first in New York, her mother told the Dürer story with a good deal of invention: Sylvie waited at the door with maids and the cook for the Bishop's departure with a young priest who bestowed a final blessing on all. She was summoned to watch the emissary drive off in the big black car flying the Austrian flag—red, white, gold of the imperial eagle. Or that may have been her mother's invention, but this memory was Sylvie's, told at last to Louise: the day her father and brother were taken, she had watched her mother dissolve in tears. *Mommi, Mommi,* she cried, as her mother's gray-green eyes blinded with sorrow. Her full lips, ripe for laughter, puckered to a sore. Sylvie would dream her mother's face over the years, drowning in tears, gasping, *Otto. Otto.* The last time Inga would speak her son's name, casting Sylvie off with a swift thrust of her arm to quickly compose herself, Frau von Neisswonger on the phone with arrangements, a forgiving smile for her girl who believes it was this day when her mother, no longer Mommi, became Inga, co-conspirator and pal. And they had lived on in the villa for some weeks, eating like mice in the kitchen, spare meals brought in by a loyal maid. Packing and unpacking their bags, would they need lavender soap, warm hose or sturdy sandals? Inga, silent and calm in preparation as though they were going to take the waters, splash about in the refreshing Seebensee.

Flying over the vast expanse of America, Sylvie indulges herself in this dream tour of a house, polished copper pots in the kitchen, full canisters—*Zucker, Kaffee, Honig*—while many were lucky for a potato, a crust of bread. No good can come from this scrapbook of plenty. She stands at the door of her father's study where bound books lined the walls, each with its gold title, and the atlas lay open to the map of the Austrian Republic, 1918, the beautiful blue Danube fading on the lectern by the window with a view of the untidy garden rippling in sunlight. Now she enters the pretty bedroom of a small, scrappy girl, her Steiff animals outgrown, her dolls abandoned at a tea party, suitcase packed for the life of exile soon to come. Her father and brother taken. Neisswonger had spoken against the Chancellor, who stalled for time while Austria welcomed the invasion. Papa wrote letters against that very Cardinal who played word games with the Vatican, trifled with Mussolini, which gave a bitter twist to Inga's amusing story: how easily her Ulrich was swept away like so much dross from his silver mines. And could he not see that Catholic

Austria was running out of time like the hourglass in Dürer's engraving? *Melancholia,* the hefty goddess with her scientific apparatus, unable to figure life-and-death equations? But why her son swept into the ashes of history? And what good to never say his name? *Otto.*

No good at all figuring, not even as an unburdening, though once the villa was revealed in detail to Louise Moffett, who's as close as Sylvia Neisswonger Waite will ever come to having a daughter. No relation at all. Louise is the wife of the grandson of her lover, Cyril O'Connor, which is more distant than the second cousins twice removed recorded in the genealogy of the Neisswongers, all those lofty connections. Louise did not mourn the vanished Dürers, or a little girl's room with a tea table and white coverlet on the bed, or the anxious weeks out of time lingering on in the villa, but cried for the spoiling, the word Sylvie chose to convey her memory of the soldier's rough hands on her body, the harsh scrape of his brass buckle. He had not taken his tunic off, only pulled down his britches to accomplish the act. *Beflecken,* too often in recent days, the German word came to mind, would not allow the plain English. She, who once had the gift of tongues, a translator at the UN, German to English, English to French. In telling of the soldier's weight upon her, she lapsed into the concealing hush of childhood, what must never be known. She believed he had bristle-blond hair, that his eyes were ice blue, though he covered her face with a pillow; then she heard his boots stomping downstairs, coarse laughter. Whispering to Louise as though Cyril stirring in the cradle might hear that her father's books were thrown off the shelves, his wine cellar desecrated, the silver service carried off, and, most surely *Melancholia* and *The Passion of Christ* wrenched from the dining room walls. That night, when the soldier was through with her, she had wiped herself on a soft linen towel embroidered with the von N. Then, possessed of a miraculous will, she dressed in the inappropriate velvet frock her mother had set out for their voyage, woke Inga from a deep sleep, led her down the back stairs, out across the terrace and neglected parterre through a hole in the garden wall, thank God never mended. For years Sylvie would hate her small body, shun intimacy, though later she slept around, as they used to say, strictly unserious business, until she met Cyril O'Connor, but that was another story not told to Louise Moffett, only that she was loyal to her husband, Bob Waite, who took care with her, was attentive and kind.

The lost city is no longer real, Innsbruck only a setting for a fable told to her friend—the towering Alps at a distance, the villa garden in disarray. *Unnatürlich,* her father called the clipped box laid out in a stiff maze. The handless statue of a goddess blessed a plot of roses gone wild. Thorns and a dry fountain. She was allowed to play with a few friends in this confusion while Inga poured tea *à l'anglais* for their mothers.

On the terrace always, those ladies.

Lou listening to a story more mysterious than a whodunit read before bedtime, a tale that would never provide the desired solution with each strand folded into an end. Otto would always be framed as a boy, lifeless as a studio photo; or the faint human skull, a prop in Dürer's staging of a depressed angel with that skinny dog sniffing her feet. Two women together in a loft on Lower Broadway, tea bags soggy in their mugs, not art history with slides and a term-paper answer—Louise had cited Panofsky—to demonstrate that reason is defeated by imagination, or was it the other way round? In *Melancholia,* that is, not the insoluble history of this afternoon's tale.

And how my father disliked the order of that garden, its geometric paths, labyrinth that tricked no one. He had been, in his youth, a mathematician. But Sylvie took that no further, returned to Inga working better millinery at Saks to pay for their rented room before she assumed her glamorous refugee disguise.

Inga, the farm girl with the stench of goats and sheep still in her nostrils, was not much for nature, and not much for pouring tea. Did she long for the shops and cafés of Vienna? For the operettas and balls she presumed as her marriage portion? Surely she had bargained for more than a husband who closed the door to his study to read journals written in a language of numbers and signs. The city on the river Inn no longer honored Ulrich Neisswonger. His mines had been appropriated by the state, though once he had walked with his daughter to the Silver Chapel, not with Inga or Otto, just the two of them, an occasion so rare. It seemed strange even then, walking through the old town, her father in his British tweeds worn each day, now that he did not go to his office. He tipped his *Tirolerhut* at merchants and bowed to a lady in mourning along the way. Yet so informal with his daughter in tow, the many smiles of that morning, *Guten Tag*. When he pulled back the leather curtain at the door of the church—not the church Inga took his children to on Sunday while he read of problems in his mathematical journal—the altar shone upon them, a girl and her father not come to pray. *From our Alpine mines*, he said proudly, all of the silver latticework on the high altar before them gleaming with Christ and triumphant signs of the zodiac. Sylvie looked long at the prettiest figure, Virgo, the month when she was born.

We were tourists in our very own city, that's what I believed, that he took me as a treat, a special day for his girl. But that was not so. Or I believe his taking me along may have given my father an ounce of protection. We seemed to be waiting, just waiting, and then a priest came from the darkness behind the silver altar. It was planned, you see, this meeting, and my father took papers out of his leather pouch, the bloodproof bag he carried when hunting. They spoke French, a language I had only begun to study in school. Still, they turned from me, and for a long while they spoke together. Then the priest, old, very old with creases all round his dim eyes and purple spots on his hands, put the papers in the folds of his cassock. He went back into the shadows he came from, and my father said I should look at the crab on the altar, how perfectly the scaly ridges were formed, and that he, Ulrich Neisswonger, was a Scorpio, which meant he kept secrets, did I understand?

But I never found those secrets, only guessed them from movies, from novels. I know he was angry at the Cardinal, who ordered the Nazi flag to fly over the chapel, and that I wore a dirndl that day, costumed for a dark plot, not Sound of Music.

A story told when she traveled to the loft to help out with Cyril sleeping in that wooden cradle, the possession of all those Waites on their hill in Connecticut. It was the one thing she appropriated from their store of useful Yankee things. Now Cyril was in school, and when it came cradle time for Maisy . . . she recalls the apologetic sigh when Louise returned it, beautiful certainly, no longer useful. Maisy lay in a padded Moses basket woven of plastic straw, an ingenious contraption with many pockets, zippers, and handles to haul her about. Louise had carried the cradle down to Sylvie's Jeep, parked illegally on Lower Broadway. A packing-up day, the time of the Freemans' move uptown to be near the University so that Artie might go on with his studies, his note of purpose redressing his truant past. On the day Sylvie told of her childhood home in the Tyrol, she did not give the full tour of her father's study. Louise was invited to view the map of the Hapsburg Empire well in decline, but her guide left out the mathematical journals neatly stacked by her father's reading chair. To touch even their pale blue covers was strictly verboten by order of the silver-mine master who turned through their problems at night. The cradle was returned to its proper station by the fireplace in Connecticut, an artifact for a phantom child.

Now Sylvie walks the aisles of the plane as instructed by Bob Waite. So march she does up to the blue curtain denying her entry to the superior classes. She takes in her fellow passengers sleeping or enduring this time out of time. Seat-belt signs on, she lurches through turbulence, gives way to the moment of fear that Bob Waite laughed at, then delivered the stats proving safety in flight. Jed has stowed his computer, put up the small screen with the plane consuming the red line through eastern Pennsylvania, where a flight on its way to destination unknown—White House? Camp David?—met its fate. Bob had died well before that terrible day, his statistics never figuring hijacks or security fuss at airports. *Mein lieber.* She had lived under his protection, a stranger in the national landmark of his house, his history of good family with names of teachers, bankers, ministers recorded in the Waite Bible never consulted, their worth, worthiness—*Wert, erhaben* haunting the purity of Federal rooms. The stale breath of humankind is heavy in the cabin. After her marriage Sylvie flew first class to visit her mother in one extravagant new house or another, improbable as pictures in slick magazines. Inga Meyer, channeling Ingrid Bergman with a touch of Zsa Zsa Gabor, had made her fortune by way of husbands. The silver mine, a brave if failed start; then on to the rewards of Hollywood and Texas—movies, born-again oil—a true American story. The Baroque mansion in Houston, where she finally came to rest, was fitted out in Secessionist glamour, Austrian bentwood chairs, a mantel clock (Adolf Loos) that flung the minutes away with a sleek brass pendulum, all said to be like if not the very treasures confiscated from the villa. The depressing Dürer woodcuts were banished from Inga's story. The dining room in River Oaks displayed George Grosz's decadent posturing, while her daughter, the prim translator, cut into a bloody steak.

Louise laughed, *An improvement over* The Crucifixion? She was, let's recall, an artist, or had been when she first met Sylvie. Something wistful about her quick judgment, the pleasure she took dwelling on Grosz's dark romance, the arrogance of many self-portraits.

And pricey Paul Klees. My mother's claim to a life never lived in the Tyrol.

Sylvie's account depends on doubtful stories told by Inga. As a student, late nights in the Public Library would never reveal that her father was called Herr Professor, a title he sharply rejected as he did the von. He came back to Innsbruck from his studies to run the family silver mines, and there Inga was, a village girl with aspirations. The mines' picture-book village sat at the bottom of a valley below the Neisswongers' hunting lodge, and at every turn there was Inga radiantly pious at Sunday Mass, flirtatious in the tavern where she washed up the steins, his with the family crest, eagle rampant. He came upon her each day on the path going down into the village, or at the bend in the one narrow street. She seemed always to be in his way that first season. He was reviewing the accounts, learning to manage the workers in the mine. This lovely girl's smile distracted him from the reality that times were already bad, quite bad, that he may never go back to the University, listen to the arguments of his scientific betters. Inga had been once to Innsbruck with her confraternity for a procession—Immaculate Conception, Epiphany? The feast day was movable when Inga told of her meeting young Neisswonger on such an excursion. And wasn't he surprised to see her in town looking smarter in her loden jacket than any village girl? Her "professor" became more than he ever could be, her Ulrich, who published one paper discrediting the uncertainty principle in a popular scientific journal. Why would Sylvie, a child transported to New York, not believe in this legend, yet still believe that her father followed the news of the brilliant men who practiced Jewish Science, as the Reich would name it. Sylvie telling Louise the story of her father's great learning, his degrees, a man so certain—isn't that odd?—that National Socialism with its diseased anti-Semitism, its anti-Christian program would never take hold in *Catholic Austria*. In going back over her father's miscalculations about the fate of his country, his silence, then his defense of the Jews, she avoided his lonely pursuit of mathematics, knowing Louise fears that her husband might never run the course, that Artie's makeup exam may prove to be a layman's fiddling with numbers, much like her father's.

Oh, how Papa lectured Inga and Otto that the failed artist with the comic mustache would never . . . I was too young to fully understand what might never in Catholic Austria. It happened right in front of Papa's nose.

And on another day Louise turned the page of a coffee-table book sent years back to Sylvie, gift from Inga to her daughter intended to enforce her tale of Bauhaus good taste. A glamour shot of a slim crystal carafe (Otto Wagner, date uncertain) faced off with a silver broach set with moonstones (Josef Hoffmann, 1919).

You understand I was shamed by my mother's claim that such objects were part of our life. I was ten years old when we finally left the villa, escaped through the garden wall huddled in Inga's fur coat, the two of us linked together like kids in a three-legged race. Kinderspiel. *Martha latched to her brother. Gerald.*

Gerald?

The other Waite child, not my son.

But the story not told—one woman to another, working girls who found their way in the big city—was of Sylvie's lonely investigations of the vanished life on the river Inn. She had wanted more than a postcard world of cuckoo clocks, a lost realm of kitsch and personal memory—Otto in lederhosen. When she was well enough grown in New York, Inga took off, made her way out to the émigré movie crowd in sunny California. Then Sylvie designed a course of study outside the curriculum at Hunter College, carefully tracing the marriages and bloody wars that redrew the borders of Austria again and again, adding and subtracting Venetia, Dalmatia, Lombardy, Bohemia. Her father had turned the page in his atlas back to the Holy Roman Empire. Poor Papa: the borders he finally believed in were erased. His repeated claims for the honor of *Catholic Austria* now seemed more than an annoyance to his daughter, more than a scratch in the record of his wife's favorite Strauss waltz stuck in three-quarter time. It was far too late when he changed his tune. That is what she presumed, too late defending the Jewish bankers, and Rosen, who sat on a high stool over his ledgers, green shade sheltering his eyes as he once figured the ounces of silver mined by the elder von. The mines now property of the Reich. She further imagined that her father spoke up for his teachers at the University who were relieved of their posts, that he defended his café companions not practicing Aryan science. Now he became the elder; the line had run out save for his son, Otto, and why, she would ask, taking notes in the Reading Room of the New York Public Library, why turn through pages and pages of the Nuremberg Trials, the verdict clear as to crimes against humanity, but with no hope of the answer? Why take a boy? A miscalculation from hell, his name set down with his father's, by a simpleton following rules? Simple is evil, is death by paperwork, damnation filed away. By the year Papa Neisswonger's daughter graduated with honors from a city college in New York, the map he honored, give or take a slice of northern Italy, was in place once again. But his lectern by the study window was no longer in her dreams.

She had taken to the books. March 12, 1938, the date on which Austria was annexed by the Reich. The players who led to Austria's downfall—Chancellors Dolfuss, Schuschnigg, the German ambassador, Papen—could not answer her question: when did Papa wake to the nightmare of Catholic compliance? Did he speak against the very prelate who laughed at his Dürer story? They ordered him to work his mines for their benefit two years before the *Polizei* led him out the front door with his son. The camp where she presumed her father and brother were taken was enlarged early, December of '39. She worked on in the library at 42nd Street until the lights dimmed, then took the subway uptown to a rented room, the maid's room in a big drafty apartment. The accounts of the war were not sorted into the arguments and fables of history. She discovered a portrait, Marie Elizabeth of Austria, radiant child who, disfigured by smallpox, became an abbess, d. Innsbruck, 1808; Emperor Ferdinand I required a yellow patch to be worn by all Jews, 1551. Protestants denied citizenship, their lives endangered with the punishment of heresy, 1527, according to Catholic state law.

Searching for a family story, Sylvie copied down notes in her neat hand: the operation of silver mines, Hapsburg political marriages, the Vienna Boys' Choir (est. 1498, held in contempt by Otto, an athletic boy). Her ledger was thick as a poultice to sooth the pain of her father's fate. Had she really expected to discover a record of that meeting in the Silver Chapel, the nature of the documents passed to the old priest? The chapel with the luminous silver altar was carefully preserved in memory. She went to mass every Sunday, obedient to her father's political belief. There came one night when she discovered that titles were passed out liberally by the Hapsburgs long before they settled into their palace in Innsbruck. Best not pass that item to Inga, or that von, *often a mere honorific,* was now prohibited by the Austrian government.

Want these books put aside?

She had turned back three volumes on the Treaty of Versailles and a rant claiming Hitler was indebted to Nietzsche, and to Descartes's *Meditations* in which the philosopher questions if we can ever come up with the answers. Bright Sylvie said clearly—*No thank you.* She walked the long block to Broadway, took the bus uptown. A couple with theater programs, flirting madly, just out of a show, or perhaps, in the heat of desire, they'd left during intermission. Cut out to make out at home. Well, her home was that narrow maid's room in the apartment of an old refugee couple. Each week, she paid twenty dollars in cash, passing an envelope to them before sunset on the Sabbath. They had little to say to their boarder with a cross on her neck in search of a family story, reading history to solve yesterday's crimes when any day she might see that Solomon's watchband did not fully conceal the numbers on his wrist. Inga had discovered their vacant maid's room through a friend of a classy friend, then gone off to California, where yet another friend dealt her secretarial work for swank émigrés. Later Sylvie would understand that she took a page from her mother's book, Inga writing her own script, a quick read that instructed: get on with your life.

> *Wo, o wo ist der Ort—ich trag ihn im Herzen—,*
> *wo sie noch lange nicht konnten, noch von einander*

Study your languages, pass the exam to translate.

> Oh *where* is the place—I carry it in my heart—,
> where they still were far from mastery, still fell apart
> from each other, like mating cattle that someone
> has badly paired;—

The UN was plain and sturdy, no mirror tricks of Versailles. No more fiddling with lines of Rilke, better treaties securing the here and now. Her inner ear could not connect with the poet's feeling. It was a sort of deafness that plagued her, more troubling than the deafness that would come upon her late in life.

The altar of the Silver Chapel with its shimmering zodiac was not revealed to Louise on the day she flipped the pages of an extravagant book, a storybook really: how superb the Austrian designers before the First World War at the modernist game, how their artifacts—beautifully photographed—vases, candlesticks, gems worked into silver, each crafted with the vision of the maker upon it—predicted a future unburdened with the sodden bourgeois trappings of the past.

The villa, you see, was as my father must have it, as it had always been in his time. Biedermeier curves of each sofa, his ashwood desk. My room of the spoiling was kitsch, Tyrolean cute. He had no anger against his privilege or trappings of his class, not a dollop of sour *schlag. Not a worthless Austrian mark.* Turning now to the page with: *Silver clip in the form of a maple leaf for a fräulein's hair,* and: *a slim Wiener Werkstätte mirror. Unburdened with a view of the past. Meine Mutter so clever—refurnishing memory. How we do live the life set forth by our tables and chairs.*

* * *

Sylvia Waite is on her way to JFK, then on to the white house on a hill in Connecticut. Her late husband, an airline executive, had been a pilot in the war—their war, she calls it. He led his squadron of Spitfires halfway to Dresden. *Then we turned back.*

Turned back?

We had only enough fuel to escort the bombers off on their mission. Escort them through dogfights. I lost half my squadron one night. Bob Waite gave no personal details, which she found troubling, the way the firebombing of a city could be no more than an order carried out. *It's all in the books,* he said.

In time she came to believe in her husband's reserve, though answers she sought were not in the books. She had married something of a hero, a widower with a ready-made family, enjoyed his gentleness in the old bed with creaking wooden slats. Passion would not come until she met Cyril O'Connor, shared a cab on a rainy day at the UN. Cyril had served in the Korean Conflict. Their emotional extravagance might have been shot as a war movie—lovers on *Waterloo Bridge,* tearful parting. They returned to their dutiful married lives until Sylvie, of all the unimaginable things, came back into his life. The sleeping prince—ailing eyesight, sparse white hair—was kissed back to life. Not her boldest move; that would always be the flight through the garden wall with *Mommi.* Still, finding their loved ones had passed, she took a chance that in matters of the heart there might be a second chance duty-free. Now their caresses were tender, the way kids courted a millennium ago. Sylvie runs the story off. Her visions—the love of her men in varying degrees. Of her father who she mourns in the full knowledge of his folly.

Soon after they met, Bob Waite took Sylvie to his house listed as a historic treasure. She raised his kids, lives on there in comfort though carpenter ants are back at their mischief. It is not truly her house: never can be. *Wer jetzt kein Haus hat, baut sich keines mehr.* Translate to the language you live in. *Whoever has no house now, will never have one.* How her beautiful mother of the *grun-grau* eyes came to quote Rilke with ease though she had no education to speak of. But that was in California, where Inga took tea with Thomas Mann, did more than frolic with Peter Lorre by the pool. Then Inga Meyer, moving on, was married to Billy Ray Boots by a Baptist minister in Houston and must be put to rest with many artifacts of genuine beauty, forgiven at last by her daughter. *Wer jetzt allein ist . . .* Translate: *Whoever is alone will stay alone.*

As they prepare for descent, Jed tells all, fesses up. He's not on his way home to the baby girl on the laptop screen. Going to visit the teenage boy he left behind. Sylvie, pert with an encouraging smile, yes, the fairy godmother with a halo of white hair, is comfortable hearing his familiar story of ambition gone wrong, midlife crisis, the office affair. She has listened carefully to the security guards at Martha's Institute, how one Perez son is premed, the other hijacks cars. Lola visits him in prison. Bonfilio must keep at the course in bookkeeping to get on with his life. His heart is invested in tango. Weekends he competes. Mrs. Waite has seen the head shot, hair slicked, throat gleaming with sweat in the passion of the dance. Jed has no picture of his boy left behind—a moody dropout, will not welcome this visit from his father. Below the clouds now, ordered to turn off all electronic equipment. Jed back to business. His personal story now seems impersonal. Sylvie recalls the name of the actor he resembles, a sentimental fool in old movies, eyes tearing up, the flesh wobbling on his moon face. Jed cutting her off, scribbling numbers on a scratch pad, reminds her of Gerald Waite, never her son. She feels the flight has been a waste of her seatmate's time, not finishing his thriller, chatting up an old lady, movie out of mind before the credits run. Perhaps it will never come right, these awkward visits with his son. Gerald Waite has written himself out of his stepmother's life, that little prince of his private school who never took to Sylvie. Each year on the Christmas card, he covets the Rhode Island highboy, though inappropriate for his high-rise in Hong Kong. Gerald is corporate, self-posted to Asia.

Martha put it simply: *Gerald needs money the way we need air. The whole nine yards. You know the expression?*

I know it. Gerald needs more than his father's considerable salary, more than his grandfather's take from a distinguished legal practice in the city.

The little plane has nibbled to the very end of its trail on the screen. Pressure pops in her ears, and for a moment Sylvie's hearing seems restored, that same baby crying above the pilot's landing instructions—advice for descent, Bob called it.

Offering a stiff apology, Jed's jowls quiver. *Sorry for the personal stuff, laying it on.*

Not at all, carry-on baggage.

Returned to the strained silence of her deafness, she thinks this is what we have, perhaps it is all—the telling, telling each other our stories. In the quarter hour that remains, she sets her watch to Eastern Daylight Time, flips pages in the airline magazine that offers, for a price, comforts never imagined: a robot vacuum, an electric corkscrew and a miniature trident, the three prongs of Neptune's weapon to spear lint. Lint? *Your clothes dryer may be clogged. Are you aware of this danger?* Now the darkening sky wavers through Sylvie's tears. It is too foolish, this fear of fluff, yet she finds it so sad, the claims of this product offering a life free of weightless debris. She remembers he was called Cuddles, the Hungarian actor who made you laugh when you should have cried. The plane is waiting for a runway, circling the city. She sites the Triborough, Randall's Island, buildings along the East River—the towers of New York Hospital, the brick of old Bellevue and in between the UN, where she worked as a young woman, a translator double-speaking the principles and arguments of international agreement. In that upended matchbox of hope, she met both her husband and her lover. She can't remember which committee Cyril, still in uniform, reported to, but she was translating areas of dispute between French and German fisheries. She must tell Martha: the commission was called Law of the Sea.

The neighbors have turned on the porch light, left the door off the latch. The mail of the last two weeks lies in the Chinese export platter on the hall table—catalogs pushing Christmas before the first frost, Doctors Without Borders, Coalition for the Homeless and Peace Folk, as Louise calls the many organizations begging money, as well they should, given the headlines Sylvie glanced wheeling her suitcase through the airport. FAMINE, GUANTÁNAMO TORTURE. DEATH TOLL RELEASED.

She is suddenly *bone tired,* speaks the phrase aloud to the heavy silence of the house. *Now, what does that mean?* It's the spirit that's tired; still, she must call the neighbors who doused the plants to death, thank them for their kindness. They have turned up the thermostat, set her tea mug next to the electric kettle, propped up a card of a smiley cat— *Welcome!* Sylvie sits by the fireplace where the Waite cradle resumed its proper place. A pale patch on the floor reveals where the Connecticut clock stood for nearly two hundred years, a grandfather clock that now ticks its inaccuracies in California. Alas, the finials have been taken off to accommodate the low ceiling in Martha's cottage. Gerald Waite, the banker still building his firm's business in Hong Kong, is the only one who gives a damn about the antiques, in particular their value. Last Christmas card went beyond the highboy to the Pilgrim hutch and Duncan Phyfe chairs. In a frivolous moment Sylvie sent Gerald the Canton punch bowl, never heard if it arrived back home in one piece. She'd as soon ship him every spindle and scrap, the sampler ill stitched by some long-forgotten girl, the coverlet sturdy as the day it was woven pre– Jacquard loom. Her very life is overfurnished. Alone in the house, deafness her companion, she listens to herself through worn bone. Well, there is not much flesh on her though the limbs are sturdy; didn't she make it uphill with a spring in her step, up from the parking lot to Perez and Bonfilio, to their courtesy each day? Now she must call Louise. She gets Artie. Maisy is ill again. Each night plagued with that cough. His voice—low-pitched, solemn.

Sylvie in a whisper: *Tomorrow I will drive into the city. I should never have gone away.*

She prepares a tray of white toast and tea. For the first time, the stairs are not easy. She sets the tray on the lowboy next to the pencil-post bed. Oh, it has a verified date, this uncomfortable bed where she slept beside her late husband and with her lover, Cyril O'Connor. The call to Martha's A-drive is not forgotten.

I'm in the lab, Martha says, *making up for lost time.* She does not say time lost with Sylvie's visit, their weekend jaunts up to the mission in Santa Barbara, down to the Baja Peninsula. Martha is working on a pet project, classifying sea cucumbers that thrive in a frigid canyon deep down in the sea.

Sylvie says, *Well, it's cold here, too. The leaves are turning.*

Remember? Martha asks. *Home again, home again, jiggity jig.*

The last line of a ditty she chanted to the Waite children when they came from the beach in wet bathing suits, sand in their shoes. They were beyond such nursery jingles, but what did she know?

Yes, she remembers. *Home again, home again, all in a day.*

BUG BOX

> *And so Gregor did not leave the floor, for he feared that his father might take as a piece of peculiar wickedness any excursion of his over the walls or the ceiling.*
>
> —Franz Kafka, *The Metamorphosis*

On Riverside Drive the wind whips up from the Hudson. Artie takes his son's hand. *First real Fall day!*

His exuberant words blow away. The boy looks puzzled. Dad walking on air? They are both on their way to school: that's Cyril's delight. His father will leave him off, go on to his classroom, where he writes numbers and squirrelly letters on the blackboard. His father has homework most nights. Sometimes Cyril pretends he has homework. Last night he wrote his name on his backpack, wrote it all out—Cyril Moffett Freeman, a name like no other kid at his school. Cyril is the name he comes by from the grandfather who is dead. His father had no father. He was not supposed to know that. When he asked, his mother said, *You're ours.* Well, of course. What did that have to do with the man who disappeared off the face of the earth? Moffett was in there because his mother must not leave out her parents in Wisconsin. They lived on a farm he visited every year of his life. That grandfather had almost no hair and a loud voice like a man his parents watched every night on the news. Too loud when he came to New York, showed a movie at school telling about the rows and rows of cows hooked up to his milking machines. A calf sucked milk from its mother's udder. *Direct Delivery,* his grandfather said, laughing in case you didn't get it. Milk was pumped into a big steel tanker to travel to the next machine, boil it up and ship it to market. He knew more than anyone in his class about pasteurizing when Grandfather Moffett ladled milk from a can for every teacher and student. The farm was cleaner than anything in New York City, so Grandpa said. He taught dairy. That was just weeks ago when Professor Moffett passed out ice cream cups for the whole lower school. For some days Cyril was made much of, then taunted by older kids—*Cyril 2%, Fat Free.* Well, he was skinny, and besides, his teacher, after a conference with his mother, advanced him to reading and math with the second grade. It was still early in the school year, and one day he broke from his class line after recess, to watch a chess game, to advise a third-grader how a pawn could block a bishop. Before he fully understood the kid's mockery, much mooing was what he put up with. Now the best part of the day was walking hand in hand with his father.

There's a kid wearing a black mask on the steps leading up to school, sweater tied round his neck for a cape. Captain Marvel, looks like maybe he's got a sore throat. Now that his father sees the black mask, he goes on about the calendar, how we should respect it, not let the merchants take over. By merchants he means all the shops on Broadway with plastic pumpkins and ghosts in the windows, and all the creepy ads on TV.

A full week till Halloween. Why blow it before the real day?

Five nights, Cyril corrects his father. It will be night when he goes out to spook the world. He is going to be a beetle, in fact. Today he has a ladybug in with his snack and a note to the teacher. The note says that they, the Moffett-Freemans, may be moving away within the school year, so save all records as to his progress to be transferred. Cyril had tipped a beetle into his bug box when they were in Connecticut looking at property. It was already dead on the doorsill of a dusty house where someone had died (not supposed to know that), just tipped it with a touch of his pinkie into the plastic box, which has a magnifying glass set into the lid so the bug looks larger than life, a monster black beetle with sharp horns. The hard wing case is unbroken. Too bad he never saw it fly and might not see a live one

now that there's frost, his mother says, but when they visited Sylvie in her old house, she showed him a chair which had been eaten by beetles, little holes in the wood.

Tells you how very old, she said. *Please, not to sit in that chair.*

Which made sense, because the beetles could still be in there chomping. He plans to be the black beetle in his box. His mother must make horns out of cardboard, but he has not figured the carapace, how it must cover his wings, how he can scare the kids at school and still carry a bug-looking bucket, a nest or hive for the treats the merchants sell.

He's Artie to his students, often theatrical, over the top today. They have finished the problem in linear algebra according to plan, but he does not plod on with the syllabus.

Today *your teacher will turn back the clocks.* Turn to his antic self, more likely, to Freeman who got kicked out of Yale for posting answers to the difficult calculus exam on primitive e-mail. *Because it is the process,* he wrote back then, *not the answer. The rush is working it out.* No longer a smart-ass, just wanting to say to these engineering, business majors, tech-masters-to-be, that they must take care with time. In a short time, the up-and-coming time of this November, Congress has decreed that they will walk to class in the dark. They will play, let's say Frisbee, an educated guess, in daylight saved for that purpose. He hops to the blackboard, the old miscreant Artie, to begin his lecture that has nothing to do with the job market, the one which is suddenly less healthy, the market he's in, though how could they guess from this acrobatic instruction that leaps from Daylight Saving Time back to long shadows cast at Stonehenge to the Aztec calendar and the Julian, to leap year and the missing half minute of time, to Mark Twain who marked time in a paddleboat on the Mississippi? When he doles out Heisenberg, he gets a groan from the sharpest girl, the loveliest, who never lets him walk her home when she baby-sits the kids: *We cannot know, as a matter of principle, the present in all its details. I'm down the rabbit hole late, late for a very important date, stopwatch and all. I come to rest, ladies and gentlemen, at the commercial countdown to Halloween, to the politics of time, the principle being that we have one more hour of sunlight to stop at the mall, so Congress has decreed. Meanwhile the alarm clock, do we use them anymore? But time being personal, I will hold you no longer. There's a war on. It is evening in Baghdad. As a matter of principle, we wait in the dark for the morning news.*

Late-night comic spinning off script, or a karaoke assault on the captive audience, he bops on to the abuse of constitutional powers, Bible study in the White House, or just another peace rally, war protest, one of how many? Their teacher ranting, bringing it down, the uncomfortable day-to-day problems they must either solve or leave unanswered in all their details. Artie, in self-destruct, is running late. They look at the time on their cells. What's the next assignment? Patient, amused at his apology, which they accept as no apology at all. Class dismissed.

In the cavernous hall below, Artie is faced with Gottschalk having a good laugh, a hearty rumble off the old tile walls. He'd thought our leader never laughed, just meted out sourballs to children with the indulgent smile. Gott, waylaying him at the door of his office, *I see that you were amusing in class today.*

Artie reckons the half minute it takes to run down the spiral staircase. *Telepathy?*

Texting. It did give me a laugh, a student sending your tangent. You've been critical—pause for mock harrumph—*of my insistence upon pencil and paper. It's too easy to take answers off the screen, post them, send them about, as a miscreant just now broadcast your performance. We had to figure, in my day. In my day, the answer was inked on the palm of the culprit's hand. In any case, an enjoyable excursion. Time, you old gypsy—*

Artie dare not look at his watch. The hands of the old clock affixed to the wall are stopped in Western Union Time, five-fifteen of a day or night long gone.

In my day goes on with good humor; then Ernst Gottschalk strikes a serious note. In that moment Arthur Freeman understands that his leader, grudging as ever with his slant smile, will deal him another chance to pick himself up, brush himself off as in his grandmother's hope invested in God and Fred Astaire. Gott—it's only a spec—has a job up his sleeve. Artie must remember to tell Lou that this kindest of men was wearing a mixed message, bush jacket and cargo pants, perhaps working his sartorial way toward Halloween.

He's late to pick up Cyril, the last child in the bright kindergarten room. The harvest is in place, cornstalks and pumpkins, humongous gourds. Cyril is counting, slow and steady, to a thousand.

Mrs. Goldberg tells Mr. Freeman once again, *He does this to see how far he gets until you arrive.* She does not say, *Late as you often are.*

Artie damns his performance, time lost in Mathematics Hall.

Seven hundred twenty-five, seven hundred twenty-six, twenty-seven . . .

Sorry Mrs. G.

No need to be sorry. Not closing the shop.

Course not. She tidies up after the children the many days he's been late, never as late as seven hundred and twenty-eight. She gathers the scraps of construction paper, collects the blunt scissors, clamps the paste pot left open. She's a pro—brisk, not motherly, a comfort to the children in her care. In the world of her room, each child's name is spelled out in capital letters, numbers envisioned as red apples and golden pears. Amusements blend into Mrs. G's lessons as she tracks the daily progress of every child, so particular in its triumphs and failures.

Such a bright boy, I am sorry you're moving away.

Spoken clearly, it comes as a shock to him. Not really. They have nearly settled on a house in Connecticut not far from where he lived as a small boy before his mother drowned in that boating accident, before he preserved her in legend, her mahogany hair without a streak of silver, her voice uncertain in song, folksy strumming.

Mrs. G going on about Cyril, her brightest student in years, how the Freemans must be careful with their gifted boy.

Pacing himself now—*seven hundred and thirty-five.*

Oh, come off it, his father says.

On the way home, it's not OK. His father doesn't reach for his hand at the crossing. Cyril digs in his backpack for the bug box. *How much bigger does the magnifier make my beetle?*

His father is somewhere else. *Hard to tell.*

Late to pick him up at school not surprising, but the brush-off Cyril will remember, the chill of his father's silence as they headed round the corner to Riverside Drive. His fear that he must not say it: *Seven hundred and thirty-six.*

Beetle was the best, better than the fright wig of mad scientist last year. A pizza pan painted by his mother became his rusty black shell, jaws and legs black, belly of bubble wrap, Ping-Pong balls bulged with the many facets of insect eyes. The Beetle won "Most Original." He carried a trick-or-treat hive, brown paper totally incorrect. Spider-Man, "Most Popular," was everywhere in school, on Broadway, on the block, nothing like a spider, just a costume merchants sold in the shops. His mother soothing: *Comics trump* Insects for Girls and Boys. Cyril had better get used to that. He tore the antenna from his head. Late enough now to be dark. He dodged between taxis honking, braking with a screech. In Riverside Park, he burrowed down between rocks, sucked three Milky Ways before his father found him, a dung beetle weeping chocolate from his sticky mouth.

FAMILY TREE

Louise makes ginger tea, splits a bagel with Sylvie. Mother and daughter scene, but they are nothing to each other. Their odd circumstantial connection prompts Louise Moffett to draw a tree as she listens once again to Sylvie's adventures in California, great tacos in Santa Barbara, Bonfilio stomping his solo on the steps of the Institute, Martha's softness this year, never too late for the girlish gleam in her eye, heavy equipment fellow on the plane. Drawing: Louise is drawing on the newsprint pad that belongs to her boy, says his name in bold caps. She has flipped past Cyril's airplanes, rockets, a spaceship to Mars, finds a blank page. Maisy sleeps on the couch. Sylvie, head bobbing, trails off in midsentence. She was saying about a cave under the sea, how like a story she read to the children, Waite's children. She never suspected that the caves in the story might be real. Now Martha may go down many leagues to measure a dark pit with her mentor. Sylvie repeats her stories. Her sentences lose words, but today Martha's sea adventure comes with a fable for children.

The charcoal pencil feels strange in Lou's hand, but the tricks of dimension and line—the smudge and shading reliable. The sketch comes along. It's a tree. Not a tree she might bring into focus when sighting a bird. Those trees she observes in detail, each node, crook of a limb to harbor a nest, bark broken where woodpeckers dig for their grub. This tree is puffy and perfectly round, a simplified picture-book tree. She believes she is drawing it for Sylvie, who must insist once again that Martha and Gerald are not her children. Louise has seen their photos displayed on a sideboard, sturdy girl in cap and gown, conventionally handsome boy, blazer and school tie. She writes *Family Tree* on top of the page, big page so a kid can draw freely. When the tree is finished, she inscribes a bold line under it, writes the names of Ulrich von Neisswonger and his wife, Inga, from which dangle Sylvia and Otto. Then Sylvie affixed to Bob Waite (deceased), from which, on a slant, Martha and Gerald, from Gerald a wife and two children unnamed, a second offshoot from Sylvia to Cyril O'Connor (deceased), from which Fiona with mate unknown, the begetter of Arthur Freeman, impossible to place as a piece of white cloud in a jigsaw puzzle, from which sprouts their boy connecting to Louise Moffett, from which Cyril and Maisy with side line to Pop Moffett and Shirley out there in Wisconsin, to her brothers so often deleted and a firm sidebar to Pop's sister, Aunt Bea. Now the tree which spreads above must have leaves, and caught in the crotch of the branches, a corporate jet, powerful as Bob Waite might will it, then Fiona's pleasure boat, the death vehicle, upended in turbulent waves. $$$ fluttering for both Gerald and Inga, and why not the stockbroker, Cyril? A moo cow for her father and an equation—here the artist is out on a limb—a problem, might have been solved by the von or by Artie, two guys who share the math gene. The cheap newsprint does not take to fine lines, but she must have the speckled ruff of a wise owl, as though she could go back to her bird, the one she drew as a girl, the owl that won her first prize. She has left out, quite by accident, Artie's sainted grandmother, Mae.

Lou turns the page. With a stroke she gets Maisy wheezing in perfect peace, lips slightly parted, the gentle curve of her cheek, the scramble of pale curls. Gets the humpback of the old couch, the stick figure of Sylvie in her proper gray suit, mouth slack as in death, as though words might not come again. Lou, alone with these sleepers, feels she's never been so alive, not even on the bus she flagged down to leave the farm, not even in her first studio apartment in this city. Back then she was fearless, her intentional distortions sharper than binocular blowups, than the camera's eye. Alone with pencil on paper, she sweeps a line cross page, pure pleasure. She's forgotten her work's satisfactions. Call it art, the intentional smudge, lump of clay, streak of acrylic. Making something out of nothing.

Was I saying about the cave? Sylvie's voice a soft whisper. *I am not sure what Martha . . .* now she speaks up *. . . what they are looking for, Martha and her mentor, but in the story, a man is kept in a cave under the sea.* Eine Fabel, *a spell, you see. This drunkard, not worthy of the King's daughter.*

Maisy smiles at some turn of events in a dream.

I changed the story for the children. That I remember. He smelled of dead fish, but when the spell broke, the princess married him. His eyes crusted with salt, her wedding dress, seaweed. I was saying about Martha and her friend exploring caves under the sea. I'd never tell them the bitter end as it was written.

Seems right. Lou closes the pad. *We do tend to make nice.* The family tree intended for Sylvie now seems sentimental. So she takes the hard path, says what she must finally say. On this day Louise announces they are leaving the city. *I wish it could be different.*

Sylvie touches a trembling hand to the useful aids in her ears, first one, then the other. *I know about moving on.*

I think you invented it.

No, that would be my mother, the beautiful Inga.

Lou has never quite believed the legend of that woman's beauty, sees only the silver delicacy of Sylvie's old age. *We will have a house,* she says, *with a shed. Cyril claims it. Enter at your peril.*

Wunderhaus.

I'll have a barn, size of a garage, nothing like my father's setup in Wisconsin. A barn nevertheless with a loft, a few stalls.

Für der Kinder?

No.

For your work, then? About time. She has never let up urging Lou to go back to her art. *And the boy?* A slip of the tongue, but so Artie Freeman was tagged when his grandfather was alive. *He has finished his studies?*

He may or may not—finish.

As though just another cup of tea, a repeat of Sylvie's travels—the best tacos and the old Mission in Santa Barbara, another day in which deflating birthday balloons (Maisy's) begin one by one by one to fall to the carpet; in which the hamster rests beneath the wheel in his cage; in which Louise Moffett Freeman, just another night, turns to the end of her mystery to find out who fired the antique rifle point-blank at the Colonel, thereby missing the pages that told her why. Why kill off the old gentleman, so decent to his servants in Singapore?

Arthur Freeman discovers the family tree in the trash. Though it is signed Moffett, dated this day in November, it seems a relic of what his wife used to do, make sense of their world in scrapbook art—here's where we came from, some of us intact, some children of disconnect and misfortune. The paper tears as he hides it in the drawer of his grandfather's desk. He will find it again when they are about to move out of the city, when the children have their valuables packed, Maisy's doll of mixed race with its infant paraphernalia, Cyril's bugs labeled, his butterflies pinioned under glass. For weeks the children have been ready to go, waiting for their parents to get it together. In the future they will have their own rooms, a backyard, a dog—think of that. The backyard is a ruin, not cared for in years, but the property goes back, back to a small barn, nothing like the Moffett spread in Wisconsin.

Looking over the property, Cyril spotted a horned caterpillar, a sphinx eating the first fresh leaves of a birch, and a turquoise beetle not documented in *Insects for Girls and Boys*. It is his last night in the bunk bed, staring at the ceiling. He will never again hear his sister's soft mewing in a dream, her phlegmy cough that begins the fevers once again, though who knows what lies ahead in the white house with a wreck of a shed, KEEP OUT OR ELS painted on its side by a child who died in that house. He is not supposed to know that. He will take possession of that shed—chess table, specimen cabinet, pincers and slides. He can see himself peering through a lens, the slight flutter of wings as he measures the thorax of a queen bee. He imagines a cot set up under the window facing the quiet street where he will be allowed to ride his bike, but never gets to the sad story of carpenter ants. If he could read the Latin words in his book, he might know why they have eaten his shed at the foundation. When you touch the doorframe, there at the bottom, what looked like wood crumbles to dust. He hears his mother in the kitchen packing dishes with gold rims, never used.

Artie Freeman has left the desk for last. The usual records, household insurance, bank statements, marriage certificate, last will and testament of one Cyril O'Connor, photo of his grandmother, Mae, in a white linen dress now yellowed with age, the tree he'd forgotten. It's flimsy, like the list of the war dead Lou discontinued in the kitchen. He folds the sketch of the family tree in with past taxes, not his wife's best work, still, not worthy of the trash.

So—musical chairs. A game Sylvie knows. She had, indeed, thought to move into New York, help care for those children, though never to hover. To teach them to pray, not as she prayed as a child, kneeling, crossing herself with belief in Catholic Austria, just pray, or something like it, as she prayed time would reverse itself after they ordered her father and Otto out the front door. Not a bad thing; call it wishing, simple enough, to wish the Alps would be snowcapped as ever, that the seas would withdraw in their assault on the shores. She would like to hear the crashing waves of the Pacific once more, can't hear the gentle waves lapping the Connecticut shore.

Moving on became clear on the day when, making her bed, she discovered a little rip in the quilt at the center of the big star where all the scraps of the quilter's remnants come together. She will patch it before she goes, leave everything in this house museum perfect. Sell up. Move back to the city, Upper West Side, where she first lived with Inga, studied English grammar at night, read books meant for kids half her age. It will be the third edit of the life she has made for Sylvia Neisswonger, a Catholic girl of good family. She showers, puts on fresh clothes, buttons up a warm sweater, recalling at this moment the snowflakes on her Alpine ski sweater as the mantle of a survivor. There had been that argument about the Jacquard loom, repetition of pattern, something to do with Otto. That memory had lost its power. This evening's sweater—cold end of day—scratches at the neck and wrists, a cheap thing bought at the mall in Stamford where, during the winter Cyril was with her, they had gone on an errand that seemed urgent, but the lights of the pleasure palace were further blinding to him. Piped-in Muzak clotted her ears.

When the music stops, you must find a chair. She will sit on a bench in Central Park with a book she always meant to read. It concerns the triumphs and failures of the great scientists trained at Vienna and Göttingen, but she will not find her father's name among them, not even in the record of their exuberant youth in the cafés, arguing late into the night. So best close the book, for he may have been an everyday alchemist, extracting silver from veins of Alpine schist. And looking up at the tree above, she will be still when she sees the birds, for her friend has said you see more when you look from one point, one steady view, see the fluttering contraction of the tail as they alight—the warblers, the hawks, old owls with aging feathers—but she will not hear their song, *natürlich*. She will sign her name, Sylvia Neisswonger Waite, in the book at Goethe House upon the occasion of the anniversary of Bertolt Brecht's death fifty years ago when she was translating documents at the UN. She takes her seat in the auditorium, is given the wireless device that will broadcast his *Jungle of Cities* into her ears. *Auf deutsch*, no need of the translation, yet she will hear, pretty much hear, a staged reading in English, Brecht's dark laughter and brutal mockery of Hollywood despair, while dreaming back to the days when her mother was with Meyer, a cameraman who worked with Lubitsch and Billy Wilder. Inga, having married into that aristocracy, bronzed and charming in yet another costume of a survivor—white linen slacks, the striped jersey of a sailor. Living at the crest of a hill on the Pacific Palisades, Inga had experienced vertigo looking down at the sea. Her grandest role, serving contraband Riesling to the likes of Thomas Mann. *Mutter* living it up with this distinguished crew, her day in the sun. Sylvie, her girl now on Fifth Avenue listening to Brecht's jovial despair, one old lady among an audience of mostly students brought to this improving event. They laugh in the wrong places. *But will you still be here when we come back?* Would the play-wright have been amused? Could they imagine the audience eager for his work fifty years ago, for the political passion of his theater? Or might they learn it? Perhaps today they will be startled into listening, really listening, when the shot goes off in his cultural jungle, though it is only a play with gangland debauchery, a simple parable compared to the Götterdämmer-ung of nightly TV. Frau Waite will straighten the electronic apparatus on her head; Sylvia, who remembers the plain girl, Inga's daughter come on a visit from her studies in New York, remembers the scrunched little Brecht in his workman's jacket, his sly squint of a smile, the ash trembling at the end of his cigar flipped onto the plate she was clearing. At home—that is, her sparsely fitted-out apartment on Columbus Avenue—she will now and again miss the empty house in Connecticut gone to the highest bidder, a quick sale much like her mother's unloading the villa on the river Inn. The lesser pieces of Waite furniture stored for Gerald when and if he comes back to this country, the finer pieces auctioned at Sotheby's. Sylvia, yearn-ing for her language, will take Brecht's early work off a shelf, find *Jungle of Cities* in the original. *Sind Sie nock hier, wenn wir zuruckkomen?* She will read, then begin to translate with ease, as in her working life long ago—*the remnants of a family, a pretty moth eaten family*, recalling Inga's bold strokes of survival and at last, long last, Sylvia will admit undeniable love for her mother who she so readily mocked, made her endurance into a skit, a poor show. Translates: *To be alone—that's a good thing to be. The chaos has been used up. And it was the best time. Es war die beste Zeit.*

REVISION

> *I never blame failure—there are too many complicated situations in life—but I am absolutely merciless about lack of effort.*
>
> —*The Crack-Up,* F. Scott Fitzgerald to his daughter

> *Maximum honesty in regard to oneself.*
>
> —Fritsch, *Sketchbook*

That night I could not sweep my dreams into an easy narrative. Midlife (when was that!) I learned to make sense of these fragments, to translate my sorrows and the gold sticker of triumph into subtitles running at the bottom of the screen. *Why so hard on yourself?* he asked when we were first together, my husband sleeping soundly beside me. What would that be like, the sleep of the just? He's entitled, the good man who rescues me daily from the brink with his dose of reality, but I'm given to self-drama—to mockery of my ambition, the little life I will soon leave behind. That's the subplot left out in reporting my trek in the Park, the exhaustion as I climbed the slope up to the hippo playground. Had I ever told myself, as I looked long at the façade of the refurbished El Dorado, that this day might well have served up my last adventure? Throwing off the quilt, I pad into the back room where work confronts me—half written, half told—yet another of my stories offering a little love, a taste of war *like a sampler box of dark chocolates,* a harsh reviewer once noted, *some chewy, all bittersweet.* Looking down at the bare floor littered with postcards and yellowed clippings, curling with age—anniversary of D-Day, uranium 235, a note on the owl, mine as I now see him, from *The Audubon Guide: Well into Autumn and Winter the big bird perches by highways and may be sighted in parks. From a mile away, its tufted ears pick up the faint rustle of the small creatures it preys on.*

Shuffling in the bits scattered among my own discarded pages, I do wonder if my mother ever read that rug woven with scraps of the past. Bill's old tweed jacket worn only on weekends. When he presented state's evidence in the courtroom, it was in three-piece suits, seat of the pants shiny with age. The cuffs could no longer be turned. My own Spring coat of robin's-egg blue, a hand-me-down-from the neighbors, was cut into coarse ribbons. The checked riding skirt, rescued from better days when my grandfather's workers boosted Loretta Burns up into the saddle to ride the trails of Beardsley Park. Yet somehow the strands in the rug came pleasantly together in my mother's craft of making do; and there it lay on the bedroom floor for Mimi, alias Maureen, to trip over when she took up her post to skim Tolstoy's novel, consigning the Napoleonic Wars to delay of the love story, passion to settle for domesticity, while ten thousand men had just died on the beaches of Normandy.

Still in search of that ultimate honesty, I look round my back room at the shelves and toppling stacks of books as though the landscape is new to me, yet I work day after day in this disorder, my fortress against reality. Often, as now, I get up in the middle of the night to mark down a word, a phrase that might be useful come morning. The streetlamp lights my way through the litter of journals and notebooks. Next to the phone a novel, my own, *Liebestraum*, love story with a slick jacket. Next to the chair that holds the imprint of my plump body: the reading lamp. Tonight: unfinished business. Long, too long delayed. I pick up the book, switch on the lamp, open to an earmarked page.

Levin lifts a shattered hand to his throat where the dog tag covers his Star of David. Against regulations. As death takes over, he thinks how he wore it on the landing craft no safer than a boxcar he built in the garage, that the star's magic would save him. Paper stars, flannel stars pasted on the Jews by the Reich. His star is *gelt,* a gift from his mother. Blood mixing with sand and grit covers the metal tags of his identity. His mother had given him the star the day he read from Torah in the little synagogue by the Housatonic River. All those memorized Hebrew words and a new suit. His father drew a prayer shawl round his shoulders, thin white wool with a fringe the Rabbi called *tzitzit*. The word stuck in his teeth like the knots of the fringe which had rules and prayers tied in them. What were the rules? He would ask the Captain, the Captain knows everything though he is not a Jew. He knew that the star or the cross should not be worn with the dog tag, against regulations. The right side of Levin's face was hot and cold; how could that be all at once? He would ask his father, the only pharmacist in town, or he'd know when he studied biology in college. He had lied himself into the army by a half year he never lived. There was noise from the constant bombardment. There was wet from the landing. Private Levin had lost his jaw on the right side of his face. Miriam, his tough little sister who beat boys at kickball, cried when he made his bar mitzvah speech on the wooden platform in the temple. He read slowly in Hebrew to the few chosen on a Saturday morning in 1940. The Germans had just then invaded Holland. He had explained the parable, Ezekiel 37:15, "Then take two sticks and write upon them and join the sticks together that they may become one in your hand." It is about the tribes of Israel, the boy said to the lawyers, the shopkeepers, schoolteachers, to their families and to Miriam, who cried tears of envy and admiration.

You gave me that scene, though your bar mitzvah was far from Levin's. You did not read from Scripture. *All those memorized Hebrew words and a new suit.* You had signed on early as a dedicated nonbeliever. Your gold star lives with tarnished cuff links, pearl buttons, a Kennedy half-dollar, and the wedding ring of my first marriage in a Florentine box bought for just such tokens we can't part with, can't throw away.

Chill in her workroom. A shawl covers the back of the reading chair. I wrap myself in it. Old lady in a flannel nightgown, Mother Goose with her tales. Those geese, if that is what they are, skimming about on the water with their proprietary air. In all the years taking in the view of the city from the Reservoir, I've never seen one falter in flight, never seen a dead bird in the growth around the shore. But then, I had never seen a soldier dying except—a big exception it seems to me this night—in the movies back when I invented Levin's story—the battlefield as on D-Day littered with bodies—oldies, *Red Badge of Courage, Paths of Glory, Platoon.* I was never sure how long it would take him to die of his wounds, only that I must get on with the Captain's story, confident that in my scheme of things he had answers for the boy beyond those of his own father, the trusted pharmacist in the Berkshires. In the aftermath of that bloody invasion, Captain Warner would find the body of the kid, which was near impossible, and clip the chain from round Levin's bloody neck, send the gold star back to a drugstore on a generic Main Street in Massachusetts. *Old Mother Goose when she wanted to wander . . .* My Captain suffered superficial wounds to take him out of action, transfer him to the army of occupation. The German of his student days was useful, assigned Warner to reading page upon page of documents supporting evidence that "Hitler's Bomb" in the works, was two years behind the Project at Los Alamos. Writing on, I had known this much—how unlikely a leap from the slaughter of Omaha Beach to a desk job. The Captain requested the transfer for the sake of my story, for the curtain to go up on the opera singer in Bayreuth he'd fallen for, lost his head completely when a student in Leipzig, where the talk had been all uncertainty, not isolating heavy waters that might make the bomb. The novel optioned before the general acclaim, but Hollywood was in a brief period of denazification, one might say, coasting with gangster epics homegrown, turned on by dazzling possibilities of special effects. The script, rewritten—less war, more sex, bodies wrestling in the sheets, a persistent *achtung,* in scenes never shot. The soprano with flaxen hair, what was she up to after the war? Taping whatever the Captain discovered about Nazi scientists while she mourned the defeat of her country. Sleeping with the enemy, the American officer who spoke with enthusiasm of Einstein's Relativity. Everything she learned from Warner was passed to her German lover, a detainee with the true secrets tucked away, the sorry information they never achieved the critical mass. Procuring the components, could not assemble them, to become death, the destroyer of worlds. *Deutsche* Science had failed. But how do you cast a Wagnerian soprano, one that is slim with cupcake breasts, with a delectable ass pumping smoothly as she positions herself above her American lover? How confuse such sport with the soaring Wagnerian score? Reads like a treatment. There was, of course, the Captain's all-innocence wife and two little boys in New Jersey, a treat for the reader, dark chocolate to flavor the tolerably happy end.

Adjusting my shawl, Mother Goose *would fly through the air on a very fine gander,* crone with a silver voice spewing out words to readers who might as well be children. That's my thought as I flip through the book in hand. The pages are marked with a system of elisions and stops, the better to read it time and again, clear and loud to an audience. Shamelessly. I filch a yellow legal pad that belongs to my husband, to write as I did before the secondhand Remington, a black office machine with the question mark and brackets missing. The rewrite comes quickly with scratch-outs of deletion. In reparation I will scribble my way to a redemptive conclusion. My handwriting, no longer schoolgirl, is illegible, damaged by years at the computer. This night and the next, I steal out of bed. Undoing is not daytime work—that's the Park with its wide-awake stories of pantomime lovers, the mathematician and his artist wife, of an old lady born in Innsbruck, the Elysian Fields of Frederick Law Olmsted, the chill splash of Bethesda Fountain on a wind-whipped day. This is night work, a Penelope task, not dreamtime, far from it. No reward, no penance. Plain personal, though not confessional, my yellow pages must stand as my defense.

The basement of the house in Somerset is fitted out as a game room—dartboard, pool table, hoop set low for little kids now grown taller than their father, desktop IBM from the Dark Ages. On one wall the shelf with trophies from prep schools the boys attended. The playroom runs the length of the house, which is large. Seen from the road, we are struck by its Georgian Brick grandeur. Look at that one, we say, preferring it over Tara or the Renaissance Castle. Get the circular drive, the Monticello lampposts. Yes, it's late, the lights are timed to go off. In a moment there will be only the dim illumination in one basement window. Above, every room lies in darkness.

Doc Warner has come down to the game room, finding his way through the house he has known for half a century. One son sleeps in his boyhood room. He has scheduled his flight back to California by way of Newark to visit his father. He thinks the old man should sell the place, settle into a retirement community, stay at the Harvard Club when he goes to

town, town being, for Doc, always and only New York. He
has been taught to make little of his father's awards. Doc, he
doesn't know incus from Inca, dorsal from dormouse, so the
jokes went when he and his brother were kids. Until recently,
Doc has been an honored physicist at Bell Labs from the early
days of his work on high-speed memory to his late paper on
fractional quantum effects, his home away from home which
we might call AT&T, but he prefers the old name, the old days,
prefers to live alone in this house, his wife of many years dead,
his boys long gone to their professional lives. This visiting son
lives in Marin County. He is a pediatrician with a wife who
cares about the suffering out there in the world, with a grown
daughter currently reinventing the druggie indulgences of the
Sixties. He sleeps in this mausoleum of his parents' marriage
under the slant ceiling of an eave, well out of the way of family life, which is how he always liked it, far above the flow-
ery chintz, the soothing greens and cheerful gold that never
graced the big house with the warmth his mother yearned for.
He wakes when he hears his father's stumbling footfalls below
as Doc heads for the stairs known to be slippery, known since
his mother turned her nose up at the idea of carpet over the
beveled lip, the lovely oak rise of each step. Doc has a knee
prone to collapse, a fractured disk in his lower spine. The real
doctor knows that the banister wobbles, not sturdy as it was
when he slid down it to his mother's annoyance. His father
is going to the rec room, an old ritual that he will honor. He
will wait till he hears Doc slapping back down the hall in his
slippers, then sleep again in his room with the premed text-
books, photos of a trivial first love and tennis teams left far
behind, nothing that matters.

Doc Warner is still in the game . . . faint praise for the
old man when he drops in at the Labs. The elevator is no longer
where it should be, security a nuisance. Recently he suffered
the insult of a uniformed kid demanding his visitor's pass. He's

made it to the kitchen stooping through the low door leading down to the playroom. Heat from the furnace, new in 1982, is trapped, not rising this first cold night. He thinks of his son who has delayed his trip home from a conference on attention deficit disorder to check him out. Does the boy remember his mother stored the extra blankets in the chest at the bottom of her bed? His son is a proper pediatrician who can take care of himself. In any case the old Doc's made it down two flights of stairs to the hi-fi, a turntable hooked up to a dusty black speaker. He takes the LP out of its sleeve with the profile of Wagner on the cover faded to a ghostly negative, the composer facing off with a bare-breasted Rhine maiden, her thick thighs straddling a golden horse. How carefully he places the record on the turntable, lifts the arm with the needle.

Here the revision reads like liner notes. . . . *Much like the broken promise to Freia, goddess of youth, love is denied, the treasure lost,* and so forth with dwarfs and the deadly curse that doesn't play well in the game room.

Doc's waxy eyelids close tight as green twilight rises in the Festspielhaus in Bayreuth just as the composer dictated each and every aspect of the production. Then darkness, deep slashes of the coming light. He finds his way to the chair, the one and only taken from the back terrace, placed here for his purpose. His purpose is to listen to *Das Rheingold,* to hear the maidens' mocking laughter . . . *hei-a! hei-a! hei-a!* . . . till Freia swims upward toward the watery spill on the rocks.

Varner, she called him, one letter short of genius, but maybe he was a genius, the student who came from America to study *Deutsche Physik.* "Secure then are we and free from care. . . ." The flowers, the wine, the long train ride from the University at Leipzig all paid for with his small stipend. He was her prize, a young lover to stick like a flower behind her ear. And when he returned to her not long after the war, it was with combat

ribbons and medals of victory pinned to his chest. He carried
with him the picture of a little boy with his mother, a common pie-faced girl, pretty enough in an apron over a maternity
frock. There is this in his favor: the medals and ribbons were
only on display when he first went to visit his soprano still in
Bayreuth. She was now teaching, but there were few students.
At night she sang in a cabaret, cynical lyrics dodging defeat. He
brought her food, not flowers, brought her news of his discoveries, ongoing intelligence, poor foolish man no longer a student
telling her that Hitler never had a go at the bomb, never had
the magician's pot of uranium 235, implying the Science *Volk*
never had the wit or the nerve, not even the man he had studied
with, the great Heisenberg. And when the Captain went back
to his work on the secrets that would never be fully disclosed,
just bandied about in biographies and thoughty plays, Mother
Goose who flew through the air on a very fine gander, sits this
night in her workroom above Central Park turning the page
while the Rhine maiden—*ha . . . ha . . . ha . . . ha*—accuses
he who the sway of love for-swears. . . .

I take a turn round my room, tripping over the rag rug, shuffling in
my slippers through printouts and postcards, return to my desk, to the
pad stolen from my husband, work on to the end

> —as the soprano, the wanton in darkness, having wrapped
> her strong thighs around the body of Varner, *ach Varner, meine
> liebe. Turn the page:* that bitch now reaches to the black tele-
> phone, whispers to her lover, the loyal party member who
> had worked on the German rockets built by concentration
> camp slaves. And with misinformation on the bomb never
> made, he attempts to discredit the testimony of the American
> Captain in the name of their Führer . . .

But now the storyteller, given to happy endings, throws off the shawl,
flips to a fresh page.

In the cellar of a grand suburban house, an old gentleman—much honored, the life of the lab with his discoveries behind him—sits so straight in his chair with the sharp pain of a ruptured disk, he might be a man of military bearing. He has taken off his flannel bathrobe, folded it neatly in his lap as though he is at a performance. For the purpose of this story, he is in the second tier of the opera house designed by Richard Wagner to suit the grandeur of his work. The record that Doc listens to is as perfect as the day he bought it at Sam Goody's on Sixth Avenue, one of his many trips to the city for Bell Labs that combined business with pleasure. He remembers his delight in discovering it, the Deutsche Philharmoniker rerecording of *Das Rheingold*, of course. His interest is in the opening scenes in which his Freia abandons herself to laughter—*hei-a ja he . . . hei-a ja.* He believes he can distinguish her sweeping high notes from those of the maidens, believes that she was in her prime, though the original recording was cut at the end of her career. She is young to him always. *Die Minne macht ihn verrückt . . . ha!* The cruel pain of her laughter, yet he would give his heart for the gold. He grasps the stiff arms of the chair. Tonight, the slow retrieval, the smudged vision of his wife, bundled in her bathrobe when she found him sitting Indian style on the floor of the playroom, head bowed to the magnificent rise of the maidens' mockery, his eyes tearing up.

"It is that sort of music," he said.

Next day she placed this stiff iron chair close to the speaker, breaking up the set perfect for lunch on the patio. When matters cultural were on the table, as though they both must shoulder the blame, she confessed her addiction to museums, reported with an indulgent smile, "My husband is devoted to Wagner, from his student days, you know." Apparently she found his emotion reasonable, never questioned why only *Das Rheingold* in the game room—*hei-a . . . hei-a*—for love had lost him his wits!

I throw the yellow pad aside. My scrawl unreadable as a secret code of childhood. Drawing the shawl close, Old Mother Hubbard, Gammer Gurton makes her way back to bed, heart thumping. I have breathed upon the old catastrophes, the mutilations and disfigurements of my story, perhaps not in vain. Now, now the old inner tube will give out, as good a time as any for that drama. My husband turns toward me in his sleep, mumbling, arms held forth as though begging an embrace. I tap him lightly. He flips back to his dream. A streetlight stripes the ceiling through venetian blinds. How efficient the linen shades in my parents' bedroom closing out the sun the whole Summer long. Natasha at last came to love Pierre. My heart returns to a neat pit-a-pat, its constant revision. See again, Captain Varner at attention, the record spinning. Or see the son come down to save the old scientist who taught him to respect predigital, the value of 78s. *All that old stuff.* Grandma moving in. I understand how I came to be in the creaking wicker chair with the delicate scent of my mother's eau de cologne defeated by the ash of Lucky Strikes, Bill's butts in the souvenir ashtray, '39, the World's Fair.

Daybook, October 31, 2007

Intermittent drizzle, seasonal chill. Today, a mild bout of the blues. My brother mangles a song: *Tomorrow, tomorrow* . . . a persistent strand of gray, the offending book not quite forgotten. If gloom settles in, I'll attempt to climb to Belvedere Castle at the topmost pinnacle of the Park. Scanning the panoramic view—Ramble, Shakespeare's Garden, Sheep Meadow, Zoo—I'll sight the arrogant towers of El Dorado and the looming skyscrapers of midtown, which could not be imagined, not by Olmsted or Vaux in their precisely drawn perspective, nor by the German laborers blasting the natural rock ledge to perfect a greensward in the uptown wilds of the city, nor by the Irish squatters who, with their rutting pigs, were displaced from the swamps, nor by the black folk of Seneca Village—all sent packing—many who owned their parcels of land, treasured their houses, stores, churches, and Colored School No. 3, all removed for the people's Park. No chance against the might of Eminent Domain. So, the Park and its urban surround. Perhaps the mythic dimension of our city of the future would not come to mind until the Great Depression when Willy Pogany dipped his brush into a pot of tarnished gold to illuminate the mural in our lobby.

I'm walking over the bones of the villagers; their lost Seneca dutifully posted, its legend on a placard of Central Park green, determined to record the shapeless present with its small discoveries in this my book of last days. Let history with its monumental events tell its own story. No soul-searching in the merely personal. In my pocket an old postcard, a tinted photo of Bethesda Terrace sent to my mother by some chap, not my father. 1912, *Dearest Loretta, Class for me? Well I guess. Matt Leary.* The trees bleed green into the washed-out sky. Paint-box blue, the healing waters of the fountain. She would have been only sixteen. I head south with my map of byways and overpasses. Raincoat, binoculars—fitted out for this day's discovery I follow the Bridle Path to Strawberry Fields where the lone word says it all: IMAGINE. The worshippers are out early, enchanted by this spectacular memorial of their past where the truest stories live on.

Where were you when the madman killed Lennon?

Teaching *Moby-Dick* to freshmen who gave me grief. I believe we had come to Sunset, XXXVII, or choose to believe it now, Ahab's *all loveliness is anguish to me, since I can ne'er enjoy.*

When a man first walked on the moon?

Santa Barbara '69. The baby-sitter pulled granny glasses down on her nose. *My father's got moon dust.* I never believed a sample of the precious grit was dealt to an untenured astronomer, a dented Ford Escort dead on its rims in his driveway.

Your witness to history is wisdom of hindsight.

Score one for my brother.

We have closed the house, the Levittown ranch in the Berkshires, pre-Sheetrock. The garden nearing its end. A daylily protected by the fence held its final bloom tight. Lady's mantle gone soggy. The first time we've done this, drained the pipes, cleared the fridge of cheese ends, onions, celery best not to mention. Bitter marmalade, ketchup transport to the city. Crackers in a tin, denied to the mice, though in the Spring we'll find stuffing pulled out of the sofa, books chewed at the spine, candles gnawed to the wick. The few will lie dead in their tracks. The little house sits across from the town cemetery. You went for a last walk through the gravestones to the top of the hill. It's not much of a climb.

You said: *Best not chance it.*

Not even for the view stretching to yonder? Last time I was allowed to garden, digging in the new laurel, a funeral procession drove up to the height where the old families of the town are laid to rest. The bagpipes sounded cheery, then wheezed to a dirge.

Well beyond the middle of the journey of my life, I'll not come to a dark wood, just the loop in a clearing of memory. Back-braiding to the college girl who tossed Greek tragedies away and took Dante as her poet. I find her wonder and despair at the discovery of greed, usury, fraud unconvincing. She misplaced her faith, that's all. Hell passed in a term, became plain-spoken outrage at corruption whatever the current scene. Soon she will find some relief in preparations for the terrarium, for the grandchildren, of course; here and now will see again the stars. Pebbles sprinkled with charcoal from the iron stove in the country, soil tamped with sphagnum moss. They will choose stones and sticks to create their landscape, form hills and ravines. Wood ferns and lichen brought down from the garden; from the florist, a bromeliad and the bird's nest fern that delighted Columbus, all to be arranged in the giant brandy snifter, well misted with tap water. A rain forest sporting botanicals, the exotic blooms that heaven allows. The Park across the street not yet in Fall glory.

Daybook, All Saints', November 1, 2007

Your wax teeth, my fright wig, cheap goods meant to fool no one. Amusing the children who came to our door last night, that's all we were up to. You had no patience with teenagers who grabbed the Mars Bars and Snickers, leaving the stale corn candy for little kids. Two polite girls—twelve, thirteen?—done up in tawdry silk rags, rattled their UNICEF canisters. You stuffed dollar bills through the slot of goodwill.

Gypsies?

Summer of Love. We don't do Gypsies.

In the lobby I've seen these girls exchange conspiratorial glances, sniggering at El Dorado inmates. An unearned innocence in their crisp school uniforms, Academy of the Sacred Heart. Still, they alone collected for the world's hungry children. You were left with a wad of singles.

We feared superheroes, believed in their transformation. So truly other, unlike the actor who paced in front of our building this afternoon as I was about to take off for the Park. Cell phone at ear, shouting—*Pay to play, pay to play?*—impatient with the doorman who could not conjure a taxi out of chill air. Saint or sinner, he plays himself always. To be kind, which I'm not these days, I see him as an accomplished Everyman, his face a rubbery mask, different yet always the same. An honorable tradition: Cary Grant, John Wayne. I'm disclosing our addiction to old movies. Chaplin then, his performance trumping the limits of time, conjuring laughter from pratfalls, his sly smirk of victory. Same old, same old, yet a tear trickles down my cheek when the little fellow in the bowler hat struts down the road to his next adventure. Twirling his cane, undefeated, he is incredibly brave. I'm hopeful for him always as the screen reads THE END.

When you left for the office with those singles stuffed in your wallet, I squirreled away our feeble disguises, the presumption they will come into play next year—your nerdy wax teeth with exaggerated overbite, my Raggedy Ann wig of orange wool, forgetting I still wore the retro note, my mother's graduated pearls. Our jack-o'-lantern deliquesces on the front hall table. Old fools, not ready to cut out the fun, nor wise enough to distinguish holiday from holy day.

The first of November was once holy to me. It's my backdrop, you know, a worn tapestry hung in a ruined castle of faith meant to keep out the cold, or simply to display the daily rituals of the church. Now faded and frayed, yet the RC calendar with its surfeit of stories can still be read. All Saints, honoring the list of miracle workers, virgin martyrs, self-flagellates, popes not on the A list, Jesuits converting the indigenous to the blessings of their Lord. All of them winners, all saints, thus the crowd scene: (Apocalypse 7:2–12) the tribes, each with their twelve thousand believers in white robes, their foreheads marked with the indelible tattoo of Salvation. A spectacle best seen in high definition, but in the days of my belief we had only the grainy black-and-white TV. Often a ghostly gray shadow drifted across the screen, a twelve-incher set in the sun parlor, that chill appendage to our little house with uncomfortable cane chairs and struggling plants. Let me put it this way, I will attempt, in defiance of the doctors' orders, to honor the day by walking the full distance to view secular saints of my trade, the choice few in the Park who stand watch over the language they honored.

LITERARY WALK

I set off on my way to Shakespeare, leader of the pack. He stands alone in his circle at Poets' Corner, go figure. I can't honestly say I was breathless in anticipation, just tentative as usual these days. I had lingered in my back room, writing notes toward the possible end of my days, or end of my Park project, turning through old photos of the Mall freshly planted with scrawny elms, of Ladies strolling the broad Promenade in fine shawls, girly girls chasing hoops, gents in fine equipage. I leafed through plans of *The Greensward* as submitted to the Park Commission by Frederick Law Olmsted and Calvert Vaux, 1859, but found little satisfaction in my CP collection—the sepia photo of a single boat upon the Lake, an overexposed shot of *Mall in Its Prime,* or that tinted postcard of Bethesda Terrace sent to my mother (1910). The print on our bedroom wall—*Skaters in the Park,* Winslow Homer, *Harper's Weekly Magazine*—no longer enchanted. I wanted to sit on a newly refurbished bench under the mighty elms that lead to the poets, not saints but they would have to do. Or simply to prove that I might, like the little tramp, go on to the next adventure.

Well aware of the paternal note in your voice. *Take a cab.*

Or the bus to 59th, then walk across? That would be cheating in the game of can-do.

I stalled in my back room, looking for a note on Fitz-Greene Halleck, one of the poets portrayed beyond life size, the only one you might not know. Then again, your head is full of curiosities—orts, bits, Scrabble words, the full complement of jurists on the Warren Court, lyrics of "Red River Valley."

Halleck, the popular poet?

Absolutely. But the only poet with the indignity of a small sign of identification stuck in the ground. We have forgotten his newspaper versification, devalued his celebrity. The stiff cloak thrown over his chair might be that of a Roman Senator abandoned in a schoolroom play. His ink has solidified, pen hangs in midair.

Where's Whitman?

Good question.

Where's Emily?

Smoothing the folds of her lawn dress as she climbs the stairs to her virginal bedroom in Amherst. She'll look down from the narrow window above her desk, a moody saint on a bright cloud of words.

* * *

So, a luminous Fall day, sun riding high when at last I walked directly across the street from our sandstone twin towers. I checked out the fading leaves of my favorite viburnum in the world, turned right on the Bridle Path, cut down to the grassy knoll, once Seneca Village. A woman sat on the cold ground, book clutched to her breast. Sobs choked in her throat, then spilled forth. The low pitch of her wailing.

Dismissing my inquiry and all I had to offer, crumbled Kleenex. *No, no thanks.* A tidy woman, even in her distress she smoothed a strand of pale hair off her forehead, brushed at the knees of her gray flannel slacks. Her smile apologetic, as though to admit how shameful, crying in public. She tapped the book, the cause or answer to a sad story?

Marie Claude, Marie Claude! She called as though scolding a child. Whatever tragedy started the waterworks in the Park, she turned from me in her sorrow, then caught at my sleeve, a deliberate gesture, as though to say, *Take note: I'm in control now.* Giving me the once-over. I wore the old black coat, splattered jeans. She allowed me to help her up, her mist-gray sweater the softest cashmere. I don't often traffic with strangers in the Park, nod at a permissible distance, offer faint smiles to children. But we were not strangers. We were known to each other by caste. There, I've said it. We shared the downward glance of well-brought-up girls, feelings guarded, protective demeanor.

Raw red eyes. Twirling her rings: *My husband died last night.* Then: *Four o'clock, this morning.* Steady, cultured voice delivering these few words with a hesitant smile. Was she crippled by gentility, unhinged by grief? Plain crazy? *Uncle Tom's Cabin* slipped to the ground. Well, that's a weeper.

Anything I can do, spilled from my mouth. Tears stung my eyes for no possible reason. We could not move beyond this moment of mutual pity, a recognition scene, daughter and mother long lost. *Anything,* arms open in an idle gesture. When the frame flicked forward, we were nothing to each other.

Her false smile, *It's done, managed.* Choking sobs came upon her again.

She left at once, with a determined efficiency ran toward a massive outcropping of stone, an adornment hauled into view by Olmsted's design, never a natural feature of Seneca Village. The flat land the settlers built on is a footnote in the elaborate history of the Park. I watched her lean on the mighty stone, arms outstretched as though embracing a tomb, then stomp the ground, a display of anger before she briskly headed toward the Ramble, where a weeping widow might easily lose herself in the plotted wilderness. She had left *Uncle Tom* behind. I'd come to the Park for an encounter with the poets, a look-see at Robby Burns, Walter Scott, Longfellow— recalling inappropriate lines of *Evangeline* memorized in high school.

> *This is the forest primeval. The murmuring pines and the hemlocks* . . .

I was on my way to those gentle rhymers set *in perpetuity* on their plinths, All Saints, more or less. Did I remember each and every poet settled to his work in mighty bronze chairs, pens poised above unflappable pages? Was Longfellow among them? And why should I want to check it out now, lost clue to my scribbler's life launched more than a half century ago with an outpouring of abysmal undergraduate poetry? To my credit, I abandoned Calliope, that carnival imp of a muse, for plain prose, which I believed to be more honest than hip-hop iambs never torn from my soul. I knew for certain that the Bard stands on his own in the Olmsted Circle, playbook in hand, contemplating his next scene:

> *And as imagination bodies forth*
> *The forms of things unknown, the poet's pen*
> *Turns them to shape, and gives to airy nothing*

The following line lost in the dust mouse of memory along with CP marginalia, the year of our No Nukes march to the Sheep Meadow—- '82 or '83?; though I am clear on the Preppy Murder, Gay Pride, and the Polish Pope blessing an overflow of the faithful on the Great Lawn, urging them to multiply. I started again for the Mall when, suddenly overcome with the flip-flop thump of my heart, I turned back, took the distraught woman's place on the cold ground. A tandem on the roadway swiveled out of control, the bikers righting themselves, not taking the spill. Mother and daughter live in our elevator bank. They pedal together in perfect trust. Always helmeted, safe home from their risky business. I have seldom seen them apart. Suddenly a moody sky. Caretakers gathering their charges. I began to leaf through Mrs. Stowe's popular novel, could not recall when I first read it. Why would the newly minted widow bring *Uncle Tom* as a comfort to the sloping fields once Seneca Village? The blacks at this location having been turned out of their homes for the construction of the Park. As though on cue, or just coincidentally, I noticed a human bundle on a bench, awarded it my fleeting attention.

A huddled figure in a puffy vest, shawl thrown over his head, woke to the cold light of day, foraged through his shopping cart until he came up with a respectable hat, a black Willie Nelson prop, hitched the strap under his chin. In the daily drama of the Park, he was not an unusual figure. When the ground I sat on was the Village, a drifter might have been taken in by the black citizens with boardinghouses and a public school in the basement of the African Methodist Episcopal Zion Church, that mouthful of redemption. But such thoughts only come now after the road not taken to Literary Walk, its proper name. Shameful, calling upon the cover of history to excuse my not seeing the young man with grizzled dreadlocks, assigning him a role—homeless, indigent. In the desolate tract that lay above the Village, he might have boiled bones, eaten slops with mostly Irish squatters, many parishioners of St. Lawrence O'Toole—an exiled Archbishop of Dublin, appropriate to my contemplation of martyrs on this first day of November; or he might have camped in the northern swamps that Olmsted drained for the painterly effect of his greensward, then flooded by design for his lakes. I cast my eyes down, not to witness the vagrant getting his act together, presuming he'd soon wheel his cart through Mariner's Gate to be in the company of the homeless who stake out nightly ports of safety on the benches along Central Park West. Till the cops move them on. The widow's tears, my idle offer of consolation, the forgotten line from *Midsummer Night's Dream*:

> And gives to airy nothing
> A local habitation and a name.

The turf I sat on was newly seeded. I had not noticed the tender lawn that might or might not get through the hard season ahead. Still, I sat firm, flipping through the abandoned novel. Early passages were marked in the margin with a thin pencil line. The weeping woman had written single words of notation in a minuscule hand: *accurate, clever*. I made out *stunning* set on the page where Eliza, the beautiful quadroon, leaps across on the ice floe to freedom, child in her arms. Soon after its publication, *Uncle Tom's Cabin, or Life Among the Lowly* had more copies in print than the Holy Bible. That I did know, but who reads it now? Assigns it? Purveyors of catch-up culture demoting or promoting the antebellum best seller? A curiosity, a send-up like Barnum's display of freaks and moral dramas?

And why would a woman, claiming to be widowed this very day, choose to sit with *Uncle Tom* in the Park? Straining to make out her cramped hand, I began to read where she marked a page with a shocking pink Post-it: *Tsk, tsk, Mrs. Stowe!*

> Tom, who had the soft, impressionable nature of his kindly race, ever yearning towards the simple and childlike, watched the little creature with daily increasing interest. To him she seemed something almost divine; and whenever her golden head and deep blue eyes peered out upon him from behind some dusky cotton-bale, or looked down upon him over some ridge of packages, he half believed that he saw one of the angels stepped out of his New Testament.

Tom's awe when first looking upon the bewitching blond child, Little Eva, who *looked down upon him*—and don't you know he can read his Bible, though a note informs the student of the prohibition in the South against teaching coloreds to read, thus promoting: Classroom Discussion. Looking up from the instructive page, I witnessed the close of this working day, men and women in business suits and sneakers, students heading home with mighty backpacks. I joined them on the roadway to the clearing where Bridle Path splits from Reservoir Track. There, on the curve of benches that face the public water fountain, my vagrant was conducting a class, strumming his guitar in the twilight, cowboy hat tipped back as he sang. He was quite at home instructing an intense young man who had laid aside his IBM notebook and a mother with twins sleeping side by side in their stroller.

They strummed, oh they strummed together, the students straining to see the score between them in the dying light of day. The wind rustling the reeds on the bank of the Reservoir accompanied them in a dreamy autumnal rendition of "Honeysuckle Rose." A small audience assembled. One sing-along girl fished in her purse for a dollar, but this was not a charity affair. The class became a session when the Park lights went on. One by one we drifted off, leaving their music to fade in the brisk evening air, and I heard the opening phrase of "When the Saints . . ." Or only imagined it, as I tend to in retouching the picture, for I wanted to be in that number, to set one last stroke to the story of this day when the saints come marching in.

So tell me, your poets?

Got caught up in Seneca, you know. Well, of course you know.

I repeat my stories. The raw deal when the Village was taken from the rightful owners lot by lot, the goodwill of the proposal for a People's Park reduced to city politics, real estate deals. Many gentlemen of the Union League Club, strict abolitionists, figured that displacing the black settlers might work to their advantage. We'd not be here in the third wave of uptown development were it not for the eviction of the citizens of Seneca Village. You knew I'd never made it, the distance to the Mall. It was an evening like so many, clips of the war, your incessant switching channels, just like my brother, as though the dumb machine might yield more than the nightly serving of media porridge. But dinner, in fact, was quite nice—lamb chops and mashers; so was your day in the office—profitable.

All Souls' Day, November 2, 2007

In the morning I discovered the inconsolable *Marie Claude, Marie Claude!* to be the second wife of Hans Gruen, sometime scholar at the Kennedy School, who had served as an Undersecretary of the Treasury in the Carter administration. The obituary tracked his career from Harvard to London School of Economics, professor of political economy to a post at the World Bank. A long list of his accomplishments. As in a perfectly cast world, firm jaw, full head of silver hair, yet with a touch of a schoolboy grin for all his harrowing travels to those in need of his attention. For many years Gruen, Senior Fellow, had dispensed the liberal care of his foundation. The notice was fresh, not dated. He had recently returned from the Sudan, assessing the lockstep of oil revenues with human-rights abuses. Gruen had been criticized for favoring divestment market merchandising, a term you will explain. His longtime concern: child soldiers, boys for hire, that note tacked on along with his near Pulitzer, a debunking of Reaganomics. So, the weeping woman had scolded herself, running from her husband's death. Marie Claude Montour, associate professor of American history at a college in Jersey City. Odd, very odd, yet there was my answer to the puzzle of *Uncle Tom,* her questions written in a neat hand—*Read chapters assigned as serial novel. Romantic racism?* The cool classroom inquiry did not meld with the fresh sorrow of yesterday. I thought to return the book with her scant teaching notes, mail it to the foundation. Marie Claude, that sandy flop of yellow hair, younger than her husband, it figured. I clipped the *Times* obit, filed it away with my collection of Park notations, though my chance meeting with the second wife of Hans Gruen was merely personal, nothing to do with my attempt to document the landscaped garden of my earthbound Metropolis, my final, if limited, view.

All Souls' Day troubled me beyond the passing of an admirable man whose life never touched mine. On this day, turning back to the front page where the gotcha game of uranium spinners was playing itself out, I feared the Last Judgment; shouldn't we all? At The End will we skip through the killing fields, player piano sending us off? It was then I recalled a way down, down the rabbit hole, gray hair escaping my Alice band. I went to the shelf where I stack Marina Warner's exploration: *From the Beast to the Blonde, On Fairy Tales and Their Tellers* with Ovid, Yeats' Irish Tales, the Brothers Grimm, and *My Sunday Missal,* a little black book, the worse for wear by a pious girl, with the stories that once fed her unblinking faith day by day and turned to—

The Souls of those who departed this life in the grace of God, but with debts still owed to His Justice, are purified of stain in Purgatory.

Debts still owed? I was told to believe it as a child. Not by my mother or father: they were surprisingly free of such blessed instruction. I asked my brother why I bought into the accounting system of salvation then, at an early age, began posting credit in my favor, assigning myself the star role in the family story; and now believe I must pay off my debts in this exhausted confessional form.

Debased, not exhausted. Lighten up, Mimi. Get Out of Jail Free. And then he consoled me: *That book, your D-Day extravaganza, overreaching it's true, but reading* War and Peace *as a kid, you were trifling with subjects eternal. You had*—his whisper recharged with a cough—*even had a go at Apocalypse.* I imagine a gnomish smile as he toddled across the room with his pronged cane, faced the shelf with every word I've committed. A touch of purgatory waiting through his slow progress as he came back to the phone, then began to read the embarrassment—how Bible-deprived I was in my youth, confined to the upbeat story of redemption, chapter and verse of the terrifying Old Testament withheld in my little black book that tracked the liturgical calendar, an anthology adjusted to each passing day, an almanac of sorts. He had ferreted out my attempt at a personal take on the Bible, my reading of scarifying last things in Revelation no less.

Jubilant, my brother settles to his task: *Listen to this!*

Then, in a lilting voice mocking mine, he reads the damning performance: *I worry myself to death writing against the doctrine of continuous narrative. I'm all for multiple stories, splicing it together in biblical fashion.* Silence. I imagine that in this pause he turns to discover the date, '88, then proceeds to give me grief about highfalutin blather written to please a dreary conference on intertextuality, fashionable that year. *Poor old Bible,* he says, and picks up with my—*Is it a presumption, or a transgression, to read the Good Book as cobbled together stories, one episode playing off another?*

A transgression! Plain old sinful, telling in your own words, Mims, his laughter choking, out of control. *Forget the forbidden King James Version: same story in our homespun translations. You told in your own simple words the fantastic tale of Daniel in the Lion's Den, his buddies thrown in the fiery furnace. And how did you get into Apocalypse then? Apocalypse now. If you want to worry yourself to death read the morning paper. Where's the festering outrage?*

I was simply . . .

Not simple enough. Just say it. We were Catholics.

We never read the hard lessons. All stories skipped along to the Resurrection.

He suggests the Crucifixion. It's like arm wrestling on the kitchen table, though neither one of us has the strength to pin the other. I hear him speak to his arthritic chocolate Lab in their consoling private language, then clearly to me: *All Souls' was a day off from school. End of the Halloween candy. We're all grown up now, aren't we?*

Sent back to my room to lighten up or to memorize the multiplication tables, a task I could handle. I should never have put my ignorance on display, not at that conference, which I believe embraced hypertext, welcomed the search-and-employ manipulations of early Internet exploration. I put the little black Mass book back on the shelf, not sure whether to blame its coercive calendar or praise it as enduring folklore. Washed in the blood of the lamb, am I let off the hook by the ingenious idea of Purgatory? Like Green Stamps, if they're still around, calculating points for the promised day when I can cash in my prayers and good deeds for the microwave, airline mileage, season's pass through the Pearly Gates. Or just take my place in the bleachers on this day, All Souls'.

You draw a blank, the old mystified look; actually blinking your eyes. What in the world, not in the world, am I talking about? Purgatory! Your smile is indulgent, a pat on the head for an investment you can only consider as cultural baggage. Risk management.

Chastened, I turn to the daily encounters in Central Park. I swear to owe nothing to the mother lode of memories, a photo recently found of our parents walking hand in hand down Fifth Avenue. Delighted to be released from Bridgeport, just for the day. Who snapped them? All that old stuff. I am under self-imposed orders: pay attention to here and now, to the deal they are pulling off in the oval office, placing the money on black, spinning the wheel of misfortune. It is not a game of skill, don't we know! We've seen the footage with coded signals, the pitcher idling, twice touching the tip of his cap, the catcher bouncing his butt. Low ball. Shouting through the megaphone a cheerless message, he has wandered in from another game without the call of safe home, the sweeping gesture of forgiveness. Lately he has called out for *nuance,* for *closure.* If he uses these words three times in a sentence, he will own them.

But I'm advised not to carry on about the present, not to speak of all that old stuff. Time out of mind, that OK?

In any case, my brother said, reading my mind always, *if your angst is about our parents, they lie side by side in St. Michael's Cemetery. All is forgiven.* I heard the dog collapse at his feet, the snort of its pain. His master's grunt as he reaches down to soothe the gray muzzle. *Day of the Dead has come and gone. They do it up in style down Mexico way. Food for the departed and music, call them back for the party. Weren't you writing the view from your window? Daily walk in the Park, that sort of thing?*

I thought to e-mail a tart response, a recently updated accounting of our dead in the Battle of the Argonne, our father's war, thought better of it, found a CP postcard, the statue of Hans Christian Andersen, big storybook balanced on his knee. In the flowering plaza, the ugly duckling is the only one listening to his magic tale.

I wrote: *The present is prelude to the past.* Thought better of that, saved the stamp.

But it will never end between the two of us, till the end. His e-mail posted in the morning: *Hope, ye unhappy ones: ye happy ones, fear.——The Anatomy of Melancholy*

No answer to that. I head to my dig, Seneca Village. "Melancholy Baby" signals my husband's call.

Hi! I can't call up my sins of omissions.

Say again?

Am I allowed to rage against the mercenaries waging our wars?

You feed me new material. *Oil's up and gold.* Then: *Taking care?*

Seneca

West of the reservoir, within the limits of The Central Park lies a neat little settlement known as "Nigger Village." . . . It is to be hoped that their removal will be effected with as much gentleness as possible.

——"The Present Look of Our Great Central Park,"
July 9, 1856, the *New York Daily Times*

The truth, if told at all, must need be dreadful.

> —Harriet Beecher Stowe, *A Key to Uncle Tom's Cabin*

Hans Gruen died at 4:13 in the morning. Precise about arrivals and departures, he was often at the mercy of meetings running late, airport delays. He liked a drink with his wife at six-thirty. They were not together for dinner often enough. His children knew that their Sunday call must come just after nine o'clock his time, whether he was in Brussels or in Cambridge or New York with the wicked stepmother. Charles, always the gentleman, set up his kid brother for the first call. This practice went back to their college days, when he gave his father a weekly account of his accomplishments. Ned charmed for the money. Weeks might go by when Gruen was inaccessible, or his schedule rearranged by the breaking news. He would have been amused, not annoyed, by the inconvenient hour of his death, too late for the *Times* obituary that day.

His wife stood at the foot of their bed, let the boys close in on his last indulgent smile, his final breath soft as a sigh. They wanted more of their father, always. When they were growing up, he had been absent so often, tracking economic disaster in general, in particular the fate of children hungry and abused. It was Charles, the sturdier son, who broke down when he closed his father's eyes, then threw himself on the bed in a primitive keening, a supplicant, though now he would never get the attention, never be praised for the soccer trophy, the *magna cum laude*, the tree house he built on his own. With an unnatural strength, his stepmother pried him away, led him to the window to look down upon blank silence offered by the city in the middle of the night, unsure that view was a comfort.

Amanda, the younger son's wife, had been in these last few days, showily incompatible with grief, leafing through *Vogue* until she knew the gaudy allure of each handbag by heart, ducking out of the vigil to meet friends for lunch. Claude—that was Gruen's wife—now directed Ned and the girl—Hans persisted in calling Amanda the girl—to touch the cool flesh of her husband's hand. Marie Claude had been christened MC, Mistress of Ceremonies, when she first took charge of events beyond Thanksgiving and Christmas—taxes, car insurance, yes, really, the rental of their cottage on Nantucket, all home economics to the man who, just back from the Sudan, would support targeted divestments in the petroleum sector, but did not live to elaborate on that moral scheme. The wicked stepmother: his joke when he brought his sons to meet Claude, a lifetime ago. The younger son now held her in his arms, Ned, the simpler boy who sought a replacement mother from the day he was born.

She called Gruen's office, could not bring herself to leave on tape the message they were expecting. The doctor said he would come at once to the apartment, death not officially closing the case. Claude proposed that in the morning Charles' wife send the children to school. There was no need at this point to shepherd them in from Connecticut. The hospice nurse gathered the last vials of medication. She asked if Mrs. Gruen would like tea. Lili had been on night duty with Gruen in New York Hospital and here at home. A tidy body from the Philippines with a lilting accent, she spoke to her patient in a whisper each night of the crisis, bathed his dry lips with a sponge, begged a smile when she placed his finger on the silver cross on her neck, never guessing that Mr. Gruen had no use for her Christ on the cross, only the good works of human effort.

Her role was not finished. *Recording final dosage:* the last rite of her service. The teapot was warm, as though Lili had known the hour of his death was upon her patient and his family. Skilled in consolation, she doled out the half spoon of sugar for Claude, who wanted the nurse and these grown boys to leave her alone with her husband but could not bring herself to say it.

Amanda fussed about a particular black dress she had sent to the cleaners, and wondered if a coat might be needed.

Her husband spoke softly not to offend. *Why needed? No funeral.* Ned had known for some years he'd married a brittle porcelain doll, self-absorbed like his mother, a guilt-free queen of décor and the bountiful gifts of the mall. He is the handsome son, slight and reedy, disfigured with a scraggly beard. The adventure capitalist, his father called him, bailing him out time and again. There would be no again.

There would be no funeral in accordance with Gruen's wishes.

When Claude was finally alone with her husband's body, she knelt by the bed, their bed where he lay, the journey for best boy in the class over, resting in peace from the final trip he should never have taken. His weak lungs—he recently suffered a brief bout of pneumonia. Claude begged him to pass the job to an eager young woman, the one who spoke Arabic.

Arabic not needed this time out. Just dollars and common sense.

Dr. Do-Good.

I will be—said as a complaint—*escorted wherever I go. See only what they want the old man to see. Led about like a rock star or visiting congressman.*

Then why go?

He held out his cell phone displaying his doctors' numbers—office, home, weekends.

Not about to believe that excellent medical advice would be carried out in a refugee camp, sub-Saharan, she scolded, *In case of an emergency take two aspirin, drink plenty of clean water.*

Don't be foolish, my dear.

Had he said *my dear*? Hans playing Daddy Warbucks over the years to her Annie. She gave up, gave in to his determination.

Smoothing the dent in his ring finger, she cried at her loss. In the hospital Lili had removed his wedding band, *for safety.* Time warped; the sun did finally rise, yet there would be the long day to get through. First, the doctor with kind words signing the official death certificate, dealing out Xanax to alleviate bereavement, dismissing Lili as she served more tea. Then on to phone calls, mumbled condolences, to arrangements that the Mistress of Ceremonies was, at this moment, not famously good at. She recalled the elaborate business of death, had buried, as they say, her mother and father. This past week she canceled her classes, no trip on Jersey Transit to the gritty school where improbably they first met, Hans Gruen and Claude Montour. His sons spoke with due solemnity of a memorial service, disposal of ashes. Charles reviewed the prepared obit for the *Times.* It was known that Gruen had entered the hospital, cause of death an aneurysm. Claude diagnosed it as exhaustion, years hooking up life support to the incurable world. Hans admitted to abandoning his routine on a long flight—skipping the Sudafed, not walking the aisles, perhaps knew he was dying. In his rush to get home unescorted, he crashed into economy class on the final link from Paris. A clot formed in his lungs, traveled to his brain, that generous brain. The doctors double-talked his inoperable chances. Hans demanded living, living so far as he was able, his last days at home.

To Claude it seemed not their home, neighbors hovering, brandy and soda before breakfast. A wisp of a young man in a waiter's jacket followed her back to the bedroom, a servant Mrs. Gruen had not called into play. Looking upon the dead, he blessed himself. It came back to Marie Claude from childhood. She performed the swift crisscross gesture she'd been taught by her aunts. Then the discovery came upon her—abandoned. And when abandoned as a child, she had refused the comfort offered, ran away from a home not hers, a spook house where she was billeted while her mother pursued an episode of true romance. The slight man in the white jacket mumbled in Spanish, a fragment of prayer. He cast his eyes down, asked at what time lunch should be served.

Kneeling by the bier that was their bed, she heard the girl, Amanda. *She must not be left alone.* Then Marie Claude shut the door, said good-bye to her husband, clear and plain, not a whisper or a quick buss on the slack cheek, fleeting like the kisses bestowed when he hailed a taxi for Penn Station, packed her off to her classes in New Jersey. In recent months she looked back to see if he was steady as he walked along with the computer slung on a strap over his shoulder, balancing the old briefcase in hand. Saw his little two-step of recovered balance as the driver helped him into the car that would take him to the foundation where he had served his time. At the end of this year, he would graduate from Senior Fellow to Emeritus. *Alive, alive-O,* that became their sing-along at the breakfast table as she doled out his meds for the day: *cockles and mussels, alive, alive-O . . . Sweet Molly Malone,* Molly, the name of the mother who abandoned her to territory unknown in the Berkshires; idling with great-aunts, not a great passage in a girl's shattered life. Raised on extravagant love and neglect, she was left-baggage in a ruined house. When she inherited its sagging ceilings, loping stairs and leaning tower, Hans had said raze it. Sell the ground it stands on as commercial property. She couldn't *find it in her heart*—remembers speaking the wistful phrase—find it in her heart to demolish the old wreck, named it Mercy House as in—have mercy. For years it has been Mercy Learning Center for Women. As though she could roll back the emotional insolvency of her family, make amends, share with illiterate women what little she earned as a teacher. The house was in restoration when she married Hans. He called it a folly, her blue-chip folly.

How long did she kneel by their bed? How fiercely insist she must watch as Gruen's body was efficiently placed on a gurney, wheeled down the back hall, out the kitchen door to the service elevator? So that's how it's done—by two young attendants trained in the comfort of their neutrality. Left alone, she went at once to her Victorian dresser, its stained marble top facing off with Hans' sleek Scandinavian wardrobe. *Complementary,* he said of their possessions, books in particular. His first editions of Ricardo, *Das Kapital*, all of Keynes and Galbraith; her worn copies of *Mrs. Dalloway, Walden, The Autobiography of Benjamin Franklin*. Day by day, his facts, her fancy. She grabbed a gray sweater, the one he brought from London midsummer, presented to her triumphantly: *Costly, now the dollar is down*. As long predicted. A gift he could easily afford. There was always some prize in his briefcase, a cowrie-shell necklace, a vial of precious saffron, a glass paperweight with a cricket trapped inside.

Today was Friday, almost midday. For days she hadn't done a lick of work. How did that come to mind? Her work was why Hans first loved her, so she supposed, when she was still starry-eyed with trust in the historical record, wondering if she could truly care for this man who asked with an arch smile, *The truth will set us free?*

Now that he was gone, her every move seemed planned—slipping the book from the bag with student papers, following the route of her husband's body. Stealing—back hall to kitchen door where she let herself out, rang for the service elevator, thanked the bewildered operator for his kind words. The half block to Fifth Avenue, then on to the Park, finding her way across the drive to Seneca Village, where she would read dry-eyed her preparation for class. *Marie Claude* (her childhood name) was good at hard lessons.

* * *

Amanda said, *We were about to call the police.*

Appropriately, Claude cried. She had been gone for an hour—longer. Her husband would have clocked it exactly. *My loss, now isn't that foolish? His leaving me.* Gruen left so often for extravagant good works, this last time for the oil proposal and to observe thousands behind the chain-link fence of no-man's land. He would write a report not limited to financial aid, give in to the old passion before he was elevated to Emeritus.

Why, against my pleading—a sharp edge to Claude's words—*for God's sake, as though a dose of economics, a shipment of rice . . .* She stopped mid-sentence not to offend staff from his office. They were family arriving without invitation. Not to say your big checkbook will never end a long history of revenge, she recalled his care for child soldiers, those killer kids his concern well before Rwanda. Visiting the camps, Hans could spot the one child in a gang perhaps redeemable. She brought to mind the apocryphal story of an appealing boy. *Handed over his machete.*

Kalashnikov, Ned's correction.

In any case his weapon, to the American about to take notes on his education in violence. That boy, safe as sheet-metal houses, last heard of teaching school in Swaziland. If there was another rescue this last time out, Hans did not live to document the appeal of a child now truly lost. Delivering this impromptu eulogy, Claude ushered the mourners toward the front hall. They lingered. It seemed she would never reclaim a moment alone with her sorrow. The Park had provided confrontation, not comfort. She understood why they'd come. Her husband knew each caseworker, each volunteer by name, meted out generous praise for their efforts, his care for their lengthy reports on the useless distribution of beans without access to clean water; this renewed anger at the diminishing promise of Oil for Food, UN millions ripped off. He dropped his professorial cool raging at the low estimate— twenty thousand children kidnapped—Liberia and Sudan.

She said: *Armed boys malnourished, living in camps.* Then fell silent. The wisp of a servant: *Lo siento mucho, lo siento,* poured more tea in Claude's mug than a body could bear.

What's he say? Amanda, patting the bump of her belly, suggested the Xanax: *Which you know I can't take.* The girl, at long last, expecting a child. *My bubble dress at the cleaners, perfect for the reception.*

Reception?

Charles took control, brought Claude back to the bedroom where his father had lain in state through the long night. Gruen's bathrobe lay at the ready on his reading chair as though he might rise to scan a report, search out the briefcase that traveled with him the long flight from Khartoum to Paris to home.

Always, the tidying. She picked up his slippers, worn at heel. *You might want . . . ?* She was ripping the sheets off the bed, Lili's job surely, and couldn't help but think that in records of the colonial past she once scoured, the American past in the diaries of women, accounts of washing and dressing the bodies of their husbands, often with the help of neighbors.

She said: *The best shirt would be laundered, hands folded over the chest for the viewing. The boots polished, passed along to a son. Though, of course, it was more often the wife or mother who died.* It was a relief to talk in this schoolmistress way, a clip of history taking up the sudden slack of emotion. All true, she told Charles, the christening gown was not buried with the dead child, saved in a chest for the next one sure to come along. She told Hans' middle-aged boy, beefy and broad, once an athlete with the trophies to prove it, that she had, after all, met his father at a seminar table.

He lectured. Emerging markets, I remember. And I challenged him, what gall. It should never have happened, his coming to that limp branch of a city college.

Charles brushed a twig out of her hair: He said: *I'll stay with you tonight.* His wife would drive the children in from Greenwich in the morning.

Now Amanda stood in the doorway, eyes fixed on the tear in Claude's slacks. *You going off like that so upset me.* She offered the Xanax in its plastic bubble.

Claude said: *Why should I want to dull my loss?* Yet, she must say something about her absence and with that purpose went to the dining room, where the last of the visitors had reassembled, the boy techie from Hans' office among them. Dr. Gruen had valued his instruction. Tea party sandwiches were cleared from the table.

Charles took the calls. A congressman, then a photographer his father had an affair with long before Claude came on the scene. The black dress at Madame Celeste could be picked up in this emergency. Then *Newsweek* presuming there might be more to the story.

More than my father's death? He drew back, dealt politely with the journalist pushing inquiries with the body still warm. PetroChina drilling beyond AU allotment? Gruen toured illegal mines in the Congo? *Not this trip.* Charles pushed through the swinging door to the kitchen, with one hand manipulated the wallet from his back pocket, overpaid the little guy. *Lo siento, siento,* storing away the sandwiches. No story beyond Gruen's long career monitoring what, in Africa, he might call the growth industry of human suffering. He had stolen that phrase from his father, hoped the journalist would not use it. *Nineteen thirty-two. My father would have been seventy-five this month, still saving the world.*

When he returned to the mourners, Claude had taken up her place again at the head of the table, telling Ned, Amanda, the neighbors they had always meant to visit and the fresh delegation of volunteers from Gruen's office that in her grief she ran off to the Park, where they often walked on a Sunday to admire the Conservatory Garden. She thanked Hans's assistant for the stiff arrangement of flowers, so unlike the casual bouquets she ordered to greet the golden donors and powerful guests for dinner.

I'll be fine now. We'll come together tomorrow. She had no idea what that meant, *come together, fine*. Then, to call a stop to sighs and anecdotal remembrance, thought she must say something about Hans for these good people and the sake of his children. *A loving husband and father,* chill, fit for a headstone. She said, *We shared him, we all did.*

End of the interminable day, Charles brought her to the spare room where she had been sleeping since her husband was transported home from the hospital. Fussing over towels and soap, he set Claude up as a guest. The night light cast him as a looming shadow of the father who eluded him all his life. The reliable son, clocking in more pro bono than his law firm allowed: for his sake she hated her lie about the Conservatory Garden. He must know from the rip in her pants, the disorder of her hair, she had not walked up Fifth Avenue to look at flower beds perfectly groomed. She now saw herself in the mirror, a smudge of dirt on her temple. On the Sunday before his final African trip she tore Hans from his work to come with her to the Park. Her loving, though often distracted, husband agreed to a cab up Madison. They walked the short block to the Vanderbilt Gate. In the garden, lilies were making their last gaudy show. They watched a hummingbird levitate over a red flower. *What flower is that?* City people wondering at the bird's small iridescent body, its helicopter wings. The overbred blooms of hydrangeas nodded in the breeze, a thousand clowns. Hans had tired. Silenced in their disagreement of what might come to pass on his last African adventure, they settled on a bench, soaking in the heat of Autumn. They spoke, predictably, of global warming. Why hadn't she told Charles the simple truth? That she was foolishly clear in her purpose as she ran the short distance to Seneca Village. Indeed crazed, plopping down on the grass, reading through tears, knowing that *Uncle Tom* trimmed to bare bones would not make the medicine go down for her class in Jersey City.

Yo, Mama Teresa, improvin' my black ass? Always one hoodie with the nerve to mock the gangstaspeak he aimed to leave behind. The girls were so pleased at Miss Montour's cool. They could not guess her husband's patronage, honoring her for teaching inner-city kids. Some would make the grade. One girl had actually read Mrs. Stowe's novel, all 450 pages: Felice, a Haitian far ahead of the pack. Proficient in Toussaint's Rebellion, searching for news of our Civil War, she asked who might be labeled *Uncle Tom*. She'd heard that expression.

A Supreme Court judge, a Pullman porter. His trade went out with the last guilty laugh at Stepin Fetchit. But then Miss Montour had to gloss Pullman, provide footnotes for pandering and the stupefying vaudeville performance.

Gruen honored her equally for the grit of her teaching and for playing the gracious lady with foundation folk. It simplified matters for them to believe they were in the same game: for Hans to come home and mix drinks at the set hour, for Claude to report, as on the day before his departure, which kid sassed her. For her husband to confess there's almost no one to salvage in a parched village in Chad. *Dignity*: as far back as Mozambique, he found the word useless in speaking of rehabilitation of the millions behind the barbed-wire enclosure of their history. Often he looked with pride at his wife's notes scattered on the couch. Never class notes. This past year she was attempting to write a paper tracking the fate of a runaway slave hidden here in the city.

Looking into was the phrase Claude used, demoting her academic work to something like a hobby, her papers published with little notice. She was currently looking into Bill Dove, a smart house servant, young at the time he ran from a tobacco plantation in Virginia. She was looking into stations of the Underground Railroad in this city that sent the fugitives on to Quakers in New England. Dove's name in faded ink on letters in the New-York Historical Society suggested he may have been hidden in the cellar of a house owned free and clear by Alonzo See, a cartman who lived with his sister in Seneca Village. *William Dove we called Billy*, in Betha See's gliding hand, written from Riverside Heights after the Civil War, *was a sweet man to behold at our table. Billy moved upcity with us for a season. Wind off the river blew away his fancy. He went from me on his onward journey.* Claude figured Betha had fallen for the lively Dove, his charm, his antics, though back in the Village wooden board houses were propped on stone, so perhaps it was in Alonzo's shed, not cellar, where she kept him like a prize pony, a handsome and entertaining boy who danced jigs, sang songs of the plantation. Not a scrap of evidence in *Uncle Tom* touched on the city life of a figure like Dove. Claude assigned the novel to herself as well as her class. Mrs. Stowe in her pulpit, self-ordained:

> The negro, it must be remembered, is an exotic of the most gorgeous and superb countries of the world, and he has, deep in his heart, a passion for all that is splendid, rich and fanciful, a passion which rudely indulged by an untrained taste, draws the ridicule of the colder and more correct white race.

The passage often cited as clear evidence of the novelist's condescension. Claude thought to play it again as she searched out the flamboyant figure of Bill Dove. How long had he lived with the Sees in the settlement on the Heights, a prisoner of Betha's affection? *This day I have sewn the last stitch on a Sunday shirt of fine cotton for our Billy.* Then he's gone missing, four years, five. Talk about stitching: the gaps in Dove's history patched by guesswork—New York saddled with the Fugitive Slave Act, though unofficially not in compliance. Further supposing his wiles, she finds Dove hired by Boss Tweed, living once again as a domestic. In one of those rare moments, a historian's dream, she discovers her Billy as porter for the Boss. Four "coloreds" worked in the household of this powerful man known for his Negrophobia. Thing is, Hans loved her discoveries, how she read history in the little guy's unheralded work and days. Appropriating the past, he called it. Her essays, not all of them pleasantly anecdotal, might be read as small stories despite the apparatus of bibliography and endnotes. The indentured servant of the widow Eliza Tibbs, her education and subsequent freedom. The Parisian tailor of Benjamin Franklin. The midwife who wrote each day in her journal while plying her trade through blizzards and haying, paddling swollen rivers on her journeys to stillbirth or new life in New England cabins.

Now Claude thought she must never publish the charming story of a runaway who came up in the world to serve a corrupt politician in the Gilded Age, ushering Tweed's guests into the drawing room on Lower Broadway. The night before he died, Hans rallied to speak of her project as though they might go on with the old routine, catch up on discoveries of her day. With great effort, he told of the millions Tweed's ring ripped off the city. *That would be*—the effort of his breathing as he converted the Boss's take to today's currency—*that would be eleven million, small change. Missionaries,* he said falling into a sleep.

Though in fact, the 11 million was aid lost to warlords in the country he had just looked into, far less than Tweed's 45 swiped from the coffers of the city. *Missionaries, that's all we are*, her husband often said. *Let it be known to celebrities discovering Africa*—his good humor avoiding despair—*missionaries, throwbacks to those innocents sent to convert the lost tribes. Your Jesuits, my minister in a pith helmet.* His Lutheran grandfather had made Christians of the Chinese. They claimed the term lightly. *Missionary work,* he called the life she was currently looking into, her appropriation of this entertaining Bill Dove—*Take care, no minstrel show.* Claude would never enjoy her first reader again, bask in his admiration. Impossible to tell his boys, even Charles who might defend her from the charge of History Lite, that his father loved her persistence, hanging in with uncharted lives, small truths—well, at least stories that may not set us free. Her reading of Miss See's diary placed Dove in family living quarters, not the pigsty or hen coop of speculation. She sat on the edge of the guest bed, not ready to give up this final day, heard a shrill whistle, a coach making a call on the television in Hans' study. His big boy settling into a game; but Charles came to her door rumpled, beer in hand. His pleasure as he handed her the framed shot of his father with a crop of rusty hair going white at the edges. Gruen, chin up for the photo op with the smiling Nelson Mandela.

I know. With wounded children in Darfur. *Oh, I know.*

In the Park she had run to the very spot, the banished Seneca Village, where her subject, Bill Dove, was hidden from the authorities who might ship him back to Massa, shackled not beaten. Frederick Law Olmsted had written about the Slave States when cotton was king. Mrs. Stowe praised him as a fellow abolitionist. Hans would understand that she must sort it out, whether to cite Olmsted as a good guy carefully recording testimony of a Virginian he'd known at Yale who fed him a conciliatory line: free men were better workers. You could get an Irishman for $120 a year, cheaper than a slave's board and keep. Olmsted laid it all out, the Southerner hedging his moral bets—you really wanted nothing to do with a slaver, a man who traded in flesh.

As though not a club to belong to, Hans said.

That was it, and why was she impatient with Olmsted's paternalistic chatter allowing that, if free, the Negro should be reprogrammed— morally brought up to snuff, but not granted the vote? She put the landscaper's early career down to lively reportage. Claude knew what her husband might say of cotton economics, that Irishmen were cheaper in the long run, a proposition that allowed the Virginia gentleman to barter back his soul. Something like that, so she'd think about Billy Dove, perhaps shackled if captured, sent back to serve in the opulent accommodations of Tara, not beaten. Though why would you want him when an Irish house girl came for $6 a month? The Virginian had thought the figure of Uncle Tom false, sentimental. That was in his favor. He would never be charmed by her story of Billy. Coming to Seneca was the nearest thing to having Hans with her; show-and-tell time as on an evening when they sat with their drinks before supper, her notes scattered on the couch. The old economist would know to cite Olmsted as a good guy.

How long did she sit where Alonzo See's house, so thoroughly gone, cast its faint shadow, the new sweater not warm enough over the soiled shirt she had worn for days? Not long. Then that old lady came upon her, poked into her sorrow.

She throws the quilt Charles has folded at the bottom of the bed over her shoulders, not to sleep, not to let it end, this livelong day. The quilt is a ragged thing. Little diamonds forming a star shed their batting, the work of one of the aunts who cared for her those years ago when she was abandoned. The one who sewed, not the one who played the piano. Today's lesson, Miss Montour: memory trumps invention. Plopped down on the cold ground in Central Park, her grief was about the old hurt, not the imagined history of Dove brushing silk top hats of the corrupt gentlemen visiting the Boss of Tammany Hall, nor the lashes delivered in *Uncle Tom,* nor the architects of the Greensward, nor the honored gentleman who had been her husband. The Park blurred as the woman came toward her. That wondering, clueless gaze, as though with simple inquiry she might help.

So, Marie Claude ran away as a child. She had been left by her mother with two maiden aunts, dumped in an old house with mildew rampant, creaking floorboards. Abandoned, the child felt worthless as the yellowed lace petticoats and corsets, the wills, marriage certificates, letters with family history thrown in trunks that once traveled the world. She ran through the woods, storybook girl tripping over limbs of fallen trees, hair tangled in vines that devoured her grandfather's garden. She could hear the old ladies, their fluty voices calling, *Marie Claude, Marie*

Claude, then only the swamp suck of limp ferns, the croak of night creatures. Tripped up, she fell just as she did today, scraped her knee running from the spook house. Light at the end of the trail, the oily yellow of a kerosene lamp in a shanty with a family of squatters. She was no one to these people, a girl from the house through the woods, a big old house in advanced disrepair. The mother took her in, fed her, washed the wound, put her to bed with her little girl, Sissy. In the Park on this day of her bereavement, Claude recalled that worn woman, the baby blessed with golden curls, Sissy, dirt poor but with family. The father drank from a pint bottle, wiping the spill of whiskey off his lips. She had no one in the world—not true, but true to Marie Claude. Her father a minor diplomat off to a new posting; her mother pursuing which love affair? But on the day of her husband's death, Claude does not question her recall of that abandoned girl, though no shack is left standing, only the memory of a coached bedtime prayer. Squatting on the ground once Seneca, the subject of her inquiry, she cried softly as the woman approached offering help, looking like she needed help herself, her black coat worn but good in its day. Claude's mother had trained her in matters of quality, the informed judgment of fine shoes and good haircuts, even a lack of pretension reflecting a woman's comfortable place in the world. A legacy she hated, but there it was in a teary eye blink, the assessment of this woman, the *lady pearls* of refinement around her dry neck, the boast of old jeans, her soft hand with the slim wedding band comforting her. Claude ran from the kindness, embraced a hill of stone, shamed that she guessed more of this woman's history than she ever would construct of Bill Dove's, the story of his free life and honored place in the household of Boss Tweed. She believes she has found his later life in an advertisement for Barnum's American Museum—*Negro Song and Dance Straight from the Plantation!*—The BLACK DOVE strutting down the broadside from EDUCATED WHITE RATS and THE RENOWNED HAPPY FAMILY. That would be correct: the war well over, six hundred thousand dead, Emancipation finally signed and sealed, Boss Tweed coming into full power. Why, in this time of mourning, had she recalled the song-and-dance man, Dove's place in our culture of entertainment, one of her appropriated lives?

Because, Hans said of this work in progress, her paper with its plotting: *You might call it "American Pastimes."* Now she takes his words to heart, her fiddling with time past was what he meant. Kindly, of course. And then there was Sissy, the angel child now well grown, working for her at Mercy House. He so loved the story of that girl. *The Golden Legend*, he called it. Not unlike her missionary work.

In the narrow bathroom meant for a maid, Claude strips for a shower. Under the three-corner tear in her slacks, her knee is swollen. The new sweater, Hans' gift, has come through the painful incident just fine. What seemed to be a smudge of dirt on her temple now shows itself as a bruise. The water is scalding, then chill. As she towels off, it's half-time. The blaring staccato trumpets of a high-school band: "What Now My Love?" Charles, gone shy, comes to tuck her in. Amanda has placed Xanax on the night table.

Isn't she awful? he says.

Yes, the girl.

This day must end. Tomorrow Charles will cancel a fund-raiser, black tie. He is perfectly clear that the senior partners in his firm believe he overinvests, defending the barely defensible, scanting billable hours, but he is Gruen's son, bad form to complain. Tomorrow he will get into his father's computer. Tonight it will do to open the briefcase. He figures all urgent papers have been delivered to the foundation. There are published reports: environmental stress on nations surrounding Lake Chad; the inefficiency, or questionable loyalty, of hybrid peacekeepers; a note free of time and place——*Long Term Development;* a slim bracelet of woven straw wrapped in Arabic newsprint. There is the cell phone with Dr. Gruen's core numbers——work, family, the doctor who allowed him to die at home, and a run of photos on the small screen of a boy with scant flesh on his bones, the black knobs of his knees and elbows painful to behold. The kid wears a camouflage T-shirt, floppy white sneakers. Here he bends over a bowl, hand scooping gruel into his mouth; here with a whip in hand; here brandishing a grenade, then a rifle, a machete in a PowerPoint display of the weapons he has used in his war. Gruen about to make his case for the boy before he became a cause? Or just a last encounter, one boy among many playing with guns. And here is this photo—bright sun against the frail reed fence—the boy with a man in a dated safari jacket. Gruen sickly, smiling. The thin smile his sons had been awarded, not often enough. In the morning Charles will scoop the *Times* up from the doorstep, see how it reads, his father's life. Tomorrow his children will be brought into the city.

His daughter, sucking her braid, lets Claude kiss her. It's Saturday. Missing his soccer game, Charles' son tugs at his team jersey, doesn't have to be coached: *Sorry, really sorry he's gone,* that last, almost a question.

She had taken the long route home, daring the Ramble. In the confusion of paths, Claude came upon a flock of birdwatchers. Running, she ruined their silence. The leader threw a handful of seed. A greedy flutter of wings. She ran on in this picture-perfect wilderness, climbed the hill from which the wide screen of the city could be seen blurred by her tears. Below—the serenity of the Lake. The Angel of Bethesda Fountain, on duty blessing the waters, directed her to the straight path of the Mall, but Claude must find her way home through this tangle, past boathouse and playgrounds.

The man came round a curve from a path plotted to invite a stroll, in fact a ramble downhill. He was bent though not old, his shaved head glossy black with the sweat of his climb. He wore a running suit that had seen better days, carried a gnarled walking stick that he raised when he saw her. Hans Gruen had died. Now there was no one for his wife to tell how the stranger twirled his stick high, how she ran back down the embankment, stumbled through undergrowth, fell on sharp stone. Her head, thrust forward, came to rest on a pillow of twigs and dead leaves. He came toward her, laughing. His front teeth broken, she would remember; all but one, the one capped with gold. He rapped his stick on stone.

What you think I was goin' to do, girl?
I don't know. I don't know.

* * *

Seneca: Lucius Seneca I or II, father and son, Latin poets. The father, a rhetoritician, looked back to a Golden Age in which private property, as in the Village bearing his name, did not exist at all, nor did slavery. He disapproved of his son (d. AD 65), a strict vegetarian who drank only water, tutor of Nero—morals, not the fiddle. Seneca II fell out of favor, committed suicide, a noble act, having been directed to do so rather than suffer political humiliation, thus the poison draft. He was spared the later commentary on his poetry, *too lofty by far.*

More likely, the village named after the Senecas, an Iroquois tribe that wisely prepared for war with the French, hiding their children and the elderly in the woods, burying crops of the last season, stripping their towns of everything of value. Or *Seneca,* a password of the Underground Railroad. Or Seneca Falls, where abolitionists flourished before and during the Civil War. I know this by way of a boy, twelve or thirteen, black kid in a poncho, scholarly glasses, notebook in hand. We were on a walk through Central Park, courtesy of the Conservancy, maybe a dozen history buffs, half that number by the time we reached Seneca Village that was. The guide leading our dwindling group was determined to complete her assignment on that cold, wet day. Her umbrella took off for the Diana Ross Playground, a black bat flapping against the chain-link fence. Undaunted, she called out what little information she had at her command.

Ink dribbled down the boy's page. He carried on without notes, asked a question. *Water?*

Yes, they think there may have been a well.

The mysterious *they* of guesswork, of diggers for shards in Thebes, divers for pirate gold. They, a couple of groundsmen poking for moles or chipmunk trails, may have found a bubble of springwater that serviced the Village.

The boy said: *They better have. We're in an estuary here.*

He would be in high school now, that eager kid who knew why we built a Reservoir on this island, in this Park, why our water, then as now, must be piped down from upstate. We're afloat in seawater here, so . . .

So, the coopers, the rain barrels, the cartmen of Seneca Village hauling water into the churches and school, servicing the vegetable patches and those who might afford a bath.

Did I say the boy was with his mother, who preened? And a little brother groaning with boredom, M&M's supplied to shut him up, a roly-poly lagging behind as we climbed to the next site, Vista Rock. His game—tripping the bright boy who will be an annoyance all his life.

I trust that notebook has filled up with answers that do not wash away.

Daybook, November 11, 2007

LITERARY WALK

Unfinished business, the popular poet, Fitz-Greene Halleck:

> *Green be the turf above thee,*
> *Friend of my better days!*
> *None knew thee but to love thee,*
> *Nor named thee but to praise.*

> *Tears fell, when thou wert dying,*
> *From eyes unused to weep,*
> *And long where thou art lying,*
> *Will tears the cold turf steep.*

And so forth, elegy for his friend and collaborator, John Rodman Drake. Halleck—journalist, humorist, poet, banker and in that role confidential agent to John Jacob Astor. He moved in with the lonely millionaire, regretted the loss of his muse:

> *The power that bore my spirit up*
> *Above this bank-note world——is gone.*

But retired to Guilford on Long Island Sound, wrote *Connecticut*, a long, now and then amusing poem that reflects nothing of the industrial state where I was born, where the manufacture of guns and invention of the cotton gin were to play significant roles in the Civil War. Nevertheless, ten years after his death (the designated passage of time to confirm posterity by Order of the Park Commission), Halleck was installed on Literary Walk. One of our forgettable presidents, Rutherford B. Hayes, and Frederick Law Olmsted in attendance.

On the other hand, Shakespeare, encircled in late blooming mums, is smaller in scale than Halleck, Robert Burns, and Walter Scott, though he's afforded a more decorative plinth to set him above us. The inline skating *proficienados* on their way to the plaza fronting the bandstand to compete in splits, flips, airborne waltzes know the Bard and a fragment of verse, if only lines from a movie. *Maria! Say it soft and it's almost like praying. . . .*

Oh, leave them alone; don't heckle, lick your old chops at their presumed ignorance while your fingers, a touch arthritic, fumble at the cell phone, which begs for your password. The call home aborted. *In the Park,* all I meant to say. Obsessed with the Greensward, I plump myself down in its stories, the neat rectangle of its map morphing into the uncertain turns and loops of the natural world, slopes and summits plotted.

As I descend to the Terrace, the Lake appears two dimensional against a painted backdrop of an enchanted forest as in *Midsummer Night's Dream,* but we are well into November. Movietime, Mickey Rooney played Puck, but who was Titania, Queen of the Fairies?

> *Come, sit thee down upon this flow'ry bed,*
> *While I thy amiable cheeks do coy,*
> *And stick musk-roses in thy slick smooth head,*
> *And kiss thy fair large ears, my gentle joy.*

Many trivia questions remain unanswered. You remind me our little life's not a game show. No buzzer of defeat. No cash prizes. My adventures in the Park across the way from our apartment seem all too solitary, enacted in the geography of my imagination. Virginia Woolf gave up on a friend who was addicted to Solitaire, laying out the cards in a dreary game the Brits call Patience. Well, I have no patience with life dealt out in med milligrams, scaled down to my daily walk: to the yield of small encounters, a scrapbook of facts and fables, though I have included you along the way, begged your advice, as in: *What am I to do with terra incognita above 96th Street?*

You said: *Anita Louise played Titania.* Ashamed you knew that, then: *There's something odd going on with you. Some evasion.*

Dusting me off, you switch to an old story, this day's further deflation of the dollar against the euro, then recall how we lived it up, traveled on two cents plain when we were kids. Our mighty dollars cashed in on the black market.

Expensive gelato in the Piazza Barberini.

Raspberry tart, rue Monsieur-le-Prince.

A hundred bucks sent from home . . . I bought pantomime figures in the dusty bookshop on my way to the British Museum.

Switching channels, you assume the editorial voice: *Gold will top $800 an ounce. The banks have gone begging.*

My tightrope walker, jugglers, clowns have never faded all these years. I love those theatrical folks trained to amaze, take chances.

We talk a Mad Hatter's babble avoiding what we intend. If we didn't speak at cross purposes, I'd admit that I'm silenced by candidates now up and running, not one of them reflecting my angst as night by nightly news broadcasts our failure. My mistrusts of Sunday morning pundits. Last week, fellow with the plastic hair had the buzz: *The war's not front page*. His easy skip to inflation. At my wrath, you pleasantly turned to the commodities market. Copper, corn, oil $$$ a barrel, the Chinese paying top price for iron. Tiffany & Co. interest in gold digging, though seven hundred thousand pounds of waste a day gives the corporation pause. Gold has nothing to do with my explorations in the Park written on devalued paper. No mention of uranium, or my angry outburst last month against the war, carrying on like a braless girl lost in Woodstockian fields of love is the answer. Your voice dipped to a whisper, a calming suggestion—*El Dorado*.

Seems a year since my brother calmed me down. *A little warm milk before bedtime, Mimi. Do Columbus.*

And now you accused me of evasion, ask, *How was your day?* Drama queen no more, I report that I gave full attention to my computer, then took the grandchildren to the playground that lies in the earthworks across the street. Longitude and latitude same as always on CPW, though you still refer to the 8th Avenue Subway. You grew up in this city. I did not. You climbed the Park's massive rock formations with the janitor's boy before he was thrown out of PS 6, years before Bimbo, your nefarious playmate, had a record, before they sent you to the private school with proper teams, playing fields. No more make believe in the Park above 96th—bang, bang you're dead—no private adventures.

Yes, I spent my fish-and-chips pence on comic cutouts of Columbine and Pierrot, those quarrelsome lovers, and prints of my tightrope walkers who never worked with a net. I'm a girl from the circus town of Bridgeport, where my grandfather, getting on with his life, carted water and hay—seventeen dollars for the season—to elephants shivering in Barnum's winter quarters, longing for dust baths and a wallow in warm African rivers.

See here, on the bill of sale: ALL GOODS SOLD AT PURCHASERS RISK. *Now, wasn't that smart of Grandpa?*

He left out the apostrophe.

He never made it to eighth grade. You know there's a statue of the Hatter in the Park. He smirks while Alice presides for a sane moment.

The kids?

Yes, after school with the children. We're lucky to have them nearby. Just suppose we were in some sunny place with elder persons? Golf cart gliding us about the links, Happy Hour for Seniors, the lively arguments of a book club . . .

Come off it. The playground in your Park?

Yes, the one with decks, child-safe. Nicholas dangling from a rope swing—no hands! So, a full report: The playground was desolate, the bench I sat on littered with leaves that should have fallen weeks ago. The lone baby tender on the phone neglecting her charge, a bandy-legged toddler eating cookies coated in sand. Kate, beyond playground, stood aloft on the deck, my binoculars aimed at our building, the windows catching the brass light of sundown. *Hoping to see their terrarium.*

She can't see round corners.

That's worth a fleeting smile. Our argument is winding down. True, we live in the rear of our building. With an angling of the head pressed to the window, I am afforded a partial view of the asphalt entrance to the Park, where you fear I've invested unwisely in a bear market of legends, unreal estate of my last place on earth. As for Kate, she wanted to spritz their terrarium, the brandy snifter in which they have created an alternate world—tropical, lush as the virgin forests of Guiana, which reminded Columbus of Valencia. You know perfectly well that it sits on our windowsill sweating the seasons.

That was my day. Now will you answer my question? What's above 96th?

You're back to the weak dollar, to gold mined mostly for jewelry. Whole hillsides destroyed, wetlands reduced to ash for rings on our fingers, bells on our toes. Not mine, no way José in Peru with lungs collapsing from tons of toxic waste. I am sanctimonious, but my outrage at those who think it's OK to slam a prisoner's head into water, bobbing for rotten apples, folks, doesn't have the old huff and puff. I'm reduced to a litany of complaints. You have not separated paper from plastic while I have taken bottles to the bottle people who live on the returns of our trash. And have you noted that the smirk of Cheney's smile has dipped to new lows? Never called Veep. That would lend him a pinprick of cozy: and the detained may never come to trial. The deflation of their captors is the best we can—I can—hope for, the stale breath of their dark secrets, slow wheeze of their hot-air balloon, the sorry spectacle of its bladder on *the green breast of the new world. Its vanished trees . . .*

At the end of *The Rings of Saturn,* Sebald's walking tour of the east coast of England, having embraced the near and far reaches of history, personal and public, he returns to home and garden, recalls the elms devastated by the Dutch elm disease:

> One of the most perfect trees I have ever seen was an almost two hundred-year-old elm that stood on its own in a field not far from our house. About one hundred feet tall, it filled an immense space. I recall that, after most of the elms in the area had succumbed, its countless, somewhat asymmetrical, finely serrated leaves would sway in the breeze as if the scourge which had obliterated its entire kind would pass it by without a trace; and I also recall that a bare fortnight later all these apparently invincible leaves were brown and curled up, and dust before the autumn came.

This year, next year . . . will mark the hundred years since the elms were planted to arch over the Mall. With great care and expense, many are still standing, some replaced, each tree endowed, money down against disease. Olmsted understood the American elms' formality, the grandeur of their welcoming arch to the people of the city, high and low. Saplings demand patience.

In the morning you leave a report on the front hall table. It is a research update on the **Eldorado Gold Corporation.** So we spar, paper-doll lovers, kiss and make up. *Product development toward year end. No new ounces added to the reserve.* Read as a message, I understand you would like me to nest on the sill, flourish under glass like the ferns in the children's terrarium, and entertain no dangerous exploits above 96th Street. Stay put, here in the El Dorado. Next you may advise meditation—ooom, ooom—and renew the prescription: no exercise beyond the short walk in which I turn and see them looming, the safe towers of home. But today I'll push on in the Park to 72nd across from the Dakota, determined to investigate the report that IMAGINE is sinking, the tiles at the edge of the magic circle sucked into sandy soil. By the time I reach Lennon's memorial, I'm bummed out, the heavy heartbeat throbbing as I join a busload of tourists, baby boomers honoring their bonged past. And the crazies always, humming as they lay tulips round about in a mysterious pattern. I'm foolishly encouraged. IMAGINE has been shored up, as certain in this uncertain world as Radio City, Ellis Island, St. Patrick's Cathedral.

Imagine there's no Heaven
It's easy if you try . . .

Down the slope to Strawberry Fields, NYPD reads the *Post*.

It's Armistice Day. No mixed emotions. My father wore the poppy in his buttonhole but would not march. Something about the pomp after the circumstances he'd seen in France; and you've never told me why you trusted the sodden parachute that sucked you down. There were alligators and the scum of algae in Florida's warm waters, never told your air force career as a terrifying story. Last year a vet home from Iraq stood by the memorial in the corner park just down from our little house in the country. Veterans Day, we now call it. He spoke of his friends, those left behind, shuffling through his words, not attempting eloquence, while old vets in their overseas caps and scraps of uniform buttoned over the bulge stood at attention. Then Taps, truly moving, followed by the ear-shattering salute that made the babies cry.

Daybook, Thursday, November 18

There will be a water shutdown from 10AM until 4PM in the CD line. Please make sure all taps are closed. We are sorry for the inconvenience.

Old pipes give out now and then, don't I know. I draw water in the pasta pot and big salad bowl, laundry day in the village. Almost immediately I'm thirsty. I drink from the brass dipper that hangs on the kitchen wall, a decorative item. Thirst quenched, our lives are too easy, don't we know. *Meditation and water are wedded forever.* Ishmael, about to go on his journey in Melville's big book that would succeed, though not in his time. I haven't the heart, literally, or mind for meditation. In this arid world, the waves lapping against the shore of the Reservoir may be too gentle, the still mirror of the Lake cold, unreflecting. *The November of my soul.*

So, in the parched season at the El Dorado, I'll stay home as you once again advised. Oh, the familiar warning was in your voice as you put on your wool cap.

Don't venture. That's how you put it, no need to say more.

Heart pumps a heavy beat. Ankles and wrists swollen, shipping water. My vials of medication, sleepless nights, heavy rain against the kitchen window advise against panning for choice nuggets in the Park today. So it's follow the yellow brick path, stake my claim in El Dorado. For Columbus there was no gold, only the discovery of parrots, pumpkin seeds, cinnamon bark, the useless glisten of mica and the trade-off of measles for syphilis—until the third voyage. At last, a gritty find up the Orinoco. By then Christoforo was out of favor. He believed in El Dorado, the name of an island where a gilded man rose from the river once a year. As though to sustain his belief in Christ and the Madonna, he honored the story of a god never seen.

This day, in a tower that's lost the legend for which it was named, I am confined with my books to take up this endgame of discovering where I am in the world—not Kansas, not Bridgeport. An outlander, I arrived in this city in my college kilt and polo coat fifty-five years ago. You understand that the Park will always be new territory under my surveillance; not so for the kids in the playground, not for you, city boy. So my archives: tinted postcard of Bethesda Fountain, a clipping from the *Times* flaky at the edges—John Paul II blessing the adoring crowd through safety glass of the Popemobile, bird lore aplenty, a sepia photo of real sheep in the Sheep Meadow, shots of the young guys from your office playing softball, Nick's birthday piñata spilling its treasures in the Pinetum, and *The Gates* of 2005, their citrus grandeur flying free of critical commentary, General Sherman gilded anew, and you, misty-eyed on the Great Lawn cheering *Nessun dorma* . . . *O Principessa*, holding my hand when Pavarotti hit high C. Who took the picture?

You will know at once that all views and encounters are true as the arc of the Bow Bridge though carefully engineered as a cascade in the Ramble, inevitable as statues along the way. I will never, under oath, convert the Park to an attic or yard sale for the El Dorado, just file the cache of mementos as travel stories, tickets for safe passage to the end of my days. When I make the call, isn't that how you do it? No investment too big or too small.

THE HISTORY OF THE WORLD

Like Sir Walter Raleigh, who packed a trunk of books when he went to sea, I depend on books in my back room—too often, you say. Landlocked, I could never invent Raleigh's bogus search for El Dorado, or predict his downfall having betrayed the Virgin Queen by loving a maid. His story often told between scholars' covers and popular bios with portraits of the great courtier himself, pearls sewn into his weskit, gilt buttons, Orders of Merit. And here's the heartbreaker in silk stockings, a Gentleman of the Crown with his son Wat, dwarfed by Dad's glory. A girl would easily lose her heart to Sir Walter's bright eye, the curl of his rusty beard, but the Queen's Maids of Honor were never to marry. Too many books in my cell: I take down *Aubrey's Brief Lives* (c. 1692) in which the gossipy biographer gives Shakespeare short notice, though he's enchanted at some length by Raleigh's amorous adventure.

> He loved a wench well; and one time getting up one of the Mayds of Honour against a tree in a Wood ('twas his first lady) who seemed at first to be somewhat fearful of her honour, and modest, she cryed, sweet Sir Walter, what doe you me ask? Will you undoe me? Nay, sweet Sir Walter! Sweet Sir Walter! Sir Walter! At last, as the danger and the pleasure at the same time grew higher, she cryed in the extasey, Swisser Swatter Swisser Swatter. She proved with child, and

I doubt not but this Hero took care of them both, as also that
the Product was more than an ordinary mortal.

About the Product, more later.

In *The Loss of El Dorado*, Sir Vidia Naipaul sifts through Raleigh's *The
Discoverie of the Large, Rich, and Bewtiful Empyre of Guiana, With a relation of
the great and Golden Citie of Manoa (which the Spanyards call El Dorado) And of
the Provinces of Emeria, Arromaia, Amapaia, and other Countries with their rivers, adjoining. Performed in the year 1595. by Sir W. Ralegh Knight, Captaine
of her Majesties Guard, Warden of the Stanneries, and Her Highnesse Lieutenant Genrall of the Countie of Cornwell*, to declare the book *part of the world's*

romance and its details *fatally imprecise*. Like Raleigh's first readers, I'm charmed while I mistrust the writer of *The Discoverie* but will testify that he threw his cloak down on a puddle so the Queen might not muddy her royal shoes. How did this story of gallantry find its way to the lower grades of a working-class Catholic school in the last century? It was said by Sister Philomena that Raleigh may have been of the Catholic faith! A shy woman, fingers fumbling with her rosary when the Monsignor came to bless us once a year. Movies have made much of Sir Walter romancing the Queen (best Tudor pick, an unleashed Bette Davis in *Elizabeth and Essex*, '39, in which Raleigh is demoted to an ex). Fool's gold in the Hollywood Hills, or on the banks of the Liffey:

> *Sir Walter Raleigh, when they arrested him, had half a million francs on his back including a pair of fancy stays. The gombeenwoman Eliza Tudor had underlinen enough to vie with her of Sheba. Twenty years he dallied there between conjugal love and its chaste delights and scortatory love and its foul pleasures.*

> —*Stephen Dedalus, June 16, 1904*

In the books, it's a real estate nightmare; Raleigh's lordly house and estates awarded to him were now swept away, his many titles and privileges discounted. He had written clever sonnets, failed at setting up the colonial settlement in Virginia, introduced the potato to Ireland, deported the Irish as slaves to the West Indies; then, to patch a tattered reputation, he set sail with a hundred Englishmen to discover the place called El Dorado. How does a life so documented become a costume drama? A naïve question you'd say, but you're not here to keep me in line, manage the facts. Sir Walter's legend outwits history.

Godlike in naming the new world, he embellished the many pages of *The Discoverie* with maps of mountains and rivers, the exotic customs of each stop along his way in the Empyre, titles of tribes, names of chieftains. He returned with the glitter of marquisate in worthless schist to ornament his big book with authenticity, most particularly when reporting the wonders of Manoa, a city never seen. *And if Peru had so many heaps of Golde, whereof those Ingas were Princes, and that they delighted so much therein, no doubt but this which nowe liveth and raineth in Manoa, hath the same humor, and I am assured hath more abundance of Golde, within his territorie, than all Peru, and the west Indies.* Writing his way out of failure, his account is hearsay of a crystal city, rumor that a secret door in the side of a mountain, when opened, would reveal the treasures of El Dorado. War had depleted the Queen's coffers. Sound familiar? Ordered to bring back gold, he had only a book writ out in a bold bluff of words. That there might be little or no gold was contemplated before he set sail: the report of his Caribbean adventure would then be worse than a lie, a fiction. He lived in disgrace, though not for writing his *Discoverie,* a best seller. The Faerie Queen—bloodless in old age, blanched as we see her on-screen—*passed,* as we now say. The Elizabethan world over, the Stuarts were now free to find cause. King James committed Raleigh to the Bloody Tower on a conspiracy charge long delayed. Sir Walter collaborating with the Spanish! Not likely. Confined in comfort, he turned to the possible certainties of science. Something like a gentlemen's club in the Tower: poets dropped by for a visit; chemists worked their experiments in half-light cast through narrow windows. Aubrey tells us that here the mathematician Hariot wrote to Johannes Kepler on the refraction of light, solving the mystery of rainbows. Lady Raleigh lived comfortably with her husband, Wat, and their servants. The prisoner wore elegant cloaks, lace ruff at his throat. By a little shed next to his garden, he worked on his herbal elixirs and the desalination of seawater. In this pleasant confinement, he wrote *The History of the World*; how's that for reach? Can we understand that in the entanglement of what was now Jacobean politics, the King demoted Walter to schoolteacher, sent his son to be tutored by his prisoner? *The History* was in part a textbook for Prince Henry, who loved working with Walter, did not love his father. Imagine the young prince leaving the great world of the Court for the Tower to read along with the scholar who began his course with the Creation, proceeded ever onward, invoking the wisdom of Aristotle, Virgil, Sir Francis Bacon. The myth maker Ovid, of course. Yes, Sister Philomena, Sts. Paul and Augustine were among those called upon to verify Raleigh's version of First Days, which has a geography beyond our schoolroom imagination, as in a chapter: *That Paradise was not the whole earth, as some have thought, making the ocean to be the fountain of four rivers.* Mapping Eden, spinning the globe, sweeping the ancient nations of the world into the timeline of each day's lesson. Turn back and you will find politics in the Preface. A pair, these two, Prince and tutor devoted to the stories that give the lie to the Divine Right of Kings, to the very King, Henry's father, who was the historian's jailer. While the other boy, Wat, took himself off, attempting to get bloodied as a soldier in imitation of his father. *The Historie of the World* ends in 168 BC, long after the expulsion from Paradise, the waters parting, the Flood, the glory that was Rome, though before Cleopatra put the asp to her wrist, before the year of our Lord, before the destruction of the great Library of Alexandria, before St. Anselm proposed his ingenious proof of the existence of God. We may wonder, plying our search engines, how Walter knew so many stories—of Egypt and Macedonia, the Golden Fleece, the trials of Ulysses. He'd been to Oxford, ever bookish, don't you know? But that doesn't answer the question how he proposed that the *Ark rested upon some of the Hills of Armenia,* or *How the Romans were Dreadful to All Kings.* He borrowed heavily from the library of the great antiquarian Sir Robert Cotton. We can imagine the couriers toting these precious volumes from Westminster to the Tower; even presume that Cotton *assisted* in the writing as did Thomas Hariot, and of equal merit, a clergyman, Dr. Burrel. *All, or the greatest part of the drudgery of Sir Walter's History, Criticisms, Chronology, and reading Greek and Hebrew authors, were performed by him for Sir Walter* . . . so says Benjamin Disraeli in a spirited debunking of the encyclopedic work which bears neither footnotes nor acknowledgments; copyright four centuries down the lane, but we need not speculate about *The Historie of the World* ending abruptly. The Prince, gone swimming—just a boy skipping school—drowned in the polluted waters of the Thames. The tutor's job ended. History came to its close, a provoked and provoking entry in the new book culture, another best seller for Walter.

He was now twelve years in the Tower. Antony would not die of love. Rome would not fall. There would be no room at the inn of some little Christmas Carol town until Sir Walter thought to spring himself with a sequel, a second search for El Dorado. Raleigh's proposal: once more for the gold! James I bought it. Sir Walter, now old and ailing, was up for the fund-raising, not for the voyage. I believe the writer of *The Discoverie* was taken in by his own story spun of dross. He could turn its pages, *Imprinted at London by Robert Robinson, 1596,* to find, in the sparkle of his own words, marcasite turned to gold. How pleasurable to open a book of our own making. Or how shameful, until he thought to spring himself with a sequel. That war, this war depleting the treasury, as with Columbus' repeated search for El Dorado.

Never should have begged and borrowed so liberally from his wife's fortune, to commission the ships. Still, he was sprung from the Tower. He took the Product with him, his son Wat still yearning to be a soldier in the grand manner of his father, his once upon a time hero who now sent him off with the faithful Lawrence Keymis, an Oxford professor who gave up a scholar's life for belief in gold, who had sailed with Walter first time to Guiana. Never should have Swisser Swatter, Swisser Swatter sent your boy up the tricky Orinoco. Sweet Sir Walter had mapped his bailout from the Tower by pure conjecture, the historian rewriting his past. Old soldier with a hacking cough, cruising the waters off Trinidad, old gardener searching out botanicals for his elixirs, idling while Keymis and his son were long gone on their adventure, days slipping by on their quest.

Time is displayed in a half dozen places in our bourgeois mother lode here at the El Dorado—on the bedside table, pantry wall, computer screen. In the corner cabinet, each hour my father's self-winding pocketwatch guards my mother's handiwork—her clay figures of Joseph, Mary, Babe in a cradle—time on my computer and on my wrist the sleek, numberless museum watch you gave me years ago. It's half past whatever as the morning hours of my incarceration slowly tick by; no wonder that in Trinidad, waiting for word of good fortune, time stretched long and lonely for Raleigh. *Will that kid ever come home?* Surely you remember me sleepless, waiting for our girl's key in the door. Well, time had stopped for Wat, an ordinary mortal, ordered to stay clear of the Spaniards his father taught a harsh lesson at Cádiz, the enemy who, after the century of bloody battles, were now to be pals. King James desired more than diplomatic relations with the handsome Spanish

Ambassador, more than close friendship. But Wat, up for a fight, provoked the Spaniards, was ambushed, the bare truth of it according to Keymis, who killed himself having failed as the boy's protector, his suicide a great sin against God according to Walter, who cruelly condemned him, which supports Sister Philomena's claim, fantastic and girlish, that the Courtier was Catholic. She turns from me, flips her veil so as not to soil it with chalk dust as she approaches the blackboard, or not to hear me complain: *How was he a Catholic, Sweet Sister, when often charged as an atheist for liberal views?*

When Sweet Sir Walter wrote to Keymis, the moment of forgiveness had passed; and in a letter to Lady Raleigh: *I was loth to write, because I knew not how to comfort you, and God knows, I never knew what sorrow meant till now.* This was the true end of his spirit. We may find it painful, his story carrying on and on. Home again, home again, nothing to show but debts and pre-Columbian trinkets plundered from the Spanish, you know. I'd rather not tell the story of his feigned sickness, or his botched attempt to escape across the Channel to France with that pair of fancy stays, just give in to gossip. The King, a fop troubled by his loss of the Spanish Ambassador, as well as his unpopular rule, moved in on Walter's case, tried him for trumped-up crimes, old and new. Back to the Bloody Tower, a short stay.

Never loved by the Irish, those with recall of his ruthless injustice when, still the Queen's favorite, Raleigh ruled over them. Sister Philomena might find cool comfort in more than the legend of his cloak thrown on a puddle, if she ever thumbed through an early chapter of his *Historie* to discover *That man is (as it were) a little world: a digression touching on our mortality.* Though he is loved for the soft spoken reserve of his last days, and for revising an early love poem to his wife, writing it out in his Bible. In my confinement, I search for your Viking Portable Elizabethan Poetry with a broken spine.

> Even such is Time, which takes in trust
> Our youth, our joys, and all we have,
>   And pays us but age and dust,
>   Who in the dark and silent grave,

> *When we have wandered all our ways,*
> *Shuts up the story of our days,*
>   *And from which grave, and earth, and dust*
>   *The Lord shall raise me up, I trust.*

Each line a penance. And Walter is loved for his dignity as he was led to his death. Dressed in black silk and velvet for heaven and history, he spoke to the crowd: *So I take my leave of you all, making my peace with God. I have a long journey to take and must bid the company farewell.* He felt the honed edge of the ax. *This is sharp medicine, but it is a sure cure for all diseases.*

Nothing in his life became him like the leaving of it, but those are Will Shakespeare's words, the butcher's son, as Aubrey noted, an actor of some merit who was writing of another soldier's death.

Daybook, November 20, 2007

The old pipes will not splash our way till four. Inconvenient for laundry, and for infants, a new crop wheeled through the lobby. We have multiplied. I nod until my white moon face comes into focus to fetch their smiles. Family, mostly a friendly sort here, though I am wary speaking of family: you, my love, the correction officer my brother, the dear departed, and grandchildren who live nearby are fair game. But I will not puff with pride or disapprove of our grown children, run to third-person honesty in tattle time. Two out of three are killing themselves with nicotine. The stepdaughter dresses as if she is sixteen, not fifty, knows the names of the supporting actors on cop shows. One fuses bok choy with tamarind while he performs the lost art of joinery; the third, my own, educates me with a subscription to *ARTFORUM.*

See here: the self-reflexivity of modernism versus artist as criminal Duchampers. We're let loose to plunder the world, don't you see, quo-quo-quoting. You even quote yourself!

When we lived on 10th Street, pre–El Dorado, we saw Duchamp every day. He crossed the street early to put in his time at the chess emporium. He gave up art long before you were in third grade.

All three children run, lift weights, are given to excessive self-preservation. They are sure I court sedentary death in the clutter of my back room, that my addled head will slump onto the keyboard or I'll fall to my death reaching to a top shelf for a book I didn't really need, did I? Need that shard of information—*Mercury lent his winged shoes to Perseus. Bulfinch's Mythology,* weighty, slipped out of my grasp. I tottered, scattering the El Dorado clippings, *New York Times,* May 23, 2005: more residents ante up for the Democratic Party than in any other apartment house in the city. Head shot of Natalie Wood cast as Marjorie Morningstar in film of that name taken from the novel: Puttin' on the Ritz, the Morgensterns moved down from the Grand Concourse to the El Dorado. Gene Kelly, male lead . . . but really who cares if his theatrical snare captured the heart of an enchanted Jewish princess?

I've come down on this day for the tour. To give thanks for the etched-steel elevator doors, for the gilt and silver trim—sort of Egyptian or Aztec—on the lobby's high ceiling, for the marble fireplaces of no place like home and the latest generation of deco furniture, and for the imperial desk from the set of *Duck Soup* (Groucho Marx, loony president of Freedonia). I head back through our Promenade, where the mural of El Dorado lures the eye to a slick mountain of gold. First stop: Perseus. You see, it was necessary to reach over Calvino and Cather, above Austen and Auster, where mythology lives with those fairy tales aforementioned. Turn round in the soft light of the lobby and you will find his statue in an alcove stippled in gold. There on a marble pedestal, Perseus holds Andromeda in a swoon. She's had a wretched time, but is now free of her shackles. He sports those winged boots borrowed from Mercury, wings on his hat, too. He's flown down from up, up and away, or so we suppose, to be cast in the heroic moment, has saved the beautiful maiden from the Sea Monster. Her chains dangle. His bloody sword is cast down on the rocky shore where an elegant little scallop shell rests in the pebbles. Sculptor unknown who captured the moment of the young god falling in love. Till her hair fluttered in the wind, Perseus thought she was turned to stone. Misplaced but homey, the statue in its gilt cubby has nothing to do with El Dorado myth or décor. A middle-classy bronze to claim the residents were once acquainted with the classics, not Seventh Avenue,

not talking heads or rock stars, nor fans of *The Andromeda Strain*, New Age nuts fearing the galaxy just beyond ours. The Greek lovers in the lobby, fellow inmates can't possibly know, are distant relations to *The Angelus,* the bronze girl praying as the bells ring midday devotion in our dining room, an item that once held its place of honor in Bridgeport. In that grandfather's house with a broad staircase, she stood on a landing set before a stained-glass window, Tiffany of sorts. Grandpa had arrived at art. When the bells toll, the idealized peasant says her prayers.

Ordered the turkey?

Absolutely. An intentional turkey. How can a sixteen-pounder have slipped my mind? I rise to my duties, order the bird. It's the once a year call to the kosher butcher, some belief left from your childhood, though belief, as such, is far from your mind. Custom, you call it, a custom that a rabbi's surveillance improves the drumstick that you favor. The slaughter of the innocent fowl is clean according to a Son of Abraham, who kindly puts up with my lives of the saints, and at this time of the year with Advent Calendars I order for the little kids. Each day they will flip open another link of the story. Not *the* story, you say, giving advent your reality check. The dominant narrative is Pokémon cards, iPod shuffles—few candy canes in Santa's pack. So much for Mary approached by the angel of the Lord: *Do not be afraid.*

Ever cheery, the weatherman predicts sleet mixed with rain. You were right about the wind stealing through the old iron windows. Heat sucks the soul out of my struggling plants that will not be watered today while the children's terrarium flourishes, sweating in tropical splendor. I do morning e-mail—Cleo, Ed, GK, Bin and Paul tracking me down. To all: *I'm on El Dorado duty. Park not allowed today. Item: Sinclair Lewis lived in a vast apartment in the south tower gussied up at great expense by his lady love, Marcella Powers, who lived in Little Towers, perhaps a cubby tucked in line B. He called our El Dorado Intolerable Towers, though he could see the East River and the Hudson, the whole island spread before him. It wasn't Main Street, or Minnesota, Just "29 floors up in the air." Lofty loneliness, don't I know. Old friends still able to board his battered airship came round for cocktails. Americans had received his message. We are moral bumpkins, bewildered Babbitts, lynch men of hope. He'd made his move on Fascism in '35; about time, said his wife of those days. It* Can't Happen Here *was a comeback novel written five years after the Nobel, in which a Vermont journalist turns from passive belief in this country to active disillusionment, protests grandly, is sent to prison by Minute Men. You may see in Lewis' description of his hero's study, with few deletions and updating, a semblance of my own.*

It was an endearing mess of novels, copies of the Congressional Record, of The New Yorker, Time, The Nation, New Republic, New Masses, and Speculum (cloistral organ of the Medieval Society), treatise on taxation and monetary system, volumes of exploration . . . the Bible, the Koran, the poetry of Sandburg, Frost. . . .

Get the picture, though my back room is electronically amended and old toys are displayed on dusty shelves. Brave fellow of *It Can't Happen Here* is a journalist of the highbrow persuasion. With brash editorial rants, he named names—Father Coughlin, Huey Long, KKKs—connecting the homeland fascists of the day to brownshirts. Swastikas flutter in the wind. A triumph in the Depression when the Bund was still news, when the tin cup of the hungry came up empty. But in 1943, Lewis wrote a novel that irritated the critics. In *Gideon Planish*, he bashed America when we were at war. His son, Wells, died in that war on D-Day.

The day Lewis got the news, he took a girl, too young for him—often the case—kid from the Midwest, took her to the musical *Oklahoma!*, kept his loss in silence. I imagine him coming out of the show to the blacked-out lights of Broadway. I must suppose the hearty lyrics pissed him off—*We know we belong to the land, and the land we belong to is grand.* Well, it was grand to Lewis even in this forgotten novel where he had a fine time in thinly disguised portraits of Media Moguls—William Randolph Hearst, Colonel McCormick—the lethal power of their editorial clout. Planish comes on eloquent, citing greedy corporate committees, contracts signed in their interests—sound familiar?—alas made a hero, then a fool of himself. I can't say if the novelist mourned when the matinee date was packed off, a ticket stub in his cluttered life. But here's what I do know by way of Red Lewis: like Dickens, he had causes to pursue, the scold who lived upstairs for a few years; and that I'm not angry enough, just a girl of the old school who can't throw a pass. I conjure up the Cheerleader bumbling through his pep rally, megaphone concealing the folksy grin; then I reach down the paperback with messages once timely. *It Can't Happen Here?* Condi sets the mood with a Bach partita as we bid farewell to habeas corpus. Where's the body to fit the crime?

I'm well aware my soapbox is cheap wood that splinters. I expect my brother's reprimand: *Mims, don't ask easy questions not appropriate for* The Historie of the World. *Who remembers that endless rubbers of bridge and bootleg booze reigned in the White House, Harding administration? '68, student riots, April or May?*

I retaliate with silence, with visuals: The Nast cartoons of Boss Tweed that brought him down. Chaplin playing Hitler, blows the world into a balloon, flips it to destruction with the tip of his toe. In *The Disasters of War,* Goya gives each horror a one-liner—"For this you were born," "There's lots to suck."

THE " BRAINS "

Mucho hay que chupar.

Guernica gathers silence.

You call, checking to see I'm in lockup, as ordered: *The turkey?*
    Kosher organic! We talk mashed potatoes, no turnips.
    Not breaking the rules of my confinement, I descend once again to
the lobby. *I dreamt that I dwelt in marble halls, with vassals and serfs at my side:*

terrazzo will have to do, movie-
set palatial—mirrored, German
nickel frieze of arcs, futuristic leaves and sleek posies.
The good men who keep track
of us are members of Local
32BJ, Service Employees International Union, not Beefeaters

in medieval finery guarding a tourist tower. Dogs sport raincoats today. Newborn, size of a rump roast, swaddled under plastic. Psychiatrists, folders held close to their chests, go the midday route back to their consulting rooms. Hello darkness, fantasy, revenge surfacing in notes of their listening profession. Kurt Eisler—do you remember how dutifully he walked his little white dog? Keeper of the Freud papers, Dr. Eisler was not given to idle greetings. To the end he practiced analysis as set forth by the master, so we were told by a fellow who inherited a brewery, detailed the wealth of his dreams every day to Dr. Grump, who was patient with the nips of his dog. Long gone, along with the adman who jogged to death on a Christmas morning, and the Irish doormen and deskman— plump, good-humored like the boys I grew up with—and the skeletal woman working out in the gym, last seen as cult figure in an arid landscape as we switched channels, switched back to hear her hooting at the moon. More than goldbricks and gossip—no celebrities, please—as I greet fellow inmates, though never to reveal what might be called the plot with maximum honesty. Or why I must not venture, a personal story.

It came slowly, the pain. First, a muscle pull, a familiar wrenching as when transplanting the laurel with a spade. Cold days had come on, Autumn giving way to deep frost. We had retreated to the city, drawn back to the rags of time that are to end my four seasons. As though they are mine, like Vivaldi's, Poussin's, Balanchine's Four Temperaments? No indeed, like the plain *Old Farmer's Almanac* with its solo turns of useful information and oddments of stories.

The pain in my left shoulder blade, intense. You were just home from the office, said I must see the doctor. We went together in search of an immediate poultice or pill. I answered the doctor's questions. Then you were answering the same questions in the emergency room while an intern slid me onto a gurney. The boy—I say boy, having heard you report the date of my birth to one attendant, then another—moved with grace and speed hooking me up. We watched my crazy bleeps on a screen. The intern was working off his assignment in ER. How easily we chatted once the pain subsided. The heart would not be his practice.

Sports medicine, aiming for the healthy ticker. Which seemed impolitic as we watched the erratic performance of my heart.

Healthy to begin with?

Healthy at the finish line.

Recalling how I sparred with a particularly smug student. *What did you like about Kafka?*

Didn't like him at all.

I lay with others in a state of emergency. Some hoped for a bed, others to be dismissed with a warning and a prescription. The young woman next to me had been beaten by her husband, perhaps a broken jaw, a story she was eager though painful to tell. A babbling old black hat bobbed his head, his mumbled prayer joining with songlike moans of a young woman in a head scarf. All others were silent, waiting to be transported to the next lap of their journey in the belly of the beast, Mount Sinai looming over the Park. The dumb show of TV at a distance. Vials of my blood taken. You tucked the thin blanket over my toes, asked questions that seemed to the point of my pain, recorded the nurse's evasive answers.

On our way to the hospital in a cab, tears stung my eyes. Tears of pure pain, addressing the hurt at hand, differ from tears of grief. Idle tears are for memory of a grandfather's keloid half finger; for a trick-or-treat boy who lost his belief in transformation; for a villa not reclaimed in Innsbruck, sold by a wealthy widow in Houston to the highest bidder.

I said: *Lamentations.* We were holding hands. We are given to fleeting caresses, swift kisses, gestures of enduring affection—soppy, were it not countered by our well-honed give-and-take. *When you go home, you'll find the Bible . . .*

I'm not going home.

Foolish. They're taking good care of me here. In fact the doctor—not the one in training for the healthy heart—Dr. Shah is on my case. He'd like to know if I admire Salman Rushdie. He most certainly does. I'd rather have remained anon when you filled out the form. Not a vital sign, my backroom profession. You'll find the King James next to The Executioner's Song. *Often it's just where a big book fits on a shelf.*

You'd not go home till Dr. Shah turned you out. He pushed my gurney to a quiet hall. *You see,* he said, *I have little time to read.*

I did see, and that he's Bollywood gorgeous, his white coat left open, the better to display a preppy polo shirt, jeans that attain to perfection. We agreed that I'll make a list—stories and novellas only—while he went off to the next patient and the next, Shah's chosen practice being the infinite variety of emergency.

When I wake, the Park lies out my window. The very Park I must not walk in today is lit along paths unfamiliar to me, Fifth Avenue, East side of the Greensward. I'm alone with my monitor/minotaur tracking me. A nurse comes with orange juice and crackers. *Part of the rescue,* he says, then draws blood; they all do. *If you want the TV, you have to pay.*

I'll pay not to have it.

He's just come on duty. My rebuff may be first of the day. He knows how to handle me, lets me stand at the window.

The Gardens, I suggest. *Aren't they grand?*

He's never been to the Park, what with night duty, the commute from Queens. Two-thirty in the morning, the trains run seldom and late.

Well, it's all grand. Never viewed the Park from this perspective, craggy hills jutting upward. In daylight, a view of the Harlem Meer I've only seen mapped, a natural body of water, needed dredging to fit Olmsted and Vaux's Adirondacks scheme. So this is where you fished with Bimbo, threw your catch back according to the rules, though once you brought a carp home. Your mother wouldn't touch it. It lay on the kitchen table, the milk scum of death on its eye, hook still in its open mouth as if to gulp air till your father came home and wrapped it gently in the sports pages of the *Telegram*. You had wanted to read the Giants lineup against the Boston Bees. Carl Hubbell pitching.

Summer camp for that boy, your mother said, *he's best out of here.*

This story a shortcut back to the night I scanned territory unknown from the hospital window, plagiarized your memory while waiting for news of my mortality. When dawn finally came, I saw clear across the Park to the towers, just the golden pinnacles above the leafless trees. Waiting for a test we can't cram for, you found me in this room with a view, threw your *Times* aside in an extravagant gesture, read me words copied in your unreadable hand, words soon to be filed away with old postcards and Park memorabilia:

> How the gold has grown dim,
> How the pure gold is changed!
> The sacred stones lie scattered
> at the head of every street.
>
> —Lamentations 4:1

You knew as you *quoted,* that I never intended you should cart the big book across town. You had searched out a passage that would support your order, that for the life of me, I best stay home, tour the devalued El Dorado. Despite good news in the commodities market, bitter cold would come. Today, you repeated that old turn of phrase to confine me. *Don't venture.*

Turning from the love story of Perseus and Andromeda, we walk through a lofty Promenade to view the mural, our prize. There was a season in which I loitered here, rifling through my purse for wallet and glasses, ducking round to the back elevator bank to hear Pinky Zukerman in his practice room run through a rehearsal of Brahms or Schubert, his half of the Vivaldi Double, until one day when he was to play in Carnegie Hall there was silence. Billy or Patrick, one of the hall men, said: *He's moved out.* Abandoned, I consoled myself with Willy Pogany's mural, seen/unseen over the years.

Most likely the commission was handed to Willy by Emery Roth, the architectural designer of the interior of the building. Both top of their game in '29. Roth was senior. As an émigré kid, he picked up drafting skills, worked as a young man on the World's Columbian Exposition of 1892. Frederick Law Olmsted, Landscape Architect of that monumental occasion, would not have known an apprentice, but it's not beyond supposing that Roth, having come up in the world, had a mural in mind, passed the El Dorado job to his fellow Hungarian, Pogany. Murals were in fashion, the big picture rescued from the frame. Diego Rivera, Orozco came up from Mexico, where they painted history large as altarpieces, recasting religious themes. Clear political messages, that's what they were up to in the broad strokes of public art. For twenty-nine years I'd passed Pogany's *El Dorado* with a quick look-see, can't remember the day it came over me: it's theater, maybe political and not so simple. In the foreground, beautiful people—who bear no resemblance to Peruvian, Minoan, Trinidadian, or free citizens of Guantánamo Bay—are displayed in the extravagant flora and fauna of a legendary place. A dreamy girl lazing at the bottom of the canvas may be stoned on the tropical flora. Pasties on her breasts? Her double, saddled on a white steed, smiles upon a suitor serenading her with a lute. Vacant girls waiting for their cue while to stage right the indigenous are packing up to depart the scene. One fellow heaves a shipping crate onto his shoulder, same costume trunk as the extras and their vassals—pan-historical jerkins and tunics—same exotic paraphernalia of fronds and a bird never seen by Columbus or Raleigh. Even Audubon, blind and daffy in the swamps of Florida on his final search for every possible American bird, could not invent the extravagant plumage imagined in Willy's storybook scene.

A woman, elaborately draped, anxiously offers a sacred object, a casque that may contain some treasure of this fruitful place. The supporting cast may be headed for a flimsy arc that descends to—nowhere, really. Or, in Pogany's play with perspective, they're tripping to a point of darkness (8th Ave. subway?) while far above, a golden city gleams. We see the back side of the few who've made it out. Faceless figures, increasingly diminished, they appear to be everyday sorts, perhaps early residents of an apartment house, Upper West Side of Manhattan. Let's say it's Spring of '30 by the time Pogany set up his scaffold before the blank wall. He'd painted, etched, engraved beyond his wildest dreams when an art student in Budapest and Paris, illustrated a full shelf of fairy tales in London, designed Broadway sets, worked (uncredited) on Chaplin's *Modern Times*—Charlie mechanized in assembly-line frenzy. And then the murals, *Lovers of Spain,* for the Royale Theater; *Titan City* (1925)—the New York skyline from Dutch Village to cityscape of the future for Wanamaker's department store, yet another for Hearst's San Simeon, unfortunately not called into play for *Citizen Kane.*

Is it properly named *El Dorado,* the mural in our lobby? That woman to the left in the richly patterned shawl offers the sacred (?) casque, urging those pressing to exit the scene, take it along, an ornamental reliquary that might—just guessing—harbor a golden chalice, the Grail. He was a smart young man, Pogany, when he illustrated *Parsifal,* the gem of his Wagnerian cycle. He must have read each and every story to envision heroes and villains, make them particular to legends that came his way: Hungarian and Irish, *The Arabian Nights, Tanglewood Tales, Mother Goose.* I presume he did his homework in preparation for *El Dorado,* read of the crystal mountain of Manoa, painted it as a gilded glob, then lightly sketched skyscrapers on its glossy surface—faint towers, spires, maybe Emery Roth's apartment houses, so of the moment, flourishing despite bad times. Willy had just painted a mural for the grand dining room of Roth's Ritz-Carlton (1929). From that panorama of a French garden in all its rigid glamour, he next turned to the vision of our paradise lost, a futuristic ghost town looming (the building in default, rescued in a real estate deal). Why do the climbers on Pogany's frail arc want to leave their climate of plenty? Bottom of the canvas, there's plump fruit in a basket. Why sell out for the gold? Better take pleasure in theatrical allegory than lightly sketch yourself into shellacked gold. In 1931, Willy headed for Hollywood, the paint not dry on *El Dorado.* He set the pedestal twirling in *Dames,* a Busby Berkeley extravaganza of showgirls showing leg, girls as pure design in a rousing loss of identity. Synchronicity the message.

Stroll to the side doors. You discover the companion pieces. 90th Street: pattern of feathers and robes overwhelm the scene of lust or perhaps just yearning. There's that casque, and you'll find it again on 91st Street. It was just such a box, carved or bejeweled, held the Holy Grail, so we've been told. I know that legend, not from the pop novel with profane misinformation, not sexed for the screen, not even from Wagner's very long opera I once saw on a Good Friday, the tolling chorus of all those Germanic knights weighing me down with their sorrow. I knew the jeweled box that concealed the sacred chalice as I read *Percival* and *Parsifal* in college, each notable version. In my quest for more than a legend, I read into the night. My faith in the goblet with blood of the crucifixion, or a sword that bled crimson drops slow as a saline drip.

I toyed with Pascal's wager—put your money on God just in case. But insurance was for houses, the aged, not for a girl eager to chance it, flip the coin in her favor. I'd been given a single room—scholar, don't you know—squirreling away clues to support my disbelief in a postcard of da Vinci's *Last Supper* in which there's no chalice, no cup at all. Like my father mounting evidence, determined to win the case, state versus local swindler or punk. All I was up to, you see, was swapping one legend for another. Storybook for belief. Pogany's illustrations of *Parsifal* (1913) are grand, heroic yet light of hand—gossamer strokes of the boy knight's long quest, swift movement of an angel's wing.

The daughter who instructs me on matters pictorial, on what seems to float as art, balks at my scolding our muralist—*no style of his own.*

He was a commercial artist, your Willy. Why so hard on him?

I said his Parsifal *was lovely.*

Angel's wing! It's pen and ink, wash, color plates.

You haven't seen it, read it.

I'm guessing it has pretty endpapers, embossed leather binding, art nouveau tools of the bookmaking trade. Why can't you just love the murals, not search out his Holy Grail? Face the wall with your grocery bag, ice cream melting, enjoy the natives, whoever, enchanted by their props—lutes, melons, fantastic beaks of those birds. Forget the gift box, that kitsch. Maybe we're not supposed to know what's inside, what's offered.

But if they are having such a pastoral time of it, land of plenty, why leave for the city? Not a tree, not a bird in sight. Gilt hump of a deserted mountain, gloomy skyscrapers sketched in, no Emerald City. Men begged in the streets, families waiting for a handout of day-old bread. Brother, can you spare a dime?

Look, the murals aren't wallpaper, but they're not a big puzzle. They're fabulous however you read 'em. Your Pogany was versatile.

I suppose he did sign on for too many projects. In Hollywood on Parade, *he appeared as himself, that was just after* The Mummy, *before his carnival set of hell for* Dante's Inferno. *And besides he was happy.*

That may be a problem.

*I came to Hollywood where I am designing the sets for movies, which
I find very interesting indeed. I also married again in Hollywood and
I am living here in a beautiful garden, full of sunshine and flowers. I
am always working hard, because it is great fun and hard work to be
an artist.*

—Willy Pogany

In my dormitory room, my choice single, looking down on the
quad, I could see the watchman on his rounds. No Sea Monsters or Red
Knights to trouble a girl, no Peeping Tom come over from Amherst College seven miles away. My grandfather, as a young workman, had laid the
stone walks at Amherst when Olmsted's landscaping firm refurbished the
campus. That's how he heard there was this place of learning, Smith College for girls. That's why my mother was sent here to study mathematics and German, which may be why I dutifully turned from the window
to devote myself to the next adventure of Percival, the boy with a bleed-
ing lance sent in pursuit of grail, bowl, vessel or casque. The rag rug on
my floor was braided by an educated woman filling her days with craft.
She had chosen these scraps from the worn clothes of her husband, her
children, fragments with the sniff of our bodies upon them. Her thin lavender coat, the best she could afford, was looped round the red vest Bill
wore at Christmas before his waist gave way to belly. It may have been
that night when I turned from the lamplit quad, gloomy but safe, that I
first understood my mother's rug braided with memory was lumpy, not
beautiful, that it was never meant to be useful. No more than a story.

Waiting to hear from my brother, long as we're still standing. Sent
him the short tour, Andromeda, et al.

*Who is this Pogany? I gather jack of all trades, did that swell scene in your
lobby. Every post office had a mural, Works Progress Administration, courtesy of
our President.*

*Not till '34. Willy was never on the dole, but that desolate gold city, the sorry
descent of the emigrants. He may, after all, have been more than a touch political.*

*Mims, we'll be coming around noon on Thursday. Must have turnips, creamed
onions.*

* * *

I had not told you the full story when we ran through the nightly news of the kids large and small. You'd bought tickets to *Macbeth*. That would be later in the season. We spoke of missing the little house in the Berkshires, but wasn't it best, what with the price of heating oil? I could no longer manage the garden, put it to sleep for the season. We tracked the many presidentials, a fresh form of entertainment; were enchanted with one or another member of the press—last week how lame her questions, this week how sharp his reply. The message has long been the medium, an observation with no bite. Outrage was out of fashion: its gasping rhetoric of little hope. And wasn't I really, in my notes on the Cheerleader with playground permission to torture, writing an in-house memo?

In house. I had not held to my promise. My confinement in the tower these days had an alternate ending. I turned from the bleak horizon that cuts across Pogany's mural separating his road-show Eden from the chill city of tomorrow, walked back past Perseus transforming himself— killer to lover—and marched out the front door. Did it snow midtown? Had you stuffed the wool cap in your pocket? In my mini-climate it was snowing, the blustering rain swept away. Snow fell gently, translucent on the pavement. I felt a cheat not telling you, *confessing*. OK, I walked out the double doors—no coat, hat, scarf—to the doorman's wonder, crossed to the Park. As yet, the snow did not conceal the Bridle Path, or decorate dead heads of viburnum, the black limbs of cherry trees. Whiteness was a scrim, false hope the show might soon begin: prelude of lute song, paisley shawl from a trunk in the attic. Dr. Shah, free of emergency, reads a slim novella, my mother cuts a navy blue strand of my brother's confirmation suit. The set is splendid with the tropical fern of the kids' terrarium. An El Dorado kind of place with you as lenient judge of my folly. And I, an ancient Columbine, go it alone, leave this good scene, climb the slippery slope to the Reservoir Track, flirting with disaster. All I want: my footprint in the first snow of the season, faint proof that I still venture.

Daybook, December 10, 2007

ALL THAT GLITTERS

We have gone back to our custom of nightly news. Watching the world go by with a glass of wine, witnessing the heft of one more sandbag to the levee. Market up. Market down. Online, I sign up for the war to end, the one in Iraq; and—*late, late again for that very important date*—order Advent cards for the little kids, Hanukkah gelt for you, my love, your only religious observance an indulgence in chocolate coins.

Pasta pot on, isn't that where I started this account of last days?

Last of your Seasons.

I stand corrected. You want me to turn from gloom—a heartbeat away—to the comforts of my back room. Well, it's no spa—hot tub, herbal massage. I'm still mad as Quixote, the spindly knight. Lost in the tragedy of my bookishness, I share with the Don the illusion that tales are the true documentation of life. Wouldn't he be surprised to find that his flapping windmills are transformed into powerful creatures these days. Let me take Primo Levi's *The Periodic Table* off the shelf, find my place at "Uranium" in which the heavy metal of destruction appears in a story. A hoax has been perpetrated upon the writer. Cadmium, that's all the scary substance is when tested. Levi envies the liar his *boundless freedom of invention . . . now free to build for himself the past that suits him best, to stitch around him the garments of a hero.* Sounds familiar, and furthermore—the story brings to mind Hans Blix, the gallant diplomat who poked around for heavy metal in Iraq to come up empty. Best not go there, yesterday's news. Cindy Sheehan? Lost her son in the war, walked cross the country to let us know.

Furthermore, we head into the joyous season. You recall a family occasion, taking the bus up Amsterdam Avenue to St. John the Divine. Swaying to music of the spheres, we celebrated the Winter Solstice. That expedition brought on by the progressive school my daughter attended, the one that had her reading beyond grade level, that taught history—Contemporary to the Present. Contemporary was the Age of Aquarius. The headmaster kept the legends of his youth on life support for his beautiful people—his students who went on to tougher courses in life. I approach the longest night without a cyberfriend; with you in rational disbelief, with that daughter's cultural reach suggesting Christ share Christmas with the cultural devine; with my brother's wife correcting proofs of her study: *The Virgin Mary, Monotheism and Sacrifice,* Cambridge University Press.

You said: *We had a grand time at the spiritual hootenanny.* I suspect you came up with this memory of the Solstice as a distraction. You're clever in your attempt to amuse while keeping me under house arrest. For all the world, you now sound like my brother: *I thought you were attending to the Park across the street. Time running out.* **Do Olmsted,** Mims. *Go for the gold.*

FLO: AMERICAN IDOL

There is something biblical about Olmsted marrying his dead brother's wife. Or mythic—it's the way the gods behave. All is ordained—failure, death, transformation—afterlife granted. Frederick Law Olmsted limped. Trying out a new horse, he was thrown from the buggy, not the first accident in a life of recoveries. Mary and the baby were not injured. For many weeks he must heal, watch the workmen pry rocks from the soil of Pigtown, where the Irish squatters had lived in mud and pestilence before the territory was declared parkland. He watches the work in the Park from a window in the old Mount St. Vincent Convent, now split into offices and apartments for his family and his partner's, Calvert Vaux. He has recently been appointed (1859), with Vaux, Landscape Architects and Designers of The Central Park.

Directly across the avenue, the outcropping of rock is massive. It cannot be moved, must not be blasted. The Designers have figured it into the Park as God's gift, or Nature's, to wall out the city, though the city with its noise and congestion has not yet moved this far uptown. Olmsted is a moralist, not a religious man; God is assigned to his peripheral vision. When he was a youngster, he suffered some problem with his eyes, sumac poisoning suggested in the biographies, or maybe Fred did not want to study up like his brother, toe the line at Yale, where he dropped in for a semester to study chemistry. He is thirty-eight, a self-confessed dilettante, has left several careers behind—dry-goods salesman in the family store, seaman, farmer. Journalist and publisher were more to his liking. He had begged money from his father so that he might belong to the gentlemen's club of a "Literary Republic." An autodidact—man of letters, God help him, as many of his class hoped to be, though now he is a Landscape Architect, a title never figured, not even when he worked long hours with Vaux on *The Greensward Proposal,* designating Play and Parade Grounds, Lake, Terrace and woodland clusters of trees.

Mary Olmsted stands in the doorway of his room. He is bedridden, can't move to a draftman's perch to study the transverse route at 96th Street, one of Vaux's many inspired plans to keep the Park free of traffic. It is steamy August, no breeze from the ravaged land across the way. Fred can't turn to see his wife, though he knows she is there. He frets about absence from his duties. The crew clearing the devastated land should be working in the lower regions, where development is further under way. Mary comes to stand by his side. She is girlish, pretty in a white dressing gown, though remarkably pale. Before John Olmsted died, he had written to his brother, *Don't let Mary suffer while you are alive.* Early this summer she has borne Fred a son. Now he is a family man for sure. Though not experienced at this job of creation, he is confident the Park will be born of rich soil excavated where ponds are intended. All carefully planned with Vaux: *The deepening of the soil in all parts of the park is highly necessary, and the sub-soil must be loosed and fertilizing material mingled with it.* He sees that the men prying rocks out of the ground have wrapped their heads in bandannas so sweat tears of their labor will not blind them. Mary brings him accounts just delivered: Shrubs have come in beyond the estimate of 16 cents per, exceeding the $50,000 for trees at an average price of 33½ cents per. Care of trees now planted has mounted beyond the

$10,000 allotted. When pain streaks from thigh to knee to ankle, Olmsted reaches for his wife's hand. Their son will die of cholera the next week, end of August.

I turn back to his floundering youth. Fred was underwritten by his father in experimental farming. In Connecticut, later Staten Island. A farmer with literary aspirations. Like Jefferson and Thoreau, he cultivated. Like Virgil, for God's sake, in his story of a gentleman farmer who, while at war, wrote home about the planting of trees, the breeding of his cattle, of his crops and the care of bees:

> And someday, in those fields the crooked plow
> Of a farmer laboring there will turn up a spear,
> Almost eaten away with rust, or his heavy hoe
> Will bump against an empty helmet, and
> He'll wonder at the giant bones in that graveyard.
>
> —*Georgics* I

Turn back to the farm on Staten Island, family property we're told. Fred often crossed to the city, a clubman with influential friends, men with connections. Olmsted declared himself a journalist, assigned the farm to his brother, traveled to the South, territory unknown. Politically provocative, his journalism was a hit up North and in abolitionist England.

> An account in the city papers, Washington DC, of the apprehension of twenty-four "genteel coloured men" (so they were described). . . . On searching their persons, there were found a Bible; a volume of Seneca's *Morals; Life in Earnest, the printed constitution of a society, the object of which was said to be "to relieve the sick and bury the dead."*
>
> I can think of nothing that would speak higher for the character of a body of poor men, servants and labourers, than to find, by chance, in their pockets, just such things as these.
>
> —Frederick Law Olmsted, *The Cotton Kingdom*, 1855

In *Journey in the Seaboard Slave States,* fault him for Cracker and Negro dialect, but his travels were read as powerful news of "the economic mistake of slavery." Fault him for his paternalism, bringing along the blacks who, according to his plan, could buy their way out of slavery on the installment plan. *Free labor,* a lofty phrase avoiding the racial and physical brutality he observed when writing from the South. He understood the South as another country.

I'm not a fit biographer for FLO, can't come up with a dark underside or portray him as a flawed hero yet more than a superb groundsman notable for manipulating the live stuff of nature. His touch of moral arrogance—share that with him, I'm told. His dedication to modest living, book learning, the persuasive power of civility, I might call upon as a corrective to our greed, our embrace of schlock culture. My gentility is a crock; his was real.

That was a grand graduation speech, Mimi. Don't put yourself down.

I'm waiting till death do us part. He's too large, you see, yet too near. I walk in his Park most every day. Fred's not up for caricature like dear old Columbus, nor a CliffsNotes romp, life and times—Raleigh. She was right, George Eliot, the grand lady novelist who disliked biography: *the best history of a writer is contained in his writing.* FLO's urgent news written on the road from the South, his many letters, lengthy proposals, that's his best bio. At the end, his mind shattered; still, he wrote a plea that his gentle namesake, the Fred who survived, must get his fair share of the landscape business.

We're a pair, *Dancing with the Stars,* not likely, me with the cha-cha heart, Fred with that gimpy leg. When the time came, he couldn't sign up for the

war. His infirmity consigned him to the pressing trials of his job in the
Park. In *The Official Papers,* he is honest and direct, elegant as in *The Greensward Proposal,* chatty in his letters to Mary. He's entitled to lose his cool in
a resignation letter, long and very angry: *To the Board of the Commissioners of
The Central Park,* January 22, 1861. Politics—should have known—money
and authority withheld from the grand project under construction, withheld by the Comptroller of the Park Commission, Andrew Green.

> *Hard as it has been, I love the park. I rejoice in it and am too
> much fastened to it in every fiber of my character to give up, if I did
> not see that [to] go on so was out of the question—for me.*
>
> *To come back to the grand question of the cost of the work and the
> estimates. Am I responsible for the cost of the work, for the errors in
> estimates, for false information under which you have acted? Am I Sir?
> Then I am an imposter.*
>
> *I am not an imposter.*

Cut back in job and title, he directs good works of the Sanitary Commission, just founded to heal the diseased and wounded, bury the Union
dead. The name of the Commission is accurate; the circumstances on
battlefields, troop trains and ships, unspeakable. Begging for funds, he
knocks on doors in the Capital. The battlefields are littered with soldiers dying of dysentery, diphtheria, cholera. Wounded lie on the streets
of Washington. Troops in the field are poorly outfitted for whatever the
season. He appeals to the Union League Club, to women sewing shirts
for soldiers, strong-minded women who founded the relief committee.
After the defeat at Bull Run, he writes to Mary:

> *Sanitary Commission, Washington, D.C.
> Treasury Building, July 29, 1861*
>
> *Beloved!*
>   *We are in a frightful condition here, ten times as bad as any-
> one dare say publickly. . . . The demoralization of a large part of our
> troops is something more awful than I ever met with.*

Tell all our friends to stiffen themselves for harder times than we have yet thought of. Unless McClellan is a genius as well as a general . . .

Meanwhile, the elms on the Mall are settling into their second year. The Seasons are coming to life in the design of Jacob Mould, artist and engineer. Plump grapes, pecking birds, bees in their honeycombs will adorn the steps of Calvert Vaux's Bethesda Terrace. The artisans Italian, I presume.

The Park is ever on his mind. When, or if, Olmsted goes back full time, it will be to oversee finishing touches—drainage systems, a stream, a gorge. He hangs in with his Park appointment, demoted to less than half pay. The Sanitary Commission—commendable, poorly paid. He writes to Mary of the deserters, *spoiled for soldiers at Bull Run*, then adds: *Write to me and make the best of our affairs. I could not flinch from this now if it starved us all to stay.* Noble thought, yet Fred's war work is abandoned for money. Here's a cut of his life I'd like to give a swift pass (biographers not allowed): *We'll be two thousand down*, he writes Mary. In a misreading of Emerson's "Self-Reliance," he signs on to be the Superintendent of the Mariposa Mining Corporation, 1863. The Gold Rush back in '49: now all that glitters is schist (Columbus and Raleigh redux). The company's books are *beyond artifice in trade*—now ya see it, now ya don't—a shell game. He's out in California on his own, makes the best of it. It's El Dorado time.

Fred's better prospects lie with the natural world. He had gone West by way of the Panama Canal, where the flora, strange to him, was heavenly indeed. San Francisco is a rowdy port; its magisterial cliffs hover over the Pacific, bleak and uncultivated. In Mariposa he resists, then is stunned by primordial wilderness, the magnificent scale of Yo-semite, the violent cut of canyons, their towering heights, broad sweep of its valleys, the giant Sequoias.

To Mary, Bear Valley, 1863:
They don't strike you as monsters at all but simply as the grandest tall trees you ever saw. . . . You feel that they are distinguished

*strangers [who] have come down to us from another world,——but the
whole forest is wonderful.*

Grandeur before fruited trees.

Mary is spending the summer in Litchfield, Connecticut, settling into
the customs of her New England family. He writes from Bear Valley: *I
would much prefer that the children never heard a sermon, if they could attend
worship of a decorous character without it. And among sermons, the dullest and
least impressive, the better.* Often as I read FLO, he comes across as *lonely*,
the word bleating through news of his days, urgent requests for tents and
haversacks for camping, or a pause in the flow of geographic detail, lets
Mary know he is forsaken. Now she's with the children on Staten Island.
Fred sends her word of tasks that must be accomplished before the winter back home. He writes to Ignaz Pilat, Gardener in Chief of the Park,
describing in detail the tropics observed as he traveled through Panama.
Then, as though he has quite forgotten that the Park is no longer in his
care, he speaks of the pictorial and emotional use of light and shade, the
tropical density of undergrowth: *There are parts of the ramble where you will
have this result, in a considerable degree, after a few years—the lower stratum
being a few shrubs that will endure the shade and the upper low-spreading-topped
or artificially dwarfed trees, assisted by vines.*

An amateur gardener, I
count this my favorite letter,
not a biographer's choice, the
only time he writes a personal letter as a horticultur-
ist, plant by plant observed.
*Of course, it is the very reverse
of the emotion sought to be
produced in the Mall and playground region—rest, tranquil-
ity, deliberation and maturity.
As to how it is caused—I mean*
*how the intensity of it which I yesterday experienced is occasioned—it is
unnecessary to ask. . . . Because it is unspeakable.* All the landscaper's

vernacular of harmony, effect, the sublime is no use. In a show-don't-tell moment, he draws a little tree, vines streaming off its canopy to the ground.

He sends for his family. They make the best of Mariposa, live comfortably over the Company Store, camp out, take pleasure in the rugged territory of this West, its timeless lakes and extravagant mountains far from their natural habitat, the water effects and mild hillocks of the Park across Eighth Avenue.

The mines are mined out. Chinese are put to panning in streams of the Merced River for the least glitter. There's mention of an oil well, but primitive equipment can't drill to depth, no yield, though there will be in the spoilage plotted if—this year, next year, 2008—the protection of Yosemite is violated.

> *We ride every day to the top of the mountain, where Mrs. O and*
> *I are doing some child's play gardening work, and where we make*
> *tea—in sight of the Yo Semite & 5000 feet high—the change of air*
> *from the valley being delicious.*
>
> —Letter to Calvert Vaux, June 8, 1865

By this time his salary—reason he took the job—is no longer paid by the fraudulent board of the Mariposa Mining Corporation.

> *"Think of it? I think it is but a lot of granite rubbish and nasty glitter-*
> *ing mica that isn't worth ten cents an acre!"*
> *So vanished my dream. So melted my wealth away. So toppled my*
> *airy castle to earth and left me stricken and forlorn.*
>
> —*Roughing It,* but Mark Twain wrote of silver, not gold

Had Frederick Law Olmsted been hired to give stature to a bankrupt claim? Hard to make the best of that. Meanwhile, Fred improves the rowdy frontier within his reach. Discovering the culture of the Golden West impoverished, he establishes a lending library; writes a proposal to preserve Yosemite and Big Tree Grove as a wilderness park, first of its kind in our country. Out of a job, he thinks to stay on in California. To Vaux:

> *I can safely calculate on getting three times as large an interest on my accumulated capital, as I could in the East.*
>
> *Capitalists here generally regard it——the Santa Barbara & other New York Cal Petroleum companies——as stupendous swindles, ala Mariposa. I think they are not swindles but they are gambles.*

Meanwhile, Mary Olmsted plans a camping trip that will take her to fourteen hundred feet. Pert and smart, solo adventures suited Mary who did what she pleased. He invested in a vineyard, growing grapes in the sunshine, a good gamble. Why did he come back to New York, to his work in the Park? It's never explained in his letters. A speculator, not a biographer, I'm curious, the detective's daughter. In my hometown of Bridgeport, the Park City, we have two parks, Seaside and Beardsley, both by the Olmsted firm. When he was young, my grandfather broke rocks for the seawall down at Seaside. I rode my bike to Beardsley in the North End, fed my lunch to the caged deer, never knew the park maker's name. Olmsted's improvement of our city was all that we had by way of recreation: a dig in the sand with a view of Long Island Sound; a miniature zoo with monkeys, chatty parrots, a few peacocks fanning their tails. Meanwhile, Singer Sewing and GE chugged in slow motion during the Depression. By the time I was twelve and rode my bike to one park or the other, the factories had geared up for the war, that war. It would be a while before I knew that our country, coast to coast, is blessed with extensive Olmstediana, before I took an interest in Paradise Pond on my college grounds and those of Berkeley and Amherst, Prospect Park, and looked into the City Beautiful Movement with its many consoling cemeteries.

There is something unsettling about Olmsted's swift recovery from his misfortune so far from his upright Yankee world. I believe——biographers allowed?——that letters from his partner, Calvert Vaux, the more experienced landscape artist, goaded him to invest once again in his profession.

Vaux was the little guy, a transplant from England, trailing the great man, working with earnest devotion at his job in the Park. His talent was immense. I forgive his overinvestment, his devotion to storybook nature and the picturesque, and his corny rustic benches and arbors. He designed the most elegant ironworks of the era. Machine-tempered, his bridges adorn the garden across the street. Fred's swagger cast his partner in a supporting role. Vaux cared about that injury. They had it out in long letters during the Mariposa years, heated exchanges raking over the past, settling into a quibble about titles awarded to Fred: *Superintendent, Architect in Chief.* Yet they were bound to each other. Vaux's letters to Olmsted woke me from the archival swamp sucking the adjunct biographer under. As though hovering above the rectangular dream of the Greensward, Vaux viewed from on high all that the city and its people must yearn for—Ramble, Meer, Cascade, Parade Grounds of his democratic vista. He is faithful, passionate, true to his dream. For a while I believed I'd fallen in love with the wrong man. Vaux staked his impossible claims for art—a heartbreaking proposition, don't I know. To Olmsted, 1863:

> I am mixed up in these affairs and am proceeding in a very half and half sort of way for alone I am a very incomplete Landscape Architect and you are off at the other end of the world, depriving the public of your proper services as I argue. My position is that the art element ought to have been the controlling element. . . .
>
> In all this I may be mistaken. You may be no artist. You may be Nap III in disguise. You may be a selfish fellow, who would like to get power & reputation on other men's brains. You may be a money grubber. You may have no patience &c &c, but it is to be presumed by my acting as I do that I think differently and that I am under the impression that the humble modest artist spirit is within you. If so, and if you can, taking art in its widest sense, devote yourself to it, your chance was never better than it is today.
>
> I believe the Park to be the big art work of the Republic. I have always felt it would be mean on the part of its makers to let the success

be an administration success—it would seem as if they were ashamed of their work.

CALVERT VAUX

Olmsted would not take on the mantle of artist, not when he returned to resume his work on the Park, not when he was pleased with the Brooklyn Park built in continuing partnership with Vaux. Just a landscaper, difficult to place him in *Lives of the Artists,* or *Saints,* or demote Fred to almanac entry, a touch of the recoverable past, with my grandfather heaving slate stone to his design, nothing to gain as in working the pathos of Columbus begging for royal privileges, or the mythmaking of Raleigh's El Dorado preserved in our haute bourgeois lobby.

Old and exhausted by his trade, Olmsted is persuaded to sign on as Landscape Architect of the World's Columbian Exposition. He is seventy years old, could not resist the offer, was brought on board for his fame, I suppose. Built of insubstantial stuff, the exposition's White City is faux classical: imperial boulevards, Greek pillars, and many Italianate domes draw more than the calculated millions to the four hundred years of progress and entertainments on the Midway Plaisance. Olmsted attempts to soften the architectural grandeur with greenery, then retreats offshore to create his Wooded Island and Lagoon with a Japanese temple.

The man-made Lake had worked in Central Park. Why not make Lake Michigan perform? His refuge from the White City's vulgarity is planted with tropical flora he admired in Panama and Acapulco. The imports wilt in the heat of the Chicago summer. By that time he had moved household and business to Brookline, Massachusetts, where his sons prosper in the family trade. I have trouble forgiving him. We both found our way to New York from Connecticut's manufacturing cities. Olmsted had a good run, Park rupture and all. Now the Boston Brahmins sought him out for their Arboretum. It was time to think of industrial growth disfiguring the city. He designs small arboreal jewels to ring round Boston, the Emerald Necklace, and enjoys the refinement up there, I suppose.

For seven years, a long decline, he lives with Mary in the McLean Asylum, taking what pleasure he can in its conservatory gardens. Does he know he designed them? They are maintained in their glory. Dr. Bhuvaneswar, once my student, walked her troubled patients on the healing woodland paths during her residency in psychiatry. I find the famous landscape gardener online: the portrait by John Singer Sargent, weight on the good leg; weak eyes dreamy, turned inward. Fred's posted between r h o d o d e n d r o n s — buds swollen, flowering kalmia and the last blooms of shad, the native dogwood that flares white among the

pines in our scant acre in Monterey. He's on the grounds of the Biltmore, the Vanderbilt estate in North Carolina, his last commission. Olmsted was for an Arboretum, not the simulacra of an English village to be set within the grounds. He disliked the clearing, mourned the loss of trees here and across America, joined in the first efforts of reforestation. Still sharp, Fred had saved the sequoia forest back in Mariposa days, yet he now detected his mental dislocation. Sargent's portrait—moving, though I prefer a photo of the old couple picnicking at the asylum: He's propped by a tree, straw hat shadowing his vision, lost to this world. Mary's abandoned herself to a patch of bare ground, frizz of white hair in disarray.

Olmsted is not at once informed of his partner's death—a suicide, some biographers claim; that dramatic note in keeping with Vaux's passion. Arguments with the Parks Commission again: He designed, then demanded that the drive for traffic to be built along the Hudson River must have a scenic walkway. One hundred years later, the promenade is near completion. It ends at 125th Street, at a wharf with sturdy benches, frail saplings, a stunning view of the Palisades.

Olmsted's writing is the best history of him: in his papers, I find notes toward an essay never finished: *The Pioneer Condition and the Drift of Civilization.* Not surprising that he returned to his literary calling to speak of the wilderness as rough and uncivil. The Chinese serving the miners were miserably treated; so were the Indians. Olmsted's lending library was a gentleman's gesture in the surround of guns and whiskey, barroom brawls. Desperados! Ever the reformer, he aimed to take our beloved Westerns out of the West, but that show already had its run. Buffalo Bill Cody was quick on the draw at the White City. For twenty years Indians had staged war dances at Barnum's American Museum on Broadway. All he wanted, for Christ's sake—*Mimi, your language*—was a civil society. At Mariposa he had sketched out proposals for a school, perhaps a dry-goods emporium like his father's in Hartford. He suggested that a journal, the *Nation,* be founded, and served for a while as an editor. I do not imagine he expected that its liberal views would be widely distributed among the semiliterate staging their barroom scenes. For *The*

Pioneer Condition, he read up as his mind clouded, all sorts of enlightening books: Goethe, Thackeray, Washington Irving. The fragments of that essay read as notes for a sermon he could no longer deliver; yet he's fine in his overreaching to *make common cause with all who are inconsiderably abused*. Still dusting off the phrase "Literary Republic"? He surely read Mark Twain, who wrote the frontier story strong and true in *Roughing It*, 1872. Absorbed on his return from Mariposa to the unfinished business of Central Park, gentrifying the Wild West was not as pressing as slavery when he traveled the seaboard states. Like Huck, Fred lit out for the Territory but turned back to the *sivilized* city.

He treasured the albumen prints by early photographers Carleton Watkins and Seneca Ray Stoddard, who went out West to deliver breathtaking news of the scale at Yosemite, the great height of El Capitan, the massive trinity of Three Brothers, luminous sunlight on Lake Tahoe. I imagine (biographers are not allowed) that Fred came to love this landscape far beyond human design or estimate per bush and tree, though at times he was equally overwhelmed by the beauty of his Park, the great artwork of the Republic.

Olmsted finally allowed that he had raised his *calling from the rank of a trade, even of a handicraft, to that of a liberal profession——Art, an Art of design,* which would have pleased Vaux, but the letter, written to a lost love of Fred's youth, was private.

I'm urged to walk in the Park each day, a short way, no Reservoir Track, though not long ago I spotted an owl near the North Pumping Station. I disobey, find my way to the Dairy, now a gift shop, where poor children were once served fresh milk, or I settle for a favorite bench looking over the field that was Seneca Village. I seldom make it as far as the Mall, where I once again wonder at the statue of Fitz-Greene Halleck set on his pedestal, *sic transit gloria.*

I wish we could go to the Bandshell, dance to Benny Goodman on a Saturday night.

Goodman played Carnegie Hall, remember?

I remember we had a 78.

* * *

So, forgiveness sought. I never meant to cast Olmsted as a bronze of some note to take his place in the Park along with Lincoln, Daniel Webster, Beethoven, or the Angel of the Waters. I never meant to withhold him, just couldn't figure where he comes in. Everywhere—that's the trouble, public and private. I remember my mother laying out the braided strips of rag on the dining room table, then with a big needle lacing the strands together. The rug was oval and smooth. With wear the lumps appeared and a bit of unraveling, as in my dormitory room. Before she married the detective, my mother taught Latin and mathematics.

Still, there are places I must know above 96th Street, what goes on there. Someone is needed, you or a Virgil, to lead me. Olmsted said little about that territory, just, as he lay with his broken leg in a splint, that the mighty black stone should not be blasted. He had something in mind, a vision. Disabled by his injury, he watched from his window, the clearing of the impoverished land. Mary caring for him while their child was dying. The war pending.

> *This song I sang, having sung about the care*
> *Of fields, and trees, and animals, while Caesar*
> *By the deep Euphrates River thundered at war. . . .*

We are at war. We tend to forget. The *Georgics* was a civil war poem. And the bees, I think they had it figured; a near-perfect society building their thyme-honored hives, stopping in midswarm to spin a story. Working hard, of course.

> *And gloriously sought Olympian heights,*
> *Of idle studies, I,*

I tend to forget . . .

> *who bold in youth*
> *Played games with shepherd's songs and sang*
> *Of how you lay in ease in the beech tree's shade.*

ZENTRALPARK

Now Cleo or my brother will say, *Professoressa*, don't do the Walter Benjamin bit. It's simple, really, simpler than the book Fred never could bring himself to write, the big study of our American culture, its triumphs and deficiencies. Benjamin, another moralist, master of the essay as life and death force, called his work in progress *Zentralpark,* a place he'd never seen, hoping he might get to this mythic greensward in the US of A. Fleeing the Fascists, he didn't make it over the Pyrenees to freedom in Spain (1940), was turned back, paperwork not in order. That night he killed himself. The story of his famous lost briefcase often told: *You must understand that this briefcase is the most important thing to me. I cannot risk losing it. It is the manuscript that must be saved. It is more important than I am.*

I would love to have talked with him.

You said: *It wouldn't have worked out, you know. He would have been forty-eight. In '40 you were a ten-year-old girl.*

I know he was already honored and with no time granted. Later, but there was no later, he would have been old beyond listening to a college student who muddled her way through Grail legends in lousy translations. But just to talk with him, about old toys and the voyage incarnate of postcards, that's all. To turn the tin key that set my clown tumbling, admire the dolls made of corn husks, folk art of our Depression. To confess the burden of my clippings and too many books and the fetish of The Angelus, *our enslaved object, watching over us in the dining room, praying as we gobble our turkey. My acrobats risking their tricks in thin air mock her bronze immobility, their bodies unlimited. Though I would argue with him, given the nerve and the chance—You were wrong about information stealing life out of a story. That's such a romantic notion. See, it's all different now. You have to live it, live with the glut, the lottery prize of mechanical reproduction and still tell your story.*

Now we must get ready, pack enough for the journey, hope our credentials for the artwork are in order. Time bends.

Sequence of words were crystallizing events into a picture, almost a story.

—Doris Lessing, *The Memoirs of a Survivor*

She thought about Macy's ad, young men modeling sweaters—crewnecks, cardigans with zippers, no less. Her husband needed just that, trouble with his stiff fingers. In the morning she buttoned the cuffs of his shirt before he went to the office. Christmas coming on. Everything on sale now that money was tight. A trip to 34th Street on the subway was verboten, of course. She was never to go down those steps to the C line, a promise made months back. Never venture out in a storm, however light the rain or snow.

Take a cab. A chorus of them ordering her about, even Kate, who, on the day she turned ten, auditioned for her nursey role with comforting hugs, and on Thanksgiving pulled out a chair to settle the old lady at the festive table. Grandma imagined the Norman Rockwell poster with herself painted out, an enormous roast turkey levitating above the fixin's on the *Freedom from Want* table. The family assembled with her best middle-classy china, the Limoges gravy boat and the bold **B** embroidered on the Irish linen napkins.

Take a cab.

It was ten days before Christmas when she discovered the ad. She had not mentioned Macy's, just shopping.

What I need, he said, *is nothing you can buy.*

Sounds sweet, but controlling. She countered their hovering with therapy-speak. They were all on her case. She gave them an unlovely snort she traced back to the McCarthy trials, which only one of their three grown kids recalled from a PBS special. Why her imitation of the Senator from Wisconsin sucking air, heavy-breathing his discourteous answers? Why remember now? Her first political protest was ladylike, the flutter of a red scarf when Joe McCarthy spoke on campus. Different from family politics, surely. Her husband had been *enabling* when she read him entries in her daybook, cheering her outrage at the wars in progress. He joined in her despair that harsh judgment would never be leveled at the thugs in power. Now her anger was spent, a bad investment with little hope for a future rally. These past weeks had been *passive,* an entertainment of watching hopeful and hopeless presidential candidates, rating and berating their performance as they balked, strained for position at the starting gate. She had called him *supportive* of her effort to rewrite a book for her own satisfaction, the war story that won a prize, to find some honesty in her own history and lives imagined in the fiction. Still, it had been a good time, Thanksgiving packed away, Christmas looming. These brisk days, he no longer encouraged her to take a short turn in the Park. They set up a festival of silents. Yet another look back, movies seen when they were children, often seen again in art houses when out of college.

He said: *First seen at the Trans-Lux, Madison and 85th.*

The neighborhood Rialto in Bridgeport. If the Diocesan newspaper agreed that Chaplin and Keaton were no threat to our morals.

Propped in bed, they laughed once again at Charlie and Buster, delighting in the voiceless overacting, the honky-tonk sound track, fancy footwork of the great comics—the triumph of grace over klutz. The gags, famous routines—Chaplin eating his boot in *The Gold Rush,* twirling the shoelaces like spaghetti.

He said: *It was licorice, don't you know.*

For once she didn't, but knew Keaton did his own stunts. Watching *The Great Dictator,* they were again enchanted by Charlie's dance with the balloon globe, continents skimming the oceans, a fragile world awaiting Herr Hynkel's flip of destruction. Alas, he crossed over to talkies. The ghetto was a pleasant stage set, and when the Jews avoiding the camps fled the city, they settled in a land of milk and honey, pet goats and darling children, costumes country cute.

In disbelief, she said: *Nineteen forty! He's gotta be kidding.*

I faked my age to enlist in the army. They didn't take me, not then.

The Little Tramp. How could he?

Just making his movie. They watched till the bitter end. Chaplin's urgent message was delivered by the waif Paulette Goddard playing to the lens, the aura of hope in soft focus of trees and bright sky behind her: *The way of life can be free and beautiful, but we have lost the way. Greed has poisoned men's souls— has barricaded the world with hate—has goose-stepped us into misery and bloodshed.*

Stunned by the blind hope of patriotic spiel, they sat through the credits, through the warning: This Movie Not for Commercial Distribution. . . . She would have been eleven by the time *The Great Dictator* came to the Rialto. Had she accepted the clean cots and cozy blankets dealt out to prisoners when the timid Jewish barber was sent to a camp? Or, moved by the bleating finale, teared up at the warning of what might come? *If I had known then;* not the excuse of a grown girl, but of the director, Chaplin making amends for this ambidextrous movie. Not one of his silents—quite noisy, in fact—the story of our Charlie enacting pathos while Herr Hynkel was dealt the best routines? Chaplin, played against himself, failing as both the little guy and Hitler. It was a miscalculation. Blather and bladder of a deflated balloon.

But walking up Madison Avenue . . . He remembered leaving the theater overcome with purpose, *I was awed or just in love with Paulette in her peasant blouse. I stopped at a bar that served me since I was fifteen, though I couldn't buy my way into the army.*

A regime was established: an embrace of the ordinary. She was not to be treated like an invalid, not that you'd notice. Light cooking and trips down to the lobby—the big adventure, mailing small end-of-year checks to assorted good works, Mercy House among them, an old house in Bridgeport refurbished to help needy women getting on with their lives. She liked that Mercy was down near Seaside, the Olmsted Park her grandfather worked on, building a seawall when he was no more than a boy. She took out his studio portrait, the one in which he wears the diamond ring on the injured hand with that stub of a finger. They had moved on to Hitchcock,

his dark tricks, and to a production of *Macbeth* staged in a warlike present
with electronic projections. Why not tread on the Bard in old Desert Storm
issue? And why not, taking care, meet friends for dinner? She insisted on
six, six-thirty, tops—knowing she'd tire, not follow the comfortable chatter,
too weary to twirl the pasta, cut the steak on her plate. Often table talk
eluded her. She seemed to be somewhere else, though once, in a moment of
bright recovery, she let go a less than sympathetic remark on the Murrays'
grandson in rehab. Her praise of the other child, the scholar, was lavish.
That girl—no secret she was bright—now reading *The Gallic Wars.*

*All Gaul is divided into three parts! The Gauls didn't succumb to ruination
by way of Rome, the decadent culture. We must take note.* Her schoolroom
remark hovered in the air, then: *And take care with our children: They're all
we've got. We're finished.* That erasure of the Murrays' ongoing lives, Joe's
pacemaker, Sue's hip replacement, called for a change of subject.

He said: *The boy who painted our fence in the country sent us an e-mail. He's
in Afghanistan now crawling the mountains, not the Berkshire hills. I miss his
simple messages ordering brushes and tarps.*

Wasn't that a year back?

*Two years. They just moved him up from Iraq. He disapproved our choice of
paint, Gettysburg Gray.*

One night at the Kleins', she dozed off while Naomi enacted scenes of
a Broadway musical she suffered when her sister came up from Florida.

Mims?

She woke in alarm to dead silence, a hush of pity.

In the cab going home: *It can't have been more than a moment.*

It was nothing, he said. *Naomi trashing the teen musical was tedious for us all.*

He began, a stealth move, entering the back room where she worked.
The lockup, as she called it, was off-limits. Still, he made bold to shove books
stacked on the floor to the side so she'd not trip. Colette, Marguerite Duras.

Scrap them, she said: *I'll never read those French women again. Licking their
wounds.*

All of Gertrude Stein? Once adored.

Poor Gertie. The roundabout of her stories is too grand altogether. Her Irish
put-down pasted on Stein discards. A surfeit of biographies to go, four
of Lincoln, three of President Wilson. Benjamin Franklin and V. Woolf

saved; all murder mysteries of the genteel British variety out, every professorial turn and turn again that smacked of a time when she was into cultural geography, simulacra. *All that old stuff, untranscendable horizons.*

Head bent to the side, he read off the titles of a potpourri concocted for a seminar. Her final time out, she'd faced off with homegrown reality— *Parents and Children, Sentimental to Scathing*—the daily bread of family life had been her concern: Dickens, Kafka, Welty, Flannery O'Connor. She had called the course an indulgence, published an offbeat piece on Rudy, the dead child of Molly and Leopold Bloom, "The Phantom of the Liffey." Her close reading imagined the boy as a shade, most probably a suicide. Joyce wrote him into the dumb show of memory. And what did the scholars say? Go back to your tales, don't tread on our dreams. He puts the "Phantom" offprints aside, but not on his life would he touch his wife's clippings or postcards; or her old toys, still treasured. She had dusted them off for Christmas—a celluloid Santa, tin clown on a tightrope, windup Loop the Loop plane, a mini semaphore that properly belonged with the old train set, her brother's. The little kids would find them under the tree, where they'd have a brief moment of attention before LEGO City was torn from its wrapping. Just that once, he made brave to tidy the discards and duplicates, then retreated to the evening news when she called him *invasive.* All in good humor of course, of course.

The dark red cardigan zipped right up to the neck. She should call, have it sent, shop online, but the trip to Macy's was planned as an adventure. She plotted the day. Avoid the subway as promised. On the corner, catch the bus. Her view had been so limited to Park and apartment, to doctors' offices, the favorite restaurant with friends. The journey midtown might now seem unknown to her, unreliable as the city dealt out to tourists on a double-decker, a bus that stopped across from the refurbished El Dorado to tell tales out of school—who's prime time in the towers, which actor has reconciled with his wife. Old news: Faye Dunaway, the writer of a *Superman* script, Groucho Marx had all lived there, a child actor quite forgotten. Robert Mitchum, Marilyn Monroe, golly! And Patricia McBride, the prima ballerina of the New York City Ballet, not in the guide's spiel, the vision of her remarkable body, once upon a time, in the C/D elevator. And would they care about the woman journalist, seldom in residence, risking her life in Pakistan? Unreliable news: a member of the City Council, under investigation for misappropriation of funds, grows heritage tomatoes on his terrace. There would be such tattle, tourists in pursuit of their holiday, post-Towers New York. When she settled herself on the M10, it would pass the Park all the way to 68th, turn toward Lincoln Center, then down to Columbus in his Circle, past the daylights of Broadway to Macy's at 34th. A harmless excursion proving she took pleasure in the city, in public transportation, not a back-number housebound. No taxi, thanks a lot.

Shopping days flipping by, when she finally geared up, went down to the lobby, a grand specimen of blue spruce was jammed against the high ceiling. Professionals were trimming the tree with large silver balls—glass bells, silent and chill, dangling between them. From the bottom branches, icicles skimmed the surface of empty boxes officially wrapped, blue satin ribbons on silver.

So Bloomingdale's, she said to Pedro. Pedro had been with the building since he was a boy. Well, a young man just out of high school. Peter, he had been called then. At times she reverted to the old name, as she did now. *Peter, remember the origami?*

Beautiful, he said. *Sure, I remember.*

They watched an agile young man in a Santa hat climb a metal ladder. He clipped the top of the tree. Still the star did not fit. He clipped again and there it was, the Star of the East, shimmering plastic. On the front desk, four bulbs were lit in a tasteful menorah.

Pedro remembered that people had come from all round to see the origami tree. The folds of paper in many colors were magic. *It was done by an artist,* he said, *Japanese.*

She had thought the origami was the work of a single mom who lived with her pierced daughter, north side of the building. But no, their only role was to place the creatures great and small on the branches. *It was an artist,* Pedro said.

She remembered the many cranes mixed in with tigers, birds, unicorns. She sat on the bench meant for visitors or for residents of the building expecting children home from school, or waiting comfortably inside while Mike hailed a cab. Well, she was just getting her breath before the journey. Tonight she would remind her husband of their origami encounter, not of the cold-comfort tree in the lobby. They had gone one evening to the Ducal Palace in Genoa. A tribute to a local painter, the mayor was to speak. They arrived early with a group from the Villa dei Pini, a haven for visiting writers and artists, and for the historian combing through the Ligurian resistance (1943–44) to the British bombardment of Genoa's port. He had found an old fisherman with war stories more compelling than the dry record in *i documenti diplomatica*. Properly invited in both English and Italian, the group from the villa wandered through the local master's retrospective—vintage oils of the old city, what was left of it, genre views of the Mediterranean surround. The artists from New York had been restrained in their judgment.

A limited palette.

He catches light on troubled water, fair is fair.

That evening her husband had worn a tie and blazer. For the first time, she put on the black dress bought in Rome. They were chauffeured down the twists and turns from Bogliasco into the city. Now they idled in the grand piazza, waiting for the *omaggio* to begin. Someone said: *There's time to see the photos.*

What photos?

Of Hiroshima.

A different exhibit altogether. Dazed by scene upon scene of destruction, they shuffled slowly by the dead—dead in the rubble, dead on the road, the scorched eyes of a mother standing above the body of her child, a pack of felled dogs and the hollowed-out wall of what may have been a temple. No building, house or field spared. They had seen such pictures soon after that war, though not so well framed. Hung row upon row on partitions cleverly forming a gallery within the restored walls of the Palace, they were—stunning. The photographer, Magnum she supposed, though no name, no titles, no commentary given. Not needed. When they emerged in silence to the bright courtyard of the Palace, they came upon origami papers being set out on a table. A student, appropriately solemn, handed them notice of *One Thousand Cranes*. Years ago she read the story to her daughter—not read to the grandchildren, not yet, perhaps never— about a girl with leukemia, one of many in the aftermath of that infamous day. Sadako had folded a thousand cranes in hope against hope of good fortune, folding until she died. Her story became a book, a documentary, a Peace Project, and here they were, *i stranieri* in their finery attempting to add to the millions upon millions of cranes. The artists from the villa folded swiftly, flapped the paper wings as though their birds might fly. Her husband had attempted folding flap over flap, then stuffed lire in a lacquered box for the cause.

Mike was in his doorman's uniform, vaguely military—brass buttons, gold braid on the cuffs and lapels. *You OK?*

She was just fine. A small audience of residents and staff going about their day had now assembled, waiting for the tree to be lit. *Tutti Genoa* had waited in the piazza outside the Ducal Palace. Waiting was part of the show, a time to be seen, to see those invited. Then the black cars arrived with many officials. She caught at words in the mayor's praise—*molta brava, sempre con cuore*. Receiving the honors of the city as his due, the artist had a touch of old-time Bohemia about him—trim white beard, silk ascot, above-the-fray importance. He set a floppy straw hat aside, the familiar headgear of Matisse, who painted just across the border in France, which brought to her mind the exuberance of the master's bright rooms with harem women, bold patterns of rugs and shawls, windows open to sunlit views. That night after dinner, they had left her fellow artists and scholars, walked under the tall pines. The garden sloping down to the sea was the pride of the villa, though seldom used. Planted years ago—no one quite remembered when—its famed succulents were now monstrous, swollen.

Unearthly, he called them.

They sat in a grotto. Broken pillars and shattered urns mimicked a ruin, once a romantic setting of decay, now merely spooky. A heavy breeze swept up from the shore. He took off his blazer, placed it over her shoulders. Tomorrow he would fly back to New York, back to business.

She said: *I'll be fine. Get you out of my way.* She was writing, attempting to write about a local boy, Columbus. Though how was she fine when touring in recent days she could not climb the streets of Genoa with ease? Here in the garden, her breath gave out on the trail leading up from the shore, so they sat in the damp of the grotto.

He asked: *What did the mayor say?*

Extravagant things. The artist captured the soul of the city, l'anima della città. *I doubt the painter knew he shared the palace with a thousand cranes.*

There's some comfort in being provincial.

From their perch in the grotto, they could see the last ferry of the day coming into the Stazione Marittima. They had wanted to cross to Tunisia while he was with her at the villa, but there was more to the hillside towns along the coast than they had imagined, more Roman ruins, more breathtaking views. And she was here to work, after all. The lights in the *sala da pranzo* had gone off in the villa. The fellows had finished their coffee and little glasses of Amaretto. The garden, abandoned to moonlight filtering through the old pines, was illuminated once again by light from the library above. Now the historian would be telling the novelist and her partner, newly arrived from Glasgow, the old fisherman's story, how he'd row out with his father as if for the catch, how they had signaled to the gunners on shore.

Can you figure, she asked her husband, *which side the fisherman was on?*
Fascist.

Partisan. It makes a better story. A little band in the hills alerting the Royal Navy.

As they made their way up to the villa, she put on his blazer. In the pockets she found the crumbled origami, his failed crane.

Snow was predicted. The last possible day for the venture to Macy's was bleak, though you'd never have known it when the Christmas tree was turned on in the lobby. *Ahs* of wonder. The natural beauty of the spruce outplayed the glitz. Now she would go to the bus stop wearing her green puffy, feathers escaping at the seams. Not a coat to wear out to dinner, or to the theater in their regime of ordinary pursuits. They had tick-ets to late Beethoven tomorrow—or next week?—their old custom, a Christmas concert. The quarters in her purse were heavy, sixteen in all to get to 34th Street and back with the dark red sweater. In the confusion of her back room, she had not found her senior bus pass. Or the taxi gang had taken it away, looking out for her welfare. Slush in the gutter was fro-zen. She took care not to fall. If she had remembered her cell phone, she might stomp her feet, call her daughter at work in the gallery, sputter with laughter at her adventure. Waiting seemed forever. Finally an M10 approached.

Going the wrong way, uptown. She ran across the street against the light, a cab swerving to get out of her way.

He whispered, not expecting an answer. *What in God's name were you up to?*

Not God's name. What I'd figured all along. Unfinished business.

A man walking his corgi had found her at 106th Street, halfway down the steep steps glazed in ice, quarters scattered. She thanked him in what he recalled as *a lively fashion,* took her home in a cab, the playful corgi nip-ping at her boots. He would not take the cab fare offered by Pedro or Mike. Rummaging through her purse, she found a dog-eared notebook, took his name—a Mr. Kunkel.

The kindness of strangers, she said. Kunkel was the butcher in Bridge-port who was, of course, plump, while this Mr. Kunkel was lean.

What were you up to?

She would never forget waiting with her mother while German sau-sage poured from the grinder. *It glistened, all that fat. Such innocent times. I was handed over by Mr. Kunkel, escorted upstairs by Eduardo.*

He begged her to cut the false brightness. *It doesn't cover your crime.*

On the following day I was lonely. Not like Olmsted yearning for the comfort of family. They'd all come to see the ruins: an aged wife and mother who breaks the rules, hadn't she always? The little kids brought the chocolate treats they like best. When the pleasant surveillance was over—then I was lonely.

Daybook I wrote on the yellow pad but did not record the month, the year. I was missing my people, not family. You will think I'm heartless, or just headed in the wrong direction again; unbalanced as in a pratfall down icy stairs. I could not return to a spill of words that charted the passing of this year. I looked to the usual suspects posted on the wall of my work-room to find Borges—the blind poet; V. Woolf, eyes avoiding the camera, gone mad in time of war; Raleigh in fancy dress—always. Only Dickens held me to account. On the old Christmas card, he's without desk, pen or paper; slumped in a chair, eyes closed though not dreaming. Figures, alive in his stories, are sketched all about him. What was next for the rumpled old man in house slippers? I lay aside my legal pad. Found a story I started years ago, ballad of a lonesome girl never finished. There was a scene in the Park, snow and a soldier, a love story perhaps, one I might honestly tell.

I'd lost my Park City of Bridgeport, was scaled back to Central Park, the limited view. I once had the whole spread, quo, quo, quoting myself— with revisions:

> *Thus the attractions of our city will never diminish, for they are continuously satisfying, as though we have dreamt them in one of our pleasurable dreams, and the vision, perhaps richer in texture if we recall for an instant the picturesque urchin—Sissy settling on a stoop with her grungy gear, her wandering nights and days, endurance without calendar. She seeps through the cosmetic skin, enters the host body, the city unscathed.*
>
> —*A Lover's Almanac*, 2000

But we cannot turn back to those innocent days.

Earth Angel: The Waif's Prologue and Tale

Sissy believes she remembers the black smudge on her brother's face and the smell of scorched wool. Her mother said the scar on her arm would go away. It's nothing dreadful; a patch of thick skin on her right shoulder. Her mother had plucked her out of bed, wrapped her in a blanket, the fire traveling fast, eating up air. Perhaps she remembers her brother playing with matches or an old picnic table with candle stubs stuck in oily tuna cans. No electricity, they were that poor. The cottage was not theirs. They were squatters. She spoke of the fire as an accident, not a crime. It wasn't memory, just what her mother wanted her to say about the family coming to an end, how they had set themselves up in this abandoned place, hiding out till they were evicted, how her father had been arraigned for arson. Rich people had no use for that cottage. Now no one would ever live there again.

Her mother had an eye that strayed. Sissy could never tell when she was looking at her or at some place far away. Well, the fire was the end of Lyman; that was the father's old Yankee name. They never found him those years ago, just that he ran off; that was the story. The fire was written up in the *Eagle* with the little one treated at the hospital for second-degree burns, but that item—so sad—got her mother work in the paper mill. They waited for Lyman to return. In time Rachelle, that was her mother's name, settled in with a man who trucked in pulp to the mill. Then it seemed Sissy and her brother became left baggage. Did she remember that her mother was pretty, despite the wandering eye? Father Rooney said it was a gift from God, the eye finding its own way. Rachelle had been raised strict, a Catholic Canuck. The priest was especially nice to Sissy, though her mother wasn't married and had a baby by Matt Baegler. That was the trucker's name.

Many years later Sissy would ask her brother why, just like her father, she ran away. Was it taking care of that colicky baby while her mother and Matt tanked up at the tavern on Lake Pontoosuc? As though she could begin her story the day she got on the bus, not when her own father struck her or Matt felt up the bumps on her chest. She was visiting her brother before he went on trial for just a small stash and DD violation. He couldn't say it was the continual screech of that kid or just she was flunking out of school. Stay out of trouble, he told her when he gave her money to get out of town. She had a plan, going to find her friend Debby who sent her a postcard from New York. Debby had a baby, one that slept, never cried, and why didn't Sissy come on down? They could make it together. Now, she does remember that the fake ID said she was sixteen and her name was Margaret Phelan. She had been just the sister in her family. Sissy stuck. In the Port Authority, a woman at a newsstand asked, real sweet, like she was lonely and wanted to talk: *Why aren't you in school?*

Well, I am, Sissy said. *I'm doing a project.* Should have said, *None of your business.* She picked up *Newsweek,* leafed through it to show she was smart. Asking her way, she had walked to the place Debby wrote out on the postcard. It was a store where the woman spoke Spanish. An old man slumped on a cot behind the counter. She showed the woman the postcard Debby sent up to Pittsfield.

Cariña, the woman said when she looked at Debby's postcard, a tabby cat kissing a mouse, but knew nothing of that baby and mother. The old man sat up straight to say, *Nevah, nevah,* in English. And Sissy understood that he must say it often to people who came to the shop—*Nevah, nod here.* There were saints and candles, a smell—the weed Matt Baegler smoked, only heavier, sweeter. The statues were of Mary and her Baby, of St. Christopher carting the Holy Child across a stream. Tin hearts pierced by arrows hung on the wall. New York had seemed like she expected, walking uptown from the bus terminal, too many people. Louder than the city on TV, but she had not figured the distance. What had she expected of Debby who wrote down the name and number of this street? She stood in the heavy perfumed air of the shop thinking no place to go, nevah back home. It was as though she'd always known how to palm a Milky Way and mints. Later she would find out why the candy was stale; that bodega on Amsterdam didn't sell sweets. It was when they saw her spit out the mint, she met Little Man and Tony. They saw the tag tied onto her gear up in Massachusetts to get her on the bus safe to New York. She would tell Father Rooney they were not bad guys, Little Man and Tony, only street people like her for a while. Not the full story. It was cold toward the end of the year. She had packed up on Christmas. Her mother sat watching the snow with one eye, massaging the baby's belly so it wouldn't cry. But it did, it did cry. They had not named it yet. It was a girl. Sissy had been given a red wool cap, that's all, and she put it on for the holiday visit with her brother, who asked, many years later, how she stole out of there, out of the company house near the mill with her big canvas zip bag. Their mother wasn't looking. *You know how she was, off somewhere.*

When she came back, Father Rooney pulled off a deal. He dealt with the mother. *You get that baby baptized, I'll take care of Sissy.* He arranged for foster care, wouldn't be the first time, till she was eighteen. He said: *Till your ID isn't fake anymore, Margaret Phelan.* The priest was the only chance she had in this life, a plump dude in black pants and a Patriots jersey makes him one of the guys, a smooth dough face too often smiling. But as he drove her to Springfield, to a childless couple who needed the money for her care, he's wondering, keeping their last hours together light with "Stardust," "One for My Baby," Matt and Mama's music she hated, he's wondering what would become of the girl. The girl who was half dreaming of her time in the big city, of Tony picked up by the cops in the Park on New Year's Eve, how she dodged the crime scene with Little Man, who wasn't the meanest. How she had kissed a soldier, just this guy, kissed deep in his liquor mouth. It was no joke—Happy New Year. He held her, and they fell in the snow. He pushed off her hat, kissed her hair. Wore that cap soldiers wear, and he wasn't a soldier. For some days, she stalked him, knew where he lived. It was like love, she supposed, wanting Soldier to see her, to see Sissy, the girl picked him out of a snowdrift, kissed him, tongued him. She had Soldier's cap with silver bars.

Captain, her brother said, *where'd you get that?* Has it still in her zip bag with clean jeans and sweaters for whatever, wherever Holy Rooney is taking her.

How's about we stop for a burger?

One more for the road, Sissy said.

Father Jack wondering what will become of the girl.

Sissy waits for Miss Montour, coming with a companion. She comes alone every Fall, drives up when her tree turns, other times, too, but Sissy's only seen her twice since she's been working at Mercy. Each year they set out the green canvas chair by a little table for Miss M's morning tea. This year she's late: Her husband has died, and she stayed sorrowful in the city until the bright leaves of her sugar maple are mostly gone. There has been a discussion, almost a meeting: to rake or not rake. Some of the students say she might like the rustle of leaves. The rakers won with their argument for tidying up and put out a pot of sunny chrysanthemums. Two canvas chairs are set side by side on the grass gone brown for Winter. Sissy's job will be to show their visitors the rooms ready for them up in the tower. Miss Mon-

tour will sleep in the administration office on the foldout couch, queen size. Her stepson is assigned to the little waiting room just beside. A cot has been donated by Rich's on Main Street for the occasion. Smiling at Sissy, she will say, *Call me Marie,* as she did last year, but that's hard, hard to imagine they are just pals talking over the season at Mercy, planning ahead for the cold season. Like, please can we turn up the heat at six-thirty? Mothers come early with their kids if they have jobs, even if they just work here at their lessons; their fingers go stiff at the keyboard waiting for hot coffee, muffins not out of the oven.

But, of course, use common sense, Miss Montour laughing at Mrs. Laughlin, who runs Mercy, Pat who's too shy to find anything funny, too sorrowful about the whole world. So, it's warm in the playroom when mothers park their children on a cold day in Fall and cool in the Summer with central air-conditioning, an extravagance in the Berkshires. Miss Montour billed for whatever the cost. Sissy in Target jeans, turtleneck, new windbreaker, looking smart with her hair clipped close, bright golden hair always her problem, something of a come-on she never intends, a local girl, no Madonna. Chill day, Mrs. Laughlin, Pat, wears the navy blue suit makes her look like a nun, which she was before she fell for Mr. Laughlin.

Now he's gone of pneumonia last year, and she's moved into the back parlor of Mercy, her saints on the bookshelf, her small-screen TV, the closet stuffed with not one pretty outfit.

Sissy is waiting on the porch of the old house where she works teaching women to learn English, read, cook good food for their children, to take care of their bodies, temples of the Lord. That's what Father Rooney calls them, not women with breasts or heavy butts. She's not laughing, not really, when he turns away from a mother breast-feeding her child. Pat says he's a throwback to holy innocence, not even a priest of this time. Sissy calls it arrested development. Not a term allowed in the classroom. She is taking Human Growth and Development at the Community College, the emphasis on normal growth in the human life span, three credits. Holy Rooney is very old but like a child needs structure, the matins, what's that? Evensong no longer remembered. Has needed the Church, a system outside the family, though he's been her father, all she ever had. His life stage is nearing death. It is stupid to think of people that way, like a chapter in a book. Turn the page. What's her life stage, trapped twenties, living with her wall-eyed mother who flashes the credit card at Sears, with the crybaby and biker brother in trouble again, and caring for kids at Mercy parked in the playroom while their mothers punch the keyboard—*ay, linda,* they call her—switching off with a volunteer, guiding achievers through Microsoft Excel. This morning Sissy should be reading the dynamics of conformity, stupid stuff—how we follow the leader like mice in the Pied Piper story. But then she may not be going to class tonight to discuss how we all kiss ass to whatever's going down. It's a special day, very, with Miss Montour coming and Father Rooney's last visit to Mercy. He will be somewhere nearby where old priests live together doing their thing, praying and watching the Red Sox win the pennant in a replay from heaven. He's skinny now, like the air's been let out of his body. For a while he has not been all here, forgetting her name, his car keys, and why he has come to the front hall of the house where photos of Spanish families and black women in graduation gear hang on the wall. He is now driven by a parishioner to visit Mercy, where he taps the heads of the children and slowly flips through the easy books the women are reading, like they were written in a language he never learned.

At last a car turns in to the circular driveway, a silver SUV. Miss M calls out to Pat and to the women who have come onto the porch waiting with Sissy for their patron's arrival, the staff eager to thank her, the students to show off their children, their skills. The man with her is reality handsome with a shadow beard like he's on vacation, jeans poured tight on slim thighs. Laughing as he comes round to hand Miss Montour down from his car. So what's funny? The flock of women with an old priest propped on his cane? Someone back at the rectory has got Father in full clerical dress-up. Miss Montour, call me Marie, goes first to Pat Laughlin with the peck on the cheek, then to Sissy, kissing, ruffling her bright hair. Miss M's different from before, gray at the roots, her face stiff, unsmiling. The death of her husband chills the Autumn air. To the north, clouds threaten Mount Greylock. The widow turns to the leafless tree, her maple you would think here from the beginning, at least from when her family built the house. Not so; at great expense she had it planted full grown when she restored what was left of the grounds, turned the house into Mercy. Father Rooney has lost track of his mission. Just as well, the dear departed who married Marie Claude Montour worshipped at the altar of World Food and clean water, had no use for his prayer. Without Father's blessing, the tour begins of the nursery, study rooms. Lights in the computer lab blink for attention.

You're Sissy, Ned Gruen says.

So they say, her flip answer a conscious decision. Initial care to be taken: the dynamics of attraction must not be put into play. They have made it up three flights to the tower with overnight bags, just Sissy and the man who's not Miss M's son.

Heard about you, he says, expecting an answer.

Here's your bed. It's a cot. Hope you don't mind.

With a slow burn of a smile, he takes in every inch of the girl, tousled bright hair to new sneakers scuffing nervously at the carpet. Longing to go back to her duties, to the safety of the lunchroom with the special treat of pizza or mac and cheese, both if you feel the need. And why would he care for Pat Laughlin's report—four Colombian women have passed high-school equivalency, or flu shots once again free. The silent auction beyond expectation. There would be talk of an elevator to the tower. Sissy would like to be there, do her take on Pat puffing upstairs.

The house set on fire, he asks, *where was it?* He stands at the curved window of the tower looking down on the old public school with boarded windows.

Other way. So now they are facing the strip mall, only the bakery and thrift shop still open, nail salon come and gone. The house set on fire, will she ever hear the end of that story? It is now Miss M's to tell and tell again, how, as an angry girl, she ran through the woods and there was this little child in a cottage with golden hair. Now this guy knows it, so thinks he knows Sissy, the angel baby of that tale. Well, the middle is left out, no-show father, dead flesh of the burn on her shoulder, making out with her body in New York, the loco parentis who fostered her. What she remembers of two years in Springfield, cleaning their loveless house, swiping their moldy tub with Clorox, closing her door against the clattering *Wheel of Fortune*, the siren screech of *ER*, then being ordered to close her book, turn off her light, so costly. Approaching eighteen, she was allowed to come home, home to her mother who could not look her straight in the eye.

She thinks to say the little house where she lived with her family, the house that went up in flames, is now the ramp where a cop car cruises to the bypass, bypass to highway. She says, *It's safe here for the women and the kids. Some come on buses.*

Yeah, I know. He knows who pays for that service and that Marie Claude has looked into the price of an elevator. Glad he's made the trip up here. It had always seemed improbable, a house by this name. Sorry his wife did not come.

Hey, she was invited. Six months down the road, going to have a baby, so.

So? Felice Martinez comes down from Lanesborough in her dinged Toyota with twins in her belly, every day writes down new English words, but why would Sissy, an angel, want to say that? She hands over

Pat Laughlin's best towels and lavender soap, how after the long drive he might want to wash up.

He catches her going down from the tower. Their hands touch on the newel post, withdraw in a swift avoidance of flirtation. Lunch is followed by Pat in her best classroom manner leading preschoolers through *deer, a female deer,* much rehearsed. Their high voices fill the front hall with a desperate cheer, a faltering then recovery of *doe, a deer,* the audience joining in. Cupcakes are passed round by two elderly volunteers helping out before heading for points West or South to avoid Winter.

I am a teacher, Miss M begins, makes that point each time she comes, that she instructs her mixed bag of students at a school much like the schools the successful graduates of Mercy, and so forth. It is not quite true, but they love her for speaking of their progress, urging them to take their place in the community, take pride in their economic self-sufficiency and so forth. The late Dr. Gruen's death is finally mentioned, just a note of thank-you by his widow for their condolences. Though the duties of his professional life prevented him from witnessing the students' achievements, his heart was always, and so forth, until a catch in Miss Montour's voice cuts short her usual pep rally for the learning season to come.

Ned, I'm Ned, takes over. Prime-time slick and easy in his role of *we're in this together,* how he'd never been much for the books as a kid but now values. . . . Sissy thinks what a crock: now he *values,* and clueless besides, as if these women were ever given a choice to value more than a few pesos in their pockets, and goes on to his remarkable father's reach to the ailing world, and of family too good to be true, then falters. He is one of three men in the gracious entry hall of Mercy: Ned, Father Rooney who's nodded off in a high-back chair of time past, and a handyman, plumber's wrench at the ready. *I'm Ned* shuffles up a few stairs, and of course he's a charmer, his sappy embrace of Pat Laughlin, then scooping the kid in a wheelchair into his arms. *Guapo, guapo.* More than Sissy can take, and she pokes the good Father, hustles him fast out the door. No formal farewell was planned. What is it she wants? Not to let Father mess up his final blessing. These people come up from the city don't know him as the parish priest who never outgrew his belief or life stage of plain kindness.

As she settles him into the car with his driver, *Doe,* he asks. *Doe?*

A female deer. She sings on as she buckles him in, Father Jack Rooney.

He looks her straight in the eye. *Margaret Phelan?*

That's me. I'm Sissy.

Marie Claude has two views from the tower of the old house, now so nicely updated to be of use, not the relic of her heart-tug family story. There is nothing left of the pond or trail through the woods. How did she tell it? One way to her husband, with the terrifying details—branches slapping at her face, the roots of ancient trees tripping her up, mud sucking at her shoes. Or was it bare feet? Their shrill spinster voices calling— *Marie Claude! Marie Claude!* Most certainly a black night, starless, but then the flickering light from the gardener's cottage, the gardener of legend who once cared for the grounds of an old man's estate. And in the cottage, this family of squatters who took her in; at least the mother did, one of those hollow-chested women who might once have been sweet, her face drawn tight. A man and a boy cut of the same threadbare cloth, gray—that's how she sees the family—and the baby with bright hair, somewhat off balance toddling toward their visitor, Marie Claude. The child's name, don't you know, Sissy.

A story told to Hans Gruen, her husband, who then spoke to her of the Brothers Grimm, Wilhelm and Jakob, how they had gathered tales mostly from one woman of Kassel with an amazing memory. That was before the philologists got hold of folklore, he said, cutting off the brutal end of his wife's tale. The police had found her sleeping that night in the cottage and taken her back to the maiden aunts. Sissy and family then evicted, but not before candles caught the curtains, the father stinking of drink and kerosene, sirens in the night. Mrs. Gruen, née Montour, had not said in her remarks today that her prince did come, just once to the tower. That's a motif, for heaven sake; she might put it that way to her class or to Sissy, now in college. Hans drove up the Taconic, found his way to the old house she inherited just as she was about, about to kiss the young lawyer handling the estate which is now Mercy. Not today or any day ever did she tell that part of the story, though when rescued, she married Hans and they were contented and happy, of course. Though her husband, ever the economist, said *Grimm's Fairy Tales* was first published during Napoleon's retreat from Moscow, when fantasy didn't sell, that footnote of history, as so often, diminishing the personal story.

Turning to her sugar maple, the crown of its branches, though leafless, perfection enough, the pot of yellow chrysanthemums, a nice touch though barely visible from above. They sit in the canvas chairs, her stepson and Sissy. Ned is the younger son, the boy running on charm and good looks, often in need of a handout. He may be telling her that he now works for his older brother, had better keep at it, the grunt work of a paralegal. Married late after fooling around, his wife now expecting a child. She is, to be kind, like a child herself. His father called her the girl. Sissy tells him his stage is midlife crisis a little early. *Turn the page.*

Ned and Sissy are drinking the bottle of wine meant to go with supper. Pat Laughlin, exhausted by the day's festivities, had ordered in roast chicken. She is preparing, overpreparing, for a meeting of the board: a local builder, librarian, school principal. Hans called them doctor, lawyer, Indian chief. So Ned is pouring the cheap Chardonnay in the dusk of a chill evening. He pulls off Sissy's red cap, roughs up her hair. Marie Claude looks away to a scattering of early stars, attempts to spot Venus. The show below her window is more compelling. They are laughing, their movements caught in the network of bare limbs. Lights turned on, both driveway and front porch on a timer. Day and night the old house is connected to the fire station, the precinct. It's safe at the house of learning. Now they get up and come forward, as if onstage, her stepson and the young woman, Sissy. Their kiss is prolonged. She caresses his beard, then gives in to the scrape of it. Marie, *call me Marie,* remembers their need. Believes nothing will come of it. They drive off in the SUV borrowed for this trip from his brother, Hans Gruen's reliable son. In the backseat a soccer ball, skateboard, a book she meant to read tonight, *Billy Budd,* attempting to lay that war story on her class in Jersey City.

She fears that the students will favor Claggart, the mean master-at-arms, not Billy, the Handsome Sailor, too good to be true. *Favor* is not the right word, not a possible response to a complex moral story, not even to a fireside tale of the scholarly Brothers Grimm.

She has looked on their need, watched the instant lovers drive off. Now it is full night. The security lights of the old house do not banish the stars.

The next week and the next, Sissy Phelan waits for a call, an e-mail, a postcard would do, then one day she gets up before her mother wakes. She scrubs Clairol, dark burgundy blush, into her hair. It sticks like clotted blood in the sink, the answer to what's needed. She heads to her job at Mercy. Pat Laughlin, wouldn't you know, cries when she sees her. That night Sissy registers for the Spring semester: Western Civilization I, Mesopotamia to the Middle Ages, 3 credits. Turn the page.

ABOVE 96TH STREET

Her glasses lay on the mouse pad—for reading, not for the screen. In her CP files, he discovers the last document. At the head of the page: Longitude 74, Latitude 40, temperature approx: 34° in Central Park, wind east from the Hudson. Now locating herself as she had when she first fashioned her almanac, stories within stories with threads of useful and amusing information. Tracking the plot of days, the seasons—nature's way of insisting on change. Same old death and survival, late bloom against the odds, the bud nipped by the frost, puffs of hydrangeas bobbing, leaves ravaged by hail. More recently she set herself in time with the Daybook. Since the heart failed her—

He recalled the questions she'd posted early in the Fall—*Where were you when?*—and discovered she had started that parlor game again.

Daybook, December 20, 2007

When the Russians sent monkeys into space? My students recalled the sudden attention to math and science, the Sputnik makeup exam. When Maria Estrada, the Cuban girl, brought a tape to class. Where were you when Springsteen was just this kid from New Jersey? When Dolly was cloned?

He read on in the posthumous file, calling it that only to himself. She was no longer here to correct him, to say she was wired as she wrote her last days, fully alive as she spritzed the terrarium, the little kids caught up in the season, writing to Santa. Kate, in newly acquired script, had her doubts about Prancer and Vixen stomping the roof on 90th Street. A whiff of Pascal's Wager here—believe it, girl, you've nothing to lose: *Please drop by with my first cell phone ever.* Finding her way into last thoughts, perhaps believing they were passing thoughts, she directed a note his way: *Nick likes hermit crabs, the pet store on Broadway. A turtle less boring. Check the house in the Berks for mice. Exterminator in Pittsfield*—New Age kills with kindness.

Fragment: This is not a story.

If I'd taken a cab, it would not have been to Macy's. I'd have left the Christmas tree gala in the lobby, given my destination as Fifth and 72nd, overtipped my Muslim driver, 'tis the season, then found my way past the empty arc of band shell, a few chairs loitering long after a show; walked the length of the Mall past poets great and small, the arching beauty of the leafless elms etching the leaden sky. After the dog walker with assorted breeds, after the lovers—brave couple on this single-digit day, their down jackets in a slithery embrace, I would come at last to the bridge overlooking the Terrace where one baby stroller bounced up the broad steps, the mother's *up-we-go, up-we-go* ditty vaporizing in cold air while down I'd go, faltering yes, down past Jacob Mould's birds carved in a marble nest, his fruits of Fall, each season noted by our maiden lady poetess, Marianne Moore, "*Autumn a leaf rustles. We talk of peace. This is it.*

One notices that the angel hovering over the pool is really hovering, not touching the water." Why is Miss Moore not here? Memorialized in her tricorn and cape.

The *Angel of the Waters* is well draped and girded. Perhaps when not healing the lame, halt, or head cold, a troubling thought may occur. Unlike Magdalene and Cassandra—her myth may have outlived its time. Energetic flow of bronze gown, an athletic girl, sturdy bare calf thrust forward, a goalie protecting us all. I'd have the Angel to myself in the abandoned living room of the Terrace. There is no one about, no gentle young man just arrived in this place called Bethesda—recognizable fellow with a clipped beard, eyes burning bright, who asks: *Do you want to be cured?*

I've come to the healing waters without my cup.

Olmsted, my Fred, had the sculptress, Miss Stebbins of a very good family, in to dine with her friend, Charlotte Cushman, the greatest actress of the day. He was propped on his cane, stumbling from that accident, trying out a new horse and gig. Two months back his newborn son had died. Forgive Mary for going off to visit her family, not facing the monumental gravestones across the way, natural to her husband's Park. Emma Stebbins has been awarded the privilege of creating a statue for the Greensward. Her brother is the Commissioner of the Park, don't you know?

The actress and the landscape-architect-come-lately perform for each other. Little Miss Stebbins is flustered by the might of these two. She's in a romantic friendship with Cushman, turbulent waters. They live an arty life in Rome with women free of American decorum. They have come back to New York for this grand *balabusta* with the mug of a pit bull to enchant Broadway. The actress "plays the breeches" as Romeo, as Hamlet, though keeps her nightdress on to rage as the bloodiest of all Lady Macbeths. Whether I can bear to imagine Cushman's elocutionary delivery of great tragedy is beside the point of her stunning career. Her breast cancer harbored both pain and the lovely angel for our Park. Emma nursed her lover through slow agony, following Miss Cushman from engagement to engagement, all triumphal, not attending to her own considerable talent. The maquette of an angel stowed away in her heart, the tribute she would create for Charlotte.

If I'd taken a cab, I'd have found my way to *The Angel of the Waters,* not working that day, idly dripping icicles from her wings. Baby, Baby—pity the naked cherubs in her pool.

Do you want to be healed?

I'd snap off a sharp dagger of ice. *Verily, verily, the waters melt in my mouth.*

Take up your pallet and walk.

The fragment seemed to him story enough. She had gone back to her Park puzzle, not to forget Emma. Hard to decode his wife's handwriting, ink on yellow pad as if tracking back—before the old Remington, upgrade to Olivetti, before her anxious love affair with Windows. Where are you now?

The children, the grown ones, all three said they would help him clear up her back room, keep what might be of value—*the personal stuff.*

It's all personal.

When he bought the cell phone, he said, *Black will do* to the clerk promoting pink. Those first days, he heard his wife having the last word, the last laugh. Then the silence of his sorrow was heavy as stone, as the dark outcropping she had scaled that day in the Park to feel the height and weight of the place unknown, a semblance of wilderness plotted by Olmsted and Vaux. She should not have awarded herself the pleasure of that final misadventure. In the North Woods, there was a sign posted on the lone circle of lawn: PASSIVE ACTIVITIES ENCOURAGED.

She had been fine till the end of her adventure, until the slippery steps led down to Duke Ellington Boulevard.

Not called that when I was a boy chasing Bimbo.

Of course not. But the Gate, remember?

He had not remembered. The entrance to the Park above 96th Street is called *Stranger's Gate.*

She had fallen, been vetted by the doctor, no hemorrhage; an appointment set up for a look-see at a troublesome artery. He'd brought her home from the cardiac center in a cab, of course, tucked an afghan around her as she lay on the couch. She threw it off to go down the hall, back to her workroom.

The children, little and grown, were bickering in the living room—should, should not, have a tree. *She would have wanted* seemed to be winning over gloom of the empty corner where they put up their tree from time immemorial, at least since they called this place home.

Not allowed to play with her antique toys. Remember?

Of course *she* had remembered when the Loop the Loop plane did its trick before the key was lost; when the corn-husk doll wore a Mammy turban; when Pinhead, Beano and Buster (the dog) stood their ground as the red rubber ball came their way in a bowling game pre-Disney. Always such elation in her display of the tin trolley, the inevitable story: how her grandfather, aloft in his Locomobile, directed his workmen ripping out the trolley tracks on Main Street, making way for the future.

I opt for the tree, he said to the children. *Bring on the clowns, her tightrope walker, the dancing bear.* One cymbal missing. He left them to their grief, having discovered soon—too soon—that sorrow came over him solo, could only partially be shared. He stood at the door of her back room, Stranger's Gate indeed. Only days ago he had pushed the towers of discarded books out of her way. She had fallen on her way home from the Park, above 96th Street, forbidden ground. He opened a manila folder on her desk. She would have noted his hands trembling as he adjusted his glasses to read an article from *Science Times.* It seems the universe is expanding. He could not follow why dark matter doomed the theory of everything. Why we need new laws of nature. If you can't do the numbers, must we take it on faith? What use would she make of this prediction, which was surely beyond her? Science for the general reader, nothing to do with the Park. He thumbed through what had seemed an unmanageable mess of clippings, photos, postcards, her scrawl in notebooks half empty, half full. She had called this room her estate of confusion. In days to come, he would figure that the accumulation seemed to have a method, even a message, if he could decode it. But now Christmas was immediate, inevitable. When he flipped through her calendar, each day of the countdown was leavened with predictable pleasures—the kids' pageant (*apron for Mrs. Cratchit*), her baking duties: Glo's biscotti, bread pudding laden with rum. *Family Not Invited* to his office party, the firm cutting costs. Lightly penciled in, the midnight Mass at St. Greg's. Every year she hedged her bets. Should she sign on as a Christmas-carol believer?

Not this year, though she had posted an e-mail from Cleo, her brother's scholarly wife. St. Anselm's Argument, right over her desk with the gallery of ghosts she believes in.

1. God is, by definition, a being greater than anything that can be imagined.
2. Existence both in reality and in imagination is greater than existence solely in one's imagination.
3. Therefore, God must exist in reality: if God did not, God would not be a being greater than anything that can be imagined.

She insisted on singing *O holy night* . . .
Mimi, you never could carry a tune.
He places Mary and the Babe into position on the front hall table. The familiar story comes to mind, how her mother modeled these clay figures attended by chubby angels with broken wings, glazed them, fired them in a mail-order kiln installed in the cellar. *Yet another attempt at art.* Well art they are, for over the years he's noted the mystery of the crackled patina, the expression of wonder on the Madonna's face, the concealing folds of her veil. A lone shepherd held a staff in his hand, but no Wise Men, no Joseph. The crèche was incomplete, or her mother's belief in the project waned. The stable insufficiently rustic, at which point the artist's daughter might hold out her glass for a refill, her Christmas Eve pleasure in the neighborhood choir at St. Gregory's forgotten or forgone. Faith put on hold by the very woman who wrote ahead in her Daybook an almanac posting: *Winter Solstice, December 22, 2007, 1:08 AM, True. Sagittarians prefer the journey to the arrival. Unreliable.*

To write ahead, what could that mean? Then a query, a one-liner on the lined page: *Where were you on the Eighth Day?*

INVENTORY

Maps: of three pretty ships halfway to America; of Cyril O'Connor's Wall Street and environs long before it suffered its scar; of the rectangular Park across the street—limited, vast; and of the watershed under the Appalachians from whence our city water, Jackie's Reservoir now for the birds; of the Fall migration, its dramatic urban stop-off in the Greensward. Sifting with care, he came upon shards—a glamour shot of their building, that studio portrait of her grandfather in full prosperity, a Chinaman with a queue porting baskets to a family, the grand vista of Yosemite behind him. *The Angel of the Waters,* triumphant above the splash. A note to no one in particular! *The last cantos of Dante's* Paradiso *were discovered after his death when he had presumably arrived at that destination.* And a poem she read to him one evening not long ago. In response to discouraging news of the market he brought home at the end of each day, every day. Was she unsteady pulling Whitman down from a forbidden high shelf? *Drum-Taps* lay, open to the page, the passage faintly marked for his reading:

> *Year that trembled and reel'd beneath me!*
> *Your summer wind was warm enough, yet the air I breathed froze me,*
> *A thick gloom fell through the sunshine and darken'd me,*
> *Must I change my triumphant songs? said I to myself,*
> *Must I indeed learn to chant the cold dirges of the baffled?*
> *And sullen hymns of defeat?*

He discovered that these lines had been read out to her brother when our President, playing do-si-do with Russia, proposed once again our antinuke missiles—useless, obsolete—be stuck in Czech soil. Had he not noted, back on the day the Supreme Court said OK to listening in,

scanning our e-mails, that her rage petered out? No place to go with a thin bleat of complaint. Let a borrowed poem say it. Let the Park flourish day by passing day—with never enough stories. She had scratched fury, turned to old recipes for comforts of the season, linzer torte and strudel. Turned back in time to when they were first together, proving herself in the kitchen, having proved themselves in bed. And here was the famous shot of Olmsted, the only man he was ever jealous of, rather a stern young fellow in a seaman's cap, primed to create a world. Well, the photo was famous to her family along with the old prints—Pierrot and Columbine, pantomime lovers in their kiss and make up routine—with her circus folk in the dining room performing their breathtaking feats, showing off for the devout maiden of *The Angelus.*

She had read to page 733 in *War and Peace,* marking the confrontation between Napoleon and the Russian emissary as they moved ahead to their bloody war. *Girlish !!!* in the margin next to the description of the Emperor . . . *a white waistcoat so long that it covered his round stomach, white doeskin breeches fitting tightly over the fat thighs of his stumpy legs, and Hessian boots.* Her notes—*his snuff box, his cologne!* trailing down the side of the page, remarked upon the brilliant maneuvers of the scene, the slippery give-take of diplomacy, the rough talk of plain take. He presumed she'd read the love story so far, though this time round, her second chance, notes in the margin revealed how closely she observed the lush setting of the Tsar's palace, the slippery make-nice that preceded war. Revise, reread, work ahead right up to the end. He must tell her brother, who maintained when she took up her post with the fat library book each long Summer day, then slept on a cot in his room—that she snored.

> *Thank you for sending back Uncle Tom's Cabin. As you may have observed, I am a teacher. Unfortunately, I do not think I will make use of Mrs. Stowe's novel again. Its arguments are flawed, its language too distant for my students. I have no memory of sitting on the ground in the Park. It was a most difficult day.*
>
> *Best regards, Marie Claude Montour*

He opened the FedEx from Macy's. On her last day, she had found time for his gift, a sweater more plum than red. It zips with ease, though his hand quivers each time he puts it on. Soon that will pass. He will simply enjoy its cashmere embrace as he looks down this day at *Short Readings for Dr. Shah*—Cather's *The Old Beauty*, Beckett's *Company*, Twain's *Mysterious Stranger*. That's the list she boldly crossed out. Perhaps not missing the point, though he had lived with her a lifetime, *perhaps* was not the right word. The point being each one of the readings was about death, immobility, angry old age, not stories for the charming young doctor who had little time to read in emergency, attending to probable death every day. The list was appropriate to herself, to finding her way out of this room with a voice not yet silenced.

> *The next talent requisite in the forming of a* complete *almanac-writer, is a sort of gravity, which keeps a due medium between dullness and nonsense, and yet has a mixture of both. Now you know, sir, that grave men are taken by the common people always for wise men.*

> *Gravity is just as good a picture of wisdom, as pertness is of wit, and
> therefore very taking.*
>
> —Benjamin Franklin, *The Pennsylvania Gazette,*
> October 20, 1737

December, 1937. At the Rialto, *Snow White and the Seven Dwarfs.* My favorite,
Grumpy.

Contrary, my father called me, wishing I'd fall for Happy or Doc, not
the Prince that's for sure. Perhaps Disney. He admired conservative gents
who made money within the limits of the law.

Our Scene neither animation nor tragedy:

> *For, as I am a man, I think this lady
> To be my child . . .*
>
> *And so I am, I am.*

A Printout: *Walden,* Is It You?

The drama of the day was not my taking the bus in the right direction
to confront at last what I'd seen in many photos of the Park, and read
of in Olmsted's papers. My venture was personal. What lies above 96th
Street? The question you never would answer.

A wilderness for dangerous games. Well, for city boys pretending to
danger, or simply for the thrill of knowing you should not be far from
your East Side home scaling these rocks with the janitor's boy who'd
steal a kid's lunch box, threatened frail old women till they dealt out a
dollar. Did you look on from a moral height? We all have need of a Bimbo
to take the rap as we watch from a safe distance.

I was no sooner out of the bus, halfway up the steep steps, so many,
when I understood I'd come not to discover the dangers of your boyhood
revelations so edited they might have been printed in *Boys' Life,* which
my brother subscribed to, stories of good-family kids escorted from the
crime scene having learned their lesson.

Halfway up the steps, bare branches glistened with ice-palace glamour. Three-thirty. I had studied the map, knew my way to the circle of lawn frosted over. Worth the climb to see in the distance the Harlem Meer, saved that for another day. I turned at once to the trail leading down to the Pool. Thought I knew the route from maps and picture books, and the stone outcropping from our scrambles up Monument Mountain. The path was lonely as promised, until the open view of the wildflower meadow mowed low for the season; and there was Vaux's charming rustic bridge over the silent stream, the dark rocks in the distance walling me from the city. I might have been where the architects wanted to place me in their pictorial semblance of wilderness—the Adirondacks, or the heights overlooking the Hudson. I stumbled—a tree root but did not fall. You see, you must see, this was not an escapist journey. It led me far beyond a disclosure of the guarded stories of your nefarious past. What struck me when I found a place to rest, was the reality of the landscapers' contrivance, not the contrivance of reality. It seemed a challenge to nature or God, whichever way you'll have it. The sun made a mirror of the water. I went close to see the clouds float by at my feet but did not see myself, nor did I want to. Nor, nor—quaint diction. There could be no charm in seeing myself. Reflection being in the mind, it came easy, remembering my way back to when I first read *Walden*.

She had been, the professor at my girl college, an officer in the Wacs, a commanding presence in the classroom. We were given our orders as to readings in American Lit. She found the writer of *Walden* feeble, a dropout spinning his lofty thoughts, "flatulent on his beans." She expected our laughter, and let us know Henry David was well fed by his relatives who left him meals he need not pay for. Thoreau was a freeloader, his economics a fraud. Was she envious of his talented instruction? I have forgotten her name but remember her brown oxfords double-knotted and the military cut of her tweeds. Seeing at long last above 96th Street the construction of pastoral beauty, I was furious all over again at the chill bluster of that woman troubling me in the wintertime of my life. Did the spoiler dislike the writer because he spoke out against the war with

Mexico when she had served in the War to End All Wars? His essay, "Civil Disobedience," was never assigned in her class. I would read it in my furious '60s, should reread it now, stand opposed to our broken social contract, beg to be put in prison if only for one night. But it would seem just another stunt, which is exactly what she called the writer's protest as she marched us back and forth across the flat parade ground of her hup-two-three put-down of *Walden*. Oh, she would never know his house, garden, pond are Paradise enough, a place real and imagined, beyond dollars and dimension.

Postcard: Wish you were here, though this pilgrimage was mine. As I made my way round the shore of the pool, the wind cut through my puffy. The heart thumped its irregular beat as it does when recorded in the doctor's office. The familiar flutter, no longer disturbing, seemed a warm throb of love. I take it back, did wish you were with me. I headed up the Great Hill. It's one hell of a climb. There was no one in this sanctuary of a vast public space and no added attractions—statues, Bridle Path, fountains or playing field, no candles to light for peace or the dead—to justify this earthly creation.

> This is the light of autumn; it has turned on us.
> Surely it is a privilege to approach the end
> still believing in something.

Here the mortal architects outwitted nature with nature itself. I was fiercely happy. It could be, don't you see, imagined. That is allowed in this forgotten corner of the Park, but not in the country beyond that encourages passive activity only; that lets Dumbos like Bimbo serve time and Big Time Offenders go free? Why had I allowed myself to flip to the concealing comforts of Literary Walk and Pinetum, to the charms of a phony castle and guarded revelations of first person?

She had lost herself in the Park. It was *The History of the World* all over again, arranging events as she wanted them to be.

Mercy is sought for my solo flights in the workroom; and the *consequent break of unity in my design*—that's Mrs. Woolf who confessed to a childlike trust in her husband, while we have been sparring. Mercy on me, RC.

On her desk, he finds the blowup of a photo, been there so long he's ceased to see it. He's in air force fatigues, not much flesh on young bones, full head of black hair. He had been trained to jump out of planes, pull the rip cord, view the world from above. Oh, just the Florida swamps. Practice only. The battalion sent ahead had been slaughtered when the Germans tried out their V-1 missiles. Then, that war was over before he got his chance.

Weren't you lucky.

Printout: November 2007 Names of the Dead

Bewley, Kevin R., 27, Petty Officer Second Class
Davis, Carletta S., 34, Staff Sgt., Army
Linde, John D., 30, Staff Sgt., Army
Muller, Adam J., 21, Pfc., Army
Ndururi, Christine M., 21, Specialist, Army
Shaw, Daniel J., 23, Sgt., Army
Walls, Johnny C., 41, Sgt. First Class, Army

Correction: December 18, 2007

A listing of American military deaths on Nov. 8 misidentified the country in which Sgt. First Class Johnny C. Walls was killed. It was Afghanistan, not Iraq.

The last e-mail to her brother: *You have surely heard of my fall. I am tidying up my back room after the incident. Though what setting things in order has to do with a skinned knee is beyond me? I'm sorting books, papers, middle-of-the-night notes to myself, the web of possibilities. The plot of the Seasons is unavoidable. It was cold in the Park that day. I had climbed the Great Hill, then cut from the path, what was left of it. Underbrush, broken limbs, neglect not foreseen in a Greensward Proposal, was beautiful to me. I saw that nature might survive our meddling, our once upon a time stories, even the artwork of the Republic. The steps back down to the street glistened in the sun, invited danger. It was then that I fell, as warned, as expected. The greater danger lay behind me, the looming blackness of the humped rock formation like a beached whale. The novel Melville started in New York is not the one he wrote in the Berkshires.*

I took your semaphore out to put under the tree with our old toys. Meddling, I dusted it, now the caution arm flops, won't give its warning of the possible train wreck down the line. Bread pudding——3 eggs, 5 egg yolks, heavy cream——is lethal. I presume you still crave your holiday helping unless otherwise directed. In my recipe files I came across fragments written back when I was into the notion that time bends. My intention had nothing to do with fast trains and synchronized clocks. Three dimensions are all I can handle. Though a math teacher had a walk-on, all I intended was the leap forward, the years flipping by like calendar pages: not where were you when we sang——We will all go together when we go? Where are you now? The more difficult question. I must have set these butter-stained pages aside as I measured out sugar and cream, not knowing the answer. Our mother taught trigonometry, which you mastered, though it was art that she favored, and craft. I suppose I can figure why I've stayed up half the night to finish this story of an artist——stayin' alive, stayin' alive, God, I loved Travolta in that movie; and why I'm sending the story to you. Time having flipped ahead. I don't intend a tearjerker. Dickens sure pulled out the stops with those Christmas Books.

His reply: *Go ahead, Mims, make me cry. On the other hand, my train set circling the sun parlor floor, the schoolhouse with a little brass bell that never rang, the church's torn cellophane windows, the fisherman on the bridge over the cracked-mirror stream, the brown cows and yellow sheep not to scale, and the policeman directing the Mitchell Dairy trucks at the crossing of North and Main means nothing to me at all, not even the uncertain headlights flickering on the engine, nothing to me at all. We're grown up now. Aren't we?*

Studio Visit: The Artist's Tale

Does one ever get over drawing, is one ever done mourning it?
—Jacques Derrida, *Memoirs of the Blind*

Everything arranged. She has placed the last postcard, posted it, you might say, with a Lucite thumbtack pinning it to the canvas. A murky photo of the Chicago Stock Yards, hand-colored before color was invented for film. The haunches of the cattle glisten, a patent-leather brown. They are being led to slaughter by a fellow with a prod in his hand, his face bright orange under a dun colored cap. The sky, washed-out blue. A dreary scene, but the postcard is one of many. The Poussin, for instance (*Earthly Paradise*), though reduced to an absurdity, is all dense Edenic growth with a sunlit distance, a small shimmering lake and a celestial figure (God, as we know him?) riding a cloud above, looking down on our first parents, naked as the day they came to the Almighty mind. Eve, center stage, points at the apple tree, urging the reluctant Adam on. You know the story; so did Louis XIV, to whom the painting belonged.

On an easel, Louise Moffett seems to have been copying the Poussin The apparatus of her craft—paint, turpentine, brushes—are displayed on a table nearby. They may be for real or props. Perhaps the copy will always remain half done, those two figures arguing, stuck in their best moment. Mealy or tart; what were apples like back then, or for that matter in 1662? Looking back to postcards posted on canvas, *The Ruins of San Francisco City Hall* (1906), the gilt dome intact as well as the classical columns at its base. Only the center did not hold. The stretched canvas that displays the postcards is painted black. A big bulletin board, that's all it appears to be.

Louise wears a painter's smock, a thrift-shop treasure. You recall the floppy garments worn so as not to soil the artists' clothes in the atelier photos of Matisse, Mary Cassatt, et al. She places a wooden palette with dabs of color—some right from the tube, some mixed—on the table, runs her hand over soft sable brushes. The smell of oil paint, a thrill.

Deep breathe it. She is a good looker heading toward middle years, her gray hair dusted with leftover gold. Winsome? That may be the word, as though something she once cared for has gone by and she wonders. . . . A sweet wince of a smile as she pins *St. Catherine of Siena Dictating Her Dialogues* (Giovanni di Paolo, 1460?) to the canvas. One more postcard may be the answer for this particular day.

The studio is an outbuilding, a quarter mile up a path from the white clapboard house where she lives with her family. Her husband is home today, caring for Maisy, down with her third cold of the season. Cyril has gone off on the school bus, no sweater, a ripped T-shirt proving he's cool. Everything now arranged. North light filters through bare branches of maples. Her studio with a sliding glass door may have been a small barn. Canvases are properly stacked in a loft above, temperature control softly humming, kettle on the boil, tidy kitchenette in a cubby once a stall. Louise, raised on a farm, knows it's too narrow for horses, perhaps goats for their milk, for cheese. Exactly eleven o'clock when the curator arrives. He has been told to follow the path back, a bit bumpy in this first November freeze. Louise has not expected the driver. Will he come in with Blodgette, who is to look over her new work for a show? She's expected a tête-à-tête. Blodge, still in the black BMW with New York T plates, looks to the driver, taps his watch briefly as if to say he'll not be long. Through the shingle side of the studio, she hears the blast of music—salsa, Afro-Cuban? No way Blodgette's choice.

Now, bussing her, one cheek then the other.

Isn't this swell? Legendary. Moffett's retreat.

The world he brings with him is of this moment, apparent in lightly streaked hair, two-day beard. Torn jeans sport their patch like a price tag. The black leather jacket, silky soft, seems live as she takes his arm, faces him toward the postcards on display. It's been some years since she's seen Blodge in the city, at openings, or at the museum properly suited for the trustees. To be fair, they are both costumed. They now stand side by side, Louise in that artist's smock over black turtleneck and L.L. Bean cords, wool socks, leather sandals. Her glasses, thick lenses, hang round her neck from a chain mended with twisties, at the ready in case, just in case she does not see the aerial view (6" × 4½") to be Wells Cathedral, or that the bombed church (Moselle, France) with the big clock face standing in rubble (Paul Strand, 1950) reads 9:35. Time of the blast?

Blodge will have tea. No milk, no sugar.

Lapsang souchong?

Beautiful.

But when steeped, poured into their mugs, the smoky fragrance mingling with the oils and turp is faintly nauseating. The music blasts its way in from the car. Like street music, do what you will, no way to silence the din, as in the city on Lower Broadway where Louise Moffett worked in her loft, mid- to late nineties. Blodge takes in the current scene. In this barn she has set up a diorama—his term, calling it that, arms spread in an expansive gesture—her postcards on canvas, tools of the painter's trade abandoned? Half-executed copies, her Poussin missing its tiny human figures; St. Catherine delivering her dialogues to an inkpot. No scribe. Louise has set her postcard next to the frozen moment of the original. Moffett's men: Duchamp without chessboard; John James Audubon birdless, eyes scummed with cataracts in his demented old age.

Christopher Blodgette leans in, examines the background, the canvas itself (4' × 6'), size of a throw rug.

Louise on the defensive, laughing. *It's not black-black, not a shroud, don't you see? More organic, like soil composted with manure.* Now why talk country to this creature of the city?

The bulletin board, as you say, is painterly.

Did I say?

For posting notices in the school hall, Louise, the essence of darkness diluting claustrophobic emotion.

She bridles at his untranslatable instruction, or (more likely) at his deep misreading of her work past and present. He goes on about her continuing vitality as though she must be propped up to carry on beyond time allotted. Music now pulsing, Pearl Jam or maybe Nirvana. Once she could have called: *Teen Spirit.* Louise claps her hands over her ears.

Blodge raps on the glass door. *Keep it down.* They watch in the blessed silence as his driver jogs round the car pursuing his puffs of cold air, then stretches against the hood.

Bing needs his workouts, sitting all day in the car.

Bing?

Back to Blodgette's curatorial business. *Truly amazing, the random collection. Great work so diminished. Then rescued with the investment of your documentation.*

Documentation?

Your reenactments, Lou, updating, bringing it all back home.

He takes up a small drawing, size of a postcard, *Washington Crossing the Delaware.* In Moffett's rendering, only the prow and founding father are sketched in. The rest of the crew still awash in the cold river?

Perfect draftsmanship.

She takes that as a cut. Since when did dusty old draftsmanship figure in his vocabulary? Since he learned to please old ladies with money, partner them at benefits, Park Avenue dinners. Louise remembers Blodgette just down from Cambridge with the proper degrees, a lanky boy scarfing the hors d'oeuvres at every opening, gobbling art world in one viewing. Fond of him, she had so looked forward to this day. They'd been friends on the rise, not close but of an age. Once they stayed up all night in her shoe-box apartment, pre-loft, drinking jug wine, last of the easy tokers, that's how she remembers it, Coltrane on a Summer night, pressing PLAY again and again, the window thrown open to the noise of revelry below. They had no interest in each other, not really. Discreet fondling, sex consumed by their dreaminess, or was it ambition? She was ahead of the game, her first postcards so carefully observed and painted, photographic in detail. Small sightings of where she came from—dairy farm in Wisconsin, the landscape of memory mocked, distorted as memory will have it.

Now the sky performs one of its tricks, quick clouds moving in. Louise gets a glimpse of herself in the glass door: the weight she's put on, the uncontrollable blink of her tired eyes while Blodge drinks the dregs of his tea as though sipping an elixir from the fountain of youth, a rather crusty cosmeticized youth, still. . . . And the show he proposes is a group show, planning stages. Louise has missed a beat in his e-mail request for the studio visit. Retro: had he not made that clear? Artists of the Nineties, Eighties if we can look back that far. He runs through a list of possible survivors, Moffett's pulled through. She must suck that hard candy as a compliment.

He speaks of the return to her strong suit, narrative, then pops *Spiral*

Staircase, Statue of Liberty off the canvas for a closer look. Two boys and a man who might be their father are trapped in the belly of this cast-iron symbol, climbing toward the deleted torch as Blodge reads it. The visit dwindles to gossip, past the demise of po-mo to talk of the art market, holding despite . . .

Christopher? Her voice barely audible. *We'll have lunch up at the house.*

Lou-Lou, I must take a pass. On the road to New Haven, *chat up the folks at the Mellon. . . .* They are distracted by the driver huffing and puffing at the glass door. He sweeps his hands toward the heavens, protests snow gently falling. He is a large, untidy boy. His sad moon face begs his release.

When they are gone—Bing and Blodge, really!—she reposts *Spiral Staircase:* unlovely industrial green, the great weight propping Miss Liberty—that's all she meant, if she meant anything at all. She wraps a shawl round her smock, begins the walk back up to the house.

Artie will ask. *How'd it go?*

Her husband never got the hang of these visits. In his world of mathematics, things mostly work. If they don't, go figure. He understands her anxiety. Lou no longer courts, perhaps fears exposure. It's not unlike . . . but there his comparison ends. Math is most often content with its equal signs, unlike art's uncertain proof of the pudding. Today she tells Artie that the visit was something like a courtesy call.

So he looked?

He scanned. Nothing on the dotted line.

Best keep it to herself, the group show with golden oldies. Blodgette's response to her installation—she will call it *Last Mailing*—was inattentive, rambling at best. He had not opened the book right there on the table, a ledger with a worn marbleized cover. On its pages lined for debit or credit, she had written messages for each postcard mounted, and for those stacked, which he did not shuffle through. On the path home, Louise experiences not anger, just the melancholy of solo flight often felt when she's working. Her ledger has no narrative at all; jottings, no story. She kicks a stone aside with the artsy sandals; now she will have a sore toe. Bing, huffing and puffing, or his friend the curator who had not been curious about her new work, just dropped by, pumping her studio full of hot air. Her bitter thought: *He must call his exhibit "Old Masters,"* not her way of thinking at all, but it lightens her way to the house, where a child is sick and needs her attention. A dusting of snow in the tire ruts is already melting away.

Then, too, a flock of red-winged blackbirds flitter across her path, birds now seen too often in the marsh encroaching on the Freemans' land. Birds that should be out of season. For a moment she longs for Central Park with its spectacular migration, that rectangular plot with less acreage than her father's megadairy. Or, on this last lap of her journey, did she long for a girl with a neat ponytail who flagged down a bus early, before milking? It stopped by the side of the road, picked her up with one suitcase and a portfolio of drawings to show the world. The bright image of that girl long abandoned, only the looming shadow in which she might see herself, sharp as a silhouette with all the forgiving details gone.

I should have said, Open the book.

Should have said? The old chestnut of regret.

Open the book. You see, it's people I'll never meet, greetings from where I've never been, but where I might like to go. To Marienbad (1923), pink clouds over the Grand Hotel. *Allegory of the Planets and Continents,* Tiepolo (1770–96). *Open the book, Blodge:* 0 through 9, Jasper Johns (1960), *the artist's numbers consuming each other in a magician's scribble. That's for Artie, my math husband, who will love my Cobb salad,* Bibb lettuce scooping still-life goodies presented on an Italian platter (Deruta, 2003). You might say an inspired show curated for Christopher Blodgette with a bottle of Beaujolais Nouveau in season.

Cyril comes in the kitchen door. It's past noon, Friday, half day of school. He hears his parents at a distance, finds them in the dining room.

What's this? Tablecloth, weird gourds in a basket. He slings down his backpack.

Salad?

No thank you. Pepperoni pizza at school, it being Zig's birthday. Cyril is ten, a scrawny kid, red hair courtesy of a grandmother long gone, owl glasses, wry smile as though he knows what's up. Maybe he does. Shivering in a T-shirt though he will never admit it. Good boy, he asks after his sister. Maisy is watching, is allowed to watch a cartoon. Odd about his parents drinking wine middle of the day, like they were practicing for Christmas when the whole dairy-land crew comes from Wisconsin. General talk of the weekend, last soccer match at the high school where afreeman.edu teaches. His father is pals with advanced nerds, writes their language. His mother offers cumulus clouds on a soupy pudding.

Floating island?

No thank you.

It is awfully quiet. Only Maisy's cough, now persistent, finds its way to where they sit at the round table with candles unlit and bread crumbs. Louise runs for the stairs, turns back to her boy.

Run down to the barn. Not calling it my studio. *Latch the door.* Pleading as though urgent, *Please put on your sweatshirt. Do it.* She never does lock up. There have been no incidents. Moffett's barn is safe as houses. But today there has been an intrusion. And who knows? In the bluster of this cold wind, could be her postcards will scatter.

Maisy watches a rabbit fool a fox, a fairly brutal episode—pops to the fox snout with one hell of a carrot. Her mother's hand on her forehead is cool, cooler than the sweat that breaks her fever. They lie together on her parents' big bed watching a cartoon they have seen many times. Lou not following the blow-by-blow script: on the path back to the house, she admitted she had looked forward to his critical eye with just enough of the old desire to show work in progress. Everything arranged, then she had not welcomed the visit. Going through the paces with Christopher Blodgette, she'd been at best inhospitable. Should she have defended her reverence for the tools of her trade? *See, I've not abandoned my craft, only given it halfhearted attention, might as well collect postcards, not a random stack. These are my people great and small. Tour my chosen places—most never seen.* As for diorama—taxidermy art, Blodge knows it. Well, she is not yet stuffed, propped behind glass. She can post her many views, change scenes. So why tears, just a few, as she trotted the path home? Tears of brisk wind, not sorrow. The fox has a net—aha!—stretched over the farmer's garden. He watches his unwitting prey chew a whole row of leafy lettuce, then makes his move. We knew the net would entangle him; still Maisy laughs and so does her mother as the rabbit digs his way out of this fix.

The studio door is latched, a flimsy arrangement. It will be easy for Cyril to break into his mother's sacred place. He thinks about it, then tests the bolt, which springs back against the shingles. Before he enters, he looks through the glass door at the setup framed just like a picture, her big dark canvas, a painting half done on an easel and all her brushes and turp on a table. He slides the door open. Warm inside, cozy. Who's to hear the tread of his sneakers, see him rub the sleeve of his sweatshirt across the snot dribbling from his nose? Catching his sister's cold? Just the chill of the day. He sits Indian style facing the night sky of his mother's painting. *Funny* and *fun,* two words fit together. He flips the stacked postcards. There's the little green one, he gets it——Adam and Eve, and the fuzzy picture of a bearded old man looking dead-eye at the camera. He's Audubon, responsible for his parents' birdwatching, for the most boring hours he's ever lived, trailing them in silence for the flap of a feather, a flick, a tweet. Fair is fair. Cyril has his lepidoptera pinned in glass cases. Slews not yet collected. Even now the pupae dig in, wintering over. That guy at the chess table should sacrifice his rook, save the queen. Old Market, Innsbruck: fat fellow with a humongous cheese. Clock stopped in the rubble, some church in France. St. Catherine doesn't look like she's talking, but the monk, doofus if ever, is writing. What's awesome is the wall above them dissolving, and who's there? Christ, that's who, coaching, cheering them on. San Francisco, leveled to ash, lies in the distance.

He opens the book. His mother's swirling cursive, the way she writes notes to Maisy's teacher, even the list of stuff she needs at the store. He reads, but only pieces that go with the pictures he likes.

The cotton picker screens his face from the camera, covers his mouth with that big worn hand. What would he say, or dare say, that isn't in his eyes or the concealing shadows?

Washington standing up at the prow. Father of our country knew with the ice floe and waters raging what any boy on a camping trip knows. Don't rock the boat. Aim for heroic.

St. Catherine not speaking, so what is the scribe taking down, pen and ink at the ready? Tempera and gold on wood. Classy medium, uncertain message.

Cyril flips pages but stops where his mother draws a little nest of numbers. He's good at math, even at this early age can deal with negative numbers. His mother has written: *Artie likes teaching his students to see the beauty of shapes and numbers. At night he is often content with his mathematical journals, or so I believe. Must believe he has survived his youthful promise. I do know I will never balance this book of my magpie collecting and spending. No final answer.*

Well, that's his mother, loopy. He closes the ledger, suddenly shy as any child should be, embarrassed by the note about his father. He shuffles the stack of postcards, comes up with a smiling lady. Her plump body takes up most of the foreground. It's hard to see the sheep, cows, and men working. *Mrs. Heelis on Her Farm* (Beatrix Potter, watercolor, D. Banner). It's sunny, so why the shawl and umbrella? She holds a quill pen in her hand. Cyril remembers when he was little, liking her stories. He takes a thumbtack, pins Mrs. Heelis right up there on the canvas, between paradise and earthly destruction.

Daybook _____

She had made out a check to Daily Bread, a worthy fund, this year recalling day-old Wonder Bread doled out to the poor, a small story recalled for Kate, who is studying the Great Depression in fourth grade. As though the yeasty smell of a neighborhood memory might take its place with *Les Misérables* or the starving children in Darfur. How Mrs. Howe stole down the street for the handout before dawn not to advertise her need; how Jack Cleary sold aprons door-to-door. His wife ran them up on the Singer—*that's a sewing machine. We had lots of aprons. It's better to read about those times than to live them.* Should he tell the kids that their grandmother was, as a girl, safely installed in the little house, not the big house next door with the sub-Tiffany window and the bronze statue of a woman praying—The Angelus now holding a sprig of gilded holly? He thinks not. That was her story.

The tree, best we ever had. Toys in attendance.

He would keep the terrarium sweating for its unnatural life. Someday in the future, he might show them a book with Magic Marker slashing down the pages; and the printout of her revision. They must know she never got the love story right, said perhaps it was not meant to be a love story at all.

He would walk with them to the Park, to the empty slope that was Seneca Village, or, in a pleasant season view the Pool and wilderness where she climbed slippery rocks though did not fall to her death. Her end was delayed mysteriously, a stunt of the body. Question is, why did she scale the heights? To see beyond her limited view of the Park and the brazen towers of El Dorado. He might say, *Come along, let's look at the mural in the lobby where golden skyscrapers are sketched in, phantoms set beyond the horizon line, the dim arena of the future raised above the fantasy life below. Do you think she preferred to stay in the foreground? Costumed, up for the performance?*

They might ask, *What's that box?*

The casque? A sci-fi device in an old movie, sends you to the stars.

Daybook, January 6, 2008

Why must she know—high-tide, crescent moon? Where are we now? That's not an easy question. But he had been married so long to the detective's daughter, he scouts the date. In the spineless black Mass book, propped up in plain view, she had placed faded red and green ribbons to mark both the Day of the Holy Innocents and the Feast of the Epiphany. Which day did she intend in reckoning time? He thought Holy Innocents, given her complaints against the war, though it might be Epiphany, the consolation of gifts brought to a stable in Bethlehem that took the prize—gold, incense. What exactly is myrrh?

RC

If it can be imagined, RC. She was so far beyond me, that Austrian student stroking the cross buried in the throbbing pit of her neck. Schande, *the shame was all mine.*

Then *RC* on an illustration scanned from Willy Pogany's *Parsifal,* the young knight having discovered the Grail. Finding the initials again and again, he believes she was back to figuring herself at the starting line in a parochial school with a crucifix over the blackboard, which had always made him uncomfortable. A secular Jew, her wager with the gods was improbable to him. Then *RC* on a turned-down page in the biography of Oppenheimer who—he is pleased to discover—studied the rock formation in Central Park when he was twelve. The mystery cleared up with the disappointing annual report of The El Dorado Gold Corporation: *Reality Check says it's old news.* That was her pet name for him when they were first together. He did not mind it, *Reality Check*—not then, not now—but minded that he had failed, for a moment, to understand she was only attempting to square the circle, to give heaven its due.

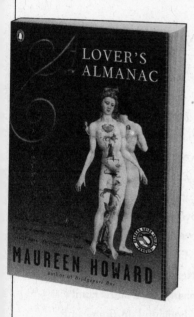

The Silver Screen

ISBN 978-0-14-303555-8

In this third novel of Howard's quartet, Isabel Murphy, who renounced silent-film stardom to raise a family, is dead at ninety, and her children are trying to break free of the lives she has dealt them. Joe, a Jesuit priest, has failed at love and the healing of souls. Stodgy Rita has found late happiness with a gangster. And Gemma, Isabel's honorary child, has grown up to experience a strange celebrity as a photographer. A darkly comic family story of guilt, love, and forgiveness, *The Silver Screen* is luminous in its intelligence and empathy.

PENGUIN
BOOKS